LYNSAY SANDS

BORN TO BITE

AN ARGENEAU NOVEL

AVON
An Imprint of HarperCollins*Publishers*

This is a work of fiction. Names, characters, places, and incidents are products of the author's imagination or are used fictitiously and are not to be construed as real. Any resemblance to actual events, locales, organizations, or persons, living or dead, is entirely coincidental.

AVON BOOKS
An Imprint of HarperCollins*Publishers*
10 East 53rd Street
New York, New York 10022-5299

ISBN 978-0-06-147432-3
www.avonbooks.com

First Avon Books paperback printing: September 2010
First Avon Books special printing: April 2010

Printed in the U.S.A.

10 9 8 7 6 5 4 3 2 1

BORN TO BITE

One

"You're late." Lucian's growled greeting made Armand Argeneau grimace as he slid onto the bench seat opposite him in the diner's only occupied booth. A "Hello, how are you?" would have been nice, but it also wasn't something he'd expect from the older immortal. Lucian wasn't known for being warm and fuzzy.

"I had some things to do at the farm before I could leave," Armand said calmly, glancing over the man's roast beef dinner with disinterest before gazing around the quiet diner. It was after nine, almost closing time, and they were the only customers. He didn't even see a waitress in evidence and supposed she was in the back helping with cleanup.

"Yes, of course," Lucian murmured, setting down his fork to pick up a warm, crusty dinner roll dripping with butter. "We can't expect that wheat of yours to grow all by itself, can we?"

Armand scowled irritably as he watched him bite into the roll with relish. "A little respect for a farmer who grows the food you're eating wouldn't go amiss . . . especially since you appear to be enjoying it so much."

"I am," Lucian acknowledged with a grin, and then arched an eyebrow. "Jealous?"

Armand merely shook his head and turned his gaze out the window, but he *was* jealous. Lucian's eating was a result of finding his life mate. It had reawakened old appetites both of them had lost long ago. There wasn't an unmated immortal alive who wouldn't envy that, including him.

"So?" He glanced back to Lucian to see he'd set aside the bun and was now chasing peas around his plate, stabbing at the little green succulents with his fork. "What was so important that you had to drive down here to see me? And why the hell did you insist on my coming out to the diner? The farm is only another five-minute drive. You could have come there."

Lucian gave up stabbing the peas and instead scraped them across the plate into the mashed potatoes. He then scooped up a forkful of the combination before saying, "I had a favor to ask you and didn't want anyone at the house to overhear."

"There's no one at the house," Armand murmured, watching with fascination as Lucian popped the forkful of food into his mouth and began to chew. Judging by his expression and murmur of pleasure, he really seemed to be enjoying the food, which was kind of depressing since the smell wasn't even tempting

Armand, and really the food looked like slop to him; brown meat, white potatoes with a brown sauce, and ugly green peas. Not very appetizing at all. Grimacing to himself, Armand asked as Lucian swallowed, "So what's this favor?"

Lucian hesitated and then raised his eyebrows. "Not going to ask me how Thomas and his new life mate are doing?"

Armand felt his mouth tighten at the mention of his son and his new wife, but couldn't resist asking, "How are they?"

"Very well. They're in Canada at the moment, visiting," Lucian answered, and then turned his attention back to his food as he asked, "You haven't met her yet, have you?"

"No," Armand muttered, watching him stab some salad and eat it.

Lucian chewed and swallowed and then asked with mild curiosity, "Did you ever get to meet Nicholas's Annie?"

Armand hesitated, but then simply said, "No. Now what's this favor?"

Lucian peered at him for a moment, but then turned his attention to cutting into his beef and announced, "I need a safe house for one of my enforcers for a couple of weeks."

"And you were thinking I could supply that?" Armand asked with surprise.

Lucian shrugged as he chewed and swallowed and then said, "You're surprised? I don't know why. You live way the hell out here in the backwoods. No one but myself and Thomas know where the farm is, and this is a rinky-dink little town where no one's likely to see her."

"Her?" Armand asked curiously.

"Eshe d'Aureus," he said, cutting off another piece of beef. "Castor's daughter."

"Castor d'Aureus," Armand murmured with respect. He'd never gotten the chance to meet the man, but he certainly knew the name. Castor was a hero to their people. Way back in the early days when the immortals had joined the rest of the world, one of their number, a no-fanger named Leonius Livius, had caused trouble for both the mortals and immortals alike. So much trouble, in fact, it had forced the other immortals to form a council and hunt down him and his progeny. It was Lucian and Castor who had slain the monster that Leonius Livius had become. In the middle of the battlefield while rogue no-fangers and the Council's fanged army had fought all around them, Lucian had pinned the man to the ground with his spear, and Castor had severed his head from his body. Both of them had been considered heroes for that, but Lucian was his brother, someone he knew on a day-to-day basis, while Castor was unknown and more of a mythic hero in his mind.

"He wasn't a hero," Lucian said quietly. "He was just a good man and a fine soldier. He was also my friend, and before he died he asked me to look out for Eshe and the others of his family should anything happen to him. Well, as you know, he died, and I've tried to look out for Eshe and it's what I'm trying to do now by getting her out of harm's way until we get this matter resolved. I'm thinking that will take about two weeks."

"What is the matter you have to resolve?" Armand asked.

Lucian sighed and set his fork and knife aside, his appetite apparently affected by thoughts of the matter. His voice was grim when he admitted, "Apparently we didn't get all the sons when we took out Leonius. At least one survived. He calls himself Leonius Livius the Second."

"You mean there's been one of his spawn running around all these centuries?" Armand asked with amazement. It was hard to imagine he'd gone without notice. If he was anything like his father, his atrocities should not have gone unnoticed all this time.

"He's been alive and flourished," Lucian assured him dryly. "The man has at least twenty sons that we know of. Or had," he added with satisfaction. "We've weeded some out. Apparently he's smarter than his father, though. That, or he has someone who has managed to keep him on a tight rein. He hasn't gone in for wholesale slaughter like his father enjoyed, or started any breeding camps. He's kept the numbers he attacks to one or two women at a time and the occasional unfortunate family. He only came into notice earlier this summer. He kidnapped two women from a grocery store parking lot up north. My men got one of the females away and killed three or four of his sons, but then had to hunt down the other female and the man who had taken her. Eshe was in on the search and was apparently spotted and recognized. Now my sources say he's targeted her for revenge for his father's death."

Armand nodded solemnly. "Has he targeted your Leigh too or anyone else in the family for your part in his father's death?"

"I don't think he knows about Leigh. In any case that doesn't matter, I can keep her safe. But Eshe is another matter. She's one of my enforcers and as stubborn and proud as her father ever was. She was ready to walk down the main street in Toronto nude to get his attention and have her chance at him when she heard he was looking for her."

"So she's like a female you, huh?" Armand asked with amusement.

"Ha ha," Lucian said dryly.

Armand chuckled at his sour expression. "If she's as bad as all that, how do you plan to convince her to hide out on my farm in the country until you catch this guy?"

"Yeah . . . well . . . that was a problem," Lucian muttered, picking up his knife and fork again. His expression was surly as he admitted, "She delights in flouting my orders as a rule. The best way to get her to do anything is to have me tell her to do the opposite. If she weren't Castor's daughter . . ." Lucian glowered briefly, but then sighed and shook his head. "Fortunately, even she wouldn't dare disobey a direct order from the Council."

"I see," Armand drawled slowly, his eyes narrowing suspiciously on his brother. "And she's agreed to stay on my farm twiddling her thumbs for several weeks?"

"I said two weeks," he pointed out, avoiding his gaze.

"And as I said, even she wouldn't disobey a direct order from the Council."

"So she isn't going to be happy," Armand surmised dryly.

Lucian shrugged. "She's too polite to take it out on you . . . probably," he added with a grin, then suggested, "Just keep her busy. Take her on picnics and hayrides, or whatever you hayseeds do."

"Hayseeds?" Armand echoed with disgust.

Lucian rolled his eyes. "Just keep her distracted and I'll call the minute it's safe for her to return to Toronto and work." He started to lift a bite of beef to his lips.

The fork was almost at his lips when he suddenly glanced past Armand and froze. His eyes widened, a curse slipped from his lips, and then he almost whispered, "I'm going to kill her."

"Who?" Armand asked with confusion, and then turned to glance in the direction that Lucian's gaze now seemed fixated. He was staring past him at the dark road outside. Armand peered at the long stretch of dark highway for a minute, slow to recognize the fiery vision approaching for what it was, a motorcycle with red, yellow, and orange LED lights around the tires and across the body that made it look like the bike was roaring up the road aflame. It was one hell of a magnificent sight.

"Eshe," Lucian snapped, finally answering his question. "That's her."

The motorcycle roared into the diner parking lot, spitting up gravel, and then eased to a halt beside Armand's pickup. He had a moment to get a closer view of the array of lights on the machine before the engine fell silent and the rider disembarked. The woman was tall, at least six feet, and she appeared to be all lean muscle in the black leather she wore. She also moved with the predatory grace of a panther.

"She looks like she was born to ride," Armand murmured, his eyes devouring her.

"More like born to bite," Lucian muttered.

Armand glanced curiously to his brother. "Why so annoyed?"

Lucian's mouth twisted with irritation, but he admitted, "I told her to make herself less conspicuous."

"Ah," Armand murmured, biting his lip to keep from grinning. It was the rare person, immortal or otherwise, who went against Lucian's orders, and he couldn't help but be amused that Eshe d'Aureus was apparently one of them. This was far away from being inconspicuous. There were probably eyes peering out the windows of every house she was passing and fingers excitedly punching in numbers on phones as word spread about the super-cool motorcycle that just rode past their place. It would be the main topic of conversation tomorrow in the diner as those who had seen it described it to those who hadn't. Not much went on in this small community.

"I'm going to tan her hide," Lucian growled as she walked past their window toward the entrance of the diner.

Armand couldn't help but think he wouldn't mind volunteering for the job as his gaze automatically dropped to the hide his brother thought needed tanning. The woman had a perfect body, with a nice round rump he suspected it would be a pleasure to touch for any reason . . . and he was contemplating the various reasons for doing just that—none of which included tanning her hide—when she opened the diner door and stepped inside, ending his view of her behind. It forced him to shift his attention to her front as she paused inside the door to undo her jacket and peer around. It was quite a nice view too, he had to admit. She still wore her helmet, so he couldn't see her face, but everything else on display was lovely. Black leather pants stretched tight over long, lean legs, but she also wore the black leather jacket now open to reveal some sort of black leather corset that left the upper curves of her breasts and her upper chest and throat on display. The woman had rich, mahogany skin that seemed to gleam under the diner's fluorescent lights as if she'd powdered herself with some sort of shimmery powder.

"I told you to make yourself inconspicuous." Lucian glared at the woman as she spotted them and approached.

"You said to make myself *less* conspicuous," she corrected in a calm voice. As she removed her helmet, she added, "And I did. See?"

Armand didn't know what Lucian was supposed to see, but he was seeing what he considered the finest-looking woman he'd seen in a long time, since his life mate had lived even. Eshe d'Aureus had huge, beautiful eyes that glowed golden with black flecks, a straight

Egyptian nose, and the most seductive lips he'd ever seen. He found her heart-stoppingly beautiful . . . and nowhere near inconspicuous.

"Eshe," Lucian growled with little patience. "Dying your hair hardly makes you less conspicuous when you're on that carnival bike of yours."

Armand's eyes shifted to her hair at those words. She wore it short on the sides and a little longer on top, and was presently running her long fingers through it in an effort to repair the flattening influence of the helmet, but it looked a perfectly natural dark brown, almost black to him. Although there appeared to be a fleck of lighter color at the ends in some places. He couldn't stop himself from asking, "What does it normally look like?"

"She normally dyes it a combination of red and blond on the end halves of the top strands so that it looks like her head's on fire," Lucian informed him dryly, and then turned to Eshe and added, "You did a piss-poor job of dying it. There's still some color at the ends."

Eshe rolled her eyes with exasperation and began to slide into Armand's side of the booth, forcing him to shift over to make room for her. "God, you're never happy, Lucian. Honestly! It's not like I had time to make a hair appointment and get it done properly. I had to do it myself and I am *not* a hairdresser. This is the best I could do in the time you allotted me." She set her helmet on the table in front of her and rested her chin on her hands on top of it as she grinned at Lucian. "So it's all your fault if you aren't happy with it."

"Couldn't you at least have come out in your car instead of that damned motorcycle?" Lucian said irritably.

"Oh yes, because a red Ferrari would be so much less conspicuous down here in hicksville," Eshe said dryly, and then glanced to Armand and murmured, "No offense."

"None taken," he assured her, and then cleared his throat and forced himself to turn away when he realized he was grinning at her like an idiot.

"Ferrari?" Lucian asked with surprise. "What happened to the convertible?"

"I sold it," she said with a shrug. "The Ferrari was prettier and I only have the one parking space at the apartment for both the bike and car, so the convertible had to go."

"A Ferrari?" Lucian looked horrified. "It was bad enough when you had the Mustang convertible, but a Ferrari with all the power it has under the bonnet? You're a speed demon. You'll kill yourself with it. You had better be following the speed limits."

Armand stared at his brother with fascination. Lucian had never been much of a talker, mostly grunting and glaring at everyone, but Eshe appeared to exasperate him into speaking. He'd never thought he'd see the day. His thoughts were distracted when Eshe said dryly, "Of course . . . Daddy."

Armand's eyes widened, but she wasn't done. Smile widening as Lucian grew grimmer, she commented, "I hope Leigh pops some babies for you soon, Lucian. Maybe you'll stop daddying the rest of us."

"Daddying?" Armand asked doubtfully. He could think of a lot of words to describe Lucian, *bossy* and *bullying* among them, but *daddy* just wasn't on that list.

"Yes, daddying," Eshe said with a friendly smile his way. "He's forever telling everyone what to do and where to go and so on. He's like a big old grumpy daddy."

"Your father—" Lucian began, but she cut him off.

"My dad asked you to look out for me and my brothers and sisters should anything happen to him and you're just trying to live up to that promise, yada yada," she said in a bored voice that suggested she'd heard that argument a thousand times at least. "That argument carried some weight back when I was a kid, Lucian, but jeez, more than a millennium later it means nothing. You're only a hundred years older than me for cripes sake. Get over it already. I'm sure my father didn't mean for you to play guardian *forever*."

"You're only a hundred years younger than Lucian?" Armand asked with surprise. "You seem a lot younger."

"Why thank you!" She turned and beamed a smile on him that had Armand almost sighing, and then she stuck out her hand, "Hello, I'm Eshe d'Aureus and you're Armand Argeneau."

"Yes." He took her hand and shook it, smiling at how small and soft it felt in his own. "So why aren't you as grumpy as Lucian? I always thought it was his age."

Eshe snorted at the suggestion. "Not hardly. Father Time over there just likes to carry the weight of the world—not to mention passing time—on his shoulders like a vampiric Atlas. Me? I enjoy life to the best of my abilities and leave Lucian and others like him to be the grump masters."

"There are others like Lucian?" Armand asked with doubt.

Eshe raised her eyebrows. "Not traveled much in Europe? Because there are a ton of them over there. Especially Britain; even the mortal males when they get older are grumpy and bossy in Britain. I think it's a law or something."

Armand was just smiling at what she said and trying to think of something to encourage her continued disrespect of Lucian—which was incredibly fresh and exciting in a turning-him-on kind of way to Armand—when his cell phone began to chirp its funeral dirge. Grimacing, he slipped it from his pocket, flipped it open, and pressed it to his ear, wincing when Paul, his manager at the farm, began to squawk in panicked tones about Bessy's labor. When the man paused to take a breath, he took the opportunity to say, "I'm on my way. I'm only at the diner. I'll be there in five minutes."

"Trouble at home?" Lucian asked dryly as Armand snapped the phone closed and slipped it back in his pocket.

Armand nodded and began to slide out of the booth as Eshe got out to make way for him. "One of my dairy cows is calving and there's a problem with the birth."

"I thought you had a wheat farm?" Eshe asked, glancing up with surprise in her eyes as he straightened beside her.

"I do, but we have a couple of dairy cows too and a few other animals; chickens, goats . . ." He shrugged. "Most farmers keep them to save on groceries."

"And what do you do with them?" she asked curiously, assuming, correctly, that he didn't eat.

"My manager takes some of the goods, but mostly we supply meat and eggs and milk to the diner here."

"We'll follow you home," Lucian announced, eating more quickly.

"Take your time. I'll be down at the barn, but make yourselves at home. The front door is always unlocked." When Lucian raised an eyebrow at that, he said wryly, "It's the country. No one bothers anyone out here and crime is pretty rare."

He waited just long enough for Lucian to grunt an acknowledgment and then smiled and nodded at Eshe and strode out of the diner. He could feel her watching him as he left and wished he could watch her too. She was a beautiful woman, and he was looking forward to her company at the farm. His manager handled things during the day and had the evenings off, and Armand was usually alone there when awake. It would be nice to have someone to talk to for a change, especially someone he found attractive. It had been a long time since he'd found anyone attractive in more than a passing-fancy kind of way. Even his second and third wives hadn't been that attractive to him. His affection for them had been based more in friendship and companionship than in pure animal lust. Armand suspected it was going to be difficult to keep his distance from the lovely Eshe d'Aureus . . . and wasn't even sure if he really wanted to anyway.

* * *

Eshe watched Armand walk out of the restaurant, her eyes sliding from his broad shoulders to the narrow waist and then down over his behind and legs. He had a confident walk with a hint of a swagger that was purely unconscious, she was sure, a natural rolling of his feet and shifting of hips as he moved. His broad shoulders remained straight, his head high. With his rugged features and silver-blue eyes, she hadn't been able to help but notice that he was a good-looking man, but then she hadn't met an Argeneau male who wasn't. They weren't all classically handsome, but they had a certain something. Armand seemed to her to have been gifted with a little extra helping of that certain something.

"You should see if you can read him."

Eshe glanced around with surprise at that comment from Lucian. He was halfway through his meal and eating quickly. She settled back in the booth to watch him, eyeing the food curiously. It smelled good, she noted, and asked in a distracted voice, "Why would I want to do that?"

"The real question is why haven't you already done so?" he said dryly, scooping up potatoes and peas together onto his fork. "I have known you a long time, Eshe, and never known you not to try to read every newcomer you encounter . . . whether they were mortal or immortal."

Eshe scowled at him as he popped the food into his mouth, mostly because he was right. She wouldn't admit this to anyone, but she was eager to meet a new life mate and enjoy the peace and passion she had enjoyed with her first life mate for several centuries. Life was terribly drab and boring without the vibrancy a life mate brought to it. That being the case, the first thing she usually did on meeting someone was try to read him. Although *try* wasn't the correct term since she hadn't yet met anyone she couldn't read. The only reason she could think that she hadn't read Armand was that she had been too busy annoying Lucian. It was a pastime she'd enjoyed for centuries. After living so long, life could get a bit boring at times. A gal had to amuse herself somehow.

Still, it was unusual for her to not read newcomers, Eshe acknowledged to herself, and had to wonder why she hadn't. The question, however, made her uncomfortable and eager to change the subject.

"So did he buy your story about me needing a safe house?" she asked quietly as she watched Armand Argeneau get in his pickup and pull out of the diner parking lot.

Lucian nodded without even glancing her way. "Why wouldn't he?"

Eshe made a face. "I suppose. It's not like he knows me. If he knew me he wouldn't think I was willing to hide out anywhere."

"Hmmm," Lucian murmured, finishing off his food. "Well, do me a favor and try not to make that too obvious while you're down here."

"Right," she murmured, and then when he pushed his plate away and stood up, she stood as well and asked curiously, "Do you really think he could have killed his wives?"

"No," Lucian acknowledged, digging out his wallet

to throw a twenty on the table. "But then I didn't think Jean Claude could do what he did either."

Eshe frowned at these words as she retrieved her helmet from the table. She followed him toward the diner door, asking, "Why don't you just read him and see if he did it? For that matter, why didn't you read Jean Claude?"

"Because I couldn't."

The words startled her so much that Eshe stopped walking. She could maybe understand his not being able to read Jean Claude who had been his twin, but Armand . . . "But you're four hundred years older than Armand."

Pausing at the door, Lucian glanced back and grimaced. "For some reason—which I've never been able to work out—there are some siblings and even one or two nieces and nephews in the family that I can't read."

"Really?" Eshe asked with interest as she finally began to move again and joined him by the door. "I didn't know that."

"It's not something I advertise," he said dryly, pushing through the door.

"No, I suppose not," she murmured, trailing him outside. "So, why do you suspect Armand? It's not just because you can't read him."

"No, it's not," he agreed, walking along the front of the diner to a dark van parked several feet past her motorcycle. "And it's not that I suspect him so much as I don't feel I can afford not to. As far as I can tell, his being their husband is the only connection between his three wives. And then Annie was his son's wife."

"And Nicholas wasn't killed, just put on the run to prevent his discovering whatever it is Annie might have learned," Eshe murmured thoughtfully. She knew the whole story. Armand Argeneau had lost three wives to "accidents." Each more than a hundred years apart and each after marrying him and giving birth to one child. His daughter-in-law had also died in a tragic and somewhat freak accident after marrying his son. She had been pregnant, but hadn't yet given birth to what would have been their first child when she died. Both had perished in that freak accident. More important to the situation was that it appeared Annie had been asking questions about the deaths of Armand's wives before her sudden death, and while speaking to Nicholas on the phone the night before her accident, she had been rather excited and told him she had something to tell him when he got home. However, she'd died before she could tell him whatever that was, and when Nicholas had set out some weeks later to ask a friend of Annie's if she knew what Annie had wanted to tell him, he had somehow ended up in his basement with a dead mortal in his arms, her blood in his mouth and a blank spot where the memory of killing her should have been.

Nicholas, a rogue hunter Eshe had worked with a couple of times before these events, had been on the run since that night fifty years ago, but had recently turned himself in to save his new life mate. However, Annie's phone call and the blank spot where the murder of the mortal should have been had been enough to make Lucian reluctant to execute him as was expected. Instead, he'd assigned Eshe the task of sorting out the mess and finding out what really happened to Armand's wives and, hopefully, Annie and Nicholas. It was a pretty demanding task, almost impossible to do, really, since Armand's first wife had died in 1449, she thought.

"Follow me to the house," Lucian said as he got into his van.

Eshe merely nodded and moved on to her motorcycle, pulling her helmet on as she went. Her actions were automatic as she mounted and started the bike; her mind was on Armand Argeneau and the possibility that he had had something to do with the deaths of his wives and then Annie. It definitely wouldn't be a happy thought to anyone who knew and cared at all for the Argeneau clan, and Eshe was one of those people. The Argeneaus were presently enjoying a happy period after centuries of misery and oppression by Lucian's brother Jean Claude, and didn't need this kind of thing to blight their happiness.

Sighing, she forced herself to focus on the task at hand and followed Lucian's van out of the parking lot.

Armand's farm wasn't far from the diner, which was probably good since—despite her best efforts—Eshe's mind was preoccupied with her thoughts, leaving her little attention for driving. She automatically slowed when the van's brake lights came on, then followed it onto a long paved driveway lined with trees. The trees were old and large, their branches stretching like a canopy over the road and blocking out the stars overhead. It was actually startling when they suddenly fell away on either side, spreading out to surround a clearing around an old Victorian farmhouse.

Eshe slowed to a stop behind the van when it came to a halt, and then drove around to park beside it on the circular drive that ran around in front of the house. Her eyes traveled over the building as she did. It was an old Victorian gabled farmhouse of yellow brick with gingerbread trim and a porch that ran its length along the front. The porch rail ran along both sides of a set of four or five stairs, leading up to double doors that were dead center in the front of the building. Light spilled from the windows on the main floor, adding to the illumination from the porch light that shone over the doors in a welcoming manner.

Eshe turned off her motorcycle and disembarked, her gaze sliding over the abode with interest as she removed her helmet. While the building was old, it was in good repair, either tended with love over the hundred or so years since it had been built, or refurbished at some point and restored to its original glory. Her guess would have been that it had been well tended rather than refurbished. The gingerbread trim and wavy window glass looked authentic to her.

"Your guess would be right," Lucian announced, appearing at her side.

Eshe scowled at him for reading her mind, a rude habit the man had and never apologized for, and then her gaze slid to the cooler he carried and she breathed out a little sigh at the thought of the blood it probably contained. Lucian's call had woken her up mid-afternoon and she'd been in such a rush to follow orders and get down here that she hadn't thought to feed before leaving. She was beginning to feel it.

Lucian smiled faintly at her thoughts and waved her forward. "Then lead the way and you can have a bag or two while I put the rest of these in Armand's refrigerator."

Eshe nodded, retrieved her bag from the CruzPac on the back of her motorcycle, and started toward the house.

"That's it? That's your idea of packing for a trip?" Lucian asked, eyeing her bag with disbelief as he followed her to the stairs.

"What were you expecting? A steamer trunk?" she asked dryly. "Besides, I wasn't sure how country folk dress. I thought I'd buy a couple of things down here once I figure that out."

"You make it sound like farmers are another race entirely," Lucian said, half with disgust and half with amusement.

"As if you don't think the same thing," she said dryly, and then added, "Besides, they are as far as I can tell." Eshe shook her head as she admitted, "I just don't understand why anyone would bury themselves out here in the backwoods. I had enough of that nonsense in the Dark Ages, thank you very much. Outhouses hold no attraction for me. I prefer city living."

"I believe they have plumbing out here now," Lucian said with amusement.

"They didn't the last time I was on a farm."

"When was that?"

"When we were hunting that rogue down in Arkansas," she answered with a shudder. The living conditions in the nest had been positively brutal to her mind. She'd actually felt she was doing the rogue and his little mini rogues a favor by putting them out of their misery. That had been one of their kill-order hunts. Where the rogues had already been investigated and judged, but their hideout just discovered.

"For God's sake, woman, that was seventy or eighty years ago."

"Not long enough ago for me to forget," she said with another shudder.

"If I'd known it was going to scar you, I wouldn't have included you in that hunt," he said dryly.

"Yeah, right," she snorted. "More like you would have made me hit all the farmhouses with outhouses after that. Why do you think I didn't let you know how much it bothered me at the time? You're a sadistic bastard, Lucian. You would have seen it as your duty to desensitize me to the situation."

Lucian's answer was a grunt as she held the door for him to enter ahead of her.

"So how long are you staying, anyway?" she asked as he moved past her and started up the long hall. It had several doors leading off it and a set of stairs on one side leading to the second level. Lucian had obviously been here before; he headed straight up the hall toward the back of the house.

"Long enough to talk to Armand again and then I'm heading back."

"I figured when I saw that Leigh wasn't with you,"

Eshe admitted with a smile as she mentioned his life mate. The two were rarely apart, and she'd honestly expected to find the woman at the diner with Lucian and Armand when she'd arrived.

"She and Marguerite are having a girls' night out, some time at the spa, dinner out, and a movie," Lucian announced as he led the way into the last room on the back left side of the house. "I'd like to be home before her if I can."

Eshe murmured acknowledgment of his comment, but her attention was on the room they'd entered. The light in this room was off, but enough light was streaming in from the hallway that Eshe could see it was a country-style kitchen with wide plank wood floors, a brick-faced outer wall, three inner walls painted what appeared in that light to be a sunny yellow, an island in the kitchen side, by the refrigerator, and what appeared to be an old-fashioned wood-burning stove. The name Elmira on the front told her that it was probably a gas stove, specially designed to appear to be authentic to the Victorian home.

Her gaze shifted to Lucian as he set the cooler on the stone-topped island stationed at the cooking end of the room. When Eshe paused beside him, he opened the container, retrieved a bag of blood, and handed it to her.

Eshe murmured a thank-you, leaned her side against the island, opened her mouth, waited for her fangs to slide out and down, and then quickly popped the bag of blood to them.

Lucian then turned to open the refrigerator behind

him. When he peered inside and grunted, Eshe shifted to peer in around his shoulder. Her eyebrows rose when she saw there wasn't a single bag of blood inside. Either they had arrived between deliveries or Armand kept his blood supply somewhere else.

Shaking his head, Lucian turned back to begin transferring the blood bags from the cooler to the refrigerator and Eshe backed up a couple of steps to give him room. The bag at her mouth was nearly empty and Lucian was turning to set two bags in the refrigerator when he suddenly dropped them and whirled toward her, his hand shooting over her shoulder and past her head.

Eshe heard skin slap on skin and a choked sound from directly behind her and quickly glanced over her shoulder. Her eyes widened incredulously as she saw the man dangling in the air behind her, Lucian's hand around his throat and holding him off the floor. He held a knife clenched in one tight hand.

Two

A curse from the doorway made Eshe glance that way to see Armand coming to a halt in the entrance. Anger flashed over his expression, but it was quickly replaced with resignation. His voice was weary when he asked, "What happened?"

"Your house wasn't empty as you said it would be," Lucian said grimly.

Armand looked annoyed, but explained, "That's Paul Williams. He's my day manager here on the farm. I expected he'd head right back down to the barn after calling me, but he must have sat down here to wait for me. Unfortunately, I drove straight down to the barn when I got here. When I realized he wasn't there, I hurried back here to find him." He paused and frowned and then asked, "But why did he attack?"

"Neither of us noticed him at the table. I started to unpack the blood, Eshe flashed her fangs and popped a bag, and he tried to stake her," Lucian said dryly, and then grimaced and said, "Although I guess it would be stab since there weren't any stakes handy and he was reduced to grabbing a knife from the butcher block."

Eshe shifted from between the two men, stepping away to get a better look at the mortal who had been about to attack her. She grimaced and tore away the now-empty blood bag from her teeth as she got a better look at the large carving knife in his right hand. It wouldn't have killed her, but would have hurt like hell had he finished his action and stabbed her before Lucian had noticed him. Grimacing, she muttered, "Friendly guy."

Armand frowned at the knife, but then glanced to Lucian and asked with disbelief, "You didn't notice him? How the hell could you not notice him?"

"The light is off," Lucian pointed out stiffly. "Mortals do not generally sit around in the dark, so I assumed the room was empty and didn't glance toward the table where he was apparently sitting. Besides, I was distracted talking to Eshe." He frowned, and then shook his head and turned to concentrate on the mortal briefly before turning to Armand and raising one eyebrow. "He has been with you since the beginning of summer, but you haven't explained about us to him?"

"Of course I haven't. He's a good worker," Armand said with disgust, running one hand through his hair in a weary gesture. When Lucian merely raised his other eyebrow, Armand sighed and said with some exasperation, "Have you ever even had to *try* to initiate a mortal to our world?" He didn't allow Lucian to answer, but merely clucked with disgust and said, "Of course not, you only keep immortals around you."

"It makes life simpler," Lucian said with a shrug.

"Yes, well, some of us need mortals who can go out in sunlight so we don't need to double our blood consumption . . . and let me tell you, it isn't easy. Nine times out of ten when you do tell them they don't take it well and have to have their memories changed and be sent away." He blew a breath out through his mouth and then said irritably, "It's a huge pain in the ass. You tell them you're a vampire and they think you're joking. You flash your fangs to convince them, and half the time they piss their pants or reach for a weapon. You take the weapon away and explain that no, no, it isn't like that. We aren't the soulless dead. Our vampirism is scientific in nature. Our ancestors were Atlanteans and they were more advanced than even the myths suggest. They developed nanos that were shot into the body to repair injuries and fight illness, only the nanos use blood to do it and to propel themselves, more blood than the body can create, and so we need to consume blood from an outside source." He snorted, and then added, "Oh right, and the nanos see aging as something that needs repairing, so keep their hosts at their peak condition and young . . . forever."

His mouth twisted and he shook his head. "As I said, nine times out of ten they don't take it well and I end up having to wipe their memory and send them on their way." His gaze shifted to the man Lucian still held in the air. "Paul is a hard worker, a good manager, but he's very authoritarian in nature. I suspect he'll be one of the nine rather than the one out of ten. I didn't want to have to find a new manager so I've been putting off telling him."

"Your instincts are good," Lucian said quietly as he took away the knife the mortal still clutched and set him on his feet. "Judging by what I'm reading in his thoughts right now, Mr. Williams will have to be wiped and sent on his way."

"It figures," Armand muttered with disgust. "And I suppose it has to be done now."

Lucian didn't comment, but then Eshe supposed he didn't have to. The level of fear the man must have experienced to have come at her with a knife when she hadn't done a thing to threaten him meant that to wipe the memory and keep it wiped, Paul would never be able to see either her or Lucian, or even this kitchen again without risking that memory's return. There was even a chance that seeing Armand framed in a doorway could spark the memory and bring it back to life. Paul Williams had to be sent away to ensure the memory didn't return.

"I will handle Mr. Williams," Lucian announced. "You have a calving cow in trouble to deal with."

Armand hesitated, and then nodded grimly. "Paul was bunking in the smaller house behind this one. The furniture stays, but everything else is his and will have to be packed onto his pickup. I'll go write a generous severance check for him and drop it off to you at the house on my way back out to the barn."

Lucian glanced to Eshe. "Put away the blood and then meet me at the manager's house."

Eshe nodded but then simply stood and watched as Armand turned and headed up the hall. Once he was gone, Lucian focused his attention on her and said, "When he comes back, I want you to try to read him."

Eshe frowned, but Lucian then marched Armand's now ex–day manager out of the kitchen, and she moved around the island to continue with the work he'd started, retrieving bags of blood and stacking them in the mostly empty refrigerator. She was quick about the task, eager to get out to the house, get the manager on his way, and start this new job.

Eshe was an enforcer and had been for some time. She hunted rogue vampires, finding their nests, capturing them and usually bringing them back to the Council for judgment. Although there had been the odd job Lucian led where the rogue had already been judged and there was no need to go to the trouble of bringing him back at all, alive or otherwise. Those jobs were usually fast-paced and brutal. However, this job wasn't going to be anything like that. This was going to be more brainpower than muscle, and she had to take her time, ask the right questions, and follow the right leads. She just hoped she found the answers that would cause the least pain to everyone involved. She didn't want to fail to find any answers at all, or find the ones they didn't want and be the reason Nicholas Argeneau was executed.

Armand gave the cow a reassuring pat on the side as she licked and cleaned her new calf. He was surprised she had the energy. It had been a hard birth. The calf had gotten itself turned around and tangled in the umbilical cord. For a while there he thought he wouldn't be able to correct the situation in time to save the calf. There had even been a moment or two when he'd worried for the mother, but he'd managed to get the calf turned and all had worked out in the end.

Straightening, he stripped off the rubber gloves he'd donned to try to turn the calf and glanced at his wristwatch, grimacing when he saw the time. It was just after midnight. It had been only a couple of hours since he'd come back out to the barn. It felt like it had been at least twice that. In fact, he was a little surprised to walk out of the barn into a starry night rather than predawn light.

His eyes moved to the manager's house first. He wasn't surprised to see that the lights were out. In the short time it had taken him to walk to his office earlier, find his checkbook—which admittedly had taken a couple of minutes, Armand was always misplacing the thing—write a check, and carry it out to the manager's house, Lucian had already gotten Paul there and had him half packed up. While Lucian himself had been working at the increased speed their people were capable of, he was also controlling Paul and making him work almost as quickly.

Armand suspected they'd probably gotten the task done and Lucian had seen Paul off while he was still trying to calm the cow so he could help her. No doubt Lucian had been sitting around for hours waiting for him to finish and return to the house . . . along with Eshe. She'd come out once to ask if she could help him, but he'd sent her away, finding her too much a distraction to be an aid.

There was something about the woman, a combination of sultriness and strength that quite fascinated him. The very way she moved held his eye and attention. She definitely would have been more hindrance than help in the barn. Now that the calf and mother were well, however, Armand found himself eager to get to the house and see her again. It had been a long time since a woman's very presence had captured his attention so. Not since his first wife, Susanna, his one and only life mate.

The thought brought a frown to his face as Armand mounted the steps to the back porch of the house. He had no desire to examine that fact further. In truth, all it did was make him think it might be best if he refused to allow her to stay with him. But he couldn't do that. Aside from the fact that you simply didn't refuse Lucian Argeneau, he had to admit Eshe would probably be safest at his home. If she went somewhere else and something happened, he'd never forgive himself.

Armand found Lucian and Eshe in his living room. She was leafing idly through a magazine while Lucian had the television on and was flicking through the few channels available with a bored expression that turned to irritation when he saw Armand entering.

"Dear God, Armand, you've only got basic cable here. What's the matter with you? The best shows are on the upper channels, and I don't know how you live without the movie channels."

Armand shrugged, amusement tugging at his lips. "I

wouldn't even have basic cable if it weren't for Agnes. My sister-in-law by my first wife," he explained for Eshe's benefit, before adding, "She ordered it for me when I asked her to arrange for the Internet out here. I'm still not sure why she bothered with cable at all. I don't watch television." He raised an eyebrow. "As far as I knew you didn't either. When did you start?"

"Leigh's got me watching a couple of shows," Lucian muttered, and then said, "Most of what's on TV is crap, but there are a couple of good ones amongst the drivel."

"Are there?" Armand asked dryly, finding himself oddly amused at his brother. It was a rare situation to find himself in. Lucian was rarely amusing, but finding his life mate had given him an almost human side that sat awkwardly on his shoulders, and was definitely bringing a smile to Armand's face. It was interesting to see. Given some time, Leigh might manage to make him almost normal. Doubtful, he supposed, but still it was fun to contemplate. Putting that possibility aside for now, he raised his eyebrows. "So . . . ? I'm surprised you're still here. Was there something else you needed to tell me?"

"Yes." Lucian turned off the television and stood. "Let's get to it, I've already been gone longer than I intended. We'll talk in the kitchen. I want more blood."

Armand smiled wryly and stepped aside as Lucian moved past him to head up the hall. It might be his home, but that didn't stop his brother from acting as if it were his own. He was like that everywhere, though, and all the time. It was not unexpected. His gaze slid to Eshe, but when she continued with her magazine, he left her to it and followed Lucian.

"You had no blood in your refrigerator when I put this in. Are you waiting on a delivery?" Lucian asked as he walked to the refrigerator to retrieve blood.

"I keep my blood supply in my bedroom refrigerator. I have a mortal housekeeper, and between her and Paul, it seemed wise not to risk one of them sticking their noses in the fridge and wondering about a supply of bagged blood."

"And the juice and few other items in there?" Lucian asked, retrieving two bags of blood and closing the door.

"Camouflage," Armand murmured as he accepted the bag Lucian held out to him and followed him to the kitchen table at the far end of the room. "An empty refrigerator would cause questions I don't want to answer. I always keep something in the fridge. I change it out once in a while, feeding the fruit and lunchmeat to the pigs and replacing the juices and milk with fresh stuff when they've passed their 'best before' date."

Lucian grunted at the information as he settled at the table. A moment of silence passed as they concentrated on feeding, but once the bags were empty, Armand took them and walked over to throw them out in the garbage under the sink as he asked, "So what did you need to tell me?"

"I've arranged for extra blood in your deliveries for as long as Eshe is here," Lucian informed him, all business now. "I'll pick up the tab."

"There's no need for that," Armand murmured. He had shares in Argeneau Enterprises and ten farms all making a profit. He could supply blood for the woman for the couple of weeks she was here.

Lucian ignored him and pulled out his wallet to retrieve a credit card. "She'll need more clothes than she brought. Is there somewhere around here you can take her shopping?"

"Of course, Lucian," he said dryly, and then pointed out, "London is only twenty minutes or so north of here."

"Hmm." Lucian didn't seem impressed and said, "She has rather exotic tastes."

Armand grinned at Lucian's pained expression, but merely said, "London has designer stores. It's a good-sized city, you know."

"For Ontario, maybe," Lucian said dryly and passed the credit card to him. "Put her clothes on the company card."

Armand raised an eyebrow at the suggestion, not sure it was exactly kosher to put a woman's clothes on the company card, but accepted it rather than argue.

"And put anything else she asks for on the card too. I don't expect you to be out-of-pocket for doing us this favor." Before he could comment, Lucian asked, "Have you tried to read her?"

Armand felt his eyebrows rise, but admitted, "No."

"Why not?" he asked at once.

"She's older than me, I'm not likely to be able to."

"Still, you should try to read her. Most immortals would try on first meeting someone in hopes they'd found their life mate."

Armand felt his mouth tighten and glanced away as he muttered, "I'm not looking for a new life mate."

"Hmmph." Lucian scowled at him, and then added, "Well, I want you to try to read her before we leave. We'll rejoin her in the living room and I want you to try." When Armand glared at him rebelliously, he added, "Just do it for me. If I call you with updates, I need to know how much I can tell you. I don't want her reading something from your mind and coming rushing back to Toronto if another enforcer gets hurt in her place or something."

"Right, whatever," Armand muttered, understanding the need for it.

"Come on." Lucian was up and out of the room in the next heartbeat and Armand reluctantly followed him back to the living room. The moment they entered, Eshe glanced up, and Lucian gestured for Armand to get to it. He grimaced, but turned his concentration to the woman, focusing on her forehead, seeing it but not seeing it as he tried to penetrate her thoughts. He wasn't terribly surprised when he failed to do so.

"Well?" Lucian asked impatiently. When Armand merely shook his head, Lucian nodded as if he'd expected as much, which he probably had since Eshe was the older of the two of them, and often it was hard for a younger vampire to read an older one. Lucian then glanced to Eshe and ordered, "See me out."

She got up at once, but managed to look as if she was doing it only because she chose to rather than because he'd barked at her like she was a dog who had to obey. She also sauntered out of the room in her own good time, rather than quick-marching as Armand suspected most immortals would have done, and he found himself admiring her spunk as well as her fine ass as she made her way out of the room. Armand was about to follow her swaying hips out the door when Lucian was suddenly in front of him, one hand on his chest to hold him back.

"There's no need for you to accompany us. She'll be back in a minute. Wait here."

Armand briefly debated flouting the order as he suspected Eshe would have, but then shrugged and moved to settle in the La-Z-Boy she had just evacuated. She would be back soon enough and he'd have her company for two weeks. He could wait, he decided, and then turned his head to the side and sniffed as he noticed that the chair was still warm from her occupancy and a trace of her perfume lingered in the air around him. It was a lovely, spicy scent that he decided suited her perfectly, and he inhaled of it deeply, drawing it into his lungs with pleasure.

"I couldn't read him," Eshe admitted in a small voice the moment the door of the house closed behind her and Lucian and they wouldn't be overheard. The fact that she couldn't read Armand was almost mind-numbing. Eshe had tried to read Armand the first time when he'd shown up in the door of the living room on returning from the barn, and then again when he'd returned from the kitchen with Lucian. She had failed to pierce his thoughts both times.

Eshe had known the second time that he too was

trying to read her, probably under Lucian's order, and had let her guards drop to allow it, but had seen him shaking his head in response to Lucian's prompting "Well?" However, her main concern had been that she couldn't read him. She should have been able to. She was older than he was and had only ever encountered one person that she hadn't been able to read: Orion. He had been only ten years younger than she and had been her first and last life mate. It seemed Armand might be her second.

Any other time, finding a possible life mate would have been a cause for joy. This time, however, with this man—a suspect in several possible murders—it was not a joyful event and she was almost in a panic at the realization.

"I couldn't read him," she repeated more grimly as they descended the stairs to cross to Lucian's van.

"I know. I could tell by your expression," he said solemnly. Lucian tapped his leg as he started across the pavement to the van. "It might not mean anything. I can't read him. Maybe he's hard to read."

"And if it does mean something?" she asked quietly as they paused beside the van. She grimaced when he narrowed his gaze on her, knowing he was reading her, and had done so intermittently all evening. She said, "I know you know I find him attractive as well."

"I wouldn't start worrying unless you find yourself suddenly eating," he said quietly, and then added, "And if you do . . ." His mouth tightened. "It doesn't change things, Eshe. You're here to do a job and I expect you to do it whether he's a possible life mate or not."

"Yes, of course," she murmured, forcing herself to at least appear calm. Clearing her throat, she held on to the van door when he opened it to get in and asked, "Any last instructions?"

Lucian settled in the driver's seat before turning to peer at her solemnly. "Just watch your back."

When she stared back blankly, he pointed out, "His last life mate didn't fare very well, nor did his wives. Just stay alert and get the answers we need as quickly as you can."

Eshe nodded unhappily, and when no other orders were forthcoming and he leaned forward to start the engine, she pushed the van door closed. She then watched silently as he followed the circle back onto the driveway and headed up the lane toward the road.

Eshe stood in the driveway until his rear lights disappeared before turning to peer at the house. Inside was a man who might be her life mate. Unfortunately, he might also be a murderer as well.

Three

The rather loud roar of a vacuum cleaner outside her bedroom door woke Eshe at about mid-afternoon. The annoying sound was one she found impossible to ignore, and she glared at the door of the guest room where she'd spent a very restless day and silently cursed Lucian for assigning her this job. So far, she hadn't made a stellar impression on the job. After seeing Lucian Argeneau off the night before, she'd spent several minutes girding her courage for what lay ahead, then had marched back into the house determined to start at once.

However, before she could ask any questions of the man who might be either her life mate, a murderer, or both, he'd greeted her with a quiet "My room is the master bedroom at the back of the house upstairs, but there are four guest rooms upstairs as well. Take whichever one you want. I need to go check on Bessy and her calf and attend to a few chores. I'll see you when you get up tomorrow. Good night."

Armand had then slipped past her and out of the house before she could even murmur a quiet thank-you. Eshe had stared after him with amazement, finding the situation rather anticlimactic after her moments of worry, but then had heaved her breath out on a sigh, collected her bag, and gone above stairs to check out the guest rooms. Each of them was nice, but Eshe's favorite had been the rose-colored room next to the master bedroom. She'd dropped her bag on the bed and then gone to poke through Armand's room while she had the chance.

Her poking hadn't turned up anything of use. There hadn't been any handy-dandy little diary with a written confession of terrible deeds, or bloody weapons that might have been used to behead past wives. In fact, there hadn't even been pictures or portraits of his wives or from the past. The room had held a bed, a chair by the fire, a bookshelf full of books both old and new, and a closet full of clothes. The en suite bathroom hadn't been any more helpful. She'd left the master bedroom knowing no more about the man than what brand of aftershave and toothpaste he used.

Eshe had wandered the house after that, noting the absence of knickknacks and memorabilia. It seemed Armand wasn't the sentimental sort. There was nothing of his past life or wives in the house. Only the office held anything that told her the man had family. It hadn't been anything out in the open. As with the rest of the rooms in the house, this one had no visible photos or portraits that suggested there was anyone in the world he cared for, but after picking the lock on the large bottom drawer of his desk, she'd found a collection of photo albums and a box that held miniature portraits. The portraits had been older, from before the invention of photography. They had been paintings of three women she presumed were his life mate and wives, and then of his children. She recognized both Nicholas and Thomas, whom she'd met through her position as hunter, and guessed that the daughter was Jeanne Louise, his daughter by his last wife, Rosamund.

The albums themselves had held much more recent images, one had held pictures of his eldest son, Nicholas, and his wife, Annie, both looking happy at various functions, their wedding, on picnics, and so on. Then there had been an album dedicated to Thomas with newer photos of his wedding to Inez in Portugal. The last album had been of Jeanne Louise, following her from her knobby-kneed youth, through her graduation from the university, and then at various family functions.

Eshe had found that discovery somewhat reassuring. She had been told that Armand had cut all ties with his children and the rest of the family after his last wife's death a century ago and had never even seen his daughter, Jeanne Louise, since dropping her on his sister-in-law Marguerite's doorstep after the death of the girl's mother, Rosamund. Those albums suggested, however, that while he hadn't seen her in person, he'd been keeping up with her life and what she was doing, and he did care about the girl. The fact that he'd hidden those albums away, however, was rather curious. The man lived alone. There was no reason she could think of to hide them anyway.

Pondering the matter, Eshe had locked the albums away back safely in their drawer, and then slid out of the room to await Armand's return, her mind full of questions. She'd waited for him to return to the house until just before dawn, pacing his living room like a caged tiger until she couldn't stand it anymore and had finally gone out in search of him. She'd found the barn that held his dairy cows, a couple of pigs and goats, but he hadn't been there. She'd then gone through the other barns searching a good-sized one that held horses, and a henhouse full of sleeping chickens that had started stirring before she determined he wasn't there and closed the door on the incredible stench coming from inside, and then she'd checked the last barn to find it held a tractor, a riding lawn mower, and various other farm equipment but no sign of Armand.

Eshe had given up after that and made her way back to the house as the sun began to crest the horizon. Tired, she'd sought out her room and got ready for bed, thinking she would start fresh in the evening. However, tired as she'd been, sleep had not been easy to claim or keep. It was bloody noisy in the country. She often heard people comment on how noisy the city was and how blissfully quiet the country was in comparison, but she would have a couple of choice words on the subject in future. They were full of crap. Her apartment in the city was soundproofed, her sleep never disturbed by the sounds of traffic or city life. The same wasn't true out here. While there wasn't much in the way of traffic on this rural road, there were a gazillion other sounds instead; the deep thrum of passing trains in the distance, the chatter and song of birds, the chirps of crickets . . . She'd had the devil of a time getting to sleep and staying there.

And now there was that damned vacuum cleaner to contend with, she thought, and glowered at the door as the sound grew louder, suggesting it hadn't been right outside her room at first but now was.

The country definitely was not a quiet place, Eshe decided grimly as something banged against the base of the door several times. Growling deep in her throat, she threw the blankets and sheets aside and slid out of bed to stomp to the door. Tired as she was, Eshe was in a fine dudgeon, and all wound up to blast Armand for his inconsideration in waking her, but was brought up short when she dragged the door open and found a round little mortal woman about to bang her door again with the head of a vacuum cleaner.

"Oh dear!" the woman exclaimed, stopping just short of running the vacuum over Eshe's bare feet when they appeared in place of the door. "I'm sorry! Did I wake you?"

Eshe stared at the woman rather blankly as she quickly shut off the vacuum she'd been running over what seemed obvious to Eshe was a perfectly clean carpet. The vacuuming hadn't been necessary. The woman had just been trying to "rouse Mr. Argeneau's guest," she read from her mind. It seemed her presence was such an oddity the woman had been waiting impatiently all day for her to make an appearance and finally gave in to the urge to bring that about herself . . . with the vacuum. And the woman was glad she had, Eshe read from her mind as the woman thought that the guest was quite a looker, and she couldn't wait to tell the girls at the beauty parlor when she went in for her weekly wash and rinse. Oh, the girls would all be aflutter when they heard the elusive bachelor Armand Argeneau had himself a beauty in his house. Perhaps there were wedding bells in the future.

Sighing, Eshe stopped focusing on the woman's thoughts and shifted her attention to her eager expression, only then becoming aware that while she had been reading her mind, the woman had been giving her the once-over. Eshe grimaced and glanced down at the overlarge T-shirt she'd brought to sleep in. While it covered everything that was important, it wasn't exactly how she would have chosen to be dressed to meet the housekeeper.

"I *am* sorry if I woke you," the woman said with a good job at feigning regret. "Mr. Argeneau did say you got in late last night and would probably sleep the day away. I guess I just wasn't thinking when I started to vacuum."

Eshe just managed not to snort at the words, but forced a smile to her lips. "That's all right, I—Did you say Armand spoke to you? He's already up and about then?"

"Oh my, yes, he was up when I got here, which is unusual for him. But I suppose what with Paul having to leave so unexpectedly to tend to family matters, he had to see to the animals himself today. Poor man. I do hope he finds a replacement for Paul soon. Managing the farm and writing his daily article for the newspaper will wear him out in no time if he doesn't."

"Writing his daily article for the newspaper?" Eshe asked with a start. Lucian hadn't mentioned that to her. He'd only said Armand was a farmer.

"Yes, dear." The woman beamed as proudly as if she were his mother. "Didn't you know? He's our own little celebrity in town. He writes a daily interest article. Everyone just loves it. I gather writing runs in the family. He has a nephew who writes novels, you know, but Armand says he has enough trouble coming up with things for his little daily article and can't imagine ever writing a book, but he's a fine writer," she assured her, and then said almost apologetically, "Mind you, he's a bit eccentric, writing at night and sleeping during the day, and really, from what I can tell, he doesn't eat enough to keep a bird fed, but then Doris tells me most writers are a little different than the rest of us, and she would know. She did read that book on the life of Hemingway . . . or was it Hemingway? It may have been someone else," she admitted with a frown, and then waved that away and said, "I can't remember now but I do recall he was a hell-raiser whoever she read about. Why, he was into drugs, and sex, and . . . Well, fortunately, our young Armand doesn't do any of that." She frowned at her own words and then said quickly, "Well, the drugs at least. I'm sure he likes sex as much as anyone else. Although we were all starting to wonder since he never has ladies around or invites any of the local girls out or anything. Doris is positive he's gay and has a 'friend' in the city that he sneaks off to visit, but now I can tell her about you and she'll just have to shut up about that," she announced with satisfaction.

"Yes," Eshe said a bit faintly, amazed that the mortal had managed to babble all that without pausing for breath. Dear Lord.

"Well now, I'll just put this away," the woman announced, bending to unplug the vacuum from a socket right beside Eshe's bedroom door. "You'll want to dress, and I'll go down and see about getting you something for breakfast. Why, you must be starved. You missed breakfast and it's well past lunch. I'll fix you something nice and we can chat while you eat."

Eshe watched wide-eyed as the little woman bustled off and then shook her head and closed the door to begin getting dressed as the woman had suggested. It didn't seem likely she would get back to sleep anyway, and if Armand was up it meant she could hopefully find him and get in some of the questions she'd wanted to ask last night. She intended to get him to talk today about his wives and how they'd died. Lucian had merely told her their deaths all appeared to be accidents, but hadn't explained what kind of accidents, and it seemed to her that it would be pertinent. She just needed to figure a way to slide such questions into a conversation without raising Armand's suspicions about the real reason she was there. *No problem, right?* she thought dryly as she pulled on her leather pants from the night before.

Eshe had her pants only half on when the realization sank in that Armand's housekeeper had said she would go make her some breakfast. She didn't eat, but that wasn't what made her freeze with her pants still only half on. It was the fact that making breakfast no doubt included the woman looking in the refrigerator. A refrigerator she distinctly recalled stacking bags of blood in last night.

Cursing, Eshe yanked her pants the rest of the way up and hurried for the door without even bothering to do them up. Eager to get to the woman before she saw the blood, Eshe practically flew up the hall and then down the stairs and up the hall to the kitchen. She arrived in the kitchen door to find Armand's housekeeper bent over peering into the refrigerator and poking around inside. Eshe was about to take control of the woman's mind when the housekeeper straightened and stepped away to set a carton of eggs and some bacon on the island, leaving a clear view of the open refrigerator and the food stacked inside. There was no blood.

"Oh my, you must be hungry, dear, to rush down here like that," the housekeeper said, drawing Eshe's gaze away from the refrigerator to find the housekeeper smiling at her widely from the other side of the island. "My goodness, you didn't even brush your hair. Well, sit yourself at the table and I'll fetch you a coffee and some toast to tide you over until I can get these eggs and bacon cooked for you."

"Eggs and bacon?" Eshe murmured, running her fingers through her short hair to bring it to some kind of order as she moved closer to the fridge to get a better look inside. Nope. There was no blood in there at all.

"I can understand your surprise," the housekeeper said with a laugh as she bumped the refrigerator door closed with her hip on her way past to retrieve a loaf of bread from the counter beside the toaster. "If you looked in the refrigerator last night you must have been horrified at how little there was in there. As I said, Mr. Argeneau doesn't eat enough to keep a bird fed, but when he told me that he had a houseguest, I hopped in the car and ran over to the market to pick up some food for you."

And to gossip to everyone about a woman in the house, Eshe read from her mind with wry amusement.

"Oh my, I've just realized I didn't introduce myself," the woman said with vexation as she dropped a couple of slices of bread in the toaster. She pushed the button down to begin the toasting and then turned to hold her hand out toward Eshe. "I'm Mrs. Ramsey, dear. Enid Ramsey."

"Eshe d'Aureus," she murmured, clasping her hand briefly and wondering where the blood had gotten to.

"D'Aureus," Mrs. Ramsey echoed with a smile. "What an interesting name. What does it mean?"

"Gold," Eshe answered automatically.

"Like your eyes, they're gold. They even seem to shine like gold when the light hits them just right. Very pretty, dear. Striking."

"Thank you," Eshe murmured, and turned to make her way to the table as an excuse to keep her from looking at her eyes too long or hard. Like those of all immortals, Eshe's eyes captured and reflected the light for better night vision. It made hunting at night much easier. Her father, Castor d'Aureus, had had golden eyes and so had been called Castor the Gold when he'd fled Atlantis with the others. He'd passed those eyes on to his children, though most of them had dark flecks in them, inherited from their mother, she supposed.

Wanting to distract Mrs. Ramsey from the topic of her eyes, Eshe sought her mind as she settled at the table, and then asked the first question she could come up with. "How long have you worked for Armand?"

"About five years now," Mrs. Ramsey answered, retrieving a coffee cup from the cupboard and moving to a still-working coffeepot beside the refrigerator. As she waited for the last of the coffee to run through the drip filter, she offered, "That's when he inherited the farm from his uncle. It was nice when he did. His uncle was never out here. He had a manager run it while he lived in the city and took in the profits. It's much nicer knowing the owner and having them in your community."

Eshe nodded solemnly even though she knew that everything the woman had said was simply a cover story for Armand. He actually owned several farms in southern Ontario and rotated his time among them, spending ten years at one and then moving to another before his neighbors noticed that he wasn't aging. Each time he moved, the cover story was that he had inherited the farm he took over, but there was no uncle for him to inherit from. She had no idea what excuse was given to the old farm community to explain his leaving. Perhaps he let them think he died, or simply said he was moving to the city and leaving a manager to run it.

"He's a nice young man," Mrs. Ramsey informed

her. "Always polite and very good about my switching days if I have an appointment on a day I'm supposed to come in. I only come out to the house on Mondays, Wednesdays, and Fridays, you see."

Eshe made an encouraging sound to keep her talking.

"I do worry about him, though. I'm not sure his inheriting the farm was that good for him, really. He works very hard, rarely leaves the farm, and has no social life to speak of. I worry he'll just stay out here and grow old on the farm, never having had the experience of a wife and children." Mrs. Ramsey heaved a sigh as she poured the now-finished coffee into the cup. She perked up, though, as she added, "Still, he's young, and now you're here maybe you can get him to bring himself out a bit more. We have bingo at the church on Wednesday nights, and the diner serves a good meal. All the locals meet there. And now that the harvest is over, there are a couple of fall fairs coming up if you're still here and can drag him to them. I know the locals would enjoy getting to interact with him more."

"I'll see what I can do," Eshe said as the woman crossed the room to set a coffee cup before her.

"Good." Mrs. Ramsey beamed at her and then turned away to retrieve a frying pan as well as the bacon and eggs to start cooking. Eshe watched her for a moment, unsure whether she should tell her not to cook for her or not. She certainly wasn't going to eat the food. On the other hand, the woman seemed to be enjoying making it for her. In fact, judging from her present thoughts, Eshe suspected Mrs. Ramsey would be disappointed if she didn't let her do it. She could always dump the food when the woman wasn't looking, Eshe decided. Besides, Mrs. Ramsey was incredibly chatty and there might be something useful she could learn from her.

"So, Armand doesn't have any company at the house?" Eshe asked curiously, leaning forward to sniff at the black liquid steaming in the cup before her. It had a rather interesting scent, a bit bitter perhaps, but aromatic.

"Just Agnes and John Maunsell. They have a farm not far from here and I gather they're his sister-in-law and brother-in-law," Mrs. Ramsey confided, and then clucked her tongue. "He must have been married very young. He was already widowed when he moved here and can't be more than twenty-six or -seven. At least he doesn't look any older than that."

Eshe murmured a sound of agreement, her curious gaze on the food Mrs. Ramsey was frying up. The bacon was smelling surprisingly delicious as it cooked.

"Oh, there's your toast." Mrs. Ramsey bustled over to the toaster as the toasted bread popped into view. She quickly shifted the slices to a small plate and buttered them, then grabbed a couple of jars of what appeared to be preserves and brought them to Eshe. "Here you are, dear. You start on that while I finish up your bacon and eggs."

"Thank you," Eshe murmured, peering down at the offerings.

"That one is marmalade, and this is strawberry jam," Mrs. Ramsey announced, pushing the jars toward her. "I make them myself at home and bring them for Mr. Argeneau. Though, truth to tell, I don't think he has even tried them. I thought he was eating them at first because the jars kept disappearing, so I kept bringing him more, but then I found a whole box full of them in the basement." She heaved a disappointed sigh, shook her head, and bustled back to the stove. "You give them a try, though, and see what you think. Everyone else raves about them."

Eshe glanced up to see her watching expectantly and reluctantly opened the jar of orange marmalade and began to spread some on her toast. She could have just controlled the woman and made her think she'd tried it, but was actually a little curious to see what it tasted like. Eshe hadn't been curious about food in a couple of centuries now, but decided not to think about that and what her sudden interest might mean. She had other matters to deal with.

"So, he only has Agnes and John over?" she asked as she replaced the lid on the marmalade.

"Yes." Mrs. Ramsey wrinkled her nose. "Agnes is a sweet little thing, but I just haven't found myself warming to John. I'm not sure why." She shrugged and then gestured toward Eshe's as yet untried toast with the fork she'd been using to turn the bacon and said, "Give it a try, then, and tell me what you think."

Eshe picked up the slice of toast she'd spread marmalade on and took a bite, surprised at the burst of flavor that hit her tongue.

"It is really very good," she told the woman honestly.

Mrs. Ramsey flushed with pleasure at the compliment and chuckled. "You sound surprised. Does it look to you like I might be a bad cook?" she teased, gesturing to her robust figure.

Eshe smiled faintly, and took another bite of the toast before asking, "Does Armand ever talk about his wives?"

"Wives?" she asked with a start.

"I meant wife," Eshe corrected herself quickly.

"Oh." She relaxed and smiled wryly as she turned back to her cooking. "No. I think it must be a painful subject. I only know he was married because Agnes introduced herself as his sister-in-law the first time we met."

"I see," Eshe murmured, taking another bite of toast as she acknowledged that she wasn't going to learn anything about the past from this woman. Not that she'd really expected to. The woman was mortal, after all. But there had always been the chance that Armand had let something slip. Then too, Mrs. Ramsey had worked for Armand for five years by her own reckoning, and it wasn't unusual for long-term servants or employees to be let in on the secret of their immortality. However, it seemed obvious Mrs. Ramsey wasn't in that rank. Eshe supposed it was because the woman was only at the house three days a week and usually while he was sleeping, if he slept during the day and worked nights as the woman had suggested. There was less chance of her accidentally discovering his secret with such minimal contact.

"Ah, you're up."

Eshe glanced around at that comment to see Armand entering the kitchen. He looked even more exhausted than she felt. Though, to be honest, the toast and just the smell of coffee had perked her up a bit. Now she watched him walk toward the table where she sat and inhaled the scent of him as he drew near. He smelled of earth and spice and male. It was a heady combination on him, and Eshe swallowed and forced her eyes away from him when they tried to dip down over his body to examine it in the tight jeans and T-shirt he wore.

"Oh, Armand." Mrs. Ramsey smiled at him cheerfully and then made a sad moue before saying, "Yes, she's awake. I'm afraid I woke her up with my vacuuming."

Knowing she wasn't really sorry at all, but was very pleased to have gotten the chance to talk to her and gather more gossip, Eshe quickly stuffed a piece of toast into her mouth to keep from snorting. The shock on Armand's face when she did so made her wish she hadn't, however. Quickly chewing and swallowing, she explained, "Your lovely housekeeper insisted on cooking breakfast for me, late in the day though it is."

"And I've made enough bacon for the two of you just in case you came back in, so sit yourself down and I'll just put in a couple more eggs," Mrs. Ramsey ordered, sounding rather like a bossy mother or grandmother.

Armand took it in his stride and merely quirked his lips with amusement as he took the seat across from Eshe. His gaze, however, slid from her to the toast she'd already half eaten and back again with speculation.

"Here's a coffee for you, Armand." Mrs. Ramsey set a cup before him and then glanced at Eshe's untouched mug and clucked with self-disgust. "I suppose you take cream and sugar in it and I didn't even think to offer you any."

Shaking her head, she bustled away to collect the items and then returned to first pour some milk in both cups and then drop a couple of square cubes of sugar in each cup as well before handing over a spoon to each of them and hurrying back to her work.

Eshe glanced at Armand, shrugged, and stirred the coffee as she assumed she was meant to do. Armand immediately began to stir his own. They both then set the spoons down on the table and hesitated, glancing at each other.

Eshe didn't know what he was thinking, but she was wondering like crazy if he would actually drink it. Or if she would, for that matter. While she'd been curious about the toast, and would admit she was curious about the coffee, she never ate or drank.

That sounded foolish even in her own head, Eshe acknowledged with a sigh. She might have been able to say she never ate or drank before she'd come down to the kitchen this morning, but she had now eaten a piece of toast with butter and marmalade on it and quite enjoyed the experience. It seemed obvious there was more to her not being able to read Armand than that he was hard to read. She had eaten and enjoyed the toast, was eager to try the bacon that smelled so delicious, and was even curious to try the coffee. The problem was she wasn't sure it would be a good thing to let Armand know that. Right now she might be able to get away with claiming she'd eaten the toast only to please Mrs. Ramsey, but . . .

She peered at Armand silently. In her experience, the best way to catch rogues was to sneak up on them, or rattle them. Sneaking up on them was, of course, the easiest route, but when that wasn't possible, rattling them could set them off their stride and make them vulnerable to attack. Perhaps rattling Armand would work for her in this case, she thought, and letting him know she was showing all the signs of an immortal having met her life mate should certainly do that. It was rattling the hell out of her, after all, Eshe thought grimly, and stared at him silently as she picked up the coffee and raised it to her lips.

Armand's eyes widened, his eyebrows rose upward on his forehead, and his hand clenched around the cup he held as he watched her drink.

"Mmm," Eshe murmured in a voice so low Mrs. Ramsey couldn't possibly hear it, but Armand with his immortal hearing would. "I know they say the caffeine isn't good for us, but that tastes as delicious now as anything I partook of while with my first life mate, Orion."

Armand sucked in a gasp of air, his face paling briefly, and then sat back with a start as Mrs. Ramsey set two plates between them.

"Here you go. You two eat that up and I'll clean up the mess I've made in here."

Eshe murmured a thank-you, still watching Armand, and then picked up her fork and began to eat watching him watch her. It was a strangely erotic few moments. His eyes were locked on her lips, watching her slide the food into her mouth, his tongue slipping out to lick his lips as she chewed, and his own throat working as she swallowed.

"Aren't you hungry?" she asked huskily after the third bite when he simply continued to watch her. Picking up a half piece of the crispy bacon with her fingers, she held it out in front of his lips temptingly. "Try it. You might like it."

Armand caught her hand in his, held it briefly, and then opened his mouth and tugged her hand gently forward to slip the bacon into his mouth. His lips brushed her fingertips as they closed, a deliberate action, she was sure. When she then tried to withdraw her hand, Armand wouldn't let her. He held it in place, simply holding it before his face as he chewed and swallowed the bacon she'd offered. He then tugged her hand forward again.

Eshe stiffened, unsure if he meant to bite her fingers or kiss them, but he did neither. Instead, his tongue slid out and rasped over the pad of her thumb and fingers, licking away the grease left behind by the bacon and sending a shudder of unexpected pleasure down her back.

"Delicious," Armand agreed huskily.

"Good," Mrs. Ramsey said cheerfully.

Eshe retrieved her hand quickly and glanced guiltily toward the housekeeper as she turned to smile happily at them both.

"Eat up then before it gets cold," she ordered, obviously in her element manning the kitchen.

Eshe forced her eyes down to her plate and picked up her fork again to continue eating, but she couldn't help but sneak peeks at Armand as she did. He was eating now too, and with a relish that said he was indeed enjoying the food he consumed. His eyes were also glowing silver-blue and he was watching her hungrily as he did. It was enough to make her toes curl with anticipation. The man was definitely her life mate and he was hungry for more than food.

So was she.

Eshe already knew the pleasures to be found in the sacred bond between life mates. Her life with Orion had been a happy time, and she often retrieved the memories and relived them, wishing she could experience such bliss again. Which made it hard to lie to herself, and she knew damned right well that she'd been doing just that when she'd told herself she was only revealing that she was Armand's life mate to rattle him. She wanted more than that. She wanted to enjoy some of those benefits of life mates while she could. Which was damned stupid, Eshe knew. It wouldn't stop her from doing her work here, but it would distract her and slow her down and just make it incredibly hard if things didn't work out happily at the end. If Armand was a killer behind the deaths of four immortal women and the mortal Nicholas had been accused of killing, then she would have to turn him in to Lucian. It would be hard, but her sense of justice wouldn't allow for anything less.

However, whatever relationship developed between them in the meantime was going to make it harder to do, and painful as hell afterward. Unfortunately, it was difficult to worry too much about that when her body was humming and aching for what Armand could give her. And he could give her a hell of a lot. He could re-awaken the hungers and passions that slowly died out for immortals when they were without a mate.

In fact, he already had, she acknowledged. From the moment she'd walked into that diner last night, her senses had wanted to focus solely on Armand. She'd found him attractive and interesting, and should have known right away that here was something different, but she'd been focused on the task ahead and relegated to the back of her mind her responses to his scent and body heat as he'd sat next to her. They were no longer at the back of her mind. The cat was out of the box, and they both knew what they could be to each other if they chose to accept it, and what they could experience with each other . . . and apparently they both wanted it. Certainly she did. Eshe was basically nothing better than a bitch in heat at that moment, and judging by the way Armand's eyes were beginning to burn more silver than blue, he was feeling much the same way.

Damn, Eshe thought on a sigh. She'd forgotten how potent it could be. Had she recalled, she would have told Lucian to find someone else for this task and left last night before her senses could be fully stirred back to life. Too late for that now, though, she acknowledged. They were awake and roaring to be satisfied, and nothing was going to make her give up whatever time she could have satisfying them . . . whether it ended badly or not.

"Good, you both cleaned your plates." Mrs. Ramsey's cheerful voice sounded just before she appeared at the table next to them.

Eshe forced herself to look away from Armand and toward the woman. She even managed a smile, though there was a slight growl in her voice as she said, "Yes. Thank you. It was good."

"Good. I'm glad," Mrs. Ramsey said, sounding pleased as she retrieved both now-empty plates. "And it is nice to see you eating for a change, Armand."

"Yes," he murmured, and then stood abruptly, almost toppling his chair in his haste. "Eshe and I are going to have a word in my office, Mrs. Ramsey."

It was all he said, and all he needed to. Eshe was on her feet at once and leading the way, moving as quickly as she could without running. She entered the office, heard the door close behind them, and turned at once.

Armand was there to meet her so that she almost bumped into his chest before stopping her turn. In the next moment she did bump his chest as he tugged her into his arms and claimed her mouth. There was no "Hello, how do you do?" The moment his mouth covered hers, her own was open and his tongue was doing a good impression of trying to tickle her tonsils. Eshe didn't protest or pull back. She wanted it. It felt so damned good to be alive again, for her senses to be feeling and responding again.

Eshe gave as good as she got, her hands reaching up to claw through his hair, her body pressing into his even as he pushed against her. She was so consumed by the sensations exploding inside her, the only way she knew he'd backed her across the room was by the feel of the desk suddenly pressing at her back. Eshe sat on it at once and wrapped her legs around him too, embracing him with her entire body and pulling his hips forward until he was grinding against her.

The man had a weapon in his pants. He was as hard as steel, as hard as she was hot and wet, and she knew then that their first time was going to be fast, furious, and mind-blowing. It was going to be a battle toward that pleasure they both knew they could find rather than a slow build to it.

Eshe didn't care. They could try the slow build the next time. Right then all she wanted was for his body to be pounding into hers as fast and hard as he could, and she reached between them to begin undoing his belt and jeans to accomplish that. The moment she set to work at the task, Armand broke their kiss to begin licking and nibbling a trail down her neck. When he encountered the collar of her overlarge T-shirt, he paused and reached down to grab the hem of it and yank it up. That's when he froze. Eshe glanced down to see what he'd discovered, and saw that her leather pants were still undone from when she'd rushed downstairs after Mrs. Ramsey. The knowledge seemed to transfix Armand briefly, and then he swept the phone, papers, and other items littering the desk onto the floor and urged her to lie back on the desktop so that he could catch the waistband of the pants and begin tugging them down. Fortunately, he had just started when a soft tap came at the door.

"Mr. Argeneau? Is everything all right?"

Both of them froze at Mrs. Ramsey's gentle query from the hallway and then turned to peer at the unlocked door. They were both panting heavily, and

Eshe suspected equally shocked by the realization that they'd been so caught up in the moment that they hadn't considered the possible ramifications of their satisfying their needs right there and then with the woman in the house.

First of all, it wouldn't have been a quiet coupling. The clatter of the desktop's items hitting the floor would have only been the beginning of it. Eshe suspected that if they hadn't been interrupted she would already be howling like a wolf and urging Armand on. Secondly, when immortals reached completion, it was generally followed by both parties passing out, overwhelmed by the pleasure assaulting them. That would have been a very vulnerable position to be found in, and sweet as she seemed to be, Mrs. Ramsey was just nosy enough that Eshe wouldn't have put it past the woman to come walking in to see what was what. She certainly would have gotten an eyeful.

"Mr. Argeneau?" Mrs. Ramsey called again.

"Yes, Enid. Everything is fine," Armand said this time, pulling away from Eshe and letting her T-shirt fall back into place as he moved to do up the belt and jeans she'd just gotten undone. "I just knocked the phone off the desk."

"Oh. Okay. I was just coming to tell you that when you asked me about a good place to shop for women's clothes this morning when I got here, I forgot to mention the Bay. It has some nice things and it's in White Oaks Mall in London, which has a lot of clothing stores in it. It might be the best place for you to take Eshe. Or there's Masonville Mall on the other end of town. It has some nice stores as well."

Eshe raised an eyebrow at Armand, but he was concentrating on the task of doing up his belt and didn't catch the silent question. He simply said, "Thank you, Mrs. Ramsey. We'll be heading there right now actually."

"Oh, that's nice. You should take Eshe to dinner while you're in town. Moxie's is nice," she added cheerfully, and then said, "I'll probably be gone when you get back so I'll say good-bye now, but I'll be back on Friday."

"Yes. We'll see you Friday, then. And thank you for the shopping advice," Armand called, finishing with his belt and reaching out to offer Eshe a hand to get off the desk.

Eshe met his gaze, smiled wryly, but shook her head and got herself off the desk without touching him. She was afraid that even that innocent touch would break the control she was slowly regaining over her body. It seemed they were going shopping. Probably a smart move, she thought on a sigh, though smart wasn't always satisfying. Still, it would give her a chance to reconsider this path she'd chosen and perhaps give her a chance to set them on a new one if she could. Eshe was starting to think that letting Armand know that she couldn't read him and that her other appetites were awakening might have been a bad one. Lucian had warned her to watch her back last night before leaving . . . which was hard to do when she was lying on it.

Four

"So what are we going to do?"

Armand glanced toward Eshe in the passenger seat of his pickup, for one moment thinking she meant about the fact that they appeared to be life mates. Of course that was only because it was the elephant that had been sitting in his mind since they'd left the house and headed out for the city and the malls awaiting there. Eshe was his life mate. After all these centuries, he'd been fortunate enough to find a second one. It was a hell of a surprise. The problem was, he wasn't sure if it was a pleasant one yet. That being the case, he was trying to decide how to answer her question when she added, "I gather we're going shopping for clothes for me, but why?"

"Oh." Armand forced his eyes back to the road and his mind to the question. It took him a minute to do so, however, and he was frowning over that fact as he said,

"Lucian said you needed clothes for your stay here. He said to take you shopping and gave me the company card to buy them on."

Eshe made a disgusted sound and then sighed unhappily. "I suppose my leathers don't exactly blend in out here."

"No," Armand agreed, his eyes straying from the road to her leather-clad legs. She really had quite shapely legs, he thought, and then acknowledged that everything about her was shapely. The brief glimpse he'd had of her upper body before being distracted by the sight of her undone pants had been a rather revealing one. Eshe didn't have very large breasts, barely more than a handful each, but they were round and perfect for all that. Besides, who needed more than a handful?

"Okay, I'll get some jeans and T-shirts," Eshe said suddenly in a voice that was almost rebellious. "But I'm not buying any flowery dresses or anything like the one Mrs. Ramsey was wearing today."

"You don't need dresses," Armand said with amusement. "Jeans will do just fine."

Eshe gave a small, appeased "hrrumph" and then fell silent again, leaving Armand to his thoughts. He was deep into a silent debate as to whether he should call Lucian and have him take her somewhere else when she suddenly said, "I'm not your first life mate."

The comment set him aback briefly and he took a moment to gather his thoughts before acknowledging, "No. I have had a life mate before."

"So have I," she said quietly, and then added, "I was fortunate enough to meet my first life mate while still quite young, only thirty. I got to spend eight lovely centuries with him before I lost him."

"How did you lose him?" he asked curiously.

"He died in battle," Eshe said quietly. "He was a fierce warrior, but luck was with the other side that day and they took his head."

"Were there any children?" Armand asked after a hesitation.

"Yes. Eight. Six still live," she said simply, and then said, "I know you have three. All of them were not your life mate's children, though, were they?"

"No," he said on a sigh. "Susanna, my first wife and life mate, she and I had only one child, Nicholas. Thomas was born to my second wife, and my daughter, Jeanne Louise, to my third."

"But your second and third wives weren't life mates to you."

Despite the fact that it was a statement rather than a question, Armand said, "No, they weren't."

"Then why did you marry the other two women?" she asked simply.

It wasn't an unusual question, but the explanation was complicated. Grimacing, he finally simply told the truth. "I was lonely, and my second wife, Althea, looked very like my deceased life mate, Susanna. Even so, I didn't plan to marry her, but she became pregnant, and single women were ruined by such things in those days."

"So she tricked you into marriage," Eshe said dryly. Immortal women didn't become pregnant accidentally as could happen with mortal women. The nanos in their bodies were programmed to keep them at peak condition, and having babies used up a lot of nutrients and blood so that the nanos apparently saw the baby as a parasite to be flushed from the body. An immortal woman had to consume extra blood to get pregnant and then had to continue to consume extra blood for the next nine months to keep the child to term.

"Essentially, yes, she did," Armand admitted quietly. "But I didn't mind very much. As I said, I was lonely and the idea of another child pleased me."

"And the idea of another wife?" she asked.

Armand frowned at the question. There was something in her voice that made him glance at her, but her expression held mere curiosity and he decided he must have grown a bit paranoid over the centuries and answered, "Althea was the daughter of a friend. I had great affection for her. And I blamed myself for not realizing what she was up to."

"What do you mean what she was up to?" This time it was definitely curiosity in her voice.

"Althea had had a crush on me since she was about twelve. The fact that she couldn't read me convinced her that I must be her life mate. Her parents explained that she simply couldn't read me because I was older and that I could read her, but she didn't want to hear that and decided they were wrong. I was the man for her." He grimaced at the memory. "It was adorable when she was young, but then my ten years at the farm near her father's ended and I hired on a manager and moved on to one of my others. I didn't see much of her after that. While her parents visited me often, they left her at home, afraid to encourage her crush. She was a bit obsessive with it even as a teen," he admitted unhappily. "Anyway, several years later a young immortal woman arrived at my farm in search of a job as maid. She said her name was Alice, and she looked a hell of a lot like my Susanna."

"It was Althea, of course," Eshe guessed dryly.

Armand nodded. "She didn't really look that much like Susanna in reality. They had the same blond hair and not completely dissimilar features, but that was about it. However, she had seen portraits of Susanna and styled her hair the same way, and then dressed in a more modern gown of a similar fashion to the one Susanna had worn for her portrait. It was enough that when I first opened the door I thought Susanna had risen from the grave and come knocking." He grimaced and then admitted quietly, "I suppose I wanted to believe it was her. Or maybe even just pretend for a little bit."

Armand sighed at the old memories. "She happened to arrive at a weak moment and I bedded her that very night. She was more than willing. Of course, it wasn't the same as with my Susanna, but it was nice and filled a little of the ache in my heart . . . until I finally gathered enough sense to read her thoughts and realized who she was.

"Dear God," he muttered with disgust at the memory of his shock and horror at the time. He still couldn't believe he hadn't recognized her at once. While it had been years at that point since he'd seen her, and she'd been a child then, he still felt he should have recognized the seductress as the knobby-kneed child he'd known. Unfortunately, he hadn't. "I didn't know whether to shoot myself or her. She was my best friend's daughter, for God's sake. And at eighteen still a child really in immortal terms. Of course I took her home to her parents at once. She begged me all the way there not to tell them what she'd done and how she'd tricked me. I wasn't all that eager myself to confess to bedding her, so allowed her to persuade me."

"But then she turned up pregnant," Eshe deduced, and Armand nodded.

"Yes. That was one hell of a memorable night, I can tell you. I wasn't pleased when she showed up on my doorstep again, but then I was simply stunned when she blurted the news. Still, my annoyance passed quickly at the thought of another child, and so I offered her marriage with the understanding that neither of us would try to read or control the other, and when she met her true life mate we would dissolve the marriage to allow for him to claim her. The same was to go for myself as well should I meet a second life mate, though I didn't really expect I would," he admitted wryly. "Of course, then we had to go explain everything to her parents. That's when the night really got memorable. I nearly lost her father's friendship that night, but he knew what Althea was like when she wanted something and eventually came around."

"The child was Thomas," Eshe said quietly.

Armand smiled. "Yes. He was an adorable baby. Always laughing and chortling at something. Smart as a whip too, walking early, talking early, and forever humming tunes. I should have realized then he'd become a composer as an adult." He sighed at the old memories of a very young Thomas dancing through his head. "I had to take him to Marguerite to raise when Althea died, and ashamed though I am to admit it, I missed him much more than his mother."

"Why did you take him to Marguerite?" Eshe asked. "Why not raise him yourself?"

"How?" Armand asked dryly. "It's not like there is an immortal nanny company out there with lists of immortal women looking for nanny jobs. And you can't leave a child that young with an uninitiated mortal woman. He'd bite. Not out of cruelty or meanness, just because he was hungry and the nanny smelled like food."

"You could have initiated a mortal nanny," Eshe pointed out.

"You can't spring something like that on them. It takes time to develop enough trust in a mortal that they can accept what we are. In the meantime, Thomas could never have been left alone with her and I simply couldn't be inside watching him with a nanny twenty-four hours a day. I had a farm to run." He shook his head. "I didn't see any other option but to let Marguerite raise him for me when she offered."

Eshe was silent for a moment and then asked, "How did Althea die?"

Armand heaved out a sigh, his gaze on the road ahead as he said, "A hotel fire."

"You escaped?" she asked, and his paranoia rose up in him again, making him glance at her uncertainly. He could have sworn there had been an inflection to her tone that . . . Armand let it go when he saw her expression was simply curious, and explained.

"I wasn't there. It was a busy time at the farm when I was outside more than in. William and Mary, Althea's parents, had come to visit for a bit. When they left, they took Althea and four-year-old Thomas with them for a short stay. I understood they were going to their farm, but apparently they made a detour to the city for what was supposed to be a few days, but the first night they were there a fire broke out in the hotel. Althea must have been trapped or didn't wake up to the shouts and noise in time. She perished in the fire."

"And yet little Thomas got out?" Eshe asked with a frown.

"He was in Althea's parents' room. Althea had been tired after the day's excursions and Mary liked to spoil the boy, so she took Thomas into their room with them so Althea could sleep undisturbed. They got out with Thomas. Althea didn't."

Eshe was silent for a minute. When she spoke again, he could hear the frown in her voice and understood it completely when she murmured, "Nicholas once mentioned that his mother died in a fire too."

"Yes," he said grimly. "Fire has been a plague in my life."

"How did she—?" Eshe began, but he interrupted, glad to be able to do so as he said, "Another time. We're here."

Eshe turned to glance out the window as he turned into the mall parking lot, and Armand felt himself relax. He understood her curiosity but he didn't like to talk about the past. Doing so had wound him up a bit. He, a man who normally hated shopping, was glad for the respite from talking about the past that it would offer.

"You should probably go to the food court now," Eshe announced as they carried her bags out of the last of the clothing stores, or at least the last of them she was willing to try. Eshe wasn't much of a shopper. She liked what she liked, spotted it quickly, bought it, and got out, and this had been a particularly quick shop for her since all she had bought were a couple of pairs of jeans and half a dozen T-shirts. She had also bought a pair of black dress pants and a dressier top in case they went somewhere fancier than the diner—like this Moxie's Mrs. Ramsey had mentioned—but that had taken only a couple of minutes.

"The food court?" Armand said with surprise, and then asked, "Are you hungry?"

"I am a little," she acknowledged, surprised to find that it was true. It must only have been a couple of hours since they'd eaten. The drive in hadn't taken much more than twenty minutes, and her shopping had probably taken an hour, but they'd also walked all the way around the mall checking out the shops available before starting the actual clothing shopping. That had been a rather interesting exercise. Eshe had been rather surprised to find that many of the things Armand had found interesting or attractive in the decorating and furniture stores were items she liked herself. She'd thought sure they'd have little in common, with his being a country boy while she was a city gal. She'd been wrong, however. They had similar taste.

Shrugging that thought aside, she added, "But I meant you should go there to wait while I finish off the shopping . . . at La Senza."

"La Senza." Armand frowned. "I remember the name. Which store was that?"

"Think lacy black and red teddy," she said with amusement, recalling the way he'd eyed the item on the mannequin in the window as they'd passed the store earlier.

"Oh! You need . . ." His eyes dropped to her breasts and then down below her waist and back, and the man actually blushed a little. Or perhaps it was just a flush of desire. Certainly his eyes were starting to glow again.

"I don't mind if you want to accompany me there, but I thought you might be more comfortable waiting for me in the food court," she admitted with a grin, and wasn't terribly surprised when he seemed to take that as a challenge and straightened his shoulders.

"I'll come with you," he said firmly, and then frowned and added, "I probably shouldn't leave you alone for a day or two until we're sure you weren't followed down here from Toronto anyway."

Eshe's grin turned into a full-fledged smile that she knew without a doubt was wicked. "Good. Then you can tell me what you want to see me in. I was only going to get panties and bras; I usually sleep nude," she added huskily, watching his eyes and pleased by the burst of silver flame in their depths as she added, "But I don't mind wearing sexy little baby dolls if it pleases you to see me in them . . . and take them off me."

Armand swallowed thickly, but his voice was still husky as he said, "Lead the way."

Chuckling, Eshe swung away and led him along the strange layout of halls until she spotted the La Senza sign ahead.

"I usually wear black," Eshe murmured, perusing the selection. She hadn't always, but it was the color she'd favored since Orion's death. She chose a see-through black lace number and lifted it off the rack to examine it more easily. Her eyebrows rose when she saw that it was actually a see-through black lace catsuit with strategically embroidered black lace patches at the groin and at each breast that would barely hide the important bits beneath.

"I like it," Armand growled, and then selected another from the rack and held it up. This one was a short gown in pure white satin with spaghetti straps, and matching and very tiny snowy white satin panties. He held it in front of her and nodded. "And this one."

Eshe raised an eyebrow, but accepted the baby doll. She really did normally wear mostly black, but supposed the white would be a nice contrast with her coloring. She glanced to Armand, raised an eyebrow, and asked wickedly, "Shall I try them on for you in the dressing room here before we buy them?"

Armand raised an eyebrow. "Not unless you don't mind being found naked, in an unconscious puddle, on the dressing room floor with me."

Eshe laughed huskily at the threat and simply laid the items over her arm as she moved on to select panties and bras. But his words had raised visuals in her mind that she couldn't seem to get out of her head, and while her hands were automatically selecting several pairs of panties, her mind was playing a short flick of her trying on the white satin number, coming out to show him, and then his following her back into the dressing room, backing her up against the wall, and—

"Is there something I can help you with today?"

Eshe blinked those naughty thoughts from her mind and turned to find a slim young blond beside her, smiling widely from Armand to her and back to Armand.

"You can start ringing up and bagging these while I grab a couple of bras," she said easily, neither surprised nor upset by the thoughts running through the girl's mind as she looked Armand over again and offered him an inviting smile. He was a good-looking man. Eshe couldn't blame the girl for having good taste. Besides, the poor kid didn't stand a chance with him now that he'd met her, so she smiled at the clerk kindly as the girl took the items she'd already picked.

"Not the jealous type, I see," Armand murmured as the girl carried the clothes back to the till.

"You read her mind too, did you?" Eshe asked with amusement, leading him to the bra section.

"Hmm." He grimaced and did actually blush a bit as he said, "Her thoughts were disconcertingly X-rated."

"Not as X-rated as mine," she assured him with a grin and then chuckled as the silver in his eyes flamed anew.

"You'll have to tell them to me when we get back to the house," he growled, his hands clenching at his sides as if he wanted to touch her right then, but didn't dare to.

"Maybe," she said with a shrug, picking out two bras in her size. "Or maybe I'll just show you."

On that note, Eshe turned away and headed to the counter, leaving him to follow and laughing as she heard him growl under his breath. She might be a bitch in heat, but Armand was no better, and there was a certain thrill of power with the knowledge that he wanted her as badly as she wanted him. It made her decide that delaying the inevitable might be fun . . . a sort of foreplay. It couldn't hurt, Eshe decided, especially since she doubted there was going to be much real foreplay once they were alone together. At least not the first time, and probably not the second or third time either.

"Do you want a drink before we leave?" Armand asked as they exited the lingerie shop.

"In more ways than one," Eshe admitted with a grimace. "You don't happen to have any blood in that cooler I noticed in the back of the pickup, do you?"

"As it happens I do," he assured her quietly, and raised an eyebrow. "Do you need to feed again already?"

"Already?" she asked, arching an eyebrow. "I haven't had any since the one bag when Lucian and I arrived at the house last night. The blood was missing from the refrigerator when I came downstairs this afternoon," she pointed out when he looked startled at the news that she hadn't fed since the night before.

"Oh yes," he said with realization. "I moved it before Mrs. Ramsey arrived this morning so she wouldn't see them and ask questions. It's in a special refrigerator I had built into my walk-in closet. I'll show you how to open it when we get back."

Eshe nodded.

"I guess we should head right out to the pickup then," Armand said, and actually sounded a bit disappointed.

Eshe shook her head. "I can wait another half hour or so without attacking anyone, and I wanted to try one of those fruit drinks I saw them making when we passed through the food court earlier. I used to like fruit and they smelled good."

"I thought so too," he admitted, smiling now.

They made their way quickly back to the food court to purchase and then watch them make the creamy fruit drinks. Eshe's mouth was watering by the time she got her hands on the drink.

"Did you want to sit down here and drink them or take them with us and drink them on the way back to the house?" Armand asked as they moved away from the counter.

Eshe arched an eyebrow at the query. "You intended to head right back to the house?"

"Well, Mrs. Ramsey will be gone by now and—" He cut himself off abruptly, and Eshe chuckled at his expression.

"And you thought you'd buy a girl a drink and then get lucky?" she suggested with amusement. "Without even feeding me?"

"Well, I—" Armand looked truly at a loss, but she didn't let him off the hook. Instead, she shook her head.

"No, no, my friend, this girl isn't that easy. You're buying me dinner at that Moxie's Mrs. Ramsey mentioned and then *maybe* I'll let you take me home so I can have my wicked way with you."

"Your wicked way with me, huh?" he asked, his discomfort giving way to amusement. "What if I don't want to let you have your wicked way?"

Eshe arched one eyebrow and reached out to run one finger lazily down his chest to the top of his jeans. Her finger stopped there, but her eyes continued downward to pause on the bulge growing and pushing his zipper outward. "Oh, you want it," she said with amusement. "And you'll get it. But you're going to work for it . . . at least a little."

"Damn," Armand breathed.

Eshe chuckled and evaded his hand as he suddenly reached for her. Dancing ahead of him, she found an empty table, set down her drink and dumped all the bags but one, and then turned to survey him as he followed her in a much lazier fashion. The man was moving like a tiger stalking a gazelle. His movements were lazy and slow, but his eyes were burning across her skin with desire as if patiently awaiting the opportunity to pounce.

"Take a load off," she suggested, gesturing to the table. "I need to hit the ladies' room. Back in a minute."

Eshe didn't wait for his response, but whirled away with the bag she'd chosen and headed away along the edge of the food court tables.

Five

Armand watched Eshe go with a frown, unsure whether he should follow and stand guard outside the ladies' room or not. This was a busy mall with lots of people around, but that wouldn't stop Leonius Livius if he was around. And aside from having promised Lucian to keep her safe while she was here, Armand himself didn't want to risk anything happening to her either. He'd already lost one life mate and two wives and wasn't willing to add to the number.

He was about to pick up their drinks and the bags she'd left behind and follow her when Eshe suddenly turned into a hall and disappeared from sight. Noting the sign hanging at the entrance to the hall with the international male and female figures that denoted the washrooms, Armand decided he could watch from there and sat down to drink his drink. It was really very good, cold and tasty, hitting the spot after their shopping. Armand normally didn't like shopping, but had enjoyed his time with Eshe today. She was an intelligent woman, and naughty as hell. The perfect combination and hard to resist, he acknowledged.

That thought made him sigh and sit back in his seat. She *was* hard to resist, but then that wasn't unusual for a life mate. It was bad luck for him, though, and made it difficult to even consider returning her to Lucian with the order to send her somewhere else.

That would be the smart thing to do, he acknowledged to himself. Women who got involved with him tended to end up dead. Armand had thought it tragically bad luck when his first wife and life mate Susanna had died. The blow had been crushing and it had taken him a while to recover from the loss, but he'd never even considered it might be anything but a terribly tragic accident. He had pretty much felt the same way when Althea had died; not the grief, while he had mourned her passing, it hadn't been nearly as bad as losing Susanna. But he had thought her death another case of terribly bad luck. However, when his third wife, Rosamund, had died, Armand's thinking had changed. Not at first. At first he'd been too upset to think clearly and had cursed God and the fates for taking yet another woman he cared about from him. For a while he'd been bitter and angry, wondering why he was so cursed, or what he had done to deserve it. It was so unlikely for one man to lose three wives as he had . . . especially when they were immortal women. Immortals weren't as fragile as mortals. They were incredibly hard to kill, and that fact was what had finally kicked him out of his anger and depression.

Armand had started to look into his wives' deaths then, quietly and as inconspicuously as possible, but centuries had passed since Susanna's death, and another century had come and gone between Althea and Rosamund, and as far as he could tell all three deaths appeared to be simple bad luck on the surface.

Still, a part of him had trouble accepting that and suspected there was something else at play, someone who was causing this bad luck. The problem was that as far as he could tell there wasn't anyone who had been present during all three deaths who could be responsible. He had no one to point a finger at. Even so, Armand had done what he could to protect those still left in his life that he cared about. He'd basically withdrawn from their lives and society as a whole, staying on his farms and refusing to see and show that he cared for his children or anyone else in the family for fear that they might suddenly become a target.

While he couldn't keep Lucian from coming to see him, and had visited with Nicholas at first, his visits with his son had always been furtive little stints when he snuck away from the farm to meet with him and get updates on Thomas and Jeanne Louise and the rest of the family. When Nicholas had gone on the run fifty years ago, Thomas had taken his place, meeting him in diners two towns over to pass him the latest photos of Jeanne Louise and himself and tell Armand how things were going.

Armand knew Thomas didn't understand why he was doing what he was. He also knew his son thought he was a coldhearted and half-crazy bastard for not seeing Jeanne Louise, but he couldn't explain. How foolish would it have sounded had he said that he just had this "feeling" that his wives' accidents hadn't been accidents at all, and that he was afraid in the absence of a life mate or wife, anyone he cared for might suddenly begin suffering accidents? If he'd said as much to Nicholas or Thomas, he suspected one or both of them would have ignored his wishes and sprung Jeanne Louise on him as a surprise at one of their visits.

To be honest, Armand would have liked that. His heart hurt over the fact that he'd never even spoken to his daughter, but since it was the women he cared about in his life who seemed to die, he was damned if he would take even a hint of risk with the girl's life.

Now he had Eshe to worry about. He'd like to think she was safe enough, that he was the only one who even knew she was at the house, but he'd be lying to himself. Armand had no doubt that Mrs. Ramsey had probably been on the phone all morning telling everyone she knew that he had female company on the farm, and that was before she'd even seen Eshe. He was equally positive that before they'd even turned out of the driveway onto the road when they'd left the house, Mrs. Ramsey had been back on that selfsame phone describing Eshe in minute detail to all her cronies and repeating every word spoken. By now, Eshe's presence would be known to everyone in the small town and the news would still be traveling the gossip grapevine. He just hoped it hadn't spread far enough to put her in danger.

The question was whether he was willing to take that risk. His three wives had died after marrying him and giving birth to a child, which might mean she was safe enough for now so long as he didn't marry her and get her pregnant. But he hadn't been willing to take the chance that the pattern would continue when it came to his daughter, Jeanne Louise, and ultimately he decided he wasn't willing to take that chance with Eshe either. He already liked her . . . a lot, and he wanted her with the passion that only life mates could enjoy. He suspected too much more time in her company would push him over the brink into love, and then he wouldn't be able to make himself send her away, and if anything did happen to her . . .

Armand swallowed and reached for his phone. It was better to call Lucian now and get her removed before he actually experienced all he would enjoy as her life mate. He wasn't sure he'd be able to send her away once he'd tasted the paradise he was sure he could enjoy in her arms.

"Who are you calling?"

Armand snapped his phone closed with a start and glanced up to see that Eshe had returned. His mouth opened to offer the standard lie, "No one, I was just checking messages." But the lie never passed his lips. Instead, his mouth simply hung open as he stared at her. She had changed for their dinner at Moxie's. However, she still wore her leather pants and hadn't changed her

T-shirt in for the dressier blouse they'd purchased earlier. Instead, she was now wearing the incredibly short, white satin baby doll as a top with the leather pants.

"I grabbed the wrong bag," Eshe said with a shrug as she claimed a chair across from him. "But once I got a look at it I thought, what the heck. It really just looks like a dressy summer top, and while it's fall, it's still pretty hot, so . . ." She shrugged again and picked up her drink to take a long pull of it.

Armand stared at her, his eyes traveling over the snowy white straps against her darker skin, before moving down to the satiny cups almost covering her breasts, and then his gaze slid to the other people in the food court. No one was pointing at her and squealing, "Eek! She's wearing a baby doll as a top." In fact, no one seemed to be noticing anything amiss at all, he acknowledged. Then again, as she'd said, it *was* an unseasonably warm day and there were a lot of women wearing very similar actual tops but in cotton and polyester rather than white satin . . . and probably not purchased from La Senza.

A husky chuckle drew his gaze back to Eshe to see that wicked smile back on her lips as she watched him, and then she leaned forward and whispered in a damned sexy growl, "I put on the matching panties too. All I need to do is shimmy out of my leathers and I'm ready for bed when we get home."

Armand's phone was back in his pocket and he was standing up and collecting the bags before the last word had left her lips.

"Oh," she said with a surprise he suspected was wholly feigned. "Are we leaving already?"

"You can drink that on the way to Moxie's. I'm hungry," Armand growled, urging her out of her seat.

"And I bet it's not just for food either," she taunted with a laugh as he herded her toward the mall exit.

God had definitely been laughing when he'd created Eshe for him, Armand decided as he hustled her out to his pickup, because she was going to be the death of him. It was surely going to kill him to have to call Lucian and have her taken away . . . tomorrow morning. He would give himself one night with her, but tomorrow morning before he retired he was calling Lucian and telling him to get her out of his home and somewhere safer, Armand promised himself. He'd make up spotting a suspicious character who might be one of Leonius's people if he had to, but he would not risk this woman who was so full of life and passion ending up dead because she was unlucky enough to be his life mate. He had decided.

It was only a short drive to the restaurant called Moxie's. Even so, Eshe managed to finish off her fruit drink and even empty the bag of blood Armand had stopped to get for her before getting into the pickup. That had been an uncomfortable experience. She'd had to feed on the bag while bent forward with her head ducked below the dashboard to prevent anyone in the other cars on the road spotting her sucking on a bag of blood. While there were innumerable benefits to being an immortal, it could be a serious pain in the ass at times too, Eshe acknowledged as she disposed of the bag in a small garbage bag between the seats and sat up to glance around. It seemed her timing had been perfect. Armand was just steering them into a parking space in front of the restaurant.

It was actually late for dinner, but the restaurant was still quite busy. However, one of the half a dozen girls clad in skintight or scanty black outfits and stationed at the entrance to the restaurant showed them to a table along the back wall. It appeared to Eshe to be one of the better places to sit, being somewhat sheltered from the rest of the place by a curtained wall that offered some soundproofing, and she wondered if Armand had put a little suggestion in the girl's ear or they'd just gotten lucky.

Eshe slid into one side of the booth while Armand took the other, and they then accepted the menus the girl offered. They were subjected to a quick listing of the restaurant's specials before the woman left them alone to peruse the menus.

Eshe ordered wine and the peppercorn steak, rare, when a handsome young waiter also in all black arrived to take their orders. She hardly noticed the overfriendly smile on his lips or the way he kept looking her over as she gave her order. She did, however, notice how short Armand sounded when he gave his own order.

"I *am* the jealous type," he admitted grimly when she raised her eyebrows after the boy had left. "You obviously didn't read his mind."

"Why waste my time?" she asked lightly. "I've already found my life mate."

Armand relaxed somewhat at her words, but still grumbled, "Half the things he wanted to do to you were illegal."

"And the other half were things you plan to do to me yourself when we get home," she suggested with a grin.

Armand smiled reluctantly, but then breathed out, visibly letting go of his irritation as he did and relaxing completely. He reached for her hand and held it between them on the table as he admitted apologetically, "It's been a while since I've felt this way."

"For me too," Eshe acknowledged quietly, and then, cognizant of the job she was there to do, asked, "Were you jealous around Althea and Rosamund too, or just Susanna?"

Armand released her hand with a little sigh that suggested he'd rather she hadn't brought the conversation around to this subject again, but said, "No. Only with Susanna. Althea . . ." He glanced away and then back before admitting, "I'm pretty sure she had affairs after Thomas was born. I didn't blame her," he added quickly. "I was always busy back then, and by that time she'd realized that what we'd all told her was true and I wasn't her life mate. She was still young. But she was a good mother to Thomas, and a good wife to me, and I didn't begrudge her looking for her true life mate, or enjoying everything she could until she found him." He grimaced, and added, "She suffered a lot of guilt over it, though, and I didn't know how to help her with that without letting her know I knew, which I think would have just made her feel worse."

"She never came to be able to read your thoughts like you could read hers?" Eshe asked, realizing that was how he'd known about Althea's affairs.

"No. She may have been able to in time, but in the end didn't get the time." He sighed and then admitted, "I was considering sitting her down and telling her she could have her freedom. The only thing stopping me was missing Thomas if she took him to live with her, but then she died and I had to send him away anyway."

Eshe considered him silently for a moment but didn't see any subterfuge in his expression. What he was telling her appeared to be the truth. Sitting back, she asked, "And Rosamund? You weren't jealous of her either?"

Armand smiled faintly. "Rosamund was a different kettle of fish altogether. Like Althea, she was young in age for an immortal, but that's where any resemblance between the two ends. Rosamund was much more mature, wise beyond her years."

"Was she?" Eshe asked, and was surprised at the harsh sound of her own voice. It suggested a jealousy that was unexpected . . . and she wasn't the only one to notice. Armand raised a surprised eyebrow and peered at her in question, but she just shook her head. "Sorry, go on. Rosamund was wise beyond her years . . . How?"

He hesitated, but then apparently decided to continue and said, "Rosamund had a plan."

"And what was that? To get herself pregnant and make you marry her like Althea did?"

"Oh no. She didn't trick me into marrying her," he

assured her. "First you should understand that we were friends for quite a while before we married and had Jeanne Louise. She was a smart girl, fun to talk to, always with an opinion on this or that, and as I say, she had a plan. She knew it could be centuries before she met a proper life mate and she had every intention of going out and finding one, but she didn't want to wait centuries to have a baby. She wanted one while she was young."

"She did, did she?" Eshe asked dryly. "And I gather you weren't averse to having a child either?"

Armand shrugged unapologetically. "It had been more than a century since Althea had died. Thomas was grown and always off exploring somewhere, and I missed having a family."

"So you married and had Jeanne Louise."

He nodded, a smile curving his lips. "Jeanne Louise was a beautiful baby."

"And Rosamund?" Eshe prompted.

Armand's smile faded. "Jeanne Louise was born in February. Five months later in July, Rosamund died."

"Fire?" she asked.

Armand shook his head. "She was decapitated when the wagon she was driving careened off the road and turned over in a ditch."

Several questions occurred to Eshe. The first was, "Was anyone with her?"

"Jeanne Louise, but she was thrown clear when the carriage rolled off the road and into the ditch. She wasn't even hurt. Apparently the blankets she was wrapped in cushioned her landing."

"Where was Rosamund headed?"

"Into town, I think." Armand frowned and then admitted, "She spent a lot of time away from the farm after Jeanne Louise was born. She'd pack the baby up and head out when I left for the barn. I didn't think much about it at the time. I was busy on the farm and we still had to hunt to feed, and I just assumed that was what she was doing, but after she died . . ."

"After she died . . . ?" Eshe prompted.

Armand shook his head. "I found out that there were a lot of times when she didn't get back until just before I did at dawn. In fact, most nights she was gone the entire night."

"It wouldn't have taken that long to hunt up a meal," Eshe murmured thoughtfully. She considered his troubled expression and then asked, "Do you think she was having affairs like Althea?"

He appeared startled by the question. "Rosamund? No, I don't think so."

"You never read her mind?" Eshe asked with surprise.

Armand shook his head firmly. "I tried not to. Marriage is tough enough without intruding on each other's private thoughts so we had a deal to try not to do that."

Eshe nodded slowly, but pointed out, "So you can't be sure she too didn't have affairs."

He sighed wearily. "No, I can't, and I suppose that would explain what she might have been doing. I just wouldn't have thought she'd have felt she had to keep that from me. We had a solid agreement that it was all right if she wanted to."

Eshe considered his expression. He didn't appear

hurt or angry at the idea that Rosamund might have been having affairs, merely somewhat startled at the possibility. He also hadn't appeared upset by Althea's affairs, but then they hadn't been life mates. She supposed that meant she could discount the possibility of his having killed his wives in a jealous rage. At least wives two and three.

"And Susanna?" she asked now, and when he glanced at her with confusion, asked, "How did she die exactly? I know it was a fire, but—"

"Oh," he said on a sigh. "It was a stable fire shortly after Nicholas was born. The family still lived in England then, and as a baron I had to make the occasional trip to court. I had put it off that year until after the birth, but the day after Nicholas came squalling into the world, I kissed Susanna and the baby and headed out. I returned as quickly as I could; still it was nearly two weeks before I rode back into the bailey. She had been dead a week by then."

Armand's expression was stark for a moment as he recalled the painful loss, and Eshe waited patiently. His expression convinced her he had loved his Susanna. She didn't begrudge him that. She had loved her Orion too and grieved his passing. It didn't mean they both didn't have enough love to welcome and embrace a new life mate.

Armand cleared his throat, the grief easing from his expression as he forced himself to continue more clinically. "It seems a fire started in the stable a week after I left. Susanna must have run in to try to save her mare. She loved that beast. It was a gift from me when we married. But the roof must have caved in while she was inside and a beam must have trapped her or . . . something," he finished wearily.

"Another accident," Eshe murmured.

"Yes," he said grimly.

"And then there's Annie," she pointed out.

Armand glanced at her with a start. "Annie?"

"Nicholas's wife. She was decapitated and then burned up in her car," Eshe pointed out.

"Yes, but that was an accident," Armand said at once.

Eshe raised an eyebrow. "So were your wives' deaths . . . weren't they?"

Six

Armand frowned briefly and then glanced to the side and sat back, drawing her attention to the fact that their food had arrived. She sat back as well to make room for the waiter to set it down, but kept her gaze on Armand as the food was placed before them. Her bringing up Annie had obviously disturbed him. As if he had assumed all this time that her death had been an accident, but Eshe's question had raised some doubt in him. His startled "That was an accident" was interesting, though. It could mean that he knew or suspected that his wives' deaths weren't the accidents they appeared to be, which would explain the way he had withdrawn from society and his family. Perhaps he was trying to shelter them and keep them safe and away from the danger that appeared to plague those who loved him.

Before Armand had told her how the women had

died, Eshe might have suspected those words had been a slip and that he knew the deaths of his wives weren't accidents because he'd caused them, but he hadn't even been around when two of them had died. He'd been several days' ride away at court when Susanna died in that fire, and Althea had been hours away in Toronto with her parents when she died in the hotel fire.

The knowledge made Eshe shake her head with bewilderment. She had no idea why Lucian had worried for even a moment that Armand might have been behind the deaths of his wives. She suspected it had to do with his twin brother, Jean Claude. The man had treated his family abominably and even broken their laws in taking the lives of mortals. Eshe knew Lucian suffered a great deal of guilt over his not having seen and put a stop to his brother's bad behavior and supposed he was now determined not to repeat that mistake with Armand. She would be glad to be able to tell him that his brother couldn't have been behind the deaths. However, this meant she now had to look elsewhere for answers.

Eshe tried to think where she should next look as she picked up her fork and knife and cut into the rare steak she'd ordered, but forgot the question and nearly moaned aloud at the burst of flavor in her mouth as she popped the first bite in. Damn, she'd forgotten how good food could be. Actually, Eshe acknowledged, it wasn't that she'd forgotten, but that the food had begun to lose its flavor after Orion's death, as if her taste buds had slowly died and left everything bland and uninteresting. She was definitely glad to have them back and working again, Eshe decided as she next tried a bite of the stuffed baked potato.

They ate in silence at first, Armand appearing slightly distracted, and Eshe herself busily trying to think where she should turn her attention and questions next. It seemed to her that whoever might be behind the deaths had been in Armand's life a long time, and also had to be relatively close by. They were halfway through the meal when she finally asked, "So is there anyone else I should know about who comes to the farm besides Mrs. Ramsey?"

Armand was silent for so long she thought he hadn't heard her question, but then he said, "Paul and Mrs. Ramsey were the only mortals who came around. Of course, Paul won't be a problem now."

"Will you replace him?" she asked curiously, thinking he'd had even less sleep than she that day as he took over the work Paul normally did. From what she could tell he hadn't gone to bed at all.

"Not right away," Armand decided, taking a sip of wine. He swallowed it and then added, "I'll wait a couple weeks."

Until she was gone, Eshe suspected. Lucian had told him she would be there for about two weeks, and she supposed he wanted to wait until she was gone to bring in a new mortal. There would be less chance of his discovering what they were that way. But it also meant he wasn't yet thinking of her being in his life longer than that. The fact rather bothered her.

Eshe took a sip of her own wine and forced her mind back to the job at hand, asking, "What about immortals? You must have visitors on occasion. Old friends you've known since England, or new ones you've made here? Mrs. Ramsey mentioned an Agnes and John?"

Armand nodded as he cut into his own steak. "Agnes and John come around once in a while, usually once a week or so to see how I am and check in."

"Check in?" she asked curiously.

He smiled wryly. "I'm the only family they have. They were Susanna's brother and sister, mortal like she was until they were turned. The rest of their family has long passed on, and of course Susanna is gone as well. So I'm all they have."

"How were they turned?" Eshe asked with surprise, and then her eyes widened with alarm. "You didn't turn them, did you?"

"No, of course not," Armand said with a laugh. "Brother or not, Lucian would have had my head had I gone against our laws."

"Oh." Eshe let out a relieved breath, but asked with confusion, "So did they turn out to be life mates for other immortals?"

"No." Armand shook his head on a sigh and set his knife and fork down to pick up his wine. After taking a drink, he explained, "Susanna was very fond of her brother and sister. She, not unnaturally, didn't want to leave them behind, and introduced them to every unattached immortal who attended our wedding, hoping they would turn out to be life mates for one of them. But, of course, we were a lot more spread out then. There were very few who were close enough to attend."

Eshe nodded in acknowledgment. Before the advent

of blood banks they had been forced to feed off mortals. Essentially, they'd had to bite their friends and neighbors or servants and peasants. Having too many of their kind in an area had meant more mortals in that area being fed on and had raised the risk of discovery. To avoid that, they had spread out across the land, allowing only one or two immortals to a good-sized area. It was how her father, Castor, had ended up in Africa and met her mother, his life mate.

"I didn't stop her from trying to find them mates," Armand continued. "I knew it wasn't likely, but felt sure that in time she'd resign herself to losing them to death."

"But she didn't," Eshe guessed.

Armand shook his head. "She didn't really get the chance to. Shortly after we were married, her sister, Agnes, became ill. I suspect now that it was leukemia, but it hadn't been named back then. Susanna got word of her illness and traveled to the convent to visit her."

"Convent?" Eshe interrupted with surprise.

"Yes. She was a nun," he explained quietly.

She felt her eyebrows rise at the knowledge that Susanna had been trying to find an immortal life mate for her sister the nun but merely gestured for him to continue.

"The convent wasn't far from our home and I expected her back by dawn, but it was the next night before she returned with a vibrantly healthy Agnes in tow."

"She turned her?" Eshe guessed solemnly.

Armand nodded with a grimace. "I had told her our laws about each only turning one and having only one child every hundred years and so on, and rather than watch helplessly as her sister died, she used her one turn to save Agnes."

Eshe nodded silently. Most immortals saved their one turn to turn a mortal who was a life mate. However, Susanna already had a life mate, and obviously hadn't considered that he might die and she might need that turn someday to turn another life mate in the future. Fortunately for her, that day had never come. Or perhaps it was unfortunate for her, since the only reason it hadn't come was that she'd died first. Pushing that thought aside, Eshe asked, "And John?"

"About a month after Susanna brought Agnes home, John arrived. He'd gotten word that Agnes had left the convent and came to see what that was about. He was angry at first, and it took some extra persuasion to calm him."

Eshe could tell by Armand's expression that what he meant by "extra persuasion" was that he'd calmed the man using their special abilities. They had several of them. Immortals could read the minds of mortals, as well as of immortals if they weren't guarded, but they could also wipe the memories of mortals or put thoughts or even new memories in their minds.

"He stayed about a week," Armand continued. "And then the day before he was supposed to leave we all went on a hunt, and he took a terrible tumble from his horse. He broke his neck. I don't think he would have survived the night if Agnes hadn't used her one turn on him."

"I see," Eshe murmured, thinking that while the woman probably hadn't considered it at the time, she'd made a huge sacrifice. But then so had Susanna when she'd turned Agnes, and indeed, as it turned out, so had Armand when he'd turned Susanna. While he had gained a life mate by turning her, he hadn't gotten to enjoy her for long before he'd lost her.

"John went home briefly after I'd taught him to hunt and fend for himself, but it was only a matter of weeks before he returned," Armand continued and explained, "Susanna's father was a baron too, but John was a second son with no likelihood of inheriting the title or property. He asked to work for me. I knew it was risky having so many of our kind in one place, especially since Susanna was pregnant and there would soon be five of us, but Susanna begged me to let him stay and in the end I said yes."

"And they stayed on after Susanna died?" Eshe asked.

"Yes. Agnes was a great help raising Nicholas, and John was my second. When it was time to move on, I took them with me, and then the next time and the next. By the time I followed the rest of the family here to Canada, I didn't even ask if they wished to join me. I just assumed they would, and they did."

"If Agnes and John were with you, why didn't Agnes raise Thomas as she had Nicholas?" Eshe asked curiously. "Why did you send Thomas to Marguerite?"

"They weren't with me anymore by then," he explained. "They both moved out when I married Althea. Agnes worried that Althea might be uncomfortable having my first wife's family around. She also thought as newlyweds we should have time to ourselves, and she said she wanted to visit the old country."

"England?" Eshe asked.

Armand nodded. "John took her back to England and they visited old haunts and then toured the rest of Europe. They returned to Canada when they heard about Althea's death, but by then I'd already sent Thomas to be with Marguerite."

"Why didn't you just bring him back?" Eshe asked. "Couldn't Agnes have helped raise him as she did Nicholas?"

"I considered that," Armand acknowledged. "But it seemed unfair to Agnes to just thrust my son on her, especially when they made it plain they didn't plan to move back in with me but were going to buy their own little farm in the next town over. Close enough they could visit, but not be a bother, John said. I realized then that he'd probably wanted to move out and have his own place for centuries, but had felt in some twisted way that he owed me."

He grimaced and then admitted, "I still might have asked Agnes if she would mind, but then I went to visit Thomas and he seemed settled and happy and . . ." He shrugged helplessly. "It seemed cruel to tear him away from Marguerite. He called her Ma and hardly seemed to recognize me."

Eshe considered that and then commented, "I'm surprised Althea's parents didn't want to raise him themselves."

"They wanted to," Armand admitted. "But they decided to move back to Europe for a while after Althea's death. I think they wanted to escape the bad memories. With Thomas at Jean Claude and Marguerite's I could at least visit him on occasion, but I'd never have seen him if Althea's parents had taken him to Europe, so I said no."

"So . . . Agnes and John were Susanna's brother and sister and they were in Europe when Althea died, but returned and have lived nearby since after learning of her death?" Eshe murmured, mentally crossing them off the suspect list. They'd hardly have killed their own sister who had loved them enough to turn Agnes. And they had been in Europe when Althea died in the hotel fire.

When Armand nodded, she asked, "But they've lived in the area since then? Close enough to visit and such?"

"Yes. John learned from me while he worked for me. He's been slowly buying up farms like I did. I think he owns five or six now himself and rotates from one to the other every ten years like I do. But all of them are in southern Ontario like mine. Far enough away from each other that he isn't likely to run into people from the area once he's left it. Although that's becoming more of a risk as time goes on," he added solemnly. "People tended to stick to their own towns when we used horse and buggy, but the more automated everything becomes, the greater the risk of running into people from the past who wonder why you haven't aged as they have."

"Will you have to start buying farms further away?" Eshe asked curiously, wondering how he would deal with the threat of being recognized by mortals from the past.

Armand was silent for a minute, his eyes on his now-empty plate, and then admitted, "Actually, I've been thinking about getting out of farming."

Eshe raised her eyebrows. "Really?"

He nodded. "Perhaps it's time for a change. I've been farming ever since moving to Canada and I find my interest in it waning."

"Do you have any interest in something else?" she asked curiously.

"I'm not sure," he said slowly. "I was thinking about going to university, maybe studying medicine or science."

"All finished here, I see," their waiter trilled cheerfully, appearing at the end of the table to begin scooping up their empty plates. "Can I tempt either of you with dessert?"

Eshe sat back in her seat to avoid his arm brushing her breast as he reached for her plate, but shook her head. As lovely as dessert sounded, it had been years since she'd eaten. Centuries even. She had already stretched her stomach to capacity. If she ate another thing she would probably burst. Literally.

"No thank you. Just the bill," Armand said, scowling at the waiter. Apparently he hadn't missed the close call with the almost boob brushing, and from his expression, was thinking it hadn't been accidental.

Eshe didn't doubt he'd read the waiter's mind and was probably right, but didn't bother to read his thoughts herself. She had lived a long time and was used to men's behavior, and really, it got a bit disheartening listening to their baser thoughts after a while. She didn't know how or why, but a mortal male could completely and utterly love one woman and still have the most staggeringly disgusting lustful thoughts about others that got caught in his vision range. It made her glad she was an immortal. Immortal mates, at least when they were life mates, didn't suffer the same problem. They might think another woman was attractive, but they wouldn't act on it, because it simply couldn't ever be as good as it was with their life mate. There might be some disadvantages in that an immortal could be incredibly lonely between life mates and that centuries and even millennia could pass before another was found, but the benefits of the shared pleasure and utter trust totally outweighed the disadvantages.

"Shall we?"

Eshe glanced to Armand to see that while she'd been lost in thought the bill had arrived, and he had dropped several twenties in the black folder it had come in, and was now peering at her expectantly.

Managing a smile, she nodded and slid out of her side of the booth to stand, surprised to find herself a little unsteady on her feet.

"You need more blood," Armand murmured, his expression concerned as he took her arm to steady her. "I should have made you have a couple of bags at least before coming in rather than just the one."

"I'm fine," Eshe assured him. "I just probably shouldn't have had the wine." The alcohol wouldn't have made her drunk, but it would have made her nanos work twice as hard to remove the alcohol from her system, using up the blood she did have flowing through her veins. She could use a top-up.

Armand ushered her out of the restaurant and to the pickup. He saw her inside, and then left the door open as he moved to the back of the pickup to the special cooler there. A moment later he was back with two bags of blood for her.

"Is this enough or should I grab another?" he asked as he passed them to her. "You probably need three or four, but I know it's uncomfortable trying to consume them under the dashboard so no one sees."

"Two is fine," she assured him, taking the bags. "I can have more back at the house."

Nodding, he stepped back and closed the door, then moved around to slide into the driver's side.

They were both quiet on the ride home. At first it was because Eshe had the bags to her mouth and couldn't talk, and then once those were empty, she simply didn't know what to say to break the silence. She was terribly aware that they were headed back to his house, his empty house where they would be alone and could finish what they'd started earlier. The thought was like a great huge boulder in the middle of her brain, leaving her incapable of thinking of much else. With every mile they drove, her body grew more and more tense with anticipation and her tongue seemed to swell in her mouth, unable to form words even had her mind been able to come up with any.

She was so wound up with anticipation that the moment the truck stopped in front of the farm, Eshe was springing out the door and hurrying for the house. She was determined to get inside before he could touch her or say or do anything that might end in their rolling around in the front yard, and then passing out there for the animals to eye curiously.

Once in the house, however, she stopped running and turned in the hall to wait for Armand. Much to her frustration, however, he was following at a much slower rate. He also didn't appear to be in the same anticipatory state as she was. A frown was carving his face, concern wrinkling his eyes, and his lips were a firm, grim line when he pulled the screen door open and met her gaze.

Armand stared at her silently for a moment, his eyes traveling her length with a hunger that was visible in the silver fire in his eyes, and then he forced his eyes away and said, "I need to check on the animals. Then I have to muck out the stalls and such."

"What?" Eshe asked with blank disbelief.

"I'll probably be out all night. There's a lot to do now that Paul's gone," he continued, turning in the open door in preparation for leaving. "Mrs. Ramsey isn't in on Thursdays so your sleep should be undisturbed. I'll see you when you wake up."

He then walked out, leaving her staring after him with amazement. That was it? After the promise of passion in the office, and their teasing while shopping, he was just going to leave her high and dry and go play with his animals?

Eshe snorted at the very idea. If that was what he

thought, Armand Argeneau had another think coming, she decided firmly. After a considering glance down at herself, she quickly pushed off her leather pants, struggling a bit to get them off over her boots. She then slammed through the door and out onto the porch in just her knee-high black leather boots, and the white satin baby doll and panties . . . only to pause at the top of the steps. Armand was nowhere in sight.

"I guess it's true that you can take the girl out of the city, but not the city out of the girl, huh Eshe? 'Cause that sure as hell isn't farm wear."

Eshe gave a start at that comment from the darkness and turned sharply to peer toward the end of the porch where it had come from.

"Bricker," she said with disgust as she recognized the man who unfolded himself from the rocker he'd been seated in and moved toward her. "What the hell are you doing here?"

"Lucian sent me to watch your back," Justin Bricker said, his teeth flashing white in the darkness as he grinned. "I can tell you appreciate the thoughtfulness."

"Thoughtfulness my eye," Eshe said dryly. "Lucian doesn't have a thoughtful bone in his body. More likely the knowledge that I can't read Armand made him decide he should send someone to be sure I didn't let that affect my work."

"You can't read Armand?" Bricker said with surprise, and then blew out a silent whistle. "Well, that complicates things nicely, doesn't it?"

When Eshe merely scowled, Bricker shifted his attention to what she was wearing. Looking her over, he asked, "So is this the latest fashion in farm wear now? Sort of slutty milkmaid or something?"

Eshe didn't even think, she just punched out at him. It was instinct. When Lucian had agreed to take her on as an enforcer nearly a century ago, a female rogue hunter was somewhat rare. Not unheard of, but rare. He'd told her at the time that if she wanted the other rogue hunters to take her seriously, she couldn't take any crap from them. Eshe had taken him at his word and spent most of her first year on the job knocking one rogue hunter after another onto his ass. She still did it roughly once a year. This year it was apparently Bricker's turn.

Propping her hands on her hips, she glared down at him as he sat up on the porch floor, and growled, "Would you care to rephrase that?"

Bricker didn't appear to be in a hurry to get up. Rubbing his jaw, he stayed sitting and let his eyes rove briefly over her black boots. He then glanced up the length of her to her face and raised an eyebrow. "Mike Tyson in drag as a slutty milkmaid?"

Despite herself, Eshe snorted with amusement at the suggestion. Sighing, she let her hands drop from her hips and then held one down in a silent offer to help him to his feet. Bricker didn't hesitate to take it.

"I forgot how hard you could punch," he muttered, still rubbing his chin as he straightened beside her.

"Yeah, well, don't forget again," she suggested dryly, turning to start down the stairs to the front lawn. Bricker was immediately beside her.

"Where are we going?" he asked with interest, matching his stride to hers.

Eshe paused and turned to scowl at him. "*We* aren't going anywhere. *I* am going to find Armand."

"You're going to seduce him, don't you mean?" Bricker asked lightly.

Eshe narrowed her eyes. "Are you reading me?"

"Well, dressed as you are I don't really need to bother reading you to figure out what you're up to, do I?" he asked wryly, and then added, "But yes, I am. You've got some hot thoughts wandering through that mind of yours, Eshe. Very impressive."

Eshe cursed harshly at the knowledge that Bricker could read her. He'd never been able to read her before this, but finding a life mate often hindered an immortal's ability to shield thoughts from others. She wasn't pleased to know it was happening with her. Forcing herself to calm down, she said reassuringly, "Seducing Armand is all part of my strategy."

"Oh, a strategy, is it?" he asked with interest.

"Yes. He'll be set off his stride by it, vulnerable to my questions," Eshe explained, wondering why it had sounded so much more believable when she was convincing herself earlier.

"Right, and this hot barnyard sex you're planning won't affect *your* stride. Right?" he asked gently.

"Barnyard sex?" Eshe asked with disbelief.

"Stable sex?" he offered.

Eshe took a moment to suck in a calming breath and then cleared her throat and said, "Look. Don't worry about it. Armand can't be behind the murders anyway. He was at court when his life mate Susanna died in a stable fire at their home, and he was home on the farm when his second wife, Althea, died in a fire in the hotel she and her parents were staying in, in Toronto. He couldn't have killed either woman."

"And Rosamund and Annie?" Bricker asked with interest.

"He was on the farm when they died too, but while I suppose that means he could have killed them, he couldn't have killed the first two women, so if they're connected he's in the clear."

"Right, because he was at court when Susanna died and here on the farm when Althea died in a hotel fire in Toronto," Bricker reasoned.

"Exactly," Eshe said with relief, glad he agreed.

Bricker nodded repeatedly and then asked, "And we know he was at court and then on the farm and nowhere near Toronto because . . . ?"

"He told me," she answered at once.

"Right," Bricker drawled. "He told you . . . and he'd have no reason to lie, right?"

Eshe opened her mouth, and then closed it again and stared at him silently, her heart sinking.

"I don't suppose he offered some proof, huh?" Bricker asked gently. "Maybe he was at court *with* someone? Or maybe he had a visitor at the farm who could prove he was there and not in Toronto at the time of the fire?"

Eshe closed her eyes briefly as she realized what she'd done. She'd simply believed him. Armand had told her his stories of his wives' deaths and she hadn't doubted a single word, or even considered doing any fact-checking. What the hell had she been thinking?

"Yeah," Bricker said carefully. "Maybe this whole

seduction thing is a bad idea. Maybe all this life mate business has set you a little off your stride, huh?"

Eshe turned abruptly on her heel and marched back to the stairs.

"Where are we going now?" Bricker asked, falling in beside her again as she mounted the steps.

"I am going to bed," she announced grimly. "I didn't get more than a couple hours of sleep this morning. Obviously that has left me a little slow today."

"Yeah, that's probably it," Bricker agreed solemnly.

"If you laugh at me, Bricker, I'll knock you on your ass again," she warned grimly, stomping across the porch to the door. "When did you get here?"

"About half an hour ago," he answered, glancing at his wristwatch as he followed her inside. "The door was unlocked, but I thought I'd better wait outside so I settled in the rocker, and fell asleep. I didn't hear you two get back, but woke up when Armand let the screen door clack closed behind him on the way back out."

"Well, you'd better go down to the barn, find Armand, and let him know you're here," she said on a sigh, leading him to the kitchen, only to pause halfway to the refrigerator when she recalled that the blood wasn't there anymore. And Armand hadn't shown her the fridge in his walk-in closet as promised.

Clucking her tongue impatiently, she announced, "I'm calling Lucian and letting him know he should send someone else, but I'll wait for you to get back before I head out."

"Calling Lucian?" Bricker asked with surprise. "I

thought it was just sleep you needed? A little rest and you'll be right as rain."

"Rest isn't going to help," she admitted unhappily, her shoulders sagging in defeat. "He's my life mate, Bricker. The only thing I'm thinking when I'm near him is how to get his pants off."

Bricker's lips twitched, but he managed to keep a straight face as he said, "Well, that's perfectly normal. You should have seen Mortimer when he found his life mate, Sam, or Decker when he found his Dani. Hell, it was boob city in the back of the van on Highway 401 with Decker."

"Yes, but Nicholas's life didn't depend on Decker," she pointed out, moving past him and heading into the hall to retrieve her leather pants from the hall floor where she'd left them.

"No," Bricker agreed, hard on her heels. "A young girl's life did."

When Eshe paused and met his gaze, he added, "I've never known you to be a quitter, Eshe. Lucian sent you down here for a reason, and you know he isn't likely to change his mind about having you here now. Just trust him and do what you can here." When she hesitated, not refusing at once, he added, "At least sleep on it. Who knows, maybe a little rest really will help. You can always call Lucian tomorrow if it doesn't."

Eshe stared at him silently, terribly tempted by the suggestion. Maybe if she slept she would be a little more on the ball. And she could stay here with Armand. On the other hand, she really didn't think sleep was going to help much. She couldn't think clearly when she was around Armand. However, it wasn't like one day's rest was going to slow things down much here, her mind argued temptingly, and she could see Armand when she woke up.

"Fine, I'll sleep on it, but I don't think it will make a difference," she muttered, turning toward the stairs. She heard Bricker's murmured good-night, but merely raised her hand in a wave as she went. Her mind was too busy going over everything that had happened since her arrival for her to expend the effort needed to say anything. She really was exhausted, but suspected it wasn't just her lack of sleep behind it. There was also the fact that she really could have used a couple more bags of blood just then; three or four would have done it. She generally needed only three or four a day, but she'd shorted herself the night before, and then the wine tonight had used up blood she really hadn't had to spare.

Unfortunately, she had no idea where the blood was. She'd already been through Armand's closet the night before after arriving and hadn't seen any evidence of a refrigerator there. Obviously it was built in, and she didn't feel like searching his closet again. Really, all she wanted to do right then was sleep. She was exhausted after what was essentially a roller coaster of a day. She'd arrived suspecting Armand was a murderer, found out he was her life mate, and spent the time since lusting after him while trying to do her job. His rejection on returning home—and that's what it had felt like to her—had been the final straw.

Her mind was still running around in circles trying

to understand what had happened there. At the mall he'd been ready to rush her back to the house and jump her bones, but after the meal he'd apparently lost interest. How could a life mate lose interest?

The question rambled through her mind on a note of disbelief and was followed by the fact that a life mate wouldn't lose interest. Which meant either that he was fighting what they were for some reason, or that he could resist her because he wasn't really her life mate. Perhaps she really couldn't read him because he was difficult to read and not because he was her life mate. After all, Lucian couldn't read him, she reminded herself. Maybe that's all it was for her too, she thought.

Of course there was the reawakening of her appetites for both food and sex, Eshe acknowledged, but then worried that that might be more psychological than anything. Perhaps she was only interested in food and sex again because she *thought* he was her life mate.

Sighing at the confusion of her thoughts, Eshe decided that sleep was really what she needed. It should clear her thoughts at least a little. In the morning she would try to work it all out again and see if she came up with something different, she reassured herself as she walked into the guest room she'd chosen.

Eshe was crossing the dark room to the bed when she caught a glimpse of herself in the dresser mirror. Pausing, she peered at her reflection for a moment, noting how short and sexy the baby doll was. It had been a good choice on Armand's part. Perfect, really. She doubted anything else in the store could have showed her off as well as it did.

"How the hell did he resist me?" she asked with bewilderment, and turned away with disgust to stride to the bed.

"How the hell did I resist her?" Armand muttered under his breath as he mucked out one of the stalls in the horse barn. He could still see her in his mind, eyes glowing golden in the dim hallway, the sharp white baby doll hugging her breasts and flowing down to barely past her hips, the skintight leather pants making her look almost nude but for the baby doll in the dim overhead light. Damn, all he'd wanted to do was throw her to the floor and—as she'd put it—have his "wicked way" with her. Instead, he'd said he had work to do and left the house, rushing down here like the devil himself was on his tail.

Armand didn't know how he'd managed to resist the urges just looking at her raised in him, but he was damned sure of one thing, there was no way he was going to be able to resist her again . . . which meant he had to get her out of there as soon as possible. He couldn't even afford to spend one night with her. Armand knew he'd been fooling himself with the belief that he could take one night and then send her away. He now suspected the truth was that one night wouldn't be enough. He'd need another and another and another until . . . until he was made a widower for the fourth time, he acknowledged unhappily. That was his fear. Telling her about the deaths of his wives had made him realize how foolish he was being. It had resurrected all his doubts about those deaths being accidents, and reawakened his worries that someone had been stalking the people he loved and taking their lives, then covering them up as accidents. It had been bad enough when he'd thought only his wives had been killed, but after their talk at dinner, Armand was now wondering about his daughter-in-law Annie's death too.

He needed to call Lucian now and get him to send someone down to collect Eshe and take her to a different safe house. His house just wasn't that safe for Eshe d'Aureus, he thought, and straightened to reach in his pocket for his phone.

"Wow!"

Armand glanced sharply toward the open barn door as a man in leather pants, T-shirt, and leather jacket strode inside and along the stalls toward him. His nose was wrinkled with distaste and his lips twisted with disgust as he met Armand's gaze.

"The smell in here is pretty rank, buddy. I don't know how you put up with it. Have you ever considered some air fresheners maybe? Or a different job?"

"Who the hell—"

"Justin Bricker. You can call me Bricker," he interrupted, offering his hand. "I work with Eshe."

Armand automatically shifted his phone to his other hand and took Bricker's. His gaze slid over the younger immortal as he shook the hand and he arched an eyebrow, "So do all of Lucian's enforcers have a thing for leather, or is it just you and Eshe?"

"I rode my bike down, and leather protects your skin better if you wipe out. Means less blood needed to repair you after," Bricker explained, and then grinned and added, "But I think Eshe has a thing for it. To tell the truth, I've never seen her out of it."

"And you won't," Armand assured him grimly, his mouth tightening at the thought of this young kid seeing Eshe undressed.

"Got it. She's off limits," Bricker agreed with a wince. "I mean seriously, guy. It's not like she'd even give me a second glance when she's your life mate, right? So do you think you can release my hand now before you break it? The healing can be a bitch."

Armand released his hold at once, feeling stupid as he realized that it hadn't only been his mouth that had tightened. Apparently he was something of a jealous idiot. Sighing, he ran his hand through his hair and then asked, "So what are you doing here?"

"Lucian sent me," Bricker muttered, rubbing his abused hand. "He thought you two might be a little preoccupied with each other, you being life mates and all, and he sent me as added protection."

"Oh." Armand sighed and then admitted, "I was going to call Lucian and suggest he take her somewhere else."

"Now you don't have to, right?" Bricker said lightly. "Now that I'm here there are two of us to watch her. She's safe as a bug in a rug."

"Rugs get stepped on," Armand pointed out quietly.

"So do bugs out of rugs," Bricker said easily. "But at least the rug offers some cushioning."

"I don't know," Armand said with a frown.

"Sleep on it," Bricker suggested easily, leaning his

arms on the top of the stall. "If you're still worried in the morning, give Lucian a call . . . but I doubt he'll change his mind."

Armand suspected he was right, but didn't say as much. He simply watched the other man glance around the stall and then the barn again.

"So, you live out here on purpose?" Bricker asked with open disbelief.

Armand stared at him blankly for a moment, and then a short, surprised laugh burst from his mouth. It seemed obvious the fellow wasn't impressed, and he asked, "City boy?"

"All my life," Bricker admitted almost apologetically. "My uncle had a farm and I used to go there, but I never quite figured out the attraction of treading through manure."

"We generally try not to do that," Armand assured him with amusement.

"Good to know," Bricker said, and then raised an eyebrow. "Is there anything I can help with?"

"It's kind of you to offer, but I think I have everything under control," Armand said wryly, thinking the boy would be more hindrance than help. If he'd never been on a farm before, he wouldn't know what the hell he was doing. "Perhaps you should just go back to the house and keep an eye on Eshe."

"She went to bed," Bricker said with a shrug, and then added archly, "Alone. Not the usual outcome between life mates, I must say. Decker and Mortimer were both like a couple of bulls in mating season when they met their life mates, and Eshe was all set to march out here in nothing but this shiny white baby doll and knee-high leather boots when I stopped her. You're welcome, by the way."

Armand stared at him with a combination of anger at the idea that this punk kid had been the first one to see Eshe properly in just the baby doll, and confusion over the "you're welcome" bit. "What am I welcome for?"

"Well, I saved you slivers in the ass from doing it out here in the barn with the horses looking on," he pointed out, and then frowned and said, "Or maybe I saved her the slivers. Either way, someone didn't get slivers in their ass thanks to my intervention."

"Gee, thanks," Armand said dryly, but wasn't sure he meant it. His mind was now full of images of Eshe in that damned baby doll and leather boots. His backing her up against the stall wall and—

"Crap!" He set aside the rake he'd been using and moved out of the stall with every intention of going inside, finding Eshe, and living it rather than imagining it.

"So, I'll just finish up in here, shall I?" Bricker offered, bringing Armand to an abrupt halt. Turning, he found the young man had taken his place in the stall and picked up the rake. He was now glancing from it to the hay on the floor with consideration.

Armand felt his shoulders slump. He had chores to do. Twice the amount he usually had now that there was no manager to do them for him. He briefly considered letting Bricker help out, but it was only very briefly. Justin Bricker didn't even appear sure what to do with the rake he now held. It seemed Eshe was going to sleep soundly tonight. But tomorrow he was going to start advertising for a new manager, Armand decided. To hell with waiting until Eshe was gone; he needed someone now so that he could spend time with her.

Seven

Harsh afternoon sunlight was peeking around the edges of the blackout curtains over the bedroom windows when Eshe woke up. A glance at the clock showed that it was just past three in the afternoon. It had been early when she'd gone to bed, but not when she'd gone to sleep. She'd lain awake in bed for hours, exhausted, but her mind fretting over her worries. It had been three A.M. when she'd last looked at the clock before dropping off to sleep last night. She'd slept twelve hours. It was a long time for her, and that alone would have left her well rested. However, she'd also enjoyed some of those shared erotic dreams that life mates were said to experience, her mind merging with Armand's as they slept and the two of them living out in their dreams what they really wanted to do in reality, which had come down to a lot of very hot sex. It was a bit embarrassing to think about now that she was awake, but Eshe was definitely better for the relief it offered from her sexual tensions. She'd even woken up with a plan on how to prove Armand had told her the truth about the deaths of his wives.

Sitting up in bed, Eshe tossed the blankets aside and got to her feet. She was even actually humming under her breath as she crossed the room to the bag she'd brought with her. While she had jeans and T-shirts now that she could have worn, leather was better for riding the motorcycle, so she pulled out the second pair of leather pants she'd brought, as well as the almost corsetlike matching black leather top, and took them with her into the bathroom.

Fifteen minutes later, she was showered and dressed and heading out of her room.

Eshe got as far as the top of the stairs and then stopped. The long sleep had done her good, but now she needed blood and there wasn't any in the refrigerator downstairs.

She swung back around to peer up the hall toward Armand's room, but shook her head at once. If she went in there and got anywhere near the sleepy-eyed, bed-headed Argeneau tiger, she wouldn't get a damned thing done today. Her clothes would be on the floor and she'd be in his bed with him before he'd finished blinking his eyes open. And despite the fact that he'd turned his back on her last night, she didn't think he'd push her out of his bed this afternoon. She'd be living out the dreams they'd shared in living color.

Sighing, Eshe started to turn back toward the stairs, but paused as her gaze landed on the only other closed door in the hallway. Obviously that was the room Bricker had taken for his own. It was the one across from hers. Eshe narrowed her gaze on the door and then nodded and strode toward it with determination.

She suspected Bricker had been up until sunrise. It was the usual sleeping pattern for most immortals; in bed by dawn, up by sunset. Of course, some immortals got up earlier or kept more regular hours. They didn't have to sleep in the day if they didn't like. They didn't even need to avoid sunlight, really. It just saved them on having to consume extra blood to combat the damage sunlight did to the skin, so most at least stayed inside during daylight.

Unfortunately for Bricker, Eshe didn't much care if he usually slept later. He was young, and she needed his help. If she knew Lucian Argeneau, he'd sent extra blood with Bricker, and she wanted some of it. And then she wanted his help asking questions of Susanna's brother and sister, and Althea's parents if they were still in the area. A quick call to Lucian should tell her where the two pairs lived.

Bricker's door wasn't locked, but then she hadn't expected it to be. As far as she could tell, none of the bedrooms had locks on them. Eshe eased the door open and moved silently inside, her eyes examining a sleeping Bricker. The boy was built like a wrestler, lots of defined muscle and flat stomach, but fortunately without the unattractive thick neck. Eshe admired his buff chest above the sheet that had been pushed down low at his waist as she settled to sit on the side of his bed, then reached out and tugged gently on a length of his hair.

Bricker's eyes opened at once.

"Eshe," he said with blank surprise.

"I need you," she whispered, not sure how thick the walls were and not wanting to wake up Armand.

A slow smile immediately curved his lips. "I knew you couldn't resist me. I'm a hottie."

"Ha ha," Eshe said, knowing he was teasing. "Did Lucian send blood with you?"

"It's down in the fridge in the kitchen. I put it there after you went to bed. Armand said we have to move it to the refrigerator in his room tonight, though, so his housekeeper doesn't see it when she comes in tomorrow."

"Good," she said, standing up. "Now get up. You're going to help me."

"Help you with what?" he asked in a whisper, sitting up on the bed.

"With finding out what really happened to Armand's wives."

"Sleep did help clear your mind then?" he said with satisfaction.

"Yes. And as long as I keep my distance from Armand it will stay clear. Now get up and get dressed. I'll be in the kitchen." She was at the door before she added, "And wear your leathers, we're going out."

Eshe didn't wait to see if he followed her orders, but the rustle of sheets behind her as she opened the bedroom door suggested he was. As the senior enforcer there, she wouldn't have expected anything less than prompt obedience, and she got it. Eshe was on only her third bag of blood when Bricker sauntered into the kitchen in a T-shirt, leather pants, and jacket, and with his hair still wet from a very fast shower.

"So, what are we doing today?" he asked cheerfully as he opened the refrigerator door to retrieve a bag of blood.

Eshe pulled the empty bag from her teeth and answered, "I'm calling Lucian to find out where Susanna's brother and sister and Althea's parents live and then we're going to go question them. They should help verify whether Armand was around when Susanna and Althea died."

"Sweet," Bricker crowed, straightening from the fridge with two bags in hand. He tossed her one, saying, "See, I told you a night's sleep would make a difference."

Eshe merely grunted around the bag she slapped to her teeth. She hated I-told-you-sos.

The moment she'd finished feeding, Eshe pulled her cell phone from her pocket and punched in the number for Lucian's home. It was early still, but Lucian was a man who never seemed to sleep. Besides, she couldn't just sit around waiting. She wanted to be out of the house and on the move before Armand woke up and her brain went south.

"Speak" was Lucian's barked greeting when he answered the phone. It made Eshe roll her eyes. There was really no reason the man couldn't try at least a little common courtesy.

"It's Eshe," she announced. "And good afternoon to you too, Lucian."

"I'm not assigning someone else to—" he began firmly, and she interrupted.

"I'm not calling about that."

"Oh." She could actually hear his frown over the line. He didn't ask what she was calling for, but simply waited for her to speak.

"I need the address of Agnes and John Maunsell and Althea's parents," she announced.

"William and Mary Harcourt," he murmured, giving her their last name, and then he asked bluntly, "Why?"

"Armand says he was away at court when Susanna died in a stable fire, and that he was home on the farm when Althea died in the hotel fire in Toronto. I want to talk to them to see if they can verify that for me," she explained, and then added, "It would get him off the hook for at least two of the deaths, which would pretty much clear him altogether, don't you think?"

Lucian was silent for a minute and then she heard a rustling sound as if he was covering the phone. It was followed by a muffled conversation she couldn't make out. When it ended, there was another rustle as the phone was uncovered and then a female voice spoke, "Hello, Eshe. This is Marguerite Argeneau."

"Marguerite," she murmured with a half smile. Eshe had always liked Lucian's sister-in-law through his now-deceased twin, Jean Claude. "Hello. How are you?"

"Very well. Listen, Lucian is getting the addresses for you, but I think I can help with at least Susanna's death. We lived not far from Armand at the time and Jean Claude and I traveled to visit when we heard the baby was born. We missed Armand, he'd apparently left the day after the birth and we didn't arrive until four days later. We stayed a couple of days and then left early in the evening on the night of the fire to head home. From what I heard afterward, it apparently happened a couple hours after we left. Armand was not home when we left, so unless he arrived after we rode out . . ." She didn't bother finishing the sentence, but instead asked, "Does that help at all?"

"Yes," Eshe murmured, trying to ignore the relief sliding through her that at least she knew that Armand probably hadn't been there when Susanna died.

"I read Marguerite's mind," Lucian announced, apparently taking the phone. "She's telling the truth."

Eshe rolled her eyes at the rather rude and abrupt announcement, but smiled reluctantly when she heard Marguerite laughing with amusement in the background. Apparently she wasn't upset by his reading her to verify that she was telling the truth.

"Here are the addresses," Lucian announced abruptly, and Eshe glanced around a bit wildly for a pen and paper to scribble the information down.

"Here." Bricker snatched a magnetized notepad off the refrigerator and slid it in front of her, along with a pen he found after a quick search of the drawer beside the fridge.

Eshe mouthed, "Thank you" to him and listened as Lucian rattled off each address.

"They're both in the area," she murmured with relief as she wrote down the addresses. Armand had said that Althea's parents had moved to Europe after her death.

She'd been worried they might still be there. But it seemed they'd moved back to the area since then.

"Do you need anything else?" Lucian asked abruptly.

"No. That was—" Eshe didn't bother to finish. Lucian had hung up the moment she'd said no. Rolling her eyes, she muttered, "And good-bye to you too."

"So?" Bricker asked, hefting himself up to sit on the island. "Where are we going?"

Eshe tore off the sheet of notepaper with the addresses and walked over to hand it to him.

"Susanna's brother and sister live closest," he commented, and then glanced at her in question. "What about breakfast?"

Eshe considered the question. She was rather peckish herself, but really wanted to get on the road. This eating business could be a bit inconvenient.

"Can you cook?" she asked finally.

Bricker pursed his lips, and then said slowly, "Yeah . . . but I passed a diner on the way out here. It would be faster."

"Good thinking," she decided, turning toward the door. "The diner it is then."

Bricker was off the counter at once and slipping past her. "I'll race you."

"I'll win," Eshe warned, following him out of the kitchen.

They served an all-day breakfast at the diner that turned out to be delicious. It was also on the table in front of them pretty fast. Eshe and Bricker were equally quick about consuming it, paying the bill and getting out of there. Aside from the fact that she wanted to get to business on the task of questioning the families of Armand's first two wives, she was also incredibly uncomfortable in the diner. It was full of locals, and every one of them seemed to be watching her and Bricker and, when not offering them wide friendly smiles, whispering wildly among themselves.

It seemed Mrs. Ramsey had been faithful in spreading Eshe's description around and everyone knew who she was, but there was a lot of wild speculation passed among the tables by the waitresses as to who Bricker might be. Some had pegged him as her lover and suspected a love triangle had developed at the farm. Others thought perhaps he was a relative. Eshe had just shaken her head at that one. As it happened she did have two white siblings who had taken on their father's coloring, but Bricker looked nothing like anyone in her family.

Eshe was uncomfortable being the center of attention and glad when they finished eating and she could hustle Bricker out of the diner.

Agnes and John Maunsell lived two towns over, a twenty-minute drive. At least it was twenty minutes with Eshe and Bricker racing each other there. The house they arrived at was a large, modern brick ranch house set back a good distance from the road, with several bright red outbuildings around it and white fencing everywhere. In truth, it looked brand-spanking-new and was obviously the latest of the six farms Armand had mentioned John accumulating.

"Nice," Bricker commented once they had both turned off their bikes and she could hear him.

"Yes," Eshe agreed as she got off her motorcycle,

and it was attractive. But she preferred Armand's place. There, a line of trees along the road and around the house itself offered privacy and made the house feel cozy and almost secluded. Here, there were no trees at all, simply the buildings set in the middle of fields as if dropped there.

"I wonder how many acres he has here?" Bricker murmured as they moved together toward the house.

Eshe merely shrugged, her gaze sliding over a small yellow sports car and a larger black van parked side by side in the driveway. "They're home."

"Yeah," Bricker murmured, reaching out to press the doorbell as they reached the door. "Now the question is whether they're awake or not."

Eshe merely grunted at the comment, but frowned as she realized they probably wouldn't be. It was still light out and a lot of older immortals slept all day, an old habit hard to break after centuries of doing so by necessity.

As they waited for the door to be answered, Eshe glanced around their surroundings again. It was late afternoon without a cloud in the sky. The sun was baking down on them, and hot though it was, she was glad she had her leathers on to prevent the sun from baking and damaging her skin. They hadn't thought to bring any extra blood with them, which was why she and Bricker both still had their helmets on with the visors down. They wouldn't remove them until they were inside, safely out of the sun.

If they got inside, Eshe thought as the wait lengthened. She tapped her fingers against her thigh as they waited, but when Bricker reached for the doorbell again, she caught his arm to stop him. "Don't bother. Most of the older immortals have soundproofed bedrooms without phones to avoid pesky calls and door-to-door salesmen." She gestured for him to follow and turned to head back to their motorcycles. "We'll go over to the Harcourts' and stop in here again on the way back."

Eshe led him back to their bikes and got on her own, but glanced to Bricker in question when he paused and peered back at the house with his head cocked. "What is it?"

Bricker hesitated, and then shook his head. Moving to his own motorcycle, he muttered, "Nothing."

Eshe glanced back to the house, but didn't see anything. Shrugging, she repeated, "We'll stop on the way back. Let's go."

Bricker hesitated another moment, but then nodded and got on his own machine, asking, "Do we know the way to the Harcourts'?"

"I punched it into my GPS," she answered. "According to it, the Harcourts' place is about fifteen minutes from here."

They made it to the Harcourts' in fourteen minutes, but then they weren't racing as they had on the way to John and Agnes's place. William and Mary Harcourt lived in a home not dissimilar to the Maunsell farm. It was a more modern ranch with outbuildings, only here trees lined the property as well as the long driveway leading up to the house.

Eshe turned onto the driveway and slowed as she

spotted the car coming toward her. The car slowed as well, the woman behind the wheel peering out at them curiously as she passed. She didn't stop, however, but continued on to the road.

"So I'm guessing that was Mary Harcourt," Bricker commented as they stopped their motorcycles on the paved drive in front of the house. "I didn't see Mr. Harcourt though."

"I'm betting that's him," Eshe murmured, nodding toward the dark-haired man peering at them from the open door of the closest barn. He looked about twenty-six or -seven, but then adult immortals all did. However, this man looked grim and unwelcoming as he watched them approach.

Eshe left Bricker to make the introductions, her gaze moving over Althea's father and then shifting to glance around the interior of the barn they were in as she removed her helmet.

"So you're Armand's new life mate."

Eshe turned to peer wide-eyed at William Harcourt at that comment.

He smiled with dry amusement at her expression. "Sweetheart, your thoughts are shrieking in my ears right now, a hazard of first finding a life mate. You'll slowly regain control of them again."

Eshe grimaced and nodded, but he wasn't done.

"Now what the hell was that I picked up about you fact-checking his alibis to be sure Armand couldn't have killed Susanna or Althea?"

Eshe cursed, but Bricker just started to laugh and said, "Well, that saves us having to ask questions."

"Maybe," Harcourt growled. "But you can damned well explain things. I've known Armand for seven hundred years. He didn't have anything to do with his wives' deaths. Hell, they were all accidents . . . weren't they?" he added, and frowned. "I know Althea's was."

Eshe peered at him closely. "You don't sound too sure."

William Harcourt avoided her eyes for a minute and then shook his head. "I don't know. I've often wondered . . ."

"What did you wonder?" Eshe asked, her body tensing.

William grimaced at her. "Oh, don't panic. I've never wondered about Armand. He didn't even know where we were. It was the busy season for us farmers, but I had a good manager, so when Mary pleaded with me to take her to see Althea and little Thomas, I agreed. We stayed a couple of days, but the girls wanted to spend more time visiting, and Mary suggested Althea come back home with us for a couple weeks. We'd bring her back after the harvest, when Armand wouldn't be so busy."

"And you agreed," Eshe guessed, bringing a wry twist to William's lips.

"I've always been a soft touch when it came to things Mary wanted, and I wasn't much better with Althea, so, yes, I agreed." He ran a weary hand through his hair. "If I hadn't, Althea might still be alive."

Eshe glanced away, giving him a moment to get past his emotion. When he cleared his throat, she glanced back to see that his expression was grim and determined.

"Anyway, Armand agreed to the visit and we left the next night. But I can guarantee you he didn't follow.

When we left he had his arm shoulder-deep in a mare's womb trying to untangle her foal that had got caught in the umbilical cord. There is no way he followed."

Eshe nodded silently for him to go on.

"Even if he'd dropped everything, changed, and followed, he would never have caught up."

"Why is that?" Bricker asked.

"Because we'd barely left the farm when the women started talking about perhaps making the trip to Toronto while Althea was staying with us," he said, and then explained, "Armand was on another farm at that time as were we. His farm was at that time northeast of London, about halfway between our farm and Toronto. A much longer journcy by carriage than it would be today. The idea of having to make the long journey there and home at a later date wasn't a thrilling one for me. I thought if we headed there from Armand's it would cut out half of the journey one way."

Eshe nodded at his reasoning. "So instead of heading south, you headed east, and Armand wouldn't have expected that so couldn't have followed unless he was directly on your heels."

"Exactly, and trust me, he wasn't directly behind us. Even if he'd given up on the mare as soon as I left the barn, it would have taken a good bit of cleanup and a change of clothes for him to follow. He wasn't on our heels," he repeated firmly.

"Then what did you wonder about?" Eshe asked quietly.

"At the time it was the fact that Althea was dead at all," he said grimly. "She was the only fatality in that hotel fire. Lots of mortals were injured. Hell, Mary and I even got a little singed, but Althea was the only person who died and she was immortal."

"How did Thomas get out?" Bricker asked suddenly. "He was only four, right? He must have been with her. How—"

"He was with us," William interrupted, telling him what Eshe already knew. "Althea said he tended to fuss through the day and Mary offered to take him in to sleep in our room with us so that she could sleep the day through without being disturbed."

"Was Althea in the room next to yours?" Eshe asked.

William shook his head, his expression tight. "The hotel was busy, the two rooms we were given were at opposite ends of the hotel; one in the front, and one at the back, away from the road and quieter. Althea asked for the one at the back of the hotel so she could sleep through the day without the annoyance of street traffic. Mary and I didn't mind which room we had so we agreed. We just wanted to get to bed. The journey back then was long and dusty. It had worn us out and we all went to bed early." William Harcourt paused, and she suspected he was looking into the past as he said, "It was a good couple of hours before dawn when we went to our rooms. It didn't take long to get Thomas settled and then Mary and I dropped right off."

He sighed. "The fire apparently started about three hours later, a little after dawn. We woke up to screams and shouts and smoke thick in the air. I went out in the hall to see what was happening, but it was mass chaos. The smoke was thick and hotel guests seemed to be panicking, scrambling to find loved ones and get out. I went back and got Mary and Thomas out of the hotel and then had to take the time to find somewhere out of the sunlight for them to wait. As soon as I had them somewhere sheltered, I went around to the back of the hotel to look for Althea. I spent quite a while searching for her among the guests stumbling around upset and confused. When I couldn't find her, I thought she must have got out and found shelter for herself. If that were the case, she could have been just about anywhere, so I took the time to go back to Mary and Thomas and move them to another hotel, then returned to continue searching."

"You didn't find her." Bricker stated the obvious.

William shook his head. "No, I kept looking until I heard some of the men saying the fire had started in the back corner room and they were bringing out remains."

"Althea's room?" Eshe asked.

William nodded. "And Althea's remains. All that was left was her charred head, but one of the ears was still mostly intact and I recognized the earring. It was one of a set we'd given her for her eighteenth birthday." He sighed and ran his hand through his hair again. "We packed up Thomas and headed straight to Armand to tell him what had happened."

William peered at her solemnly as he said, "Armand didn't kill her. I don't know if that fire was accidental and she was trapped, or what happened. But if it was set deliberately, it wasn't Armand who set it."

Eshe nodded and started to turn away, but paused when he added, "And he didn't kill Rosamund either."

She stopped and glanced back sharply. "Oh?"

"We moved back to England for a while after Althea's death. Mary didn't handle losing her that way very well and I thought a stay back in Europe would do her good. It didn't really make a difference, though, and we had moved back to the area just a couple weeks before Rosamund died. Armand was good enough to put Mary and me up at the farm until we bought a place of our own. We were there when Rosamund died. My Mary and Rosamund were in the house talking when Armand and I headed out to the fields. I was helping while we stayed with him. Didn't want to be a burden," he explained, and then continued, "I guess Rosamund went out about an hour after we left. Armand and I worked in the field most of the evening and were heading back to the house at around ten P.M. when Armand's neighbor came riding up with the news that he'd come across Rosamund's overturned wagon on the road and she was dead." His mouth twisted with dissatisfaction as he added, "They said the wagon landed on her badly and she was decapitated."

Eshe was silent, digesting that.

"I can't speak for where he was at the time of Nicholas's Annie's death," William said suddenly. "But I'm damned sure he didn't kill her either, and I know damned right well he didn't kill Susanna. No one kills their life mate," William said staunchly.

"Thank you," Eshe said sincerely, relieved by his revelations.

William nodded and then turned away, moving

toward the back of the barn and leaving them to see themselves out of the building.

"I guess that gets Armand off the hook," Bricker commented as they headed for the open barn door.

"Yeah," Eshe said, breathing freely for the first time since she'd realized she couldn't read Armand Argeneau. She'd felt like a band had been tightened around her chest with that realization. Finding a life mate was an awesome thing . . . except when there was a chance he was a murdering bastard you might lose almost as quickly as you'd encountered him.

"So, have you and Armand never met before this?" Bricker asked, and then pointed out, "I mean, you've known Lucian how long?"

"All my life," she murmured.

"Right. So how come you've never met Armand?"

Eshe paused to put her helmet on as they reached the door of the barn. "Lucian was a friend of my father's and visited us once in a while. He usually came to Africa once every fifty years or so while my father lived, but it was less frequent after that and he was always alone. Then when I moved to Canada about a century ago . . ." She shrugged and started across the yard toward their motorcycles. "I haven't been very sociable since my first life mate, Orion, died. I mostly keep to myself. I've met Marguerite a time or two in passing, and a couple of her kids. Thomas delivered blood to me on occasion, and then I've met all of the family who are involved in rogue hunting, including Nicholas before he went rogue, but other than that . . ." She shrugged.

"Hmm," Bricker murmured, and shook his head. "So if Lucian hadn't sent you on this case you may never have met Armand. Life's weird, huh?"

"Yes," Eshe agreed quietly as she threw one leg over her motorcycle. "Very weird at times."

"The good news is, now you can seduce Armand without guilt or worrying that you're doing the hoochie-coo with a killer," Bricker said cheerfully.

"The hoochie-coo?" she asked with amazement. "Are you *trying* to get yourself knocked on your ass again, Bricker?"

He grinned and merely started his motorcycle, the roar of the engine making further conversation impossible.

Shaking her head, Eshe started her own machine, but his words were resounding in her head. She could seduce Armand now without guilt. That was the best news she'd had in a long time.

They drove past John and Agnes Maunsell's place on the way back to the farm, but while it was full dark out now, there were no lights on in the house and both the car and van were gone.

"Looks like we missed them," Bricker said over the roar of their engines as they paused on the road by the driveway.

"We'll try again later, or maybe tomorrow," she decided.

Bricker nodded and throttled his engine. "Race you back to the farm."

Eight

Armand put away the steaks he'd bought at the market in town, and then moved to the kitchen door and peered up the hall and out the front screen door at the yard. Still no sign of Eshe and Bricker. Scowling, he moved back to the bags of groceries he'd set on the island and took out potatoes and onions next. Once those too were stored away, he again returned to the kitchen door to peer up the hall toward the front yard. Nope. Still no Eshe and Bricker. Armand moved back to the groceries again.

It had been past dawn when he'd finally finished all the chores and retired to his bed that morning. By that time Armand had been exhausted enough that he'd dropped right off to sleep rather than lie there lusting after Eshe . . . which was exactly what he'd hoped for. However, his exhaustion hadn't stopped him from having the erotic shared dreams immortals tended to enjoy.

Armand sighed at the memory of some of those dreams. If Eshe was half as hot in reality as she'd been in the dreams, he didn't think he'd ever be able to send her away. What's more, between those and his complete lack of sleep the day before, as well as the busy day and evening he'd had, Armand had slept through this day and into the evening. It had been after five o'clock when he'd finally woken up. He'd come below, fretting over how he would handle Eshe today, only to find it wasn't a concern. Neither she nor Bricker was there.

A quick check around had shown that while their bikes were gone, their rooms still held their possessions, so it had appeared they'd return eventually. That knowledge had left Armand rather relieved, which was odd, since he'd been ready to send Eshe away the night before.

Too hungry to worry about his own confused feelings then, Armand had poked his head in the refrigerator and then searched the cupboards in a hunt for food. The problem with eating again was that once you started, your stomach tended to demand you continue. However, he'd gone so long not eating that there hadn't been much to choose from in his kitchen. It seemed Mrs. Ramsey had used up the bacon feeding them the day before, and while there were still eggs and toast, he hadn't a clue how to cook them. After a brief debate, Armand had taken himself off to the diner for a meal.

As it turned out, that had been a most fortuitous event. Armand had found himself a replacement for Paul while at the diner. It had happened almost without his input. The townspeople were a pretty tight group, it seemed, and news had apparently spread quickly that his previous manager had been forced to leave by supposed family matters, the excuse he'd given Mrs. Ramsey. Armand had barely seated himself in a booth when a couple of men from other tables had come to introduce themselves and tell him they had heard about his problem and had a perfect solution. It seemed one of his neighbors had a grown son who had studied agriculture at the university and planned to someday take over the family farm or start his own concern. His father was still in his early forties, however, and young enough to run the farm without his son's aid, and—no doubt—still thought of the young man as a boy and treated him as such. It was thought all around that what would be best for the boy was if he helped out Armand, managing his farm for him. It would put some more experience under the boy's belt, and prepare him for when he was ready to either take over the family farm, or stake a claim on another one for himself.

Eager to have a manager so that he could spend time with Eshe, Armand had agreed to talk to the young man. He'd barely said as much when said young man had come walking into the diner. It seemed someone had helpfully called the fellow and told him to get his butt to the diner before the men had even joined Armand at his table. After ten minutes of talking to, and reading, young Jim Spencer, Armand had hired the fellow. His problem was solved; Jim Spencer was beaming with pride and eager to start, especially once he learned he'd get to stay in the manager's house, his first home away from home; and Armand finished his meal quite pleased with himself.

He'd been so pleased with himself that when he'd spotted the market's sign, he'd decided to pull in and pick up some food for his woman and Bricker, and that had been one hell of an experience. Food had been nothing like it was now when last he'd eaten. Armand had wandered down the aisles throwing one of everything that caught his eye into the cart, and a hell of a lot of things had caught his eye. The packaging nowadays made absolutely everything look delicious. He wasn't even sure what half of what he'd picked up was. Or how to cook it, and he'd left with the back of his pickup piled with groceries—and still pleased with himself—right up until he'd arrived home to find that Bricker and Eshe still weren't there.

It was then he'd started to worry. Armand supposed he should have worried when he'd first realized they were away from the house, but perhaps his hunger and still being sleepy had affected his thinking. However, he'd been fed and was wide awake by the time he'd returned home, and it had then occurred to him that Eshe was a hunted woman and their absence might mean they were in trouble. Armand had begun to worry so much then that he'd actually called Lucian. However, Lucian hadn't been concerned at all. He'd told him that since they were in the area, he'd sent them to ask questions of someone who lived in the general vicinity regarding a case some of his enforcers were working on.

Armand had stopped worrying then, but he was still

upset. They could have at least left a bloody letter so he wouldn't have worried about them, he thought irritably as he pulled a canister of whipped cream out of the bag and peered at it curiously. He knew what cream was; he had some dairy cows. Armand had even consumed cream back in England when Susanna had been alive, but that had been clotted cream on warm, soft scones with preserves. He'd never heard of whipping it, and despite his annoyance, he found himself curious. He'd always enjoyed clotted cream.

Leaning against the counter, he popped the lid off and peered at what remained; some sort of white tube with a jagged tip like fangs curving in toward the center. Quite strange. He'd never seen anything like it. Armand held out his hand, palm up, and tipped the canister over it, but nothing came out. Frowning, he peered at the strange tube again, wondering if he wasn't supposed to remove it too to get to the cream.

Shrugging, he grabbed the plastic tube, intending to try to twist it off, but dropped the canister with a start as it began to hiss and something wet hit his hand.

Armand stared down at the now-silent canister on the floor, then at his hand, eyebrows rising when he saw the white substance there. He raised his hand to his nose and sniffed at it. Noting the delicate scent, he then licked at the foamy substance, smiling as the familiar taste of cream filled his senses. It was a little different from the clotted cream he recalled. This was sweet and light rather than thick, but it was good. Licking the rest of it off his palm, he picked up the canister again and fiddled with it, pressing at the tip until he figured out how to work it. Armand then sprayed some more onto his hand and licked that off as well. He was about to repeat the action when he decided to bypass his hand, simply opened his lips, tipped his head back, and sprayed the whipped cream straight into his mouth.

It was good. Delicious. Damn, he hadn't realized he was missing such yummy—

"Oh man, I thought I was the only one who did that."

Armand straightened and turned guiltily to the door to see Bricker framed there. A heartbeat later the other immortal stumbled into the room, pushed out of the way by Eshe, who was waiting to enter. Relief ran through Armand the moment he saw her safe and sound. It was followed sharply by anger. He swallowed the whipped cream in his mouth and scowled at the pair of them. "Where the hell have you two been? I was worried sick that Leonius had got you or something. I even called Lucian. You could have left me a damned letter so I wouldn't worry."

Eshe and Bricker exchanged glances and then Eshe moved toward him. "I'm sorry if we worried you. We should have left a note."

"Yes, you should have," he agreed grimly, glaring at her as she paused before him. "And you still haven't told me where you were."

Instead of answering, she leaned up toward him. Armand froze as she licked a bit of whipped cream off his bottom lip.

"Mmmm," she murmured with pleasure and then sucked his lower lip into her mouth, cleaning it thoroughly of the sweet substance before urging her tongue between his lips to kiss him properly.

Armand was still standing there stunned when she broke the kiss and moved her lips to his ear to whisper, "That's lovely. Sweet and creamy, mixed with the taste of you. Makes me want to spread it all over your body and lick it off."

Armand forgot the question of where they'd been, swallowed, and then growled, "When?"

Eshe chuckled huskily and nipped at his ear. "Now."

Stepping back then, she gave him what they used to call a come-hither look and turned to walk out of the room.

"Right," Bricker said lightly as Eshe disappeared from view. "I'll make supper while you two are otherwise occupied, shall I?"

Armand glanced to the man with surprise when the whipped cream was suddenly removed from his hand, and muttered, "Eshe wants that."

Visions in his mind of her spraying the foamy delight all over his body and licking and nibbling it away, he tried to snatch the whipped cream back.

"Armand, buddy," Bricker said, holding the whipped cream out of his reach. "Eshe wants *you*, the whipped cream is just dressing. And judging from my experience with Decker and Mortimer when they found their life mates, you two won't have the restraint to even spray this anywhere, let alone lick it up the first time. It will just sit there on the bedside table spoiling while you two get busy. Why waste a good can of whipped cream?" he added dryly. "Now go on, hurry after her. If there's one thing I know about Eshe d'Aureus, it's that she's not a very patient woman and she's waiting . . . probably naked by now."

Armand peered at the whipped cream for a moment, Bricker's sensible words slow to pierce his lust-fogged brain. But then a couple of synapses fired and he turned and headed out of the kitchen.

He found Eshe's leather jacket on the hall floor at the base of the stairs and snatched it up on his way past. Her leather pants were on the top step and he grabbed those as well before moving on to collect her leather top where it lay in the open door to her room.

Armand straightened from picking that up and paused in the doorway at the sight of Eshe leaning against the nearest post of her four-poster bed. She wore nothing but a pair of white silk panties and a strapless white bra. Both of which he recalled her purchasing the night before in town. His gaze slid over her body, noting her long beautiful legs, her luscious hips, the curve of her waist, and then the curves of her perfect breasts rising out of the bra, before reaching her face. Her eyes were on fire, golden flames overpowering the black flecks usually there.

"I thought I'd let you finish undressing me," she said huskily.

Armand kicked the bedroom door closed, let the clothes drop to the floor, and had crossed the space separating them in a heartbeat.

* * *

Eshe gasped and shivered with excitement as Armand bored down on her, then he was suddenly there, his body plastered to hers, pressing her back against the bedpost almost painfully as he ground himself against her. She'd hoped to distract him from his questions about where they'd been, and she'd apparently succeeded beautifully. The question had obviously been forgotten by him, and she forgot that worry too as his mouth descended on hers.

Armand Argeneau was one hell of a kisser. Eshe found her toes curling into the carpet she stood on as his mouth slanted over hers, nipping and sucking at first her upper lip and then her lower. When his tongue finally slid out to join the play, she moaned with pleasure and opened to him, her hands clutching briefly at the front of his shirt, before she gave that up to slide her arms around his shoulders and delve her fingers into his hair.

He had nice, silky hair, and Eshe toyed with and tugged at it as his hands began to move over her body. They followed the curve of her back, pressing her more firmly against him before sliding down to clasp her bottom through the silk panties and urge her against the burgeoning erection pressing against his jeans.

Eshe groaned at the hardness grinding against her, and then sucked in a quick breath as his hands abandoned her bottom to slide up to the back of her bra. A moment later the scrap of cloth dropped away, slipping to the floor as he stepped back to put space between them. His hands were immediately replacing the silk, cupping her naked breasts and alternately kneading the round globes and plucking eagerly at her erect nipples.

Eshe shuddered at the warm feel of his skin on hers, her body instinctively pressing into the caress even as her hands moved to begin tugging at his T-shirt, pulling it free of his pants so that she could drag it upward, baring his chest. Armand stopped kissing and caressing her to raise his arms so she could remove it, but then rather than kiss her again, ducked his head to claim one of her eager nipples between his lips. His teeth scraped over the tip before his tongue lavished it with attention.

"Yes," Eshe breathed, running her hands over the expanse of back available to her as he bent to her breast, and then digging her claws in and scraping them across his perfect skin as he slid one hand down to cup her between her legs. She immediately shifted her legs a little farther apart, pressing into the touch eagerly as pleasure began to grow in mounting ripples within her. She knew it was the shared pleasure immortals experienced, and thanked God for it as the waves rolled over her, stronger with each pass.

"Armand," Eshe cried, throwing her head back when he nudged her panties to the side to slip a finger over the core of her. Panting for air now, she gasped, "I can't— I need—"

"Me too," Armand growled, rising up to claim her mouth as his finger continued its magic.

Desperate to feel him inside her, Eshe reached between them to work blindly at his belt and the buttons of his jeans. Getting them undone, she pushed the pants impatiently down his hips until his erection escaped, then clasped it in hand and froze as an incredible rush of excitement coursed through her, bouncing wildly around inside her and almost pushing her over the edge to orgasm.

"Christ," Armand said through his teeth as he broke their kiss. He peered into her face briefly and shook his head. "I can't wait."

"Don't," Eshe said simply, knowing exactly how he felt.

It was all she had to say. Armand immediately shifted her around the bedpost and urged her backward onto the bed, his body following. He came down on top of her, his mouth claiming hers again, and then he shifted his hips and buried himself inside her. Her panties were still on, just the strip of cloth between her thighs pushed to the side, and his pants were around his hips, but neither of them was willing to take the time to remove the items. Next time they could try it completely naked; this first time they needed to quench the fire burning inside them both, and they did so with almost stunning speed. It didn't seem to Eshe that he'd pressed into her, withdrawn, and pressed into her again more than three or four times before they both cried out with the passion burning inside them and passed out.

Eshe woke slowly sometime later to find herself alone in bed. Immediately wide awake and annoyed, she sat up at once and glanced around for her clothes. She had every intention of dressing, hunting down Armand Argeneau, and giving him a piece of her mind. A wham-bam-thank-you-ma'am was not acceptable to her mind. While the urgency and speed of the first time had been unavoidable, sneaking out directly afterward just wasn't—

"You look annoyed."

Eshe blinked and glanced around, her anger deflating as she spotted Armand coming out of the bathroom, hair still wet from a shower and wearing nothing but a towel wrapped loosely around his waist. A slow smile coming to her lips, Eshe slid her feet to the floor and sat up on the side of the bed as he approached.

"You showered," she said huskily as he paused in front of her.

"Hmm." Armand smiled. "I tried waking you when I woke but you were still dead to the world, so I took a shower rather than ravish you."

"Next time, ravish me," Eshe whispered softly, her hands reaching instinctively for the towel around his waist. She slid her fingers between the towel and his skin and used her hold to draw him closer, her eyes caught by a drop of water slipping down his chest as she spread her legs and pulled him between them.

"I—" Whatever he was going to say ended on a gasp as Eshe leaned forward and caught the rolling drop of water with her tongue. She closed her eyes as a shaft of pleasure shivered through her, the pleasure he'd experienced, and then she opened her eyes to survey his chest hungrily. He apparently hadn't dried himself off, but had simply stepped out of the shower and wrapped the towel around his hips. It left an entire field of water droplets for her to choose from. Who needed whipped cream?

"Eshe," he breathed as she began to lick and nibble

the droplets away. Groaning, he slid his fingers into her hair, cupping the back of her head as her mouth traveled up his chest. When she reached and paused at his nipples to pay them special attention, his fingers clenched in her hair and he forced her head away and up so that he could kiss her.

Eshe allowed it, but then pulled away slightly and ran one finger lightly over his swollen lips as she said, "You should have tried a little harder to wake me. I could have soaped you up."

Armand grunted and tried to kiss her again, but she held him away, turning her face to avoid his lips as she added, "Now I guess I'll have to just soap myself."

Laughing at his blank expression, she then slid from his hold and hurried away across the room, aware that his startled eyes were focused on her behind. She could feel them burning through the white panties and scorching her flesh as she walked. Pausing in the door to the bathroom, she glanced over her shoulder and grinned. "Unless you want to do the soaping?"

The moment he started forward, she laughed and slipped into the bathroom. Eshe managed to shimmy out of her panties and get the shower started before he caught up. When she then stepped quickly under the spray to prevent his stopping her, she heard his towel hit the floor and then he was joining her. She managed to grab the soap from the soap dish, but then he caught her arms and turned her in the water to face him.

Eshe held the soap out, half expecting him to toss it aside, but instead, he released her and took it to begin working up a foam. Only then did Armand set it aside. When he turned back to her his soapy hands went straight for her breasts and Eshe half laughed and half groaned as he began to soap her up, kneading and plucking at the tender orbs as he pressed her back against the cold tiles of the large shower.

Eshe closed her eyes and sighed, enjoying the contrast of the cold at her back and his body heat along her front, and then his hands suddenly left her breasts. She opened her eyes with surprise to find he'd picked up the soap again for more lather. This time when he set it back, his hands went to her sides, sliding up and down and then around to move over her stomach before dropping to find her hips.

When one hand slid between her legs to urge them apart, she bit her lip and shifted her stance for him, and then gasped as that hand rose to find the center of her. Eshe clutched at his shoulders, her nails digging in for purchase as he caressed her. The excitement came on almost as fast this time as it had the first, bouncing between them strong and hard, and Eshe was resigning herself to the fact that they probably wouldn't manage to go slow for a while when Armand suddenly withdrew his hand.

She blinked her eyes open, noting that he was breathing just as heavily as she was, and then gave a surprised squawk of surprise when he suddenly turned her into the spray, allowing it to wash away the soap he'd just spread over her. She had closed her eyes the moment he'd turned her into the spray, but felt his arm brush her shoulder as he reached behind her. When the spray suddenly moved off her, she opened her eyes to look around and saw that he'd removed the showerhead from its holster and was drawing it down on its long hose.

"I have to rinse away all the soap," he growled for explanation, but the silver glint in his eyes warned her he was up to something. Still, she wasn't prepared when he suddenly dipped the showerhead down between her legs to rinse away the soap there. Neither was she prepared for her body's response to the sharp spray pounding against her excited center. Eshe cried out and clutched at his arms to stay on her feet as her body responded to this new caress. She wasn't the only one affected. Armand had squeezed his eyes closed and was grinding his teeth together as he experienced her unexpected pleasure.

They stood completely still for a moment as the water played over her body, and just when Eshe didn't think she could stand it another moment, he cursed and dropped the showerhead, letting it spray wildly around the shower's interior as he caught her by the arms, kicked the shower door open, and lifted her out.

Eshe grabbed up a towel as he turned back to shut the water off. She marveled at the way her hands shook as she lifted the heavy cloth, but never got the chance to dry herself. The towel slipped away as Armand turned to scoop her up and carry her out of the room. They left a trail of water in their wake as he carried her to the bed.

Armand set her on the mattress, but when he started to come down on top of her, she managed to catch him by surprise and wrestle him onto his back. Eshe then sat up. She grinned at his startled expression, but when he reached out to pull her down, she reached between them and caught his erection firmly in hand. He froze at once, his eyes squeezing briefly closed. Eshe ground her teeth against the pleasure assaulting her as she touched him and quickly shifted to sit beside him so that she could turn her attention fully to his erection. She started out merely touching him, running her closed hand the length of his shaft, but then bent to take him in her mouth, little moans issuing from her throat and vibrating around his shaft as she experienced the pleasure she was giving him.

Eshe then gasped and nearly bit him with surprise when Armand suddenly caught her by one thigh and drew her body around so that he could pleasure her as she was him. The combination was too much for either of them to bear for long and then they were both crying out and clutching at each other as their mutual excitement again overwhelmed them, pushing them into the darkness that usually claimed new life mates when they made love.

Nine

Eshe stretched in bed and reached instinctively for Armand. It was something she'd done several times that night, at least the times that he hadn't woken first and reached for her, caressing and kissing her awake to join again. This time, however, rather than his warm body, her hand found cool bedsheets. She was alone in bed.

Eshe popped her eyes open to peer at the empty side of the bed and then heaved a little sigh of disappointment. It appeared playtime was over, but she supposed it was for the best. They couldn't stay in bed forever. He had a farm to look after and she had a job to do, saving his son from execution for something he might not have done.

Recalling what she was there to do, Eshe pushed aside the sheet covering her and stood to move to the bathroom. She took a quick shower, banishing the memories of her last shower from her mind when they tried to rise, then brushed her teeth, fiddled with her hair, and moved out to the bedroom to dress.

The house was completely silent when she stepped out into the hall. Eshe made immediately for Armand's room. It was empty, but she'd expected as much and barely glanced around as she made her way to the walk-in closet and the hidden refrigerator there. Armand had shown her where it was at one point during the night when they'd finally noticed they were in serious need of blood. He'd also made a run downstairs for food once and she'd woken to find him eating something called Cheerios off her naked body, placing the little rings strategically on her nipples and then sucking and nibbling them off. Eshe hadn't had any when she'd woken that time, but they'd finished them off through the night, her wishing the rings were bigger so that she could have played the same game with him, but not on his nipples.

Eshe had four bags of blood before feeling satisfied. Leaving Armand's room then, she headed downstairs, noting as she glanced out the window that it was still dark out. Knowing that, she wasn't surprised to find Bricker still up and in the kitchen, a coffee on the table and a paper in hand.

Eshe glanced from him to the clean counters and asked, "Did I hear you mention something about cooking supper as I was leaving the room earlier?"

Bricker glanced around in surprise at her arrival, but said, "Yep. Cooked stew, ate it, and then ate it again . . .

the day before yesterday before bed," he added dryly. "It's Saturday, Eshe. You two slept right through Friday . . . Or didn't sleep through it, as the case may be," he teased.

"Saturday?" she asked with surprise, and then paused to think about it and supposed she shouldn't be surprised that much time had passed. She and Armand had been kind of . . . busy. Realizing Bricker was staring at her with one eyebrow arched, she shrugged. "I guess we needed the sleep."

Bricker chuckled with amusement, and then, sounding envious, said, "Right. It was sleeping you two needed so bad . . . after you got busy. You slept, woke up, got busy again and fell asleep again, and then woke up to do it all over, and over. You probably lost count."

"I was supposed to count?" Eshe asked, arching an eyebrow.

Bricker grinned again, but she was already moving to the refrigerator to see what there was to eat. Her eyes widened at the stuffed refrigerator. "Armand bought a lot."

"Yeah." Bricker chuckled. "And most of it junk food. He must have been hungry when he shopped."

Eshe nodded, surveying the different items more closely. "So is there anything good in here?"

"Oh yeah," Bricker assured her, moving to stand beside her and peer at the contents. "Loads of it tastes good. It's just not all that nutritious for you. But I guess that's not a major concern for us. We get our nutrients from blood." He leaned past her and opened the freezer door to retrieve an orange box. "These apple strudel things are delicious, and they only take a minute in the toaster."

"Thanks," Eshe murmured, taking the box. She moved to the counter and the contraption Mrs. Ramsey had toasted her bread in the day before. When she began to fumble with the box, Bricker was immediately there, taking it from her.

"I'll do this. You pour yourself a coffee," he suggested.

Eshe murmured her thanks again and then moved to find a cup and pour herself some coffee. "So what did you tell Mrs. Ramsey to explain our absence? She was here yesterday, wasn't she?"

"She was," Bricker agreed dryly. "And I didn't have to tell her a damned thing. She could hear you weren't absent."

"Oh," Eshe said, nonplussed.

Bricker snorted with amusement. "Woman, you've got some set of pipes on you." He shook his head. "Armand wasn't much better. It was like listening to opera. You couldn't understand a word, but knew exactly what was happening."

"Oh," Eshe said again, not at all sure how she should be reacting. She supposed she should be embarrassed, but didn't really feel embarrassed. She supposed she was too old to experience the sensation. Instead, she just felt kind of warm and fuzzy all over as she recalled what had brought on that opera.

"Mrs. Ramsey was worried a couple of times though," he told her, and then added with a laugh, "Both times when you guys went quiet. She made me go upstairs and check on you before she'd leave at the end of the day. You'd gone quiet again and she wanted to be sure one or both of you hadn't died."

"You checked on us?" Eshe asked with surprise.

"Well, I didn't open the door," Bricker told her dryly, opening the box and then some sort of plastic cellophane to pull out two rectangular pastries. As he dropped them into the toaster, he added, "There was no need, I could hear the pair of you by the time I reached the top step. You were both snoring. I turned around and went down to assure her you two were fine and that she should go home."

Eshe nodded.

"I should warn you, her eyes were all sparkly and she couldn't wait to get out of here. I'm pretty sure she rushed right down to the market or the diner to continue spreading the news. Your antics are probably the talk of the town by now."

Eshe groaned at the suggestion, thinking she wasn't eating in the diner again while she was here. The last time had been bad enough. Now . . . well, she wasn't given to blushing at her age, but felt sure that would be the most uncomfortable meal of her life.

Sighing, she took a sip of coffee and then grimaced at the bitter taste and turned to open the refrigerator and look for cream for it. The coffee she'd had the first morning here had been much nicer, but Mrs. Ramsey had put cream and two sugar cubes in it. Eshe poured some cream in and then put the container back in the fridge and began to look for the little bowl of cubes.

"Speaking of Mrs. R.," Bricker said idly, "she mentioned that Armand has hired someone to replace his old manager."

Eshe glanced at him with surprise. "He did? When?"

"While we were out questioning Harcourt. I guess he went to the diner for dinner and left having hired a new man. She said he is the son of one of his neighbors. A good boy. Hard worker. Armand's out showing him around right now."

"Hmm." Eshe smiled. That would mean he'd have more free time and they could—

"What the hell are you looking for?" Bricker asked as she began to root through cupboards.

"Sugar," she muttered.

"Here." Bricker picked up a bowl of little white cubes and offered it to her, asking, "So what's the plan today?"

Eshe stared at him blankly for a moment before realizing that it wasn't going to be dragging Armand into bed. She had a job to do. Shaking her head to try to clear her thoughts, she murmured her thanks for the sugar he held out and dropped two cubes into her cup. She found a spoon to stir her drink as she tried to recall what they *should* be doing today. Well, really what they should have done yesterday, she supposed, and frowned as she realized they'd lost a day while she and Armand had been in bed.

"We still have to question Susanna's brother and sister," Eshe said finally, relieved she could think at all. This life mate business really messed with an immortal's head, and not wholly in a good way, she decided.

"Not gonna happen," Bricker announced, and when

she turned a questioning eye his way, explained, "I went past the Maunsells' farm last night and then again tonight. I only got back five minutes or so before you came down. Both times the house was dark and the vehicles gone and there was no answer at the door. I'm beginning to think they've gone away or something."

"You went there by yourself?" she asked with surprise.

Bricker made a disgusted face. "I was sent to help you, Eshe. You were otherwise engaged, so I thought I'd go question them myself. However, as I said, they aren't home." He raised his eyebrows. "Is there anyone else we can question?"

Eshe considered the question, but shook her head. "Those are the only people Armand mentioned to me when explaining the deaths of his wives."

"What about Rosamund's family?" Bricker asked.

Eshe glanced at him with surprise. She hadn't even considered Rosamund's family, but now she did and shook her head. "I doubt they werc around when he was with Susanna."

"Why not? The Harcourts were," Bricker pointed out. "How did he say he'd met Rosamund?"

"He said they were friends before they married," Eshe said slowly, recalling his words.

"Friends?" Bricker asked, one eyebrow rising. "She was what? Twenty when she died?"

"Twenty-one, I think," Eshe murmured.

"And they married a year before that, so she was twenty then." He raised his other eyebrow. "And they were friends? How?" Bricker shook his head. "I bet he was a friend of the family just like he was with Althea."

Eshe sighed, irritated with herself that she hadn't thought to ask about Rosamund's family. They might have been in Armand's life for quite a while before he and Rosamund married, and might be able to tell them something of use. It was certainly worth finding out.

"Right." Bricker clapped his hands together and then paused to ask, "I know you're the one in charge here, but may I make a suggestion?"

Eshe nodded her head reluctantly. "What's that?"

"Since we can't question the Maunsells today, I think you should go out and talk to Armand to find out everything you can. Not just about Rosamund's family, but if there is anyone else who's been in his life these last five hundred and sixty-odd years."

"But he's showing the new manager around," she reminded him.

"It's evening, Eshe. He won't make the kid work at night, he's just showing him what's what so he's on the ball for tomorrow and then he'll let him settle into the house while he does whatever it is I should have done last night for the animals." He grimaced at the thought of these unknown things, and then added, "If they aren't done already, they probably will be soon, so why don't you go change and I'll make a picnic lunch for you to take out to him as an excuse, and then you can grill him on what we need to know."

"Change?" Eshe asked with a start, glancing down at herself. She'd donned one of the new pairs of jeans and one of the new T-shirts when she'd gotten dressed.

It was all she had besides the leathers. "What's wrong with what I'm wearing?"

"It's fine," he said quickly. "I just thought you'd want to look . . . er . . ."

"Yes?" she prompted, glaring at him now.

"Never mind," Bricker muttered, turning to begin opening cupboards and pulling out items. "Why don't you find something to pack the picnic in while I make it, then, if you aren't going to change?"

Eshe continued to glower at him briefly, but her mind was on to the fact that he didn't think she looked nice. She peered down at herself and supposed the outfit wasn't all that titillating. On the other hand, she was supposed to be asking Armand questions. Wearing something titillating wasn't going to get her answers. It was difficult to talk with his mouth on hers. Not that she needed to wear anything titillating for that to happen. This life mate business really was something of a nuisance at times, she admitted with a sigh as she started to search for a suitable container to pack a picnic in.

Bricker definitely knew his way around a kitchen, Eshe acknowledged as she headed out the back door of the house some fifteen minutes later with a cooler in hand and a blanket folded over her arm. The man had been quick and efficient and packed a rather delicious-looking meal for the two of them. She'd left him seated at the table, selflessly devouring the apple strudels he'd made for her, all so that she didn't spoil her appetite and they didn't go to waste. He was such a selfless guy, she thought with amusement as she stepped off the back porch and quickly crossed the fenced yard to a small gate.

Eshe pushed through that and headed for the barns, her gaze sliding to the manager's house as she passed. There were several lights on in the building, and she saw someone moving around in the front room, so supposed that meant Armand had finished with the new guy and would be alone when she found him. That was a good thing . . . sort of. The other man's presence would have kept them from trying to jump each other's bones, which would have been handy, but he was also new, uninitiated, and would have seriously hampered her ability to ask the questions Eshe needed to ask. She could hardly start asking about Rosamund's parents and if they were still in his life, and who might have been in his life over five hundred years ago, with a mortal around.

Eshe guessed that meant she'd have to be strong, seriously strong, and not allow her body to rule her head for a change when she was with Armand. It would be difficult, she knew. But if she wanted to solve this case and save Nicholas Argeneau, it was seriously necessary. And Eshe definitely wanted to solve this case. She'd started out wanting to because Nicholas was an enforcer like herself, but now there was also the fact that he was Armand's son, and she suspected Armand would never forgive her if his son was executed and he found out she had been there investigating to try to save him and had never told him the truth. He wouldn't care that it was because Lucian had ordered it. He would see it as a betrayal, and probably rightly so, she thought with irritation. She was his life mate; she should be telling him the truth and really saw no reason not to now that he had been pretty much crossed off the list of suspects.

Pausing halfway between the house and the first barn, she set down the cooler that held their picnic, laid the blanket on it, and quickly retrieved her phone from her pocket. Eshe punched in the number to Lucian's house. It rang three times before he answered, and he sounded less than pleased to be receiving a phone call. Eshe was guessing she'd interrupted him and Leigh or something, but simply took a moment to arrange her thoughts and then said, "We've checked at John and Agnes Maunsell's several times over the past few days, but they weren't in. Bricker suspects they may be out of town. We did talk to William Harcourt, however, and he was with Armand when Rosamund died so Armand couldn't have been involved in her death. And William assured us that Armand couldn't have killed Althea because he didn't know where they were," Eshe said, and then quickly explained the tale of Althea's death.

"So Armand probably didn't kill Althea and definitely didn't kill Rosamund," Lucian murmured.

"Yes," Eshe said quickly, and then added, "Which makes it very doubtful he is the culprit we're looking for."

Lucian grunted.

"So," Eshe went on, "I was wondering if we couldn't tell Armand the real reason we're here now."

"No."

Eshe rolled her eyes. No explanation, no nothing, just no. "But he might be able to help us," she argued quickly. "He could tell us if there is anyone besides the Maunsells and the Harcourts that has been in his life since Susanna."

"No," Lucian repeated.

Eshe growled with frustration.

"Is there anything else to report?"

"No," Eshe growled, and taking a leaf from his book, snapped the phone closed without saying good-bye. Muttering some rather unpleasant things about Lucian Argeneau under her breath, Eshe slipped her phone into her pocket, picked up the cooler and blanket, and continued on to the first barn where she could see the door was open and the lights inside were on.

It was the horse barn and she found Armand in there, cleaning stalls. Her gaze slid over the mostly empty stalls and finally to the two occupied ones before stopping on the empty stall he was working in. It appeared he'd already done the mucking-out part of the job and was now using a pitchfork to spread fresh hay around. She could only think that was a good thing. Eshe loved horses, but had always had servants to handle this part of caring for them. She somehow doubted Armand would have much of an appetite had she arrived as he was removing soiled hay and manure. Besides, at this point he was nearly done and might be ready for a break.

Pausing outside the stall, she peered at the back of his head and smiled to herself as she teased, "And you're seriously considering giving all this up to do something else?"

Armand straightened with a start at her voice, and

turned to glance at her over his shoulder. Smiling wryly, he stopped what he was doing and turned to face her, his gaze moving over her slowly and then pausing on the cooler and blanket she held. He eyed it curiously as he murmured, "Hard to believe, isn't it?"

Eshe smiled and then gestured to the cooler she carried. "Bricker said you'd probably want something to eat by now and made us a picnic."

"That was thoughtful of him." Armand set his pitchfork aside and removed his gloves as he moved out of the stall and then paused and glanced from the cooler, to her, to the bales of hay at the back of the barn.

"Maybe we should eat outside," she suggested, thinking that if she wanted to get any answers at all, it was best not to eat anywhere that was conducive to reclining. Eshe knew from experience that a roll in the hay could be fun.

Armand turned back with a wry grin. "Good thinking, Batgirl."

"Batgirl, huh?" she asked with amusement as he tossed his gloves aside, took the cooler from her with one hand, and slung the other around her shoulder to steer her out of the barn. "I see Lucian isn't the only one who watches television after all. Maybe Agnes isn't the one who arranged for cable for you."

"She is," he assured her as they stepped outside and started around the barn. "But I've been known to watch an episode or two of *Batman* with Cedrick. He's a big fan."

"Cedrick?" she asked. It was a name she hadn't heard before. In fact, it was a name she hadn't heard in a hundred years or so. She was sure someone somewhere had named their poor child that, but it hadn't been popular in quite a while.

"He's my first," Armand explained, and then smiled wryly. "I guess I've never mentioned him before."

"No," she agreed, her interest more than piqued. *First* was an old expression, medieval-type old. It had usually been used to refer to the highest-ranking soldier, or next in command under a titled lord . . . Armand had been a baron. "How long has he been with you?"

"I guess it was the fourteenth century when he came to work for me," Armand murmured thoughtfully.

"And he's still with you?" she asked with surprise.

Armand nodded. "He has enough money to set out on his own twenty times by now, but seems content where he is."

"And where is that?" Eshe asked, her mind working. Here was someone else they could question.

"He's running one of my farms. He also does the books for all of them and mostly rides herd on the other managers," Armand answered, and then drew her to a halt. "How about here?"

Eshe glanced around to see that while they'd been talking, he'd led her to a spot almost under the trees a good distance behind the barns. There was a large covered stone well for them to sit on. It was a nice spot, with a lovely view of the lights from the house as well as the stars overhead.

"Perfect," she assured him and quickly laid the blanket out over the stone cover.

They settled on the blanket and unpacked the cooler.

Armand pulled out several wrapped sandwiches as well as two drinks, two bags of blood, and a small plastic container of something with a piece of tape that had the words *open last* on it in marker. Eshe shrugged when Armand glanced at her in question.

"I was busy trying to find something to pack this in while he was making it. It took me a while. I finally found the cooler in the garage, but by then he'd made and wrapped everything," she explained.

Nodding, Armand set the container aside and picked up the bagged blood. He handed her one and then took the other himself and they started with that. The moment that was done, Armand opened the two drinks, handed her one and then handed her a sandwich as well, and they began to eat. They were both silent at first as they concentrated on eating, but Eshe was also concentrating on trying to come up with a way to bring Rosamund into the conversation so that she could ask about the dead woman's family. She was still thinking when halfway through the meal, Armand said, "Tell me about your first life mate."

When Eshe blinked at him with surprise and hesitated, he pointed out, "I've told you about my wives, but we've never talked about your husband or past."

Eshe glanced down at the sandwich she was eating, and then asked, "What do you want to know?"

"You told me how he died," Armand murmured, "but how did you meet?"

"I was very fortunate," Eshe said quietly. "I was only thirty when I met him."

"And how old was he?"

"Twenty," she said with a smile, and then answered the original question and said, "He was one of my father's soldiers."

"Immortal?"

Eshe shook her head. "He was mortal."

"So was Susanna," Armand said quietly and then added almost guiltily, "It's much easier with us both being immortal."

Eshe nodded with understanding. "No difficult explanations needed."

"How did Orion take it when you explained?" Armand asked curiously, and Eshe gave a laugh.

"How do you think?" she asked dryly and grimaced. "He was horrified at first. We lived in very superstitious times. Orion was positive I was some soulless demon. It didn't help that we had to feed off the hoof back then," she pointed out dryly.

Armand nodded. "Susanna had trouble with that issue as well. Nowadays it's a little easier, but in earlier days they had to love you deeply and trust you fully to get past that part of it."

Eshe nodded.

"I gather he got past that though?"

Eshe hesitated and then admitted, "Well, my father kind of helped with that."

"Your father, Castor, helped with Orion?" he asked curiously. "What did he do? Sit him down and talk some sense into him?"

"Not exactly," Eshe admitted reluctantly, and then sighed over her own reticence. She would tell him eventually anyway. Grimacing, she admitted, "He was going to wipe his memory and send him away, but the idea so crushed me that when he read Orion's mind and saw that aside from being a possible life mate, he had really come to love me before he knew what we were, Father changed his mind. Instead of wiping him and sending him away . . . which would have left me to search for a new life mate for possible centuries . . ." she pointed out.

When he nodded, she continued, "Father took us both out into the jungle, chained Orion to the ground inside a hunting hut he'd built long ago, and then told me to change Orion's mind using everything I had."

"And?" Armand asked curiously.

Eshe shrugged. "I used everything I had. Fortunately, his love for me outweighed his fear and he came around. It was a close call though. At one point I felt sure my father would have to wipe his memory and send him away, but it all worked out in the end."

Armand was silent for a moment, and she knew he was curious about what she meant by "everything she had," but then he simply said, "And you got to spend eight centuries with him, you said?"

She wasn't surprised that he sounded envious. He'd lost his Susanna so quickly.

"Yes. As I said I have been very fortunate," she murmured, almost feeling guilty for her first life mate's longevity. She was silent for a moment and then simply blurted, "Did you know Rosamund's family as you did the Harcourts?"

Armand was obviously surprised by the abrupt change of subject, but answered, "Yes. Not for as long though. I only met them about two years before Rosamund and I married."

"Were they happy about your marriage?" Eshe asked, more out of personal curiosity than in an effort to further the investigation.

"Yes. They knew it was what Rosamund wanted and trusted me with her well-being." His voice turned grim on the last part, and Eshe reached out to cover his hand with her own.

"You've had some bad luck, but it wasn't your fault," she said, trying to ease the guilt she could see in his expression.

"Well." He smiled faintly. "Perhaps some of your good fortune will rub off on me."

"I sincerely hope so, Armand," she said huskily, and then cleared her throat and looked away when she noticed that his eyes were focused on her mouth, and the silver glow was growing in his eyes. "Where are her parents now? Do you still have contact with them?"

"No." He cleared his throat and said, "They moved back to the States just before Rosamund died. She was their fourth child. The others were all born in the States and lived in the South there. They decided they didn't like the winters and moved back that way." He smiled wryly. "They sent several letters urging us to move down there."

"But you didn't?"

Armand shrugged. "All my farms were here . . . I did consider it, though, so Rosamund could be closer to her family and Jeanne Louise could have grandparents, but then Rosamund died."

Eshe nodded solemnly and popped the last of her sandwich into her mouth. It seemed Rosamund's family would not need to be found and questioned then. They hadn't been around during any of the deaths and couldn't know anything helpful.

"Oh good, Bricker sent dessert too."

Eshe glanced to Armand to see that he'd opened the plastic container. It contained two slices of something layered with a chocolate bottom, a creamy center, and then a creamy chocolate top. He handed her a piece and took the other for himself.

"Mmm," Eshe said as she took her first bite. "Delicious."

Armand nodded with agreement, eating the treat in two large bites. Eshe shook her head with amusement but a moment later wished she'd been as quick when she felt a drop of liquid hit her hand. It was quickly followed by a second and a third large drop.

"Crap," she muttered, glancing skyward to see that the clear, starry sky overhead was no longer clear. Storm clouds had moved in quickly while they'd been distracted eating and talking, and were apparently eager to dump their contents down on them. Eshe had barely had that thought when the heavens opened and it began to pour.

"The shed," Armand said as they scrambled to their feet and began collecting the remains of their picnic. Eshe had no idea what he was talking about until he grabbed up the hastily packed cooler, caught her arm, and rushed her through the storm to the closest building, one much smaller than the others.

Eshe hurried inside, eyes sliding around the darkness as Armand followed and pulled the door closed behind them. He too then turned to survey their shelter.

"What is this place?" Eshe asked curiously, noting a small table and chairs and the lumpy old couch against the wall. It barely fit in the small building.

"I'm not sure," Armand admitted. "It was here when I bought the place five years ago. I think it was a fort or something for the kids of the last family, but I don't know what it was originally used for."

"So that couch has been sitting out here for at least five years?" Eshe asked, imagining all the little rodents that had probably scampered across it, or possibly even nested in it.

"We shouldn't have to wait long," Armand murmured. "Storms that come on this quick and hard usually move on just as quickly."

Eshe nodded in agreement, and then watched wide-eyed as he set down the cooler and took out the blanket he'd stuffed inside when packing up. She was glad his back was to her as he spread the blanket over the lumpy couch. She knew he expected they could sit there and wait for the storm to pass, but Eshe wasn't keen on the idea. While she'd roughed it at a time when today's roughing it would have been considered the lap of luxury, she was definitely a city girl now and had no intention of sitting on the couch . . . even for him.

When Armand finished and started to straighten and turn toward her, she quickly swiveled on her heels and began to pace the tiny interior.

"Come sit down," he urged quietly. "We shouldn't have long to wait."

"I'm fine," she assured him.

"Eshe," Armand murmured and was suddenly beside her, taking her arms to turn her to face him. She could see that his expression was concerned as he peered at her, and it confused her until he asked, "Are you afraid of storms?"

Eshe was about to shake her head when he suddenly said, "If so, perhaps I can distract you."

She froze then as his mouth descended on hers. Perhaps it was the rain, or the fact that he thought she needed calming, but this kiss was different from any of the others they'd enjoyed. This kiss was soft, gentle, and sweet . . . at least at first, and she melted against him with a small sigh as her mouth opened for him, and then moaned in protest when he broke the kiss to whisper, "You're soaked through. We should take this off."

"Yes," Eshe whispered, raising her arms when he began to tug her T-shirt upward. She shuddered as it came off over her head and then shivered a little when he moved to lay it over the blanket-covered couch. He then quickly removed his own soaked T-shirt before turning back to warm her with his hands and body.

Eshe moaned as his arms went around her, her back stretching and arching her breasts against him as his hands slid over her naked back, and then he kissed her again and the gentle moment passed as passion rose up through both of them as wild and violent as the storm crashing outside. Eshe tangled her hands in his hair, her mouth becoming demanding even as his did. Her body met his push for push so that they ground into each other almost feverishly, and then Armand suddenly tipped her back onto the couch. Eshe didn't even notice let alone care; her attention was on what Armand was doing as he bent to undo and remove her jeans. They had been tight to begin with, but were almost impossible now they were wet. When they finally came off, her cotton panties went with them. Armand tossed them over the back of the couch with their shirts and then scooped her up and settled on the couch with her in his lap, his mouth claiming hers as his hands began to play over her body.

Eshe moaned, groaned and gasped by turn into his mouth, her body writhing against his as his fingers moved over one breast, then another before dropping between her legs. He caressed her then with a purpose, driving them both mad with desire until she couldn't take it anymore and pushed his hands away.

"What—?" Armand began, but cut off the end of the question when she slid off his lap. The moment she was upright, Eshe caught him by the hand and drew him to his feet so that she could drop to her haunches and undo his jeans. She got as far as pushing them off his hip so that his erection sprang free and then paused to press a kiss to it before finishing removing the jeans. Armand didn't give her the chance to fold them over the couch with the other clothes, but suddenly sat down again and drew her onto his lap so that her knees were on either side of his hips.

Eshe would have dropped to sit on him and take him

inside her then, but Armand stopped her, catching her by the hips, keeping her upright.

"Such long legs," he murmured, his voice a hungry growl, and Eshe glanced down, realizing that his face was a bare inch higher than her pelvis, positioned as she was.

She peered at him through the darkness, and then realized that it was silent. The rain was no longer thundering down outside. It had been a short, hard rainfall. Licking her lips, she whispered, "The storm has stopped."

"No. It hasn't," he assured her, and shifted to slouch down on the couch, then urged her forward with his hands on her behind and pressed his mouth to the core of her. Eshe sucked in a gasp of air and squeezed her eyes closed, her head going back and hands knotting in his hair as he found the center of her excitement. Pleasure exploded inside her and then receded, only to be replaced with another stronger wave, along with an echo of the first as his tongue rasped over her. She felt his hands clench on her behind as he too was struck by her pleasure, and then she wasn't aware of much other than the passion flowing between them as he drove them both crazy.

When her legs began to shake, Eshe cried out and braced her hands against the wooden wall behind the couch and pleaded with him to stop and not to stop all in the same breath. Just when she didn't think she could take much more, she felt him press a finger up inside her and screamed as her body began to buck helplessly. She heard Armand roar with his own orgasm and felt the sound vibrate against her body. She started to collapse then as darkness swept in to claim her.

Armand woke to utter darkness and complete silence, and his face cuddled between Eshe's warm breasts. Smiling to himself, he eased her up a bit so that he could shift to a more comfortable sitting position, and then paused as a creak sounded outside. He glanced toward the door and listened briefly, but no other sound came and he decided it had been an animal of some description, a raccoon or possum. And probably an upset one if they were presently inhabiting its home, he thought with a smile as he settled Eshe back down on his lap.

The action made him bite his lip on a moan as he unintentionally rubbed her over his lap and his body leaped with excitement. It seemed he couldn't get enough of the poor woman. He would exhaust them both with his needs at this rate, Armand thought, but found that didn't stop the erection that was coming persistently to life.

Asleep or not, Eshe appeared to still be connected to him in her thoughts. She moaned sleepily and shifted against him, sending another shaft of excitement through him that had him sliding his arms around her back and hugging her close in an effort to still her. But that just pressed her breasts against his chest and stirred even more sensation in them both. It also began to rouse Eshe from sleep, and she issued a little sigh and shifted on him again.

"Eshe," he groaned. She was killing him here.

Her head lifted slowly then and she eased her eyes open to smile at him sleepily, and whispered, "Hi."

That was all it took. Little Armand sprang to full attention between them and big Armand found himself unable to resist kissing her. The moment his mouth covered hers he was lost, and Eshe with him. Their hands began to move, finding every pleasure point, and Eshe shifted in his lap, rubbing herself against him even as her breasts slid across his chest. Armand was bombarded by a double assault, his own pleasure as her wet, hot core slid across his shaft, and hers as well at that, plus little pings of added pleasure as his chest hairs tickled across her nipples in multiple tiny caresses.

Armand groaned into her mouth and caught her hips to press her more firmly against himself, then when she took over the action, raised his hands to slide them between them and catch her breasts in a fuller caress. He toyed and tugged at her nipples briefly, his tongue battling with hers in the kiss, but neither of them had much fortitude for putting off what they were heading for. He was relieved when she raised herself up slightly, allowing cool air to brush across his heated erection, and even more relieved when she lowered herself onto it properly, taking him inside herself.

Afraid he might bite her tongue in his excitement, Armand broke their kiss and quickly shifted his mouth to her neck as she closed over him. Big mistake, he realized a moment later as she raised and lowered herself again and he felt his fangs pushing outward. But it was too late, his fangs were piercing her skin and she raised a hand to cup his head, giving him silent permission as she continued to ride him.

"Yes," she gasped, as this new pleasure was added to the others and then they both screamed and slipped into unconsciousness again.

Ten

Armand woke to Eshe cuddled warm against him again, and his first thought was that she was the hottest woman he'd ever met. And not just in a sexy way. She was burning up this time, almost feverish, he thought, roasting him with her body temperature. That roused concern in him and brought him fully awake to find that it wasn't Eshe that was so hot. They were both roasting. The shed was on fire.

Cursing, he shook Eshe, but she didn't even stir. He recalled biting her then and cursed himself as he shook her again, more violently, but she was completely out of it still in the dead faint that had followed their passion. It seemed it was up to him to get them out of there. Cursing himself now, he shifted out from beneath her and set her to lie on the couch as he got to his feet and glanced around to take in the situation. It didn't take more than a glance to realize they were in serious trouble. The shed was fully alight, the walls and ceiling nothing but waterfalls of flame. By his guess they had only moments before the whole building collapsed on top of them and then they would be toast.

Turning back to the couch, he picked up Eshe, hefting her over his shoulder with little effort. He hurried to the door with her and pushed at it, wincing as the flames bit into his arm. He forgot the pain, however, when the door didn't give. They were locked inside. Armand stared at the door blankly at that realization. He hadn't locked it. It didn't even have a lock as far as he knew. But it wasn't opening.

He was distracted from trying to sort that out by the realization that his skin was beginning to bubble in the heat. They didn't have much time. The nanos made immortals incredibly flammable. Any minute now he and Eshe would burst into flame and—

Cursing, he backed up a step and threw himself at the door, turning sideways at the last moment to protect Eshe as much as he could. Much to his relief they crashed through the flimsy door and fell out onto the damp ground. Armand instinctively rolled several times, taking Eshe with him to be sure neither of them had caught flame, and then simply lay still with her head on his chest, his heart thudding madly. He stared at the sky overhead for a moment and then turned his head to the side to peer at the shed as a crash sounded. The roof had caved in, the shed was collapsing in on itself.

Sighing, he turned weakly to glance down at Eshe.

Her skin was blackened, as was his own. They'd been burned badly and needed blood. He had to get them to the house.

It was the last thought Armand had before unconsciousness claimed him again.

Armand woke to whistling. The tune was one he recognized from his wedding to Rosamund. It was one of the songs that had played at the celebrations afterward. It had been very popular at the time.

"Yeah. My mom used to hum it a lot when I was a kid. For some reason it's been in my head the last day or so."

Armand blinked his eyes open and glanced in the direction the voice had come from to see Bricker removing an empty blood bag from an IV beside the bed to replace it with a fresh one. He watched him with a slight frown, his mind slow to sort out why he was in bed and why an IV would be necessary.

"Think fire," Bricker said dryly, apparently reading his confusion.

The words had the desired effect. Armand's memory came rushing back to him at once, and he was immediately trying to sit up. Unfortunately, he didn't appear to have the strength for it.

"Don't waste your energy," Bricker admonished. Finished with the bag, he turned to face the bed and peered down at him. "You took a lot of damage. The nanos are still doing their work. Let them."

Armand slumped back on the pillows with a grunt.

The healing obviously had a way to go; that little exercise had left him panting and exhausted. His thoughts were clearing by the minute though.

"Eshe?" The word was little more than a gasp, but Bricker understood.

"In her room. Hooked up to an IV like you." Bricker grimaced. "She was in worse shape than you. Her back was a ruin. It looked like she'd been broiled."

Armand closed his eyes, knowing her position straddling him on the couch had saved him being in the same shape. The fire above and around them had been cooking her, but he'd passed out with his face tucked into her shoulder and her body covering his.

"It probably saved you both," Bricker commented quietly, unapologetic about reading his mind again. He settled himself in the chair next to the bed, and said, "If you'd been in the same shape as her, you never would have got yourself out, let alone her." He grimaced. "I always thought this passing out after sex business was like a faint. A good slap or a little splash of water in the face and you'd wake up, but it must be complete unconsciousness for her to have slept through what that fire did to her."

Armand grunted, concern sliding through him again but with guilt this time. Her unconsciousness probably wouldn't have been so deep had he not bitten her and taken some of her blood. Actually, doing that had probably prevented his waking sooner too. The extra nanos that had come with the blood would have left him weakened.

"She'll be all right," Bricker assured him. "She's already ten times better than she was when I found you both."

"How?" Armand didn't bother finishing the question out loud. His throat was bone dry and just speaking that word had hurt like a son of a bitch. As he expected, though, Bricker read the rest of the question and answered at once.

"When hours passed without Eshe returning, I just figured you two were . . . er . . . talking," he said dryly, making it obvious he'd thought they were doing exactly what they had been doing in the shed before passing out. "But when you two didn't come back by dawn I started to worry and thought I'd just pop out to the barn and be sure everything was all right. I didn't see you there, but I smelled smoke and followed my nose." His mouth twisted. "I'm sorry, Armand. I looked out the back window several times and didn't spot that shed on fire. The barns block it from view."

Armand gave a slight nod. Aside from the other barns blocking the view of it, the shed was far back on the property and to the side. The trees around the house would have helped block it too. Bricker would have had to come outside to see the fire lighting the sky.

"I'm surprised the shed burned at all with the storm we had last night, but it didn't last long. I suppose it did little more than dampen things," he muttered, and then said, "Anyway, I found you guys lying on the grass, the sun adding to the damage you'd already taken. I called Lucian at once, then carried Eshe in, and then you. It wasn't long after I got you both settled in your rooms that Anders arrived with blood. I was relieved to see him. I'd been trying to trickle blood down your throats when he arrived with the IVs. You were both so bad your fangs wouldn't come out for me even when I waved the blood under your nose."

"The insides of their noses were probably singed from breathing in the hot air in the fire."

Armand glanced toward the door at that comment to see a dark-skinned man entering the room. His eyes instinctively widened, and then he grimaced at the pain that brought about. It wasn't just his throat that was parched. His eyelids scratched across his eyeballs painfully, but he kept them open to examine the man as he wondered if this was one of Eshe's children. She'd said she'd had eight and six survived, but he'd never gotten around to asking their sex, or names. He was going to do that the very next time they spoke, he decided. Right before he sent her away with Lucian to a safer place. It seemed obvious Leonius had discovered her whereabouts. She needed to be taken somewhere safer.

"I'm not related to Eshe," Anders announced, apparently able to read his thoughts. "And don't worry about her safety. We're here now. We'll worry about that for you." He glanced to Bricker then and held out a phone Armand hadn't noticed he was carrying until then. "It's Lucian. For you."

Bricker stood and moved around the bed at once to take the cordless phone the man was holding out. He said hello, listened, and then grunted and walked out of the room still listening.

"Lucian has been delayed," the man named Anders explained as he moved around the bed toward the IV.

His back was to Armand as he apparently checked the IV, and he added, "It will be evening before he gets here. He wants us to keep you quiet and comfortable until he does."

Armand didn't comment, but he doubted it was possible to keep him quiet and comfortable. His body hurt everywhere, from his scalp down to his toes, and he was too worried about Eshe and how she was faring to sleep. In fact, he was about to ask to be taken to her so that he could see for himself that she was all right when Anders turned from the IV with an empty syringe.

"Lucian said you'd want to do that," he said wryly, obviously reading his mind as Bricker had. "It's why he said to keep you sedated."

"Prick," Armand muttered with a combination of anger and dismay as he realized the man hadn't been checking the IV but shooting drugs into it. He'd meant Lucian was a prick for giving the order to do so, but Anders apparently thought he'd been directing the insult at him.

He smiled slightly and admitted, "I've been called that many times."

Armand opened his mouth to explain he hadn't meant him, but the words came out garbled and his eyes were already closing as the drug took effect.

Eshe opened her eyes and peered blearily at Armand. His face was right above hers, a blurry wash of pale skin with silver-blue eyes. Smiling sleepily, she tried to raise her hand to caress his face, but found herself too weary, so murmured, "Armand. So sweet. Kiss me."

"I'm not Armand. I'm not sweet. And I'm not kissing you."

Eshe blinked, managing to sweep away some of the sleep or whatever scum was coating her eyes, and found herself staring at Lucian Argeneau's grim face. She wouldn't have bothered to prevent the scowl that immediately covered her face if she could have, and she didn't bother to try to stop the "God! What a face to wake up to" that slipped from her lips either.

"You have always been a charmer," Lucian said, sounding amused rather than insulted.

Eshe grunted at the words and snapped, "What are you doing in my room?"

"Perhaps you should be asking yourself why you are in your room," Lucian countered, watching her carefully.

Eshe sought her mind briefly, flushing as the memories of what she and Armand had done in the shed came to her. Obviously the man had carried her into the house while she still slept and put her to bed. Now she'd been caught slacking on the job. If Lucian was here, it must be nighttime and she should be up working.

"She doesn't remember."

Eshe opened her eyes again and raised her gaze to the brunette woman she could just see standing behind Lucian. Leigh, his life mate. Eshe had met her only a couple of times in passing since the woman had come into Lucian's life, but she figured anyone who could put up with his grumpy mug day in and day out had to be a saint, so she smiled at the woman and said, "Hi, Leigh. What are you doing here?"

"She is a saint," Lucian assured her, obviously having read her thoughts and having absolutely no compunction about letting her know that he had. He could be such a rude bugger.

"I told you the drugs would still be affecting her," Bricker said, making his presence known. Eshe glanced his way on the other side of the bed, eyebrows rising when she spotted Anders at his side.

"Jeez. What is this, Grand Central Station? Why is everyone in my room? And why does my throat hurt? And what is that smell?" she asked with disgust as she slowly became aware of the different sensations afflicting her.

"What smell is that?" Lucian asked patiently.

"Like burning pork," she muttered wrinkling her nose.

"That would be you, then," he said dryly.

"Lucian," Leigh chided, poking and prodding at him to get him out of the way. The brunette took his place sitting on the edge of her bed, and smiled into Eshe's confused eyes as she asked, "Do you remember anything at all after you and Armand had your picnic and then . . . er . . . napped in the shed?"

Eshe stared at her silently, not really seeing her as she searched her mind, but the very last thing she remembered was passing out on Armand's lap.

"No," she said finally, and then with mounting concern, "Did something happen? Where is Armand?"

"He's fine. He's sleeping," Leigh assured her quickly and then hesitated before asking, "You don't remember the fire?"

"What fire?" she asked blankly.

"She slept right through it all," Leigh marveled, glancing to Lucian with amazement.

"She was unconscious. They'd just had sex," he pointed out dryly.

"Yes, but I didn't realize we were completely knocked out afterward. I always thought it was just a faint or something."

"So did I," Bricker said quietly, and then shook his head and muttered. "God, they're lucky Armand woke up."

Lucian grunted, and glanced to Eshe. She peered back silently, waiting. Her mind was a mass of questions but she didn't ask any of them. She'd been asking questions since opening her eyes and they hadn't answered any of them yet. She'd learned more by simply listening to them talk to each other than from anything they'd actually said to her. She was apparently under the influence of drugs at the moment and there had been a fire, she *thought,* in the shed where she and Armand had taken shelter from the storm. From what they'd said, Armand had woken and gotten them out, but guessing by the fact that she was flat on her back in bed and he was apparently in his own bed, no doubt in the same state, they'd both been injured and were healing.

"That's about the long and short of it," Lucian said, still rooting around inside her head. "He got you out, but then apparently passed out again. Bricker went looking for the two of you at dawn and found you lying out in the sunshine. He called me, brought you both inside, and I couldn't get away right away so sent

Anders down with IVs, blood, and drugs to keep you both under until I could get here."

"Which was a good thing since Armand woke up right after Anders got here and we got the IVs in place," Bricker muttered.

Eshe's head shifted on the pillow as she looked for the IV. Spotting it and seeing the steady but slow drip of blood seeping out of the bag into the IV tube, she grimaced. The nanos' ability to heal would be just as slow as the speed with which they were getting the blood they needed to make the repairs. It would have been faster had they slapped the bags to her fangs and let her body soak in what it needed. She'd probably be on her feet and walking around by now if they had.

"Your fangs wouldn't come down," Lucian informed her. "We think your nostrils were damaged breathing in the hot, smoky air. The smell of blood didn't bring on your fangs. The IV was the best Bricker could do until you awoke."

"I'm awake now," she muttered, and boy was she. Drugs didn't work long on immortals and hers were apparently starting to wear off. Her damaged nerve endings were coming back to life with a vengeance.

"Get her several bags," Lucian ordered at once. "Her fangs should produce themselves the moment she sees the blood now that her eyes are open."

When Anders nodded and headed for the door, Lucian glanced to Bricker. "Go check on Armand. He may be coming around now too if you gave them the drug at the same time."

"What do I tell him if he's awake?" Bricker asked, moving toward the door now as well.

Lucian's mouth tightened. "Nothing. Just put him under again. I want to talk to you and Eshe before I decide what to do about him."

"What do you mean, what to do about him?" Leigh asked with a frown, and Eshe nodded in her bed. She was wondering the same thing herself and relieved she didn't have to ask the question now that the drugs were wearing off.

Lucian scowled briefly. He did hate explaining himself, Eshe knew. But apparently would do so when Leigh asked a question because after a pause he ran a hand through his hair and said, "I've been trying to keep Armand from knowing what was going on here. About the investigation, I mean."

"Why?" Leigh asked with surprise, and Eshe could have kissed her for it. It saved her doing more damage to a throat she could now feel was in bad shape.

Besides, it was obvious the woman was actually the only one he'd bother to answer, Eshe decided as Lucian sat down in a chair beside the bed and actually began to speak, stringing words together to make whole sentences and sentences together to make what was from him a long speech as he said, "Armand was an active member of the family before Rosamund's death. He still kept to himself quite a bit, but he would visit the boys, and join family functions and so on. After Rosamund's death, however, he dumped Jeanne Louise on Marguerite's door and shut everyone out. I thought he just needed time to heal and left him alone. I would have eventually got around to kicking his ass and getting him back into the family given another century or so, but after Nicholas turned himself in and we learned that Annie had been looking into Armand's wives' deaths when she'd died herself, I began to wonder."

"If he'd killed them?" Eshe growled, and immediately regretted speaking. Damn, she must have been swallowing flames for her throat to be so sore, she thought with a sigh.

"Don't talk," Lucian snapped, and then turned to Leigh and said, "I didn't really think he would have killed his own life mate. Or Althea and Rosamund, for that matter, but it was a possibility that had to be investigated. What I really began to suspect was that he'd shut himself off from the family in an effort to keep everyone safe. That perhaps he himself suspected with Rosamund that it was just one accident too many, and something besides bad luck was behind the deaths of his wives."

"But it was only his wives who have died," Leigh pointed out. "Why would he think anyone else might be in peril?"

"If they were murdered, as it's looking, it could have been because they were his wives, but they were also the females in his life that he cared for. You have to remember that Althea and Rosamund weren't life mates, just females he held affection for."

"You think he was worried for Jeanne Louise," Leigh realized with dismay. "That he feared without a wife to concentrate on the killer might have harmed her."

"It was a possibility," Lucian murmured.

"Apparently a good possibility, since it's looking more and more like Annie, another female in his close family, was murdered as well," Leigh murmured, and then frowned and pointed out, "But he never met her, did he? I thought they said he refused to come to the wedding or allow them to visit."

"Yes," Lucian said dryly. "But if Annie was asking family members about the murders, I doubt she stopped there. Nicholas was away a lot working for me. She could have driven down here to speak to him."

"Did you ask him?"

Lucian nodded. "He said he'd never met her and I can't read him so couldn't tell if that was true or not."

"You think he'd lie to you?" Leigh asked with surprise.

"Well, I only asked the question in passing. I couldn't very well tell him why I was asking or explain that it was important."

"Why not?" Leigh asked, and Eshe was grateful for being saved the bother herself.

"Because he can't know Nicholas is locked up in the enforcer house. He'd do something stupid. And then there's Eshe here. I only got her here under the pretext that I needed a safe house for her. I'm pretty sure he's thinking he will only give himself this short time with her and after the two weeks I told him she'd be here are up, he will send her away for her own safety. If he knew she was here actively looking for whoever was behind all these deaths, he'd have sent her away at once."

"He wouldn't send Eshe away," Leigh protested quickly, and Eshe was starting to think the woman was reading her mind and asking the questions and saying the things she wanted to say herself as Leigh added, "They're life mates. You don't send life mates away."

Lucian turned to Eshe and arched an eyebrow. "Has he spoken about a future with you, or what the two of you will do after the two weeks is up?"

Eshe's eyes slowly widened as she realized that no, he hadn't. In fact, she recalled the time he'd mentioned her leaving in two weeks, and her upset about it at the time. But she'd thought that was just a slip or something.

Lucian grunted and nodded as he read the answer from her. "That's why I wouldn't let you tell him the real reason you were here when you called me the other night; he'd have hustled you into his pickup and driven you straight to my doorstep in Toronto. No doubt he then would have bought a new farm and kept the address to himself so you couldn't find him again. Or maybe even moved to Europe or something to try to keep you safe. He's already lost one life mate. I guarantee he won't risk jeopardizing another."

Why, the dirty bastard, Eshe thought with dismay. Lucian was right. Armand thought he could send her away after the two weeks were up like some cheap vacation romance. *Well*, she thought grimly, *that man had another think coming.*

The bedroom door opened then and Eshe was relieved to see Anders returning with half a dozen bags of blood. While the IV bag hadn't done it when she'd spotted it, the sight of these bags that she knew were meant for her to drink were enough to bring on her teeth. She ground her teeth against the pain she was experiencing and managed to lift herself up somewhat, then simply opened her mouth. Lucian stepped out of the way as Anders approached, but it was Leigh who took one of the bags from him and turned to slap it to Eshe's mouth.

"Sorry," she murmured as Eshe winced at the sting of the bag against her damaged face, but Eshe couldn't respond to tell her it was all right, so hoped she read it from her mind as she let her teeth do their work.

"Are you all right?" Leigh asked once the bag was empty and she pulled it from her teeth for her.

Eshe merely grunted and gestured for her to bring on the next bag. It was Lucian who took another bag from Anders, handed it over, and said, "Don't stop. Feed them to her one right after another." He then took the other bags from Anders and said, "Go get the drugs I sent down with you. As soon as she's had the last bag, you'll need to put her out."

"Why?" Leigh asked with surprise as she slapped the second bag to Eshe's mouth.

"She's taken enough damage that this is going to be almost as bad as a turn," he explained grimly. "Better she doesn't stay awake for it."

Leigh looked horrified at the possibility, but Eshe wasn't surprised. She'd lived a long time. This was hardly the first time she'd been hurt. The worse the damage, the worse the healing was, and she could already feel her body beginning to buzz as the nanos set to work. Right now it felt like she was being stung by a million bees that had somehow gotten into her veins, but by the last bag she suspected it would feel like she was being eaten alive from the inside out. However, she needed to heal. She needed to get back on her feet and find whoever had set that shed on fire. She was *not* going to be pushed from Armand's life for her own good, and she wasn't risking his getting killed in an attempt on her life as had apparently almost happened with this fire. But she suspected she was going to have a fight on her hands when Armand woke up.

Eshe needed to heal quickly and regain her strength to win that battle. She was Armand's life mate, and he'd better get used to it because she wasn't going anywhere.

Eleven

The sound of the door opening stirred Armand from sleep. Blinking his eyes open, he peered toward it, a relieved smile claiming his lips when he saw Eshe entering. She wore jeans and one of the new T-shirts they'd purchased on their shopping expedition. She looked good. Better than good, she looked like nothing had ever happened.

His smile faded the moment the next person walked in though, and Armand scowled at his brother with disgust. "Get out, Lucian. I don't want to talk to you."

Eshe's eyebrows rose, her head swiveling to peer at the man behind her and then back to Armand in question, and he shifted restlessly on the bed, and then explained, "He had me drugged."

"It was so you'd sleep through the healing," Lucian said with a shrug, moving out of the way as Leigh, Bricker, and Anders followed him into the room.

It was getting damned crowded in his room, Armand thought with disgust, but said, "It wasn't for healing the last time. The healing was mostly done by then."

"Mostly," he agreed. "But Eshe's wasn't and you were trying to get up and go to her."

"She was screaming her head off," he pointed out grimly. "You're damned right I was going to her. Wouldn't you have gone to Leigh if the situation had been reversed?"

"Of course," Lucian said calmly. "That's why I had Anders drug you again. You needed your rest and there was nothing you could have done for her."

Armand snorted with disgust. "God, you are such an arrogant ass."

"I try," Lucian said with unconcern, ushering Leigh to the chair beside his bed as Eshe moved toward the bed itself.

Armand scowled at his brother for another moment and then glanced to Eshe as she settled on the side of the bed. He managed a smile for her, and asked, "How are you?"

"Alive. Thanks to you," she murmured, and leaned forward to kiss him, then whispered, "Thank you."

Armand sighed unhappily, knowing that if he hadn't bitten her the last time they'd made love, both of them probably would have woken sooner. In effect, he'd damned near killed them with that stunt. Forcing a smile for her benefit, he squeezed her hand when she slid it into his, and then glanced to the others in his room. "So what's all this about?"

"Time to talk," Lucian announced quietly.

Armand grimaced at the words. He'd hoped to have a moment alone with Eshe before this conversation, but supposed it was better just to get it done and over with. Kind of like ripping a bandage off in one swoop and suffering a quick sharp pain, rather than suffering the long, drawn-out effort of feeling each little pull of hair as it was slowly worked off.

"Fine," he said at last. "Obviously Leonius II has found out where Eshe is and she needs to be moved to a safer location."

The response to that was decidedly strange. Everyone in the room turned to Lucian, deferring to him . . . except Eshe. She was peering down at their entwined hands, but she was obviously attuned to Lucian, as were the others. The moment he started to speak, she cut him off by saying, "There is no Leonius to have to hide me from."

"What?" Armand asked with surprise.

"I mean there is, but he's not after me," Eshe said quietly. "That was just—"

"I sent Eshe here to investigate the deaths of your wives," Lucian interrupted.

"What?" he asked sharply, his gaze shifting between the two of them. "Why?"

"Because Nicholas's life depends on it," Eshe answered at once.

"Eshe!" Lucian snarled, glaring at her across the bed.

"He has a right to know. It's his son," she snapped, glaring right back, and then added, "Besides, he won't do anything foolish like try to break him out. He wants to find out what happened to his wives as much, if not more, than anyone."

"What have the deaths of my wives got to do with Nicholas?" Armand asked, glancing from one to the other. "And what do you mean Nicholas's life depends on it? And break him out of where? Has Nicholas been found?"

"Yes," Eshe murmured. "And there's some doubt that he killed that mortal fifty years ago."

"I know he didn't do it," Armand said grimly, and it was true, he'd been positive then and still was that Nicholas had not killed the mortal he'd been accused of killing fifty years ago. Armand had even driven up to Toronto at the time and tried to figure out what really had happened, but everything had seemed to point toward Nicholas. Still, he hadn't been able to believe it. But he also hadn't been able to prove otherwise. The story of his life, he thought bitterly.

"I'm sure he didn't," Eshe said quietly, and he relaxed a little as he heard the sincerity in her voice. When he nodded, she continued, "It seems Annie was asking a lot of questions about the deaths of your wives before she died, and in fact called Nicholas the night before her death saying she had something to tell him, but died before she could do so. Nicholas was understandably distraught at first, but some weeks after Annie's death, he recalled that phone call and tried to find out what she'd wanted to tell him. In his memory of the night of the murder of the mortal he was accused of killing, Nicholas started out heading to the hospital where Annie used to work, intending to speak to a friend and coworker of hers and ask her if she knew what Annie may have wanted to tell him. However, his memory skips from crossing the hospital parking lot to opening his eyes in his basement with a dead mortal in his lap. He's been on the run ever since."

Armand closed his eyes briefly, guilt slithering through him. His son had lost his life mate to whoever it was who had killed his own wives. He just knew it. It was all his fault somehow. The frustrating thing was Armand just didn't know how. He didn't know why anyone would kill any of the women who had died. That had been the problem from the beginning.

"Nicholas is locked up at the enforcer house," Eshe murmured quietly. "He's waiting to find out his future. If we find the culprit behind the deaths, he will be found innocent and go free. He'll get his life back."

"And if we don't?" Armand asked sharply.

Eshe shook her head and actually smiled. "That won't happen. We've obviously got someone scared, otherwise why lock us in the shed and set it on fire? We'll catch them, Armand," she vowed. "And Nicholas will go free."

Armand almost asked how she knew they'd been locked in the shed when she'd been unconscious, but then realized Lucian had probably told her. His irritating big brother had just been finishing grilling him about what exactly had happened at the shed when Eshe had started screaming from the next room. Armand had tried to leap up to go to her at once, and Lucian had pushed him back down on the bed and ordered Anders to give him a shot. Then the lights had gone out.

Now he was awake and learning that Eshe wasn't being chased by a psycho Leonius the Second, but was here to investigate the deaths of his wives and try to save his son. Obviously he needed to figure out what the hell had been going on all these years. He'd tried looking into the deaths before, but had come up with nothing, but now it was imperative he find out what the hell had happened and who would have it in for him. Otherwise his son would probably be executed and everyone Armand cared about would be at risk . . . including Eshe.

His gaze slid to her. His life mate. After Rosamund's death he'd had suspicions, but that was all. He hadn't been able to find any proof that any of his wives had been murdered. On the surface the deaths had all appeared to be accidents, and that was it. Still, he'd suspected, and that suspicion had been strong enough that in an effort to keep the rest of the women in his family safe, Armand had shut himself off from them, thinking that if he was wrong and the deaths had all been accidents, then the only person hurt by the action would be himself. However, if he was right and didn't do his best to keep them safe, he never would have been able to forgive himself.

The same still held. If someone was killing the women he cared about, then Eshe as his life mate was definitely at risk, and the best thing he could do for her was send her somewhere safe while he sorted out this mess.

Nodding to himself, he shifted his gaze to Lucian and said grimly, "As my life mate, Eshe is most at risk. You need to get her away from here."

"Being away from you didn't save Althea," Eshe pointed out, not appearing either upset or angry at his words. In fact, she was suspiciously calm as she added, "In fact, it's you that is the largest concern."

"Me?" he asked with surprise.

"Yes. I'm an enforcer. I'm trained for this," she pointed out gently, as if talking to a child. "You, however, are a civilian. And while I was probably the target with the fire in the shed, you nearly died there with me. It's probably best if you went to stay somewhere safe." She turned to glance at Lucian. "Perhaps you should have Anders take him back to the enforcer house and lock him up with Nicholas. No one could get to him there and they could visit and get caught up on—"

"I'm not going anywhere," Armand said with amazement, and then glared at Lucian as if the man had actually agreed as he added, "You aren't locking me up. This is my life. They were my wives, and I'm staying right here to figure out what the hell's going on."

"I don't know, Armand," Eshe said quietly. "I'd never forgive myself if anything happened to you because of me."

"Well, I'm not going," he informed her firmly, crossing his arms stubbornly over his chest.

Eshe sighed, but after a moment gave a small nod. "Very well. Then why don't you get dressed and come downstairs. We can talk down there and Bricker can make breakfast and coffee for all of us."

"I can?" Bricker asked dryly.

"I'll help," Leigh offered.

"I agree we should move downstairs then," Lucian said arrogantly.

Thinking he'd definitely feel at less of a disadvantage if he weren't sitting there naked, Armand nodded grimly.

"Good," Eshe murmured, and leaned forward to kiss him on the cheek. "Then I'll see you when you get downstairs.

She stood then and Armand found himself smiling faintly as she led Leigh and Bricker out of the room. The woman was walking sex, every move seductive to him. He—

His thoughts came to an abrupt halt as it suddenly occurred to him that he'd started out trying to make Lucian send Eshe somewhere safe and somehow ended up dropping that to argue defensively that he himself shouldn't be sent away. He wasn't sure, but had the distinct impression he'd been played there somehow.

"Yes, you were," Lucian said, and while his face was expressionless, there was no missing the amusement in his voice.

"She played you like a pro," Anders agreed dryly, making it clear Lucian wasn't the only one reading him. The man shook his head and said, "It was beautiful to watch. I almost thought you were going to thank her for letting you stay before she left the room."

"So she somehow turned the tables and did it on purpose?" he asked with a touch of outrage.

"Of course," Anders laughed.

"Hmm," Lucian muttered. "It was disturbingly like watching Leigh and me disagree."

"Let me guess," Anders said with amusement. "You start out upset about something, confront her on it, and somehow by the end of the argument you're the one apologizing."

Lucian nodded with a grunt of disgust.

"Women are sneaky," Anders said dryly.

"No, they aren't," Armand disagreed with a sigh as he tossed the blankets aside and got up. He had learned something in his three marriages, short as they were. Moving toward the walk-in closet to find clothes, he explained what he'd learned, "An angry male can be intimidating, especially when he's stronger, as men generally are even when it comes to immortals. I think women have had to develop the intelligence to deal with our anger. So, while we stomp around roaring like wounded lions, they use their heads as a sort of defense."

"Hmm," Anders muttered, appearing at the door of the walk-in closet as Armand dragged on a pair of jeans. "So you're suggesting they've evolved to be smarter than us?"

Armand smiled faintly at the arrogant disbelief in the enforcer's voice and said, "Only in communication skills. They can dance circles around us on that front. Or at least most of them can," he corrected himself dryly. He had met women who were failures in that area and men who had better communication skills than most. "But we've got the edge in other areas."

When Anders merely grunted doubtfully at the claim, Armand simply smiled and shook his head as he retrieved a shirt and pulled it on. The man would learn.

"So?" Lucian asked as Armand stepped back into the room from the closet. "Are you going to try to insist Eshe leave?"

Armand paused to peer at him with consideration. "Would you send her away?"

Lucian shrugged. "It's your home. I would make her leave if you wished it . . . and set her up in the motel beside the diner."

"Right, so she'd still be here under threat, but without anyone to watch her back," he said dryly and then sighed. "She can stay. We'll work this out together. But I'm not letting her out of my sight."

"We'll see," Lucian murmured and headed for the door.

Armand scowled at his back and followed.

"That was a nice bit of fast talking upstairs," Bricker congratulated as he followed Eshe and Leigh down the stairs. "You turned the tables on Armand beautifully."

"I don't know what you're talking about," Eshe said innocently, and caught Leigh's grin out of the corner of her eye as they stepped off the last step to start up the hall. In an effort to change the subject, she added, "Sorry about volunteering you for cooking duty. I'll help too, of course."

Bricker snorted at the offer. "You can't even open a strudel box. You aren't going to be much help."

"Which is why I volunteered you," she pointed out, unoffended. "I'm sure I'll catch on to this cooking business quick enough now that I'm eating again. I just haven't bothered with food for a long time."

"I still don't get that," Leigh said as they walked into the kitchen. "I can't imagine not wanting to eat. I mean life just isn't worth living without chocolate and cheesecake."

"Cheesecake?" Eshe asked dubiously. It didn't sound very appealing. Cheese was lovely, but dropping blue cheese or even old cheddar in a bowl with flour and whatnot and then cooking and icing it just sounded bizarre to her.

"You haven't had cheesecake yet?" Leigh asked with amazement.

Eshe shook her head, and Leigh gave her a pitying look that seemed to suggest she was missing something.

"If we stay, I'll pick some up today. You have to try it. It's manna," the woman assured her.

"It's a girl thing," Bricker said wryly when Eshe glanced his way in question. "I've never met a woman who didn't like cheesecake."

"And you don't like it?" Leigh asked him with disbelief.

"It's all right," Bricker said with a shrug.

"Lucian likes it. He can't get enough," Leigh announced. "But most men seem to be more into greasy foods like bacon or burgers than the sweet yummies."

"Bacon is good," Eshe said, sighing at the thought of food. It felt like days since she'd eaten real food, and her stomach felt empty.

"It has been days," Bricker pointed out, reading her thoughts. "You haven't had anything to eat since Sunday and it's Tuesday now."

Eshe frowned at this announcement. It had been

Tuesday night when she'd arrived to start this job. It had been a week, and the only thing she'd done was question Harcourt. At this rate, Nicholas was going to fry.

"Don't be so hard on yourself," Bricker said quietly as he opened the refrigerator and began removing eggs, bacon, and butter. "You questioned Armand too, and we have tried to question Susanna's brother and sister. They just haven't been around for questioning."

Eshe grunted and scowled at him for reading her mind, but he didn't notice. His back was to her as he retrieved a frying pan from a cupboard beside the stove.

"Shall I make coffee?" Leigh asked, glancing around the kitchen. "And then I could start on toast."

"That would be good. Thanks," Bricker said.

"What do you want me to do?" Eshe asked as Leigh moved to grab up the empty coffee carafe and carried it to the sink to fill it.

Bricker frowned and glanced around and then said, "You can set the table."

Eshe raised an eyebrow. "Where do you want me to set it?"

"Ha ha," he said dryly, and then his expression turned uncertain. "You are kidding, right? You know about setting the table; putting plates and silverware on for everyone and butter and salt and pepper and maybe some jams?"

"Of course I do," she said dryly, moving to the cupboard to begin searching for the items he'd mentioned. Although the truth was, while she'd heard the term *setting the table*, she hadn't been sure what that involved. Now she did and found the plates to begin counting out five of them. Anders, she knew, didn't eat, so she didn't bother with a setting for him.

The coffee was just finishing when the other three men arrived. Anders immediately settled at the table, but Lucian and Armand headed for the coffeepot to get themselves coffees.

"The cream and sugar are on the table," Eshe told them as she searched the fridge for a selection of Mrs. Ramsey's preserves.

"Come sit down, Eshe," Lucian ordered as he moved to the table with his coffee.

She set the jams on the table, and then hesitated, but Leigh was manning the toaster, and Bricker seemed to have the stove under control, so she poured herself a coffee and moved to join the three men at the table, taking the seat beside Armand.

"As you pointed out upstairs, you've obviously got someone's attention with your investigations," Lucian said grimly as she dropped two cubes of sugar in her cup and reached for the cream. "We need to figure out how."

Eshe was silent as she poured cream into her coffee and then stirred the steaming drink. Setting the spoon aside, she then sighed and admitted, "I'm not sure how. We've really only managed to question Armand and Harcourt. Although our presence has been widely noted," she added dryly, think of the reaction in the diner.

"William?" Armand asked with surprise. "You can't suspect him. He wouldn't have killed Althea. She was his daughter."

Eshe grimaced. "I agree with you on that. I don't

think he's behind the deaths, but talking to him was useful. We did learn some things."

"Yes, they did," Lucian said quietly. "Harcourt alibied you for Rosamund's death and was sure you couldn't have followed them to Toronto when Althea died. He said you were working with a foaling mare?"

Armand grimaced, an unpleasant memory obviously sliding through his mind. "We lost the foal. Nearly lost the mare too," he said, and then stiffened with realization. "You suspected me?"

"Well, as far as I could tell you were the only obvious connection between the three women and Annie," Lucian said with a shrug.

"We had to cross you off the list, and talking to Harcourt did that," Eshe said quietly. "As well as Marguerite. She and Jean Claude apparently visited while you were away, arriving after you left for court, and leaving early on the evening of the fire. She verified that you were away while they were there."

"Right." He sighed. "But William Harcourt was at court when Cedrick and I got there. He left before I did, but he was with me when Rosamund died. So if all three of my wives were killed, then he isn't the culprit either."

"So that takes both William and Cedrick off the list too if Susanna's death wasn't an accident," Eshe said with a shrug.

"What about the brother and sister?" Bricker suggested, turning from the stove to glance their way.

"Susanna was very close to her brother and sister," Armand said quietly. "That's why she turned Agnes.

They wouldn't have hurt Susanna, and they weren't even in the country when Althea died."

"It's sounding like no one could have done it," Anders said dryly.

"That was my conclusion a century ago when I started looking at the deaths myself," Armand admitted, sounding depressed.

"Well, someone did something," Lucian announced grimly. "There's some reason why you two were locked in a burning shed."

Silence reigned around the table for a moment and then Eshe glanced at Armand. "Is there anyone else at all you've known since before Susanna's death?"

Armand thought for a moment, but shook his head. "We were a lot more spread out then. The Harcourts weren't that far away, and neither were Marguerite and Jean Claude, and of course Cedrick worked for me at the castle and Susanna's brother and sister were there, but . . ." He shrugged helplessly. "That's it."

"Maybe Susanna's death was an accident and you only need to be looking at Althea, Rosamund, and Annie's deaths," Anders suggested.

"That's possible," Eshe murmured.

"I don't know," Bricker murmured from the stove. "Althea's death sounded like it could have been an accident too."

Eshe glanced to him with disbelief. "You're kidding right?"

He glanced over his shoulder with surprise. "No. It was a hotel fire. It could have been an accident."

Eshe frowned, "You didn't notice anything fishy

about Althea's death when William Harcourt was describing it?"

Bricker was frowning now too as the others watched and listened curiously. "No. Not really. I mean, it was a *hotel fire*. They happened."

Eshe shook her head with amazement and marveled, "It was obvious when he was telling the tale that Harcourt didn't pick up on it either, but then he's a man."

"Hey. I'm a man too," Bricker protested.

"Oh right," she said, and bit her lip to keep from laughing at his expression. Smiling, she said, "I just think of you as an enforcer rather than a man."

"I can't be both?"

"Maybe when you're older," she allowed.

"Gee thanks," he said dryly.

"What did you notice that Bricker didn't that makes you think she was murdered?" Armand asked, and he sounded almost eager. She supposed he would be glad to at least know one way or the other in his own mind if his suspicions had a good reason.

Eshe hesitated, aligning her thoughts in her mind, and then said, "Well, it was a hotel fire as Bricker said . . . but it apparently started in her room during the day."

Bricker shrugged impatiently. "You guys used lanterns and candles back then. One or the other probably got knocked over or fell or something."

"But it was during the day," Armand pointed out, his thoughts apparently following along Eshe's. "Althea slept during the day as a rule. But even if she wasn't, she wouldn't have needed a lantern or candle during the day."

"Exactly." Eshe smiled at him.

"Yeah, I guess that's kind of odd," Bricker allowed with a frown as he turned back to begin turning the strips of bacon.

Eshe nodded, and then said, "Except that she wasn't sleeping."

Bricker wheeled back around at once, a piece of dripping bacon dangling from the end of his fork. "What do you mean she wasn't sleeping?" Bricker asked with surprise. "William said she was exhausted, that she asked for the room at the back of the hotel so it would be quiet and Mary took Thomas so he wouldn't disturb her. She—"

"She was wearing the earrings her parents gave her for her eighteenth birthday," Eshe interrupted to remind him.

Bricker stared at her blankly. "So?"

"Althea never wore her jewelry to bed," Armand said quietly.

"William said she was tired," Bricker pointed out, and suggested, "Maybe she was so exhausted she just crashed and forgot to take them off."

Eshe shook her head. "They're too uncomfortable. She wouldn't have forgotten."

Bricker snorted. "I've slept with lots of mortal women who kept their earrings on."

"I'm sure you have," Eshe said dryly. "But mortals have pierced ears and most immortals don't."

"Yeah," Leigh said on a sigh. "I have to say that's kind of a bummer. I had pierced ears as a mortal, but after the turn?" She shook her head. "My ears healed up the moment I took out the earrings I was wearing when I turned. I tried getting them pierced again, but they just healed up again when I took the studs out."

Eshe grimaced and nodded. "You'd have to repierce them every time you wanted to wear earrings, and you'd have to do it with the earrings you want to wear."

"No thanks," Leigh said dryly.

Eshe smiled wryly. "Most immortals aren't sadistic enough to want to do that. Generally we wear clip-ons that pinch the lobe."

"Sounds uncomfortable," Lucian murmured, standing to fetch himself another coffee.

"They are," Leigh said dryly, and scowled at him as if he were at fault for her having to wear them.

"Sorry, my love," Lucian murmured, and bent to press a kiss to her forehead.

Leigh's scowl faded. "It's not your fault."

They shared a smile, and then Lucian kissed her again before turning to cross the room.

Eshe eyed the man curiously as he reclaimed his seat. It was the first time she'd witnessed this softer side of him. It made him seem almost human.

Catching her watching him, Lucian raised an eyebrow. "You were saying?"

"Right," Eshe murmured, and then regathered her thoughts. "So, anyway, aside from the pinching, the fashion back then was large, clunky pieces that would have been uncomfortable to wear while lying down. Impossible to sleep in and definitely not something Althea would have worn to bed," she murmured, and then added, "Besides, William said when they brought out her remains, the only thing left was her charred head and that's just wrong. The nanos make us highly flammable. Everywhere. She should have gone up like a Roman candle if she caught fire. There shouldn't have been anything left . . . unless the head was away from the actual fire itself."

"And away from her body when it went up," Lucian said thoughtfully. "You think she was awake and alive for some reason and beheaded like Annie and Rosamund, then her body set on fire?"

Eshe shrugged. "That would explain why her head survived mostly intact while her body didn't. It might have rolled under the bed or somewhere else where it was just slow roasted rather than going up in flames."

"Right." Bricker sighed with defeat. "It is sounding less like an accident."

They were all silent for a moment, and then Bricker said with bewilderment, "But who could have done it? William said the trip to Toronto was a spur-of-the-moment thing. For someone to have followed them to kill Althea, they would had to have been directly on their heels."

Everyone turned to Armand.

"Hey, don't look at me," he said quickly. "I was busy with the mare."

"Yes, but you were also at the farm when they left," Lucian pointed out. "Was there anyone else there? An immortal who would have left right behind them?"

Armand frowned, his expression thoughtful, but finally said, "No. John and Agnes were in Europe and I'd sent for Cedrick when the mare first started having trouble. He was there with me helping the whole night and well past dawn."

"It doesn't have to be someone who was around when Susanna died if hers was an accident," Eshe pointed out.

Armand took another moment to think, but finally sighed and shook his head. "I'm sorry. There was no one. Besides," he added grimly, "I did look into this myself after Rosamund's death. I asked questions and even read minds. None of the people you've mentioned lied to me as they answered the questions I asked."

Eshe nodded. "I read William's mind too when we talked to him. He was definitely telling the truth about the deaths he knew about."

"Then we're back to no suspects," Lucian said dryly.

Armand hesitated, but then said, "I don't suppose Jean Claude . . ." He let the sentence trail off and then grimaced when Lucian began to look like thunder. "I'm sorry, Lucian. I know the idea upsets you, and frankly, I can't think of a reason he would have wanted to hurt me like this, but I can't think of anyone who would, and he did do some crazy things."

"He did," Lucian agreed coldly. "But he didn't set the shed on fire. He's dead."

"He's been dead before," Armand muttered with disgust.

Lucian suddenly looked weary. "Yes, well, trust me. He *is* dead now."

Armand sighed. "Fine. Then we're back to square one. Four women dead, no rhyme or reason for it, and no suspects. Welcome to my world," he said bitterly.

"At least you can be relatively certain now that Althea

was murdered," Bricker pointed out. "I mean, we're agreed on that, right?"

When everyone nodded silently, Bricker shrugged. "And someone nearby is nervous about the investigation or they wouldn't have tried to kill you two in the shed," he pointed out. "I guess we just keep asking questions. Someone somewhere has to know something that can lead us in the right direction if Annie found out something fifty years ago."

Eshe noted the sharp glance Lucian then turned on Armand. She saw his eyes narrow and then he said, "I asked you this in the diner, but I'm asking again. Annie was apparently asking a lot of questions about the deaths of your wives. It wouldn't be unexpected that she'd try to talk to you. Did she ever come down here?"

"I told you no," Armand said quietly. "I wasn't lying. I never met Nicholas's Annie."

"Maybe she gave you a different name or didn't give you a name at all," Eshe suggested quietly. "Did anyone at all show up around that time asking questions?"

Armand shook his head. "No. I'm sorry."

Eshe sat back with a sigh and then shrugged. "Well, then Bricker and I keep asking questions."

"*We three* will all keep asking questions," Armand said grimly.

When Eshe glanced to Lucian in question at that, he said, "Leigh and I are returning to the city after breakfast, but I'm leaving Anders with you. I want you to split up into two pairs. Eshe, you're with Bricker. Armand, Anders will be with you. I want one pair to talk to Susanna's brother and sister and the other talks to this Cedrick fellow. Find out what they remember about the deaths and if any of them spoke to Annie. Find out everything you can and then call me in Toronto and we'll talk again." Before anyone could comment, he then turned to glance to Bricker. "How long until we eat?"

"Right now," Bricker said at once, handing a plate of bacon to Leigh as she paused beside him with a plate of stacked toast already in hand. As Leigh carried those two plates over, Bricker pulled two more plates from the oven to carry them to the table as well.

Eshe's eyes widened when she saw that while one held a dozen eggs cooked in a fashion that the waitress at the diner had referred to as "over easy," the other plate held a small mountain of hash browns. She hadn't noticed him cooking those, but then she'd been distracted by the conversation at the table.

"I want to talk to you before you leave," Armand said quietly to Lucian as they began serving themselves.

Eshe glanced at him curiously, but suspected she knew what he wanted to talk to Lucian about. She'd noticed the way he'd reacted to Lucian's assignment of pairs. She suspected he was going to argue that she be paired with him rather than Bricker. But she also knew without a doubt that Lucian would say no.

Twelve

"I want to be paired with Eshe," Armand announced the moment he'd closed the office door shutting him and Lucian inside.

"No."

"She's my life mate, Lucian," Armand said grimly.

"Which is precisely why I said no," Lucian responded just as grimly. "You'd be distracted. I need you both to have your heads on straight so you don't miss anything, and to be alert in case there's another attempt to kill one of you."

Armand blinked in surprise. "One of us? You mean Eshe. It's always my life mate or wife who has died."

"Usually after marrying you and giving birth to your child, or in Annie's case, marrying your son and being pregnant," Lucian said and then pointed out dryly, "Eshe hasn't married or, I presume, got pregnant, and this time you were present and would have died too so something has changed."

"I suppose," Armand muttered, wondering what that could be. His life had gone along in the same pattern for so long the days had begun to blend into one another . . . until Eshe's arrival in it. In fact, her appearance in his life was the only change there'd been. But while the murders had all only ever included his wives before this, and his son's wife, Annie, he *would* have died in that fire with Eshe had he not woken when he had. An interesting development.

"Why didn't you come to me with your suspicions after Rosamund died?" Lucian asked abruptly, distracting him from his thoughts.

Armand scowled briefly, but then shook his head and sighed. "Because all I had were suspicions."

"Strong enough suspicions to make you withdraw from the family . . . I presume to protect them?"

"Yes," Armand admitted with a sigh. "But they were still just suspicions, and when I looked into it myself, that's all I ended up with. I didn't even pick up on the earring thing with Althea. William never mentioned that to me."

"He probably didn't want to upset you with such gruesome detail," Lucian said thoughtfully.

"Probably," Armand agreed, and then said what had been bothering him since he'd learned that Annie's death was probably related to all this as well. "But if I'd gone to you anyway Nicholas's Annie might still be alive."

"Yes," Lucian agreed bluntly, and then added, "But then if she had come to me with whatever suspicions led her to investigate, then she might still be alive despite your silence. You both did the same thing." He shrugged. "It worked out for the best anyway. Nicholas has a new life mate and isn't now having to choose between his dead Annie and his very living Jo. That would have been a pickle."

"God, you're a heartless prick at times," Armand said with amazed disgust and then asked curiously, "His life mate's name is Jo?"

Lucian nodded. "Josephine Willan. Her sister is Sam, Mortimer's life mate."

Armand nodded; he'd met Mortimer a time or two. Nicholas had sometimes stopped to drop off photos of Jeanne Louise on his way through town en route to handle a case. Sometimes other enforcers had been with him. Mortimer had been one of them.

"Where is Jo while Nicholas is locked up at the enforcer house?" he asked, a bit concerned that if she was alone and unprotected she might join the growing ranks of dead women in his immediate family.

"I had her locked up with him."

"Why?" Armand asked with amazement.

"Marguerite thought it would help Nicholas pass the time. Besides, it keeps her from getting herself in trouble trying to break him out," he added with amusement. He raised an eyebrow at Armand. "Are we done now?"

Armand nodded silently. While he didn't like the fact that Lucian was pairing Eshe with Bricker rather than him, he understood the reason. They *did* get distracted when together. Besides, his being nearly killed *was* a new development, and it was possible he had been the target rather than Eshe since she'd only questioned William. If so, perhaps whoever was behind the attack would come after him again. He'd rather Eshe was safely away with Bricker if that happened.

"John and Agnes Maunsell," Bricker murmured. "If they aren't really suspects, what are we hoping to learn from them?"

"Anything we can," Eshe said dryly, glancing out the passenger side window of the SUV as they turned onto the road the Maunsell farm was on. It was the vehicle Anders had driven down in. He and Armand had gone to see Cedrick in Armand's pickup, so Anders had suggested they use the SUV rather than their motorcycles. Of course, Bricker had insisted on driving. Eshe hadn't minded, though, so had merely shrugged and climbed in the passenger side.

"If they're in," Bricker commented dryly, and then a moment later as the dark farm came into view, added, "which it doesn't appear like they are. *Again*."

"Turn in anyway. We can at least knock to be sure," Eshe said with a sigh, but didn't really think they were likely to find anyone at home. The house didn't have a single light on anywhere, and both the van and car they'd noticed here their first time out were notably absent. Eshe feared they'd missed them again until she spotted the man who had come to a halt in the yard halfway between the barn and the house.

"Do you think that's him?" Bricker asked as he brought the van to a stop in front of the house.

Eshe shrugged. She hadn't a clue. She'd never met the couple before, but said, "If not, he can at least tell us where John and Agnes are and when we can find them in."

"True," Bricker murmured as he turned off the engine.

Eshe opened her door and slid out, her eyes immediately seeking the man in the yard. He still stood exactly where she'd first seen him, but after a brief hesitation, he continued across the yard toward them, eyeing them speculatively as he came. Eshe looked him over in return and as he drew nearer decided this was definitely John Maunsell. He had similar features to one of the women in the miniature portraits in Armand's desk. It must have been Susanna.

Like his sister, John Maunsell was fair-haired. He was also tall, with the bulk of the warrior he must have been when he was turned. But it was his face that held her attention longest. The man had silver-green eyes and the face of an angel. Seriously, God had been in a good mood the day he'd fashioned this fellow, she decided. He had fairy-tale good looks and she wouldn't have been surprised to find him gracing the pages of a fashion magazine or used as the model for the prince in *Sleeping Beauty* or *Snow White*. It made her feel sorry for the local girls in this community. They probably fell all over themselves to try to get his attention. Actually, she realized, it was probably hell for him.

"It is."

Eshe blinked at that comment from the man as he paused before them, and he grimaced apologetically.

"Sorry. You weren't guarding your thoughts."

Eshe forced a smile as she realized that he had read her thoughts about his looks. While it was somewhat rude of him to comment on them, it was a good reminder to her to keep her guards up so that her thoughts remained private. It was something that was more difficult to do when you'd found a life mate, though no one really knew why.

"John Maunsell?" Bricker asked, moving around the SUV to join Eshe.

"Yes." He nodded and accepted Bricker's hand as the younger enforcer introduced himself. John then turned to Eshe. Before she could speak, however, he said, "And you're Armand's new life mate, Eshe d'Aureus."

When she winced, he smiled faintly and said, "I'm afraid your presence and name have been making the rounds on the tongue of every gossip between here and Armand's farm." He tilted his head and eyed her briefly before deciding, "Although I'd say you are even more lovely than Cedrick said they are claiming."

Eshe smiled wryly at the compliment. She wasn't especially lovely. She was just statuesque and not ugly and had learned how best to showcase herself over the centuries. Still, the compliment was nice and she smiled and said, "Silver-tongued as well as silver-eyed, I see."

It was Bricker who asked, "Cedrick told you about Eshe?"

"Yes. He was delighted to have heard the gossip first," John said wryly, and then asked, "Isn't Armand with you?"

"No." Eshe glanced to Bricker and then back before saying, "We actually came alone. We had some questions we hoped you could answer for us about your sister Susanna."

He nodded, not seeming terribly surprised, and she suspected he assumed her questions were based in the fact that she was Armand's new life mate, with an understandable curiosity about his first mate.

"Shall we go inside then?" John suggested, gesturing toward the house. "Agnes has gone into the city for a movie, but I'll answer whatever questions I can."

"Thank you," Eshe murmured, allowing him to usher them toward the house.

"Would either of you like something to drink?" John asked as he led them inside and began flicking on lights.

"Not for me, thanks," Eshe murmured as they were shown into a living room on the left. The room was decorated in modern furniture in neutral shades of brown. Eshe glanced around and then settled onto the leather sofa and sank into its soft cushions.

"Me neither. We just ate not long ago. A big breakfast," Bricker explained, dropping onto the other end of the couch.

Host duties out of the way, John nodded and settled in the closest chair and then raised his eyebrows in question as he glanced from her to Bricker and back. "So what is it you wanted to ask about my sister Susanna?"

"Actually, it isn't really about Susanna so much as

about how and when she died," Eshe murmured, sitting forward.

"Oh." John sighed. He glanced away, was silent for a minute, and then peered back at her and said, "May I ask why?"

Eshe exchanged a glance with Bricker, her mind working quickly, and then simply said, "It's got to do with Council business."

John stared at her for another moment as if expecting more, and then apparently realizing that was all they were willing to say, he nodded. "Right. Well . . . it was about a week after little Nicky was born." He paused and smiled wryly. "I guess he isn't little anymore."

"No," Eshe agreed quietly. Little Nicky Argeneau was now over five hundred years old. Armand's son had long ago grown up into the adult Nicholas.

"Has there been any word from him?" John asked suddenly, his eager glance sliding from her to Bricker and back again. "Any sightings even that would tell us if he's okay?"

"He's—" Bricker began, and she cut him off.

"No. I'm afraid not." It was a flat-out lie, of course. But it wouldn't make this man feel any better to know that Nicholas was presently locked up at the enforcer house waiting to see if he would be executed or not.

"Oh. I was hoping someone may have at least seen him." John looked away unhappily.

"I'm sorry," Eshe said quietly, and then prompted, "About Susanna's death?"

John nodded. "As I said, it was about a week after Nicky was born. Armand was away at court; he left the day after the birth. His brother Jean Claude and his wife, Marguerite, had been to visit for a couple days to see the baby, but they had left at nightfall to start their journey home. The moment they were out of the bailey, I mounted up and headed into the village for dinner." He paused to explain, "I still ate then, I hadn't been turned very long and I liked my tucker. Unfortunately, the cook at the castle wasn't very good and . . ." He paused and smiled apologetically. "Sorry, I was getting off topic."

"That's all right," Eshe assured him, and then brought him back to the topic by asking, "So Armand was away at court?"

"Yes. As I say, he left the day after Susanna gave birth. He should have left sooner. The king sent at least three orders for him to present himself, but he wouldn't leave Susanna until the baby was born." John grimaced. "Fortunately, she had Nicholas before the king got mad enough to send soldiers, but I imagine Armand had to do some fancy mind bending with the king to get back in his favor for not rushing to court at once when ordered."

Eshe nodded, unsurprised by this corroboration of Armand and Marguerite's stories. "So you went to the village for dinner?"

"Yes. I was probably there for a couple of hours . . . maybe as many as three or four. I liked to drink as a mortal and hadn't quite accepted that alcohol had no effect on me anymore," he admitted with a grimace, and then continued, "At any rate, it was late in the evening when I returned, probably after midnight. Most of the soldiers and servants were mortal and abed. Only the men from the wall were about and they were all in the bailey watching the stables burn."

"Just watching?" she asked with a frown.

"Yes." John nodded. "Apparently they'd tried forming a bucket brigade to the well to try to douse it, but by the time they'd noticed the stables were on fire, it was too late for a bucket brigade to help much. Of course, they'd been concentrating on watching for anyone approaching the wall, as was their job, and hadn't noticed that the stables in the bailey were on fire until it was fully ablaze."

Bricker asked, "Did you ever discover how the fire started?"

He appeared surprised by the question, but shook his head. "I suppose a torch was dropped in the hay, or a lantern knocked over." He shrugged. "We didn't exactly have forensics or anything back then, and as you know, fires were common."

Eshe nodded her head. She wasn't surprised he knew she was old enough to recall. She often could tell if an immortal was young or old. It seemed to be an instinct among them. As for fires, they had been very common back then. Dried rushes and hay were a very deadly combination when mixed with an open flame, which was all they'd had to use for light.

"How did they know Susanna was in there?" Bricker asked curiously, and Eshe found herself concentrating on John's thoughts as he answered, listening with both her mind and ears as he spoke.

"They didn't," John answered. "They only knew

someone had been trapped inside. They said they could hear the shrieking as they approached. When they told me that I assumed—as most of them did— that it was one of the stable boys caught napping in the straw as they liked to do. But the fire was burning too hot when they told me that. No one would have survived running in there to try to get them out. At least that's what I thought at the time," he murmured, guilt lining his face. "I realize now that while I might have been badly burned, I probably would have survived long enough to get her out and enough blood would have seen both of us right again. But I was a new turn then. I didn't know, and I didn't know it was Susanna. I—"

His voice broke and he turned his head away briefly.

Eshe swallowed and withdrew from his thoughts. She'd been reading his mind as he'd spoken, verifying for herself that he was telling the truth. He was, and his guilt and loss were painful to experience with him.

It was Bricker who asked, "So you don't really know if Susanna was in there? No one actually saw her enter the stables or—?"

"No," John interrupted, his voice harsh with a combination of grief and what sounded like anger. "No one saw, but it was her. We realized that when Agnes came running out of the castle crying that she couldn't find Susanna anywhere. She wasn't with the baby, or in her room." He sighed and shook his head. "Of course, I didn't want to believe she could have been in there. I wanted to believe it was someone else, but the next night she was still nowhere to be found. The fire had gone out by then and the embers had cooled, so I got several men together and we sifted through the ashes." His expression was bleak as he told them, "I found her wedding ring and the amulet Armand had given her before leaving for court as well as a couple of burned and stained patches of the gown she'd been wearing to see Marguerite and Jean Claude off. That was it, though. I gather the nanos make us burn so hot that it was amazing that those bits of cloth had survived and that the metal hadn't melted."

They were all silent for a moment, and then John added, "I was the one who had to tell Armand when he returned home from court a week later." He shook his head sadly. "The man was happy as hell to be home and couldn't wait to see Susanna. You'd have thought they'd been apart a decade instead of just two weeks. He rode into the bailey at speed, bounded off his mount, and raced up the stairs, laughing and yelling for Susanna. When I tried to stop him at the top of the steps, he laughed and said, 'Where's your sister? I got her a gift while at court,' and tried to move around me until I finally just blurted, 'She's dead.'"

John shook his head. "I loved my sister, and her passing was painful as hell for me, but sometimes I think it would have been kinder just to have staked Armand in the heart. I've never before or since seen a man so stricken."

Eshe swallowed away the lump suddenly in her throat. She'd slipped into his thoughts again as he'd recalled Armand's return and seen first Armand's laughter as he'd returned home to his life mate, and then the way he'd paled and swayed as he learned his life mate was dead. It had been difficult to witness even second-hand through an old memory. Clearing her throat, she said quietly, "Thank you. I'm sorry we made you relive such sad memories. I only have one more question."

He nodded, his expression expectant.

"You said Marguerite and Jean Claude were there earlier in the evening but had left, and I know Armand and Cedrick were at court . . . Were there any other immortals that you know of who were at the castle besides you and your sister when the fire started?"

John seemed startled by the question, but took a moment before answering. However, then he shook his head. "No. Just me and Agnes." He tilted his head curiously. "Why?"

Eshe let her breath out on a sigh. She'd been hoping for someone they could investigate, someone Armand hadn't thought or maybe even known of. Someone who had dropped by unexpectedly or . . . well, just anything. But life was never that simple, was it?

Shaking her head, she stood up. "It doesn't matter. Thank you for taking the time to talk with us. We should go now."

They were all silent as he walked them to the door. Bricker murmured a thank-you as they slipped outside, but didn't speak again until they were in the SUV. Then he glanced at her and pointed out, "You didn't ask him about Althea or Rosamund's death."

Eshe stiffened in her seat, her seat belt drawn half-way across her body as she realized he was right. She'd found the tale of Susanna's death and Armand's pain so upsetting, she hadn't thought to ask about anything else. Biting her lip, she glanced toward the house and frowned. The door was closed now, John nowhere in sight. "Well, he wouldn't know anything useful about Althea. He and Agnes were in Europe. And from what Armand and Harcourt have told us, he wasn't at the house around the time of Rosamund's death either."

"True," Bricker agreed slowly. "But still, maybe we should at least ask."

Eshe hesitated, but then sighed and let her seat belt slide back into its holder. "You're right. Let's go."

They both got out of the SUV and walked back to the house. This time Eshe rang the doorbell. She then stood, silently cursing herself for not asking questions about the other women as they waited. And waited.

"He's not answering," Bricker pointed out. "He didn't slip out to the barns or something while we were walking to the SUV, did he?"

"No. We would have seen him," Eshe said with certainty and rang the doorbell again. She was about to ring it for a third time when the sound of a vehicle engine made her glance toward the driveway. A white four-by-four with tinted windows was slowing as it pulled in beside their SUV. Eshe and Bricker watched curiously as it came to a halt and the driver's side door opened. The man who got out was plain-faced and built like a bull, with a wide chest, muscular arms, and a thick neck. A thatch of pale brown hair was cut short on his head.

Eshe shrugged when Bricker glanced at her, and simply waited as the man approached the door where they were waiting.

He paused on the sidewalk in front of the stoop they were on, tall enough he managed to loom over her and Bricker despite being on lower ground, and eyed them both for a moment before turning his attention to Eshe. "You look to me to be Eshe d'Aureus."

Eshe's eyes widened slightly, but she accepted the hand he held out and nodded before asking, "And you are?"

"Cedrick Hanford," he introduced himself.

"Cedrick?" Bricker asked with surprise. "Armand and Anders were heading over to talk to you when we left the house."

"They would have missed me then. I've been running errands," he said and arched one querying eyebrow. "And who are you?"

"Justin Bricker," he said, offering his own hand in greeting. "I'm . . . er . . . a friend of Eshe's and now Armand's," he muttered finally.

Cedrick nodded and accepted his hand in a shake, then glanced past them to the door. "Not getting an answer?"

"No," Eshe admitted, frowning at the door herself. "We know John's home. We were talking to him a few minutes ago and then started to leave, but remembered something we forgot to ask him and came back, but now he's not answering."

Cedrick grunted, not seeming surprised. "He probably went down into that basement of his. If so, you're out of luck. The damned thing is soundproof. It's where they sleep and he had it built so they wouldn't hear the doorbell, phones, or anything down there. You could blow up your SUV out here and he wouldn't hear it if that's where he is."

"Surely he wouldn't go to bed this early?" Bricker said with a frown.

"Probably not," Cedrick agreed. "But he's got an office down there too with a computer that, I gather, has every computer game worth owning on it. He's down there most nights gaming until well past dawn. The best way to get ahold of him is to leave a message on the answering machine. He'll call back . . . eventually," he added with dry irritation.

"Well, I guess that's it for talking to him tonight," Bricker muttered.

Eshe nodded, and then stepped back out of the way as Cedrick murmured, "Excuse me," and squeezed between them on the stoop to get to the mailbox. As she watched curiously, he slid a CD from his back pocket and dropped it in the mailbox, then let the lid drop with a clang.

Turning back, he saw their expressions and explained, "An accounting program to help him with the books."

"I thought John owned this place, not Armand," Bricker said with surprise, speaking what she was thinking.

"He does, but Armand frets about the boy and asked me to help him out if I could. So I do a few things here and there. This program is so he can do his own accounting. Means he'll pester me less," he added dryly, moving between them again to step off the stoop.

"I'm getting the distinct impression you don't like John," Eshe murmured, stepping off the stoop to follow him when he started back toward his truck.

She saw his big shoulders shrug. "John's all right. He's just . . . well . . . John," he said wryly, stopping at his truck. He turned back to raise an eyebrow at them. "You say Armand was looking to talk to me?"

"Yes. He's probably been to your place and left by now," she added with a frown.

"Are you headed back to the farm?" he asked.

Eshe glanced back to the silent and still house behind them. They really needed to question John some more, but it looked like that wouldn't happen right now. They'd have to go home, get his number, and call to leave a message on his answering machine. A big pain in the ass, but it looked like there was nothing else to do. Sighing, she turned back to Cedrick. "Yes. We're heading back to the farm."

"Then I'll follow you and talk to Armand there," Cedrick decided, and got into his truck.

"Do you have your phone with you, Bricker?" Eshe asked as they hurried to their own vehicle.

"Yeah. Where's yours?" he asked with surprise.

"A pile of melted plastic in the shed," she said dryly.

"Oh. Right." He started reaching into his pocket.

"Give it to me in the truck," she suggested as she moved away to approach the passenger side of the vehicle.

They both got in and did up their seat belts, then Bricker handed her his phone and started the engine. "Who are you calling?"

"Armand," she answered absently as she punched in his cell phone number. "I just want to be sure he and Anders did head home when they found Cedrick wasn't there and aren't sitting out at the farm he runs waiting for him."

"So his phone survived the fire?" Bricker asked, starting the engine.

Eshe cursed and hit the end call button and started to dial Anders's phone number instead as Bricker started up the drive and Cedrick followed.

Thirteen

'Armand's on his way back,' Eshe told Cedrick as she stepped out of the SUV to find him already out of his pickup and there to hold the door for her. They'd been bouncing around so much on the gravel lanes on the way back that she'd punched in Anders's number wrong twice before finally getting it right and getting ahold of the men.

As she'd feared, they were sitting in Armand's pickup waiting for Cedrick to return. She'd explained that they'd run into him at the Maunsell farm and were bringing him back to Armand's farm to speak with him. Armand had said they'd head right over.

Eshe had barely finished talking to him and ended the call before Bricker was pulling into the driveway at Armand's farm. By her guess, they were fifteen or twenty minutes away. She murmured a thank-you as

Cedrick closed the door for her, and then started toward the porch.

"Would you like something to drink while we wait? Coffee, tea . . . blood?" Eshe added the last with a wry twist of her lips. Saying the first two had made her feel like Little Suzy Homemaker, but offering the blood had made her feel better. Besides, no one had ever mentioned if the man was mated or not. If not, he probably didn't drink anything but blood.

"Blood," Cedrick murmured as he followed her up the porch steps. He then added, "I'm unmated still . . . and beginning to think I'll never find my life mate."

The last was said on a weary note that made Eshe frown slightly. It was hard being alone, she knew. Life started to just blend together into one seamless skein of never-ending nights. And John Maunsell was alone too, reduced to a game junkie who sat alone in a soundproofed and windowless room night after night playing endless video games. After they resolved all this, it seemed to her she and Armand should throw a big party and invite a ton of females, mortal and immortal alike, to introduce to the two men. They both seemed nice enough to her and deserved life mates. Of course, she'd only had one short conversation with John, and from the few brief sentences she'd exchanged with Cedrick, it seemed he didn't think much of John.

"What did you mean by John is John?" she asked curiously as they entered the kitchen and she moved to the refrigerator to retrieve three bags of blood.

"Maybe I should move that up to Armand's room

before we forget," Bricker muttered as he took the bag she offered him. "Mrs. Ramsey will be here tomorrow."

Eshe nodded absently, her questioning gaze on Cedrick as she offered him a bag.

"Thank you." He accepted the blood, but didn't pop it to his teeth right away, instead considering her question. Finally he sighed and said bluntly, "John was a drunken idiot as a mortal."

Eshe's eyes widened at this news. He'd mentioned he'd liked to drink as a mortal, but she hadn't taken that to mean he was a drunk. Of course, he wasn't likely to tell her that. She glanced to Bricker to see that he appeared just as surprised. He also stopped pulling bags of blood from the refrigerator, plopped the two he'd already removed back inside, closed the door, and straightened to listen.

Eshe glanced back to Cedrick, and then carried her bag of blood with her to the table and sat down as she asked, "What drove him to drink?"

"Nothing," Cedrick said dryly as he and Bricker joined her at the table. "He was just a second son with no responsibilities, no prospects, and a like for drink."

"Oh," Eshe murmured, turning her bag absently in her hand.

"He was also betrothed to the daughter of a neighboring baron," Cedrick said on a sigh. "The girl could have done better, but she and John were crazy about each other and her original betrothed had died when she was a child, so the father agreed to their marriage. The wedding date was about three months away when John came to the castle to find out why Agnes was no longer at the convent. And then of course he went on the night hunt where he broke his neck."

Cedrick's mouth tightened. "He was sober when we started out, but had a wineskin full of whiskey in his saddlebag. I caught him drinking a time or two and suggested it wasn't wise to drink on a hunt. He just laughed and said it was to keep him warm." Cedrick blew his breath out with disgust. "I guarantee you the idiot was past drunk when he took the tumble from his mount and broke his fool neck."

"And Agnes turned him," Eshe murmured.

"Yes. The little fool. I thought it a waste of a good turn at the time."

"And now?" Eshe asked curiously.

Cedrick shrugged. "Turning made John stop drinking. The alcohol had no effect on him anymore and Armand ordered everyone not to tell him about how drinking a drunk's blood affected us. I'm sure he's learned since then, but as far as I can tell he hasn't drunk since Susanna's death." He pursed his lips and said, "Guilt, I imagine. If he hadn't been down at the inn in the village, he would have been there when the fire started and Susanna might be alive."

Eshe nodded, and Bricker asked, "What happened to his betrothed?"

"Oh." Cedrick clucked with disgust. "Armand warned him to wait until he had gained the skill to read minds before he married her, to be sure she could be a life mate to him, but he was still in love with the girl and would have gone right ahead and married her if she'd been willing."

"She wasn't, I take it," Eshe said quietly.

"Hell no. He went to her the minute he left the castle and blabbed to her about what he was now. The girl was very religious, most folks were back then, and she about had a heart attack when he told her. As far as she was concerned, he was now the devil's spawn and she couldn't get away from him quick enough. If I hadn't been there, she'd have run and told her father and we'd have had an army at the castle gate with stakes and torches in hand."

"You were there?" Eshe asked with surprise.

Cedrick nodded. "Armand's no idiot. John had promised to delay the wedding and not to tell until he could read and control mortals as well as wipe memories in case she reacted exactly as she did. But Armand didn't trust him not to and sent me to follow him just to be sure. I wiped her memory, put false memories of a terrible fight with John into her mind, and sent her on her way thinking she never wanted to see him again. Then I brought John back to the castle."

Cedrick sat back in his seat and shook his head. "He was a bitter and angry little bastard for a while after that, unpleasant to everyone but worst with Agnes. John blamed her for turning him into what his betrothed saw as a monster, you see," he added dryly. "Never mind that if she hadn't he'd be dead and still wouldn't have her, but wouldn't have life either.

"That was hard as hell on the girl. Fortunately, Susanna's death seemed to knock at least some sense into the boy. He's treated her better since then, very protective of her . . . which is good since she always doted on him," he added quietly, and then asked, "Have you met Agnes yet?"

Eshe shook her head. "She was at the movies tonight when we arrived."

Cedrick smiled faintly. "Agnes loves the movies. She's a sweet little thing. I believe she's almost ten years older than Susanna was. She and an older brother had a different mother than Susanna and John, who were born to their father's second wife. Agnes's mother must have been a wee thing. The girl's short and slim and looks younger than most immortals despite her more than five hundred years. She had already taken the veil and become a nun when Susanna turned her, but of course she gave that up after the turn. It's hard enough biting friends and neighbors, and they aren't virginal brides of God," he said with a grimace.

"I've met a couple of rogues who would have thought that a delicacy," Bricker said.

"Yes, well, Agnes wouldn't have," Cedrick assured him, and then let them know he'd had enough questions for now by slapping the bag of blood Eshe had given him to his teeth.

She and Bricker did likewise and they were all silent as the bags emptied. Eshe was just tearing her empty bag from her teeth when they heard the rusty creak of the screen door opening at the front of the house and then the clack as it slammed shut. Eshe wasn't surprised when Armand led Anders into the kitchen a moment later.

Cedrick nodded in greeting and removed his own

empty bag to greet Armand with "I heard tell in town that you have a new manager."

"I do," Armand agreed, slapping the other man on the shoulder in passing on his way to the chair beside Eshe. "I'll give you his name and particulars for the books before you leave."

Cedrick nodded and then glanced curiously to Anders as he moved to the fridge to grab a couple of bags of blood.

"That's Anders," Armand answered the unasked question, and when Cedrick raised an eyebrow, added, "I'm sorry, I don't know his first name."

"Few people do," Anders said mildly as he joined them at the table and handed one of the bags he'd collected to Armand. As he settled in the chair between Armand and Bricker, he added, "Speaking of your new manager, he thinks you and Eshe were away the last couple of days. So does your housekeeper. Lucian's work," he added when Armand glanced at him with surprise. "He didn't want them anywhere near the house while you two were healing so put it in their heads that you were away and your manager should stay in his house with the television on loud except when he had chores to do, and your housekeeper should go home for a paid day off. She'll be back tomorrow though, I gather."

Armand nodded and glanced to Eshe. "I suppose you've already asked him the questions?"

She shook her head, an amused smile curving her lips at his consternation at possibly missing out on gaining info. "No. Cedrick was just telling us about John and Agnes. We haven't asked about anything else."

"Oh." He smiled faintly, his eyes dropping to her lips. When Armand then swayed toward her, Eshe was sure he was about to kiss her, but he paused when Cedrick spoke.

"Sorry to interrupt, but what questions?"

Sighing, he smiled wryly at her, and then turned to Cedrick. "We're trying to figure out who killed my wives and daughter-in-law Annie."

Eshe winced at the words. While she knew Armand didn't believe Cedrick could be behind the tragedies in his life, and while she mostly agreed, it still would have been better to leave that little bit of info out for now, just in case they were wrong and he was.

She peered at Cedrick, noting the expression on his face and that while he was somewhat surprised, he didn't seem stunned at this news. She understood why when he said slowly, "I *thought* you just seemed to have a little too much bad luck with women."

"You should have said something," Armand said with surprise. "I thought the same thing."

Cedrick shrugged. "Well, you never talked about it, and I thought maybe I was just being paranoid."

"Yeah," Armand said dryly. "I know the feeling."

Cedrick stared at him silently for a moment, and then straightened in his seat and said, "Right. What can I do to help?"

Much to her surprise, Armand turned to peer at her and raised an eyebrow, silently deferring to her. Reaching for his hand where it rested on his leg, she squeezed it gently and then asked Cedrick, "I understand you were at court with Armand at the time of Susanna's death?"

He nodded. "We left the week before and returned apparently a week after she died."

"And when Althea died you were at the farm helping Armand?"

He nodded again. "I believe it was a foaling mare. Althea and her parents left while we were trying to turn the wee beast." He grimaced. "We lost the foal if I remember correctly?" He glanced to Armand, who gave a nod.

"Were you around when Rosamund died?" Eshe asked.

Cedrick grimaced at that. "I was around in the area, but I was at the farm I was managing at the time. I only heard about it the next night."

"We don't suspect you," Armand assured him solemnly. "We're just trying to sort it out. You're my alibi for both Susanna and Althea's deaths."

"They suspected you?" Cedrick asked with surprise and then glanced to Eshe, Bricker, and Anders and assured them, "I've known this man a long time. Armand wouldn't hurt anyone, let alone kill a life mate and two wives."

"Is there anyone you can think of who might?" Eshe asked at once.

The question seemed to set him aback, but he paused and considered it for several moments before shaking his head. "He's a good guy. I can't think of any reason someone would go after his women."

"Then is there anyone besides yourself, the Harcourts, and John and Agnes who have been around since Susanna's death?" she asked. "Perhaps not directly involved in his life even, but on the fringes maybe? Someone who keeps cropping up?"

Cedrick shrugged. "Just his family. They pop in and out of his life at times. Lucian . . . and Jean Claude and his wife, Marguerite."

Eshe slumped back in her seat with disappointment. She wasn't the only one. Bricker and Armand did as well. Only Anders seemed unmoved by the lack of information, but then he was new to the investigation and hardly knew Armand. It wouldn't bother him.

Cedrick offered an apologetic grimace. "I'm sorry. I guess I'm not much help."

"You verified Armand's story," Eshe said, forcing a smile. "That was helpful."

He gave a short disbelieving laugh, and then glanced to Armand when he suddenly stood.

"Come to the office. I'll get you that information on Jim, my new manager here," Armand said quietly.

Cedrick nodded and stood, but paused to nod at Bricker and Anders, then smiled at Eshe. "It's a pleasure to meet you. I hope you sort all this out and enjoy a long happy life with Armand. He deserves it."

"Thank you," Eshe murmured. "It's nice meeting you too. And we will meet again."

Cedrick nodded and turned to follow Armand from the room.

"Well," Anders said as the sound of their footsteps faded away up the hall. "I hope you two had more luck with John and Agnes Maunsell?"

"Yes," Bricker answered even as Eshe said, "No."

Anders quirked one eyebrow. "Which is it?"

Eshe peered at Bricker. "All he really did was verify Armand's story."

"Aha!" Bricker said with triumph. "This time *I* caught details *you* didn't."

Eshe grimaced. "So tell. What did you notice?"

Bricker shook his head and stood up. "I'm moving the blood. I'll explain when Armand gets back. That way I'll have a witness to my redeeming myself and not looking an idiot like I did last time."

Eshe considered telling him he hadn't looked an idiot, but then merely shrugged and stood to cross to the cupboards and begin opening and closing them until she found the ones that held food rather than dishes.

"What are you looking for?" Bricker asked with a frown.

"Something to eat," she said absently.

"Already?" he asked with dismay. "We only had breakfast a couple hours ago before Lucian and Leigh left."

"Three hours ago," she corrected, and then added defensively, "And that breakfast was the only thing I'd eaten since the picnic Sunday. I'm hungry again."

Heaving a sigh, Bricker set back the blood he'd picked up and closed the fridge door. "All right. What do you want? I'll make it."

"I can make myself something," she said at once.

"Right," he said with open disbelief. "When's the last time you cooked?"

Eshe frowned and hesitated, but finally admitted, "Never."

"Never?" he echoed with disbelief. "Like really *never*?"

Eshe heaved a sigh and turned back to the cupboard of boxes and cans with a grimace. "My family was wealthy. And Orion was an amazing warrior. He was wealthy too. We had servants to do that stuff. It didn't look that hard though. I'm sure I can figure it out."

She picked out an attractive-looking container on the shelf and peered at the pretty image of wheat and fruit on the front. "This looks good."

"That's Metamucil," Bricker said with disgust, snatching it from her hand.

"So?" She turned to scowl at him. "What's wrong with Metamucil?"

"It's—" He glanced at the container and read, "A dietary supplement."

"That sounds healthy," she said, trying to grab it back.

"Eshe," he said, his disgust giving way to amusement. "It's what old mortals take to get regular."

"To get regular what?" she asked, and then poked him in the stomach, hard. The moment Bricker bent over with an "oomph," she snatched the container back and repeated, "Regular what?"

"Crap," he gasped, clutching his stomach.

"I didn't hit you that hard," she said with some disgust of her own.

"No." He sighed, straightening. "I meant that's what they get regulated. Crap."

Eshe dropped the can with dismay. "They buy crap?"

"Not the— It's a— Oh. For cripes sake," Bricker muttered, bending to pick it up. Shaking it in her face, he then said, “It’s fiber. Psyllium seeds or chaff or something. It regulates their bowel movements for those who don’t eat enough fiber in their diet.”

“Oh.” She peered at the container. “That doesn’t sound very good. It’s very attractive though.”

“Yeah, well, so are some cat foods but I wouldn’t suggest trying them either,” he muttered, setting the container back in the cupboard. “In fact, I suggest you let me take you grocery shopping your first time out just to make sure you don’t try to make a meal out of toilet cakes or feminine hygiene products.”

“Ha ha, I do know what feminine hygiene products are,” she said dryly.

“Do you?” he asked doubtfully, and Eshe rolled her eyes.

“I am a female, Bricker,” she pointed out.

“Oh, right, I forgot,” he said dryly, surveying the contents of the cupboard now himself. “I just think of you as an enforcer. A really *old* enforcer.”

Eshe was narrowing her eyes and considering plowing him one when she became aware of Anders’s soft laughter from the table. Turning, she glared at him, but he merely shrugged.

“I believe he just got you back for your earlier comments about not thinking of him as a man,” the man said with amusement.

Realizing he was right, Eshe sighed and decided not to hit Bricker. Moving to the table, she muttered ungraciously, “Fine. You can cook for me.”

“Gee, thanks,” Bricker said dryly, and Anders laughed harder.

"What's so funny?" Armand asked, coming into the room then. Eshe glanced his way to see that he was alone and supposed Cedrick had headed back to the farm he was running.

"Eshe was going to eat Metamucil," Bricker announced, grinning with an amusement that only deepened when he saw Armand's blank expression. Shaking his head, he pulled down the canister of Metamucil and held it out. "Did you know what this was when you bought it?"

Armand eyed the container and shrugged. "No, but it looked good."

That just made Bricker laugh again. "Oh man. I'm going to have to give you two some shopping lessons before I go."

Shaking his head, he turned back to the cupboard, saying, "Sit down. We're going to talk while I make us something to eat."

"Good," Armand murmured, moving around the table to rejoin Eshe. "I'm hungry."

"Did Cedrick leave?" Anders asked as Armand settled in the chair next to Eshe.

"Yes. I didn't think he could be of any more help," Armand murmured, draping his arm around Eshe and drawing her against his side.

Anders nodded and then glanced to Bricker. "So, Armand's here . . . Tell us what you picked up at the Maunsells that Eshe didn't."

"Right," he murmured, grabbing lunchmeat, cheese, and various greens from the refrigerator. He set them on the counter and went back for an onion and tomato as he said, "Well, he told us pretty much what Armand said, but with a little more detail."

"Yes, but it wasn't really enough to figure out if her death was murder or accidental," Eshe said, watching him pull plates from the cupboard and begin slicing the tomatoes and onions.

"I disagree," Bricker said, and then pointed out, "He said the men apparently hadn't noticed the stable fire until it was well under way because they were watching outside the wall as was their job. And that they didn't realize Susanna was in there until Agnes came out upset that she couldn't find Susanna."

"Yeah," Eshe murmured, her mouth starting to water as she watched him build several sandwiches stacked high with lettuce, onion, tomato, cucumber, meat, and cheese.

He stopped what he was doing and turned to peer at where they sat at the table. "The first thing I did when I found you and Armand out beside the remains of the burned shed was call Lucian. I knew I'd need help; drugs and blood and—" Bricker shrugged, "Hell, just someone to help watch your backs while you healed." He let that sink in and then asked, "Don't you think if Susanna had gone into the bailey and seen that the stables were on fire, she would have yelled at the men on the wall to get help?" he asked pointedly. "There had to be more than one horse in there. She couldn't have thought she was going to rescue them all alone."

He shook his head and turned back to his sandwich making. "I think if the stables were on fire before she went in, she would have been shrieking at the top of her lungs for help and the men would have known before she ever went in."

"You're right, she would have," Armand said quietly.

"Which means she didn't run into a burning stable and have a beam or something else collapse on top of her and trap her as everyone assumed," Eshe said, following that reasoning.

"All the others have been decapitated," Anders pointed out. "Only Althea and Annie were burned like her. Rosamund wasn't but was decapitated."

"Yeah." Bricker frowned as he put the last slice of bread on each sandwich and then began to cut them into halves. "I thought of that, but she was apparently shrieking from inside the stables when the men finally noticed and ran toward it. She couldn't have been decapitated."

"She could have," Eshe murmured, drawing three pairs of doubting eyes her way. She took a minute to think it through and then said. "She was the first kill. The killer might not have been very confident yet. He might not have fully decapitated her, but just sliced her throat open or even halfway through. A wound like that would have incapacitated her, prevented her escaping, probably even knocked her unconscious for several minutes, long enough for the stables to be set on fire and be fully engorged in flames before she regained consciousness and could scream."

"But if her throat was sliced, she wouldn't have been able to scream," Bricker pointed out.

"Not right away," Eshe agreed. "But the nanos' first reaction would be to repair the damage to such a wound."

"Enough for her to scream?" Bricker said doubtfully, but then murmured, "It would make sense, though. I mean, you're right, killers often use the same method, so I'd be willing to believe that there had been an attempted decapitation. I mean it would fit. All the others were decapitated and then involved in fire except for Rosamund."

Eshe nodded, and then glanced to Armand to see his troubled expression. Thinking he doubted her theory, she said, "Or she may have sustained another wound, something that would prevent her being able to escape, but not to scream."

"Either way, it seems likely Susanna was murdered too," Armand murmured.

"Bricker brings up a good point," Anders said quietly. "All the rest involved fire except for Rosamund."

"There would have been no way to explain a fire with Rosamund's death," Eshe pointed out. "William said she was decapitated when the wagon she was driving overturned. Wagons didn't have engines to catch on fire."

"I don't know about wagons, but we had a Brougham carriage when I was a kid and it had a carriage lantern," Bricker said. "If the wagon had one, it could have easily started a fire when the wagon overturned. At least that's what everyone would have thought if the wagon had burned."

Eshe glanced to Armand. "Did your wagon have a lantern?"

"Actually, it did," he said quietly. "And there were signs that there had been a bit of a fire, but it was raining that night and it apparently couldn't catch hold and stay lit."

"Even with the fuel from the lantern?" Eshe asked with surprise. It had rained the night the shed had burned too, but that hadn't slowed it down much. Although Lucian had told her that he'd gone out to examine the shed and could smell gas in the grass by the fire and suspected it had been used as an accelerant to start the fire and make it grow fast and furious.

"Knowing Rosamund, she probably didn't refill the lantern before setting out that night. She was always forgetting," he added with fond exasperation. Armand shrugged. "There may not have been enough fuel in it to be of much help."

"So if it weren't for the rain, Rosamund would have burned up too," Anders said quietly and raised an eyebrow in Armand's direction. "Are any of your acquaintances what you would call firebugs? They like fire, use it to get rid of trash or such?"

Armand frowned but shook his head. "Not that I know of."

"It was worth a try," Anders said with a shrug.

"How exactly was Rosamund beheaded in the crash?" Eshe asked with a frown.

"The rails on the wagon were wood with metal top slats. It looked as if she'd been thrown from the wagon as it overturned, and then the metal slat had come down directly on her neck with the weight of the wagon behind it," he answered wearily. "It was a clean cut that a sword could have made, but the metal slat could have made it too."

They were all silent for a moment, and then Anders murmured, "So basically all we've learned is that all four women were probably murdered, which we suspected to begin with . . . and we've questioned everyone."

Eshe started to nod, but then stopped and shook her head instead. "We haven't questioned the women."

Armand glanced at her with surprise. "You're not suggesting Mary killed her own daughter?"

"No, of course not," she said at once to ease his upset, but then frowned as she realized just what she was saying and added, "Although there's no reason she might not have. I mean if William is a suspect, so is Mary. And the same is true of John and Agnes. A woman can kill just as well as a man."

"Mary was the one in the house talking to Rosamund before she supposedly rode off and had her supposed accident," Bricker pointed out.

"Mary would not have hurt a hair on Althea's head," Armand said firmly. "Dear God, she spoiled that girl rotten. In fact, she's the one to blame for Althea's willfulness. William at least made an effort to try to rein the girl in, but Mary was always hampering him." He shook his head. "She is not behind these deaths."

"All right, I'll take your word on it," Eshe said soothingly. "But we still haven't questioned either of the women, and one or both of them might know something that none of the men do. We have to question them."

Armand scowled, but then sighed and nodded reluctantly. "All right. But I want to be there when they're questioned."

"It would be faster if we—"

"I want to be there," he repeated firmly.

Eshe stared at him silently, instinct telling her it would probably be better if she spoke to the women alone. A woman would tell another woman things she'd never say in a man's presence. Then too, if Althea was having affairs as Armand believed, her mother might not want to speak of such things in front of him. Or anyone for that matter. Sighing, she caught his gaze with her own. "Don't you trust me?"

Armand blinked in surprise. "Of course, but—"

"Then let me talk to them," Eshe interrupted firmly, and when he opened his mouth, probably to protest, she added quickly, "You can be at the house with me. But I want you to keep William and John busy and let me talk to the women alone. They might say more without men there."

Armand let his breath out slowly and nodded. "All right."

Fourteen

Eshe stretched sleepily and turned on her side, freezing when she spotted the tuft of hair sticking out from under the bundle of blankets beside her. A slow smile curved her lips. Already knowing that neither of the women was available last night, they'd merely called the Maunsell house and then the Harcourts and left messages asking each of the women to call and make arrangements to meet with them. They had then sat around chatting and waiting for phone calls that hadn't come.

Finally, at around three A.M., Armand had feigned a yawn and said that since they probably weren't going to be able to meet with the women until the next night at that point, he thought he might retire and rest. He was sure he was still recovering from their adventure in the shed and worn out after everything that had happened. He was retiring early and felt Eshe should as well.

She had agreed with such alacrity it had left Bricker and Anders chuckling as Armand had led her from the room. Eshe hadn't much cared if they were amused. Her mind had been on being alone with Armand, safely in the house where they had backup and were unlikely to be attacked.

The door had barely closed behind them before they were in each other's arms and dancing blindly toward the bed in a sideways scuttle that had probably made them look like a huge, misshapen, multicolored crab. They had slept, though . . . eventually, and no doubt long before the men had come up to bed. She supposed that was probably why she was awake now while the sun was still trying to peek around the blackout curtains . . . Which meant they had time before they had to get up and set about their day talking to the women, Eshe thought, smiling as she took in Armand's position.

He'd cocooned himself in the blankets with just a handful of hair strands poking out of the small opening at the top. His face and his body, all the way down to his feet, were hidden and enwrapped in the fluffy comforter . . . leaving none for her. It was fortunate she didn't like heavy blankets and preferred to just draw a sheet over herself, she supposed.

Shaking her head slightly, Eshe reached for the blankets, intending to unwrap the gorgeous man who had given her such pleasure that night, but paused when she opened her mouth to speak and a croak of sound came out. Dang, she was as dry as the desert and in some serious need of hydration . . . and food, Eshe acknowledged as her stomach made the most atrocious sound. Really, now that it had enjoyed the experience of having food in it again, her tummy appeared to have become demanding . . . and the rest of her was demanding blood, she realized on a sigh as she became aware of the cramping taking place in her body.

Retracting the hand that had been reaching for Armand, Eshe slid from the bed. She started toward the bathroom, tripped over the shirt Armand had been wearing earlier, and paused to pick it up before continuing on her way.

Five minutes later she came out of the bathroom dressed in only Armand's shirt, her hair finger-brushed and her mouth minty fresh, to slip silently from the room and make her way downstairs.

The house was dead quiet; no vacuum cleaners roaring away, no clank of dishes being washed, and Eshe glanced around curiously, wondering where Mrs. Ramsey was. This was Wednesday, after all, and the woman usually worked Wednesdays. Surely Lucian hadn't put it in her head not to come in all week?

Eshe frowned at the possibility. She was rather hoping the woman would make her something to eat. Although she supposed she could make herself a sandwich or something. She'd watched Bricker do that the day before and was pretty sure she could replicate the actions he'd taken to prepare it.

Eshe was trying to recall all the items Bricker had put on the very delicious sandwiches the day before when she stepped into the kitchen and spotted Mrs. Ramsey's round figure standing at the counter facing the coffeepot. It was definitely a happy sight for her.

"Good morning, Mrs. Ramsey," Eshe said cheerfully as she crossed the kitchen to her side. "How are you this morning?"

The last word had barely left Eshe's mouth when Mrs. Ramsey suddenly whirled from the counter, a carving knife flashing toward Eshe's throat. The sight was so unexpected, and frankly just so improbable, that she almost didn't get out of the way in time, but at the last moment her reflexes kicked in and Eshe leaped backward, feeling the breeze of the passing knife as it barely missed the tender skin of her throat.

"Okay. Not in a good mood today," Eshe muttered, backing away and noting that Mrs. Ramsey's face was as blank as a sheet of empty paper. Not in control of herself, then, she deduced. Realizing the woman was under control of someone else, Eshe instinctively started to glance around, but caught movement out of the corner of her eye and shot her gaze back to Mrs. Ramsey just in time to avoid another lunge by the grandmotherly woman.

"Whoa. You really don't want to do that," Eshe said, continuing to move away from her now. She then rolled her eyes at her own words. Mrs. Ramsey probably didn't want to do it, but couldn't prevent whoever was controlling her from making her do it. And that was going to make her have to hurt the woman to defend herself.

Frowning at the idea of hurting this dear woman, Eshe tried to push her way into the housekeeper's thoughts to make her stop as she moved toward her again, but whoever was controlling her had a firm grip on the woman's mind. She couldn't get in to free her, and instead had to leap back several feet as the carving knife came stabbing at her again.

Eshe bit her lip on a curse as she slammed up painfully against the opposite counter from where she'd first found the woman, and then dove to the side to get out of the way as Mrs. Ramsey kept coming. It didn't give her much respite. Mrs. Ramsey merely followed, but Eshe was getting tired of this game, and when the woman swung the knife again, instead of backing away or moving, she shot her hand out to catch her wrist, wincing but not letting go when the knife sliced into the skin of her arm.

"What the hell?" Armand was suddenly there beside her, taking over restraining the woman. He was shirtless and his face was like thunder as he asked, "What the hell is going on?"

"She's being controlled. Hold her," Eshe snapped and clasped her hand over her cut arm as she hurried past him. There were two windows in the kitchen, one over the sink looking out across the backyard, the other by the table overlooking the side yard, but the window by the kitchen sink was better positioned to see more of the kitchen, and when Eshe slammed out the back door onto the porch, she really expected to find the culprit who had been controlling Mrs. Ramsey there. She didn't, however, and cursed as she ran down the steps to hurry around the house, knowing that whoever it was would have seen her head outside and taken off right away.

As Eshe expected, when she turned the corner there

was no one in the side yard, but the bushes at the edge of the woods were still moving from his passage through them. Eshe started forward at once, intent on chasing the culprit, but she'd barely taken a couple of steps into the woods before she realized how foolish that would be. Coming to a halt, she peered around. The trees were old here and tall, their leafy branches blocking out the sunlight so that it was dark and there was no ground cover. All there was before her were dirt and tree trunks and an expectant silence that had the hair crawling on the back of her neck.

He was there somewhere, Eshe knew it, waiting, either behind one of the wide tree trunks or even up a tree in the branches overhead. Probably hoping she'd keep coming, maybe even holding his breath in expectation, and most definitely armed. Eshe just wasn't stupid enough to go traipsing where he wanted when she was injured, unarmed, and barely even dressed.

"Eshe?"

That shout from behind made her glance back the way she'd come. It was Armand, and it sounded like he was outside now. She hesitated, glanced forward again, but saw nothing, and when Armand shouted her name again, sounding closer, she began to move quickly backward for several feet before turning to hurry back out of the woods. Eshe was glad she had when she saw that he had hurried after her as barefoot as she in just his jeans and without even thinking to grab a weapon.

"Are you all right?" he asked worriedly, rushing toward her. "You're bleeding."

Eshe opened her mouth to assure him she was fine

and then paused and turned her head to the side to listen as she heard a vehicle engine start up somewhere on the other side of the woods. She briefly considered running up to the road to try to see it, but knew she'd never get there in time and turned back to Armand with a sigh. "I'm fine. Let's get inside and out of the sun."

Armand nodded, his gaze moving over the woods behind her and then to the road, but then he slid his arm protectively around her and hurried her across the yard, but heading for the front of the house rather than the back.

"What did you do with Mrs. Ramsey?" she asked as he opened the door for her to precede him into the house.

"She just suddenly collapsed. I left her in the kitchen," Armand muttered, ushering her up the hall and back into that room. He barely spared a glance for the woman on the floor as he urged Eshe toward the table. "Sit down. I'll get the first aid kit and some blood."

Eshe grimaced and removed her hand from her wound so she could get a look at it. There was a lot of blood running in trails away from the deep cut, but it was already stopping, the nanos repairing and healing her now.

"Don't bother with a first aid kit. A towel and blood will do," she said on a sigh. It would just be a waste of good bandages. It wouldn't take long for her arm to heal. Her gaze slid to Mrs. Ramsey and she sighed again as she took in her slack face. The woman would be confused and distraught when she woke, very distraught if whoever had controlled her had left her aware while doing it. It would mean she'd have to be wiped and sent away. But she was going to have to be sent away temporarily anyway, as would the new manager, if their culprit was going to start using them to do his handiwork.

"What happened?"

"What's going on?"

Eshe glanced around to see Bricker and Anders rushing into the room, both of them in only jeans, sleep still evident in their eyes. However, while Bricker was suffering a serious case of bed head, Anders's hair apparently didn't dare present itself so. Every short strand was in place. It figured, she thought, and then glanced to a half-naked Armand as he hurried to her side with a towel and several bags of blood. Here she was surrounded by beefcake and she simply wasn't in the mood to appreciate it. Didn't that just figure?

"What happened to Mrs. Ramsey?" Bricker asked with dismay as he spotted the woman on the floor and moved to check on her. It was Anders who first noticed Eshe's arm and asked, "What happened? I heard Armand shout."

"I'm not sure," Armand admitted when Eshe remained silent. He dropped the bags of blood on the table and began to wrap the towel around her arm as he said, "I woke up to find Eshe gone, came to find her, and Mrs. Ramsey was—" He shook his head, either not sure what the woman had been doing, or unable to even say it.

"I came down to get something to eat and someone

controlled Mrs. Ramsey and had her trying to slit my throat," Eshe said dryly when Anders glanced her way.

"What?" Bricker looked at her askance.

Eshe nodded her head, but when she opened her mouth to speak again, Armand brought one of the bags of blood into view, her fangs slid out, and he popped the bag on, silencing her.

"Feed now. Explanations after," he growled when she glared at him. Ignoring her then, he turned to glance at Mrs. Ramsey and told them, "Mrs. Ramsey had a knife, Eshe was cut and holding her wrist to keep her from stabbing at her again when I came into the room. I grabbed Mrs. Ramsey, and Eshe immediately rushed outside, probably to chase after whoever was doing the controlling. Mrs. Ramsey collapsed and I hurried outside after Eshe."

Anders spun on his heel, heading outside no doubt, but paused when Bricker said, "Don't bother. He's gone. She heard him drive away."

Eshe glanced his way with a start and then rolled her eyes when she saw he was concentrating on her face. He was reading her, of course, and probably enjoying being able to, she thought with annoyance, and mentally called him a little pissant when her thoughts made him smile. That just made him laugh, however, and Eshe sighed and shook her head, then glanced to Mrs. Ramsey when the woman gave a little moan and began to stir. Bricker had raised her upper body to rest against his chest rather than the floor and the woman took that in with surprise as she returned to consciousness.

"What happened?" she asked weakly.

"She doesn't remember a thing," Anders murmured quietly. "She was thinking of making coffee and then woke up on the floor or, as she's thinking, in this handsome young man's arms," he added with amusement.

"I'll take care of her," Bricker said quietly, helping the woman up. He led her from the room, his concentration on Mrs. Ramsey, no doubt calming her and rearranging her memories as they went.

Eshe watched them go, then tugged the finally empty bag from her teeth and murmured, "She can't come back until this is resolved. He might use her again."

When Anders raised his eyebrows and glanced in Armand's direction, he sighed wearily and nodded. "It's for the best. We'll have to send my new manager, Jim, away until this is over too."

"We'll handle it," Anders assured him, and slid from the room.

Armand handed Eshe another bag and sank onto the seat next to her. His face was troubled as he watched her pop the bag to her mouth and then he said, "They controlled Mrs. Ramsey because they didn't want to be recognized themselves."

Unable to speak, Eshe nodded. It was what she'd been thinking too.

"So it's someone I know," he continued, following the thought.

Eshe nodded again. She wasn't terribly surprised by this possibility. After all, strangers didn't usually fixate on a person for so many centuries without knowing them, but it seemed obvious that either Armand really hadn't thought that could be possible, or he'd just not wanted it to be and convinced himself it couldn't be, because he appeared to be staggered by the possibility and struggling to accept it.

"Who?" he asked finally, and there was a combination of pain and anger in his eyes as he peered at her.

Eshe pulled the now-empty second bag from her teeth and said, "We'll find them."

"When?" he asked, the anger and frustration in his eyes creeping into his voice.

"As soon as the boys come back we'll all get dressed and head over to John and Agnes's house," Eshe said quietly. "We'll break the door down if we have to, but we'll get in and talk to Agnes, then go to the Harcourts and do the same."

"What if talking to them doesn't get us any further than talking to the men did?" he asked quietly.

"Then we bait a trap," Eshe said quietly.

Armand's eyes narrowed. "What is the bait?"

When she merely stared at him silently, he shook his head.

"Not you," he said grimly. "I'll be the bait. I'd actually like to be. I want to confront this bastard."

"We'll talk about it after we've talked to Agnes and Mary," she said quietly. "I still think we'll learn something from them."

"Why?" Armand asked with a frown.

"Because Annie learned something somewhere so I know there's something to learn. We just have to figure out where she learned it and go there too."

"You think she spoke to Mary or Agnes?" Armand asked with surprise.

Eshe shrugged. "Or William or John. We didn't think to ask them if she'd been around to see them fifty years ago. But someone talked to her, and they said something that made her think she had the answers. We'll find those answers too," she assured him firmly.

"You sound so sure," he said almost enviously.

Eshe shrugged. "I told you I've been most fortunate in my life. I don't intend to let that change now."

Armand stared at Eshe silently, her words ringing in his ears. She had told him she'd had good fortune in her life because she'd met her first life mate, Orion, while young and enjoyed eight lovely centuries with him. And if you looked at it that way she *had* been fortunate, but now he looked at her and recalled other things. That she'd lost Orion, as well as two out of eight of her children. She had lost people she loved as he had, but Eshe didn't focus on that. Armand knew as surely as he knew himself that she had dearly loved her life mate and the two children she'd lost, and suffered those losses deeply, but Eshe chose not to linger there. She literally counted her blessings and saw herself as lucky to have the other people in her life and the other things that she considered blessings.

It was a matter of perspective, Armand acknowledged, and understood exactly why the nanos had put them together. He could learn from this woman. He could be happy with her. He could even love this woman. In fact, he suspected he already did. Eshe was strong and smart and didn't flinch in the face of adversity, but rolled up her sleeves and charged ahead to confront it . . . even in nothing but one of his shirts, he thought wryly, noting what she was wearing.

Leaning forward, he pressed his forehead to hers and whispered, "Eshe, I want to spend my life with you."

"Good," she whispered back. "That was the plan."

Smiling, he kissed her, a soft, gentle brushing of lips, and then pulled back intending to tell her he loved her, but paused and released her, sitting back in his seat as Bricker entered the room.

"I sent Mrs. Ramsey off with the thought that you two are on an extended pre-honeymoon and she is on the same extended paid leave and shouldn't return until you call her," Bricker announced, moving to the fridge to grab a bag of blood. He then glanced to Armand and said, "I hope you don't mind, but she depends on her pay from here and I didn't think she should suffer just because someone's trying to kill you and the people you care about."

"No, that's fine," Armand said quietly. He could afford it, and it was better than having her here to be controlled again. Next time the woman might have been hurt in a struggle, or even killed. He had enough deaths on his conscience as it was. And that wasn't even considering what could have happened to Eshe if the housekeeper, or the person controlling her, had gotten in a lucky stab. Armand just didn't want to think about that and was glad not to have to when Anders returned to the room now as well, garnering his attention.

"I've taken care of your manager," the enforcer announced, pausing just inside the door.

"Paid leave until I call him?" Armand asked, knowing it wasn't safe to have the manager there either. It seemed a shame to send him home to his family, though, even for just a week or so. He'd been pretty hyped about having his own place.

However, Anders shook his head and moved to the table to take one of the bags of blood Eshe hadn't yet consumed and said, "A weeklong all-expenses-paid trip to San Francisco."

"San Francisco?" Armand asked blankly.

"It's where he's always wanted to go," Anders said with a shrug, sitting down with the bag. "He's packing now. I called Lucian and he said he'd have to book the travel arrangements and charge it to you. He said he'd send a car for him within the hour."

"Right," Armand said with a shake of the head. "San Francisco."

"By the way," Anders added, tossing the gelatinous bag idly from one hand to the other and back, "he's the one who set the shed on fire."

"What?" Armand asked with shock.

Anders nodded. "He was controlled just like Mrs. Ramsey. The memories were veiled and hard to get to, but I found them."

Armand nodded. The memories wouldn't be readily available to Jim, though they might come to him in dreams. But since his mind had been controlled, all he would have were basically visual memories, like a movie he'd once seen. It was always harder to retrieve those than events the person had actually mindfully participated in.

"He blocked the door with a couple of shovels stuck into the ground," Anders announced. "Then he doused the shed with a can of gasoline and sparked a match. Whoosh." Anders grimaced. "It went up like kindling despite being a little damp still from the storm."

"Did he see who was controlling him at all?" Eshe asked.

Anders shook his head. "Just like Mrs. Ramsey, he didn't know what happened. His surface memory is watching television and then suddenly finding himself standing in his kitchen in muddy boots, not sure how they got muddy or why he was there."

"Like Nicholas," Bricker pointed out, making Armand's eyes slide sharply his way as he explained, "Nicholas's memories end with his crossing the parking lot, and then, bang, he was opening his eyes in his basement to find the dead mortal in his lap and blood everywhere."

"Nicholas couldn't have been controlled though," Anders pointed out. "That had to be due to his being drugged somehow."

"Hmm." Bricker nodded in agreement and then glanced to Armand and said, "You know, moving out Mrs. Ramsey and your manager doesn't stop whoever it is from grabbing someone in town, taking control, and making them do something."

Armand frowned at the suggestion, not having thought of it himself, but Eshe didn't seem surprised and said, "Which means we need to get this done and over with quickly before that can happen. I'm calling Mary and Agnes again. If I don't get an answer at the Maunsells', we head over anyway. We'll break the bloody door in if we have to, but we're definitely talking to them tonight."

"I'll call. You need more blood," Armand said firmly. He handed her another bag and then stood to move toward the house phone on the wall.

"Neither of you needs to call, they both called last night," Bricker announced.

"They did?" Armand asked with surprise, pausing halfway to the phone. He hadn't heard the phone ring, and glanced instinctively to Eshe in question, but she shook her head and admitted, "I didn't hear the phone."

"Well, you were probably . . . busy," Bricker said with amusement.

"Or in a post-busy faint," Anders suggested dryly, and then pointed out, "If fire burning you like broiled chicken doesn't wake you up, what makes you think a phone will?"

Armand noticed that Eshe didn't blush or look at all embarrassed. She merely shrugged and asked, "So when can we see them?"

"I took that call," Anders announced. "Agnes was available tonight. She said nine o'clock was best for her."

"What did you tell her we wanted to talk to her about?" Armand asked quietly.

"I just said you wanted to introduce her to your new life mate," Anders said. "I figured it was better not to give too much away until we get there."

Armand nodded and asked, "What about Mary Harcourt?"

Anders immediately turned a dry look to Bricker.

The younger immortal sighed and said, "I took that call. Mary was phoning from Montreal. It's their anniversary tomorrow and they apparently planned this trip well in advance. They arrived late last night and don't return until Saturday. She called home to check messages when they got into the hotel, though, and called here at once," Bricker explained, and then reluctantly admitted, "She asked that we wait until Sunday evening. She wanted a day to get settled back home. She's making Sunday dinner for all of us."

"Sunday dinner?" Eshe sounded stunned. "Bricker, we only have until next Tuesday to finish this."

"That gives us plenty of time then," he said quickly, and then added, "I considered telling her what it was about. That would have probably brought them right back; I mean their daughter was one of Armand's murdered wives and they would probably want to know she was murdered and gain justice too," he pointed out, and then grimaced and added apologetically, "But it seemed kind of crappy to ruin their special anniversary trip. She sounded really happy and excited about it. Besides, I wasn't sure either of you would approve. So I just thanked her and hung up," he admitted, and then when Eshe looked irritated added quickly, "I figured you could call the hotel in Montreal and try to convince her to come back sooner yourself if you wanted. Or even fly out there to talk to her in person if you felt we shouldn't wait."

Eshe glanced to him in question, and Armand sighed and scrubbed the short hairs on the back of his neck. The situation was critical, but he didn't really think they'd learn anything from Mary Harcourt. Armand was positive she would have mentioned if she knew anything about Althea's death that suggested it wasn't an accident or seemed even slightly off. In fact, he suspected she would have hunted down the culprit herself with a hatchet at the time. The woman had a mean streak when it came to anyone trying to hurt her children. He'd seen her in action when she thought anyone had just slighted her daughter when he and Althea had been married. Armand was positive she wouldn't have anything of use to tell them.

"Let's talk to Agnes first," he decided finally. "We can always call or go see Mary and William after if we have to."

Eshe nodded and slapped the bag of blood he'd given her earlier to her teeth. When her eyes then slid to the clock on the wall, his own followed, and Armand grimaced when he saw the time. It was barely three o'clock. They had hours to wait before they could go see Agnes.

Fifteen

"I'm thinking Agnes and John won't be expecting Anders and Bricker to be with us," Eshe said quietly, looking in the side mirror on the passenger side of the pickup to glance at the SUV following them. It was eight forty-five and they were on the way to their appointed visit to speak to Agnes. Eshe had suggested it might be better if Anders and Bricker waited at the house, but Armand had insisted they accompany them.

Now he shrugged and said, "They won't mind. I'll just say Anders and Bricker are guests at the house, which they are, and that I would have felt rude leaving them behind."

She saw him glance into the rearview mirror to peer at the SUV and then his gaze shifted back to the road as he added, "I feel better having them to watch our backs on the way there and home. I'm not taking a chance you'll be attacked again . . . or me," he added as an afterthought.

Eshe smiled with amusement, knowing he'd only added the "or me" to keep from angering her, and she teased him, "I'm glad you added the last part. I'd hate to think you didn't trust me to be able to look after myself."

"I'm sure you're very capable," Armand said a bit stiffly, and she wondered if that was a tell with him, if he got all stiff and proper when he told a lie.

"I am very capable," she assured him solemnly. "I have been training in battle since I was thirty. That's a long time. I can take care of myself."

Armand didn't bother to hide his surprise at this news as he glanced at her. "You have?"

"Yes."

He turned back to the road, his expression disgruntled. "How did Orion handle that?"

"I'm sure he was fine with it," Eshe said with amusement. "Especially since he's the one who insisted I learn to fend for myself and taught me how."

"Orion did?" Armand asked carefully.

"Yes." Eshe smiled faintly to herself at the memories that flooded over her. He'd taught her how to fight with spear, knife, sword and every other weapon as it had appeared in history before his death. Eshe's favorite lessons had been hand-to-hand, though. Those had always ended up with hot and sweaty lovemaking sessions. A fine way for life mates to end lessons.

Sighing, Eshe pushed those memories away, feeling

almost guilty for having enjoyed them when she had a new life mate. Blowing her breath out, she said, "Orion was a warrior. He was away a lot. He didn't want to have to worry about me being home alone and defenseless when he was away earning money . . . or worry about possibly coming home to a dead life mate."

"Smart man," Armand murmured wryly. "I wish I'd been half as smart and taught Susanna, Althea, and Rosamund a thing or two."

Eshe shrugged. "Different times, different places, different people. It's useless to regret things you didn't think of at the time. Everyone has a path and that wasn't theirs."

Armand cast her a curious glance. "Do you really think so?"

Eshe peered at him with surprise. "Don't you?"

Armand turned his attention back to the road and shook his head. "Life has seemed to be mostly painful chaos to me for a long time."

"Then perhaps you aren't looking clearly," she said quietly. "You're still inside the fishbowl looking out rather than standing beside it looking in."

"What do you mean?" he asked with obvious confusion.

Eshe shrugged. "When my first son died in battle, I thought it was the worst thing in the world that could happen and I would never be happy again. I felt the same when my second son died."

"He died in battle too?" Armand asked.

Eshe nodded, not surprised he'd guessed. There were few enough ways an immortal could die and most immortal males had died in battle through the ages, especially when the weapons of choice had been swords.

"Anyway," she murmured now, "with each son I thought the worst had come . . . and then my life mate, Orion, died. I knew that day that that was truly the worst thing in the world that could happen to me and I'd never be happy again. I'd never love again." Eshe sighed as she recalled those overwhelming feelings. For a while she'd wanted to die herself.

"I'm sorry," Armand murmured, reaching over to squeeze her hand. "I felt much the same when Susanna died."

She squeezed his hand back, and then as he retrieved it to return it to the steering wheel said, "I was in the fishbowl at that time. But with a little time, I began to see that if Orion had to die, the timing was the best I could ask for."

"Oh?" he asked quietly.

"Yes," she assured him solemnly. "I still had one daughter at home to comfort me, and my second son had just found his life mate and brought her home, so they were there as well . . . And Lucian brought Orion home."

"Lucian?" Armand gasped, tearing his eyes from the road. "He was there?"

She nodded. "It was one of his rare visits. He joined Orion for the battle, and when he was struck down, he hefted him over his shoulder and carried him home. He walked three nights to bring him to me. No one else would have done that. They would have burned his body with the rest of the fallen immortals and simply sent someone to tell me he was gone. But Lucian brought him home to me so that I could say good-bye and see to his cremation myself."

Armand was silent, and Eshe swallowed away the lump that had developed in her throat and forced a more cheerful tone as she said, "I made it through, though, and have enjoyed moments of happiness in the time since. And now I have you, another life mate to enjoy life with."

Armand took his hand from the steering wheel again, found hers and squeezed it gently, but then just as quickly had to replace it on the steering wheel as he turned into the Maunsells' driveway. Eshe immediately turned her attention to the house they were approaching.

Tonight was not like the other nights when Eshe had visited this farm. Tonight they were expected, and every light in the house appeared to be on, as well as several outside lights that lit up the grounds so that it almost seemed like daylight.

Eshe glanced over the house and yard as they drove up the driveway, and then to the car and van in evidence, and thought wryly that they should have called and made arrangements to meet with John and Agnes sooner. It would have saved them a lot of wasted trips out here.

Armand parked the pickup next to the van and then they both got out to wait as Anders pulled the SUV in next to them. They all then walked to the house in silence, Eshe squeezing Armand's hand when his bumped and then clasped hers.

This time there was no ringing the doorbell and

waiting hopefully; John Maunsell had apparently been watching for them and opened the door before they'd even reached it.

"Hello," he greeted them, smiling, his gaze sliding over Eshe and Armand, and then moving on to Bricker and Anders with slight surprise. "You brought company, I see."

"It seemed kinder than leaving them alone at the farm to fend for themselves. That's no way to treat houseguests," Armand said with wry apology, and then added, "I hope you don't mind?"

"No, of course not. You're all welcome. Come in." John smiled again, but Eshe thought it looked a little uncertain this time, which made her curious. However, when he backed into the house gesturing for them to enter and Armand urged her forward, she stepped inside and slipped past him to make room for the others.

"Go on into the living room there, Eshe," John murmured, still manning the door for Anders and Bricker to enter. "Agnes is in there knitting."

Eshe nodded and moved into the room he'd taken them to the last time she and Bricker had been there, her eyes curiously searching for the elusive Agnes. She spotted her at once, a slim brunette in a white blouse and black pants, seated in a rocker, rocking gently as she knitted. The woman must have heard them enter, but was slow to glance up, giving Eshe the chance to look her over.

Cedrick had described Agnes as a little thing who looked younger than most immortals, and Eshe thought his description was right on. She was slender and fine-boned and her features were almost gamine, making her appear eighteen or nineteen rather than the twenty-six or twenty-seven that most immortals looked to be. The fact that she wore her dark hair pulled back into a ponytail only added to the youthful appearance.

"Oh, hello." Agnes glanced up and beamed a smile as the men followed Eshe into the room. She set her knitting aside on a table beside the rocker and stood, offering apologetically, "Sorry, I was trying to get the row done. Otherwise I lose my count."

Eshe had never been a knitter herself, so hadn't a clue what she was talking about, but it sounded a plausible excuse, so she smiled easily. "That's all right. It gave me a chance to give you the once-over without you noticing."

Agnes laughed as she crossed the room toward them. "You must be Eshe. You're beautiful. And such honesty. I like you already."

Eshe's smile widened as she took the hand the woman offered. "It's nice to meet you, Agnes."

"And you too," she said warmly, and then turned to the men. Spotting Armand, she moved to him first, offering him a warm hug in greeting.

Eshe watched curiously, noting the affection on his face as he hugged the slip of a woman back, and then Agnes pulled away to turn her attention to the other two newcomers, asking, "And who is this?"

"This is Justin Bricker and Anders," Armand said. "They're my houseguests at the moment and I didn't feel it right to leave them at home so brought them along."

"Of course you did," Agnes said staunchly. "As you should. Welcome, gentlemen."

She offered her hand to first one and then the other and then moved back to peer over the group. "Well, I suppose refreshments are in order."

"Oh, I'm sure they won't be staying that long," John said, and Eshe's sharp eyes moved over him narrowly. The man appeared tense and nervous, his expression pained. He cleared his throat and then explained apologetically, "We don't have any mortal food here, Armand. We—"

"That's fine," Armand interrupted soothingly. "We ate before leaving the house anyway."

Eshe slid closer to him, catching his hand in hers and squeezing it hard to remind him of what he was supposed to do. She heard him release a little sigh, but then he forced a smile and said, "Actually, I'd be more interested in seeing the new John Deere you bought than refreshments. Cedrick mentioned it was delivered last week and I'm thinking of buying a new tractor myself so wouldn't mind a look at it."

"Oh." John looked nonplussed, his worried gaze moving to Agnes. "I— Maybe another time. The girls would be bored without us. I—"

"Don't be silly," Agnes trilled with a laugh. "Take them out and show them the tractor, John. Eshe and I can amuse ourselves on our own." She chuckled and added, "We'll just sit here and talk about you men. It's what women do, isn't it, Eshe?"

"A lot of the time, yes," she agreed with amusement, though she wasn't sure that was true. She and her usual partner, Mirabeau, often had better things to discuss when working together, but then as enforcers they weren't perhaps your average females, even for immortals.

"See?" Agnes turned back to John. "Go on. You boys go play with your new toy, and Eshe and I will wait here chatting."

John hesitated, but with everyone looking at him expectantly, he didn't have much choice. Mouth tightening, he nodded and turned to lead the men out of the house, leaving a vacuum of silence for a moment after the door clicked shut in the hall.

"Well," Agnes said after that moment passed. Giving a half laugh, she turned from watching the archway to the hall to meet Eshe's curious gaze and admitted, "I half expected him to come rushing back and insist we accompany them. John can be terribly protective. We're all each other has."

"You have Armand too," Eshe said quietly. "He seems to care about the two of you a great deal."

That made Agnes beam. "Yes, he does," she admitted, and then worry crowded into her features and she added, "I hope that doesn't bother you? I know it might be a little uncomfortable for you since we are Susanna's brother and sister."

"Not at all," Eshe assured her. "You're family, and I hope you'll come to think of me as family someday too."

Agnes let her breath out on a happy sigh and moved forward to clasp Eshe in a quick hug. "Oh, I just knew I would like you," she said happily, and then shifted to hug Eshe's arm as she urged her across the room toward another door and confided, "You're much nicer than Althea was. She wanted nothing to do with us."

"Is that why you and John went to Europe when they married?" Eshe asked curiously, glancing over the room Agnes was leading her into. It was a kitchen that looked as new as the house. Despite the fact that they didn't eat or drink mortal food, the room had been fitted with all the most modern conveniences. Eshe admired it briefly and then glanced curiously to Agnes as she answered the question.

"Yes, I'm afraid so. She wanted us gone. That's all right, though, I couldn't stand being around the girl," she admitted with open dislike, and then said, "You know she tricked Armand into getting her pregnant and pretty much forced him to marry her?"

"He did explain how the marriage came about," Eshe said carefully. "But he said he didn't mind."

"Of course he would say that," Agnes said, waving that away as unimportant. "He's far too polite to tell the truth about such things." She paused then, her grasp on Eshe easing as she added thoughtfully, "Of course he did get Thomas from the union and so I suppose it was worth it in the end." Shrugging, she let go of Eshe and asked, "Would you like something to drink?"

Agnes moved to the refrigerator as she asked the question, and opened the door to peruse its contents. "I know you and Armand are probably eating and drinking mortal food now that you've found each other, but as John mentioned, I'm afraid we don't have any of that ourselves." She clucked her tongue with irritation and added, "I suppose I should have run to town and bought some when I got up tonight, but I didn't think of it." Sighing, she bent to peer into the refrigerator and said, "But we do have a wide variety of bloods, if you'd like to choose one?"

When Agnes glanced her way in question, Eshe moved up beside her to peer into the refrigerator as well. Her eyes widened incredulously as she saw the marked specialty blood in the fridge. Most of it was blood she'd only ever seen in immortal nightclubs. There were a great deal of Wino Reds, but also Sweet Ecstasies, Bloody Marys, High Times, and all sorts that were concocted from blood taken from mortal alcoholics and drug users to allow the immortals to feel the buzz they couldn't through normal means. There was a small fortune's worth of it too. Such bloods were damned expensive. It seemed despite the fact that Armand had ordered that no one tell him, John had figured out how immortals could get intoxicated. Cedrick was obviously wrong, John was definitely drinking again, and she wondered if this was why John had been reluctant to leave them alone, if he'd feared Agnes revealing his secret . . . as she had.

"John buys them," Agnes said sadly. "I have tried to get him to stop but he won't. He takes several bags and sits in his room night after night just drinking himself into oblivion. It's no way to live really."

"Perhaps Armand can help him with that," Eshe murmured as she straightened, and in the next moment wondered how he could possibly do that. There were no rehab places for immortals. Yet, she thought dryly.

"Oh no, you mustn't tell Armand," Agnes said

quickly. "He'd just worry and feel bad. He's happy now. Let him be happy." She turned back to the fridge. "We have some normal blood too, if you like? But I won't tell if you would rather a Wino Red."

"No. Thank you," Eshe murmured. "I don't usually drink such things. I don't care for the sensations they cause."

Agnes closed the door and turned from the fridge to beam at her. "I'm glad. Althea liked to bite drunks whenever she went to town. Life was one big party to her. You seem much more suited to Armand." She breathed in happily and let her breath out on a gust, and added, "I'm so happy for Armand, I can't tell you. He's been so lonely for so long. I'm glad he's found you."

"Thank you," Eshe murmured, and then cognizant of her reason for being there, said, "But it hasn't been that long, a century perhaps."

"A century?" Agnes peered at her with wide eyes. "Why, Susanna died over five hundred years ago."

"Yes, but then he had Althea and then Rosamund," she pointed out.

"Oh, them." Agnes waved her hand with disgust. "As I said, Althea wasn't suitable for him. She was nothing but a sneaky whore, and Rosa—"

"Whore?" Eshe interrupted with surprise.

Agnes grimaced. "I suppose you're surprised to hear me use the word. Armand probably told you I was a nun before the turn, and I know I really shouldn't use such vulgarities, but it's what she was. Althea had scads of affairs on Armand, you know."

Eshe did know, at least Armand had told her he suspected as much, but she merely raised her eyebrows in question to encourage Agnes to continue.

"She did," Agnes assured her. "While he was out working so hard tilling the soil, she would ride into London and pick up a man and then either go to his place or even sometimes bring him back to the farm and have sex with him. She was no better than an animal," Agnes said with disgust, and then added staunchly, "Armand deserved better. I wasn't sorry when she died."

"And Rosamund?" Eshe asked.

Agnes shrugged and said reluctantly, "She was all right, I suppose. But she was always nosing in everyone's business. Besides, neither of them were true life mates to Armand. They were just . . ." She shrugged again and said, "His way to pass the time, I guess. He wanted children, you see. Armand was always a good father."

Eshe raised her eyebrows. "I understood he only raised Nicholas, and sent Thomas and Jeanne Louise to Marguerite to raise."

"He didn't want to do that," Agnes assured her. "But he was a man alone and working the fields." She shook her head sadly. "You don't know how often I wish we'd been here so he wouldn't have sent Thomas away. But I know he visited Thomas as often as he could. He used to stop in and tell us all about it on his way home."

"I understand you helped raise Nicholas," Eshe said quietly. "Armand said he didn't know what he'd have done if you hadn't been there. He said you were wonderful with him."

"Yes." She smiled, pleased. "I did help him raise Nicholas. Nicky was a good boy. He always did what he was told and never fussed about eating his vegetables. And he was a fast learner too. He was walking by one, talking in sentences by two, and feeding on his own by the time he was four. He was a brilliant baby."

Eshe smiled faintly at the proud bragging. She'd done a bit of it herself at times in the past and Agnes was talking like a mother rather than an aunt, but then she'd raised the boy and was more a mother to him than anyone. "Did you ever meet Nicholas's Annie?"

"Oh yes." Agnes's smile began to fade and she turned to lead the way back into the living room. "He brought her down to meet me before they married and then a couple times after. She's a sweet girl." She paused at the rocker and sank unhappily into it before adding, "I don't know why but he hasn't brought her around in a while. It's been . . . why, it must be more than fifty years," Agnes complained, and then shook her head with bewilderment. "We had such a nice time the last time they stayed too. They were here for a weekend and we played games and talked till the wee hours. It was nice, like a real family."

Eshe had just seated herself on the sofa, but stiffened and stared at her blankly. "You don't know why he hasn't returned?"

Agnes shook her head. "I've tried calling but the line was disconnected and I can't find a new listing for them. John says they're probably busy, but surely Nicky could at least take a moment to call?" She bit her lip unhappily. "They always say it's better to have girls than boys, that boys abandon their mothers when they find a wife, and I guess it's true."

Eshe simply stared, unsure what to do. Part of her wanted to tell the woman exactly why Nicholas hadn't brought his Annie back around, why he hadn't been back himself even, but the fact that no one, including Armand, had apparently told her what had become of the couple made her hold her tongue. There must be a reason, and she intended to discover that reason as soon as they left here.

"Do you have any children, Eshe?" Agnes asked suddenly.

Eshe regathered her thoughts and nodded. "Yes. Six."

"Boys or girls or both?" Agnes asked.

"Three boys and three girls," Eshe answered automatically.

"You're lucky then. You have the girls to keep you company when the boys abandon you."

Eshe hesitated, but then said, "You'll meet a life mate someday, Agnes, and have children of your own."

"No. I'm quite sure I won't," Agnes said quietly. "John would never allow that."

Eshe frowned at her words, but before she could ask anything or comment, they heard the front door open and the sound of the men trooping back in. Eshe glanced to the door as John led the men into the living room. She couldn't help but notice he had an anxious look on his face until he spotted them seated there.

"Well, that was fast," Agnes commented lightly.

"John isn't feeling well and insisted on returning," Armand murmured, his gaze on Eshe in what she took to be a silent message that they'd done what they could to keep him away as long as possible.

She shifted her attention to John, one eyebrow arching dubiously. Immortals simply didn't feel unwell. They didn't get sick.

"I'm afraid I haven't been feeding as regularly as I should," John murmured, avoiding her gaze. "I guess I need to pay more attention to that and less playing on the computer. As for tonight, I think I'll just have a bag or two and retire early."

That brought even more of a dubious expression to her face. It was only nine-thirty; that wasn't retiring early, that was sleeping their version of a mortal day away. But she knew she wasn't likely to learn much more from Agnes with her brother there, so took John's not so subtle hint and stood. "Then we should be leaving."

"Oh no," Agnes almost moaned. "But I was enjoying our visit so much. And I thought we could all play cards or something."

"Next time," Eshe assured her sincerely, smiling at the woman. "We will have you and John over to the house and you can plan to stay the night. That way if John isn't feeling well he can simply go to his room to lie down and the rest of us can all play cards and visit as late as we like."

"Really?" Agnes asked, standing up, and when Eshe nodded, she crossed the room to give her a quick hug as she said, "Oh, I'd like that."

"So would I," Eshe said.

"Oh, Armand!" Agnes whirled away to embrace him now. "I do like her. You were ever so clever to find her."

Armand actually chuckled as he hugged her back. "I'm glad, Agnes. I like her too."

"Oh you!" Agnes pulled back to slap his chest playfully in reprimand. "Ever the man of understatement. You don't just like her, Armand. I can read your thoughts. You love her."

Eshe stilled at those words, a little startled by them, though she didn't know why. They were life mates; love came naturally and easily between life mates. However, she'd been preoccupied by other matters such as the case and the great sex life mates enjoyed and hadn't given a thought to love developing between them.

Her gaze slid to Armand to find his expression solemn as he met her gaze and said, "Yes, I do love her."

Sixteen

'So did you learn anything from Agnes?'

Eshe gave a start of surprise at that question from Bricker as she stepped out of the pickup. Anders and Bricker had led the way home in the SUV, with them following in the pickup, and she'd spent the ride silent, her mind replaying that moment in her head when Armand had said he loved her in front of everyone. She'd quite forgotten all about Agnes and their conversation.

"Let's talk inside," Armand said quietly, coming around the truck to take her arm and urge her toward the house.

Eshe noticed the way the men suddenly nodded and glanced warily around and realized they were worried that whoever had controlled Mrs. Ramsey that morning might be there somewhere watching them. She allowed herself to be ushered into the house, her curious gaze sliding repeatedly to Armand as they went. He'd been silent on the ride home as well, and she now found herself wondering what he'd been thinking. It was hard to tell from his expression. He appeared to be in a solemn mood now.

"Should I put coffee on?" Bricker asked as they entered the kitchen. "And maybe some coffee cake or something? I think I saw some in the refrigerator after your shopping expedition."

"I didn't know whether it needed refrigerating or not," Armand explained as he ushered Eshe to the table, and then he added, "It looked good. I'll have some."

"Me too," Eshe murmured, settling in a chair at the table.

"None for me," Anders said drolly, and Bricker snorted and said, "Like I couldn't guess that."

Eshe smiled faintly. Most immortals stopped eating around one hundred and fifty or two hundred years old. Bricker was still young enough that he ate, but Anders was much older and no longer bothered. He stuck with bagged blood as most unmated mortals did. As she had before coming here and meeting Armand.

"So?" Armand said quietly as he settled on the chair next to hers. "Did you learn anything useful?"

Eshe considered the question and wasn't sure how to answer, but finally said, "I learned a lot. I just don't think any of it helps much with the case."

"Tell," Bricker said as he stuck the coffeepot under the sink to fill it with water. "We'll sort out if it's useful after."

"Well," she said slowly. "We didn't get a chance to

discuss Susanna's death at all, or any of the deaths really. But she did say Althea was . . . er . . . well, you were right, she was having affairs on you and Agnes knew it."

Armand merely nodded, neither surprised nor upset, so Eshe continued, "That and the fact that Althea wanted nothing to do with Agnes and John and apparently made that plain to them is the real reason why they went to Europe."

That did upset him, she noticed. He frowned with displeasure at the knowledge that Althea might have driven John and Agnes from his home, from *their* home.

"What about Rosamund?" Bricker asked, finished with the coffee and now retrieving plates and forks for the coffee cake. "Did she say anything about her?"

"Just that she was nice enough but nosy," Eshe recalled.

"I wouldn't say Rosamund was nosy," Armand said slowly. "She liked to talk a lot and was inquisitive, but . . ." He shrugged.

"Did you ask about Annie?" Anders asked.

Eshe scowled as she nodded. "Yes. Nicholas brought Annie down three times; once before the wedding and twice after. I guess they spent the weekend the last time and it was a lovely visit. Agnes said they played games and talked till the wee hours."

"But Annie never came down herself?" Bricker asked, and then added, "I doubt she would have been asking about the deaths of Armand's wives in front of Nicholas. He had no idea what she was wanting to tell him."

"No, I gather Agnes only met her the three times.

And," she added grimly, turning narrowed eyes on Armand, "why the hell has no one told her that Annie is dead and Nicholas is on the run?"

"What?" he asked with surprise.

Eshe nodded. "Agnes has no idea. She thinks Nicholas has just abandoned her or something and is completely bewildered as to why he wouldn't bring Annie back and visit again when they had such a nice time the last time they were down."

Armand stared at her with what appeared to be honest amazement, and then said, "John told me not to bring it up around Agnes, that it was an upsetting subject to her. He said not to even mention Nicholas or Annie to her."

"Well, John has apparently told her nothing," she said grimly. "He's just said they are probably busy to explain why they haven't been around for *fifty* years."

Armand cursed under his breath and shook his head. "Agnes loves that boy like a son. She'd understand his not visiting if she knew he couldn't because he was on the run, but leaving her to think he just can't be bothered . . ." He shook his head again. "I don't know what the hell John is thinking of."

"Probably his next bag of High Times," Eshe said dryly, bringing startled looks from all three men. "I suspect that's the real reason John 'wasn't feeling well' and wanted to 'rest.' The refrigerator there is full from top to bottom with Wino Reds, High Times, and various other intoxicating bloods. Agnes showed me but asked me not to tell you. She said you're happy now and would just worry, and to let you be happy. She's apparently tried to get him to stop but he won't listen." She clucked with disgust. "No doubt he's cuddled up with a couple of bags right now, sucking them back and getting high in that soundproofed basement of his."

Armand sat back with another curse, his hands clenching as he growled, "He always was a damned fool."

Eshe didn't comment. She didn't know what to think of John Maunsell. He'd seemed a sad but mostly nice guy when she and Bricker had talked to him. However, what she'd learned tonight had been disturbing.

"There was one other thing Agnes said that bothered me," she announced abruptly.

"What's that?" Armand asked at once.

"I said something about her finding a life mate someday and having children, but she said she was quite sure that would never happen. She said, and I'm quoting here, 'John would never allow that.' "

"John would never *allow* it?" Armand repeated with disbelief. "What the hell does that mean?"

Eshe shrugged. "It threw me too, but I didn't get the chance to ask. You guys came back before I could."

They were all silent for a moment, the only sound the hum of the microwave as Bricker warmed the coffee cake. When the humming stopped and a little ding sounded, Armand shifted in his seat and said wearily, "I see what you mean about learning a lot but nothing pertaining to the case."

Anders commented, "This information casts John in a more unfavorable light."

"But it doesn't change the fact that he wouldn't have killed Susanna and couldn't have killed Althea."

"I suppose," he admitted with a frown, and then his lips twisted with irritation. "Which leaves us again at square one."

"Which leaves us with Mary Harcourt," Eshe corrected. "Annie had to have talked to someone."

Armand grimaced, obviously displeased with the idea of bothering the woman on an anniversary trip, but said, "Very well. I guess we'll have to talk to her."

Eshe nodded and glanced to Bricker. "Which hotel did she say they were staying in?"

Bricker stiffened, his back to them as he cut the cake, but then he turned slowly, dismay on his face.

"You didn't get the hotel they were staying in," Eshe guessed grimly.

"I'll find out," Bricker said at once. As Anders began to chuckle, and Eshe dropped her head in her hands with disgust, he vowed, "I'll call every hotel in Montreal until I find the one they're at . . . In the meantime, I have cake for you," he added, hurrying over to slip a plate with a large slice of coffee cake between her elbows where they rested on the table.

Eshe opened her eyes and peered through her fingers at the cake suddenly beneath her nose. It smelled good. It looked good too, she acknowledged, but she wasn't quite ready to forgive Bricker until Armand slid his hand over her back and pointed out, "They probably aren't in right now anyway. They're probably out taking in plays or dancing or something. Bricker will find out what hotel they are staying in and we can call closer to dawn when they're likely to be in."

Eshe lifted her head and accepted the fork Bricker

held out to her with a sigh. "Right. Cake now. Call later."

"And coffee," Bricker said, spinning around to rush back and begin pouring three cups.

"Okay then," Anders said, standing up. "If you guys are going to stuff your faces again, I'm going to go see if there are any old *Lassie* reruns on television."

Bricker watched him go as he carried a tray with coffees and more cake on it to the table and then commented, "He's missing Jo's dog."

"Jo's dog?" Armand asked uncertainly.

"Nicholas's new life mate Jo has a German shepherd named Charlie," Eshe murmured. "The dog was with them when they were first on the run."

"We caught up to them at one point and managed to catch Charlie, but Jo and Nicholas got away," Bricker added. "We took Charlie back to the enforcer house with us and he took a shining to Anders, started following him everywhere, so he's been looking after him. But Anders had to leave him with his housekeeper when he came down here." Bricker shrugged. "I think he's got attached to the mutt and is missing him."

"He can't be all bad if he likes dogs," Armand commented. Accepting a slice of cake and a coffee from Bricker, he murmured, "Thank you."

"Do you like dogs?" Eshe asked curiously.

"Oh yeah," Armand said, and smiled. "I've had several of them. My last one died about two years ago. I've been meaning to get another, but . . ." He shrugged, and then asked, "Do you like dogs?"

"Yes, but I can't have them in my apartment," Eshe said with a grimace.

"Then we'll have to live somewhere else," Armand said with a shrug.

Eshe stilled and peered at him. It was the first time he'd spoken of a future together beyond the two weeks she'd originally been slated to stay.

"What?" he asked, cutting into his cake with his fork. "You thought I was letting you get away after this is over?"

"Before Lucian left you were trying to send me away," she pointed out.

"I was being self-sacrificing," Armand said wryly. "But you win. I'm going to be selfish as hell and hold on to you now."

Eshe grinned. "I think I like you when you're selfish as hell."

"You'll like me better naked and selfish as hell," he assured her roughly, reaching out to draw her nearer so he could kiss her. Before their lips could meet, however, a forkful of cake appeared between them. Eshe and Armand turned as one to peer at Bricker.

"Food now. Crazy monkey sex after," he admonished. "I went to a lot of trouble to warm this up and make coffee. You are not letting it go to waste."

Eshe chuckled at his words and turned her attention to the cake and coffee, but her toes were curled inside her boots and she was very aware of Armand beside her. She couldn't help but think it would be nice when all this was over and they could just be together without worrying about murder and saving Nicholas. But they had time for that, she assured herself. A very long time if they were lucky.

* * *

Eshe woke to the sound of someone hammering on the door and shouting for them to wake up. Rolling over in bed with a groan, she glared at the clock on the bedside table, her bleary eyes widening with disbelief when she saw that it was only nine A.M.

"For God's sake," she muttered, turning her glare to the door, and then frowned and sniffed as she smelled something cooking. Not cooking, she realized. Burning. It was at about that time she made out that Bricker was yelling, "Fire! Wake up!"

Before she could react, he gave up pounding and burst into the room. Eshe blinked at the sight of Bricker in just a pair of boxers, and then glanced to Armand as he stirred beside her.

"Aren't you listening?" Bricker roared with frustration. "The house is on fire. Get up!"

Armand was apparently much faster at becoming awake and alert. While she was just starting to look around for something to put on, he was already rolling out of bed.

"Where's Anders?" he barked, tossing Eshe his shirt and then snatching up his jeans to yank them on.

Eshe glanced to Bricker as he whirled and hurried out of the room to wake the other man and then quickly slid the shirt up her arms and got out of bed as she did it up. The shirt was short, stopping just below her butt cheeks, and Eshe picked up her own jeans then, intending to pull them on, but Armand came around the bed and caught her hand, dragging her toward the door before she could.

Eshe clutched the jeans to her chest and scampered to keep up as they hurried out of the room. They met Anders and Bricker in the hall. Like Armand, Anders had pulled on jeans, and now led the way toward the stairs, but came to an abrupt halt once he got there. Armand moved up beside him, pulling Eshe with him as he peered down into the inferno that was the first floor.

"Christ," he muttered, and then whirled and began to drag her back toward his room.

"Bricker, grab some blood from the closet while I get this window open," he ordered, moving straight to the window beside the bed.

"Blood?" Bricker asked blankly, running a hand through his disheveled hair.

"In case one of us twists or breaks an ankle jumping off the porch," Armand explained patiently as he raised the window and set to work on the screen. "Houses don't burn this quickly. The fire must have been set. If the culprit is still out there I don't want anyone injured and unable to defend themselves for any longer than necessary."

"Right." Bricker turned and hurried into the walk-in closet.

Eshe shifted her bare feet on the hardwood floor. "The floor is hot."

Armand nodded as he got the screen free and pitched it away from the house. He peered out, but then paused and cursed.

"What is it?" Eshe asked, squeezing up next to him to peer out. She saw at once what the problem was.

"The back porch is ablaze," he growled. "We can't go this way."

Eshe glanced over the burning porch roof and sighed, knowing he was right. It could collapse beneath them and leave them in an inferno of flames.

"The front porch probably will be too," Anders muttered as Armand turned away from the window. "The window in my room looks out on the side yard, though. It might be our best bet."

Armand nodded and ushered Eshe ahead of him toward the door to the hall.

"Where are we going?" Bricker asked. Arms cuddling several bags of blood to his chest as he came out of the closet, he hurried to meet them at the door.

"The porch is on fire. We're going to try Anders's room," Eshe explained, taking a couple of bags from him so he wouldn't drop them.

Nodding, Bricker slid out of the room and led the way up the hall to Anders's door. The smoke in the hall was thick now, smothering, and they were all coughing by the time they reached it. The heat was beginning to be unbearable as well.

"This'll do," Armand decided after tugging the blackout curtain open and peering outside. He yanked the curtains right off their rod and tossed them across the room, and then shoved the window up, and pretty much just punched the screen out this time, sending it flying outward. The moment that was done, he glanced her way and said, "Eshe, come here."

She moved forward at once, still holding her jeans

and the blood, but he took them from her and urged her to the window.

"Jump away from the house if you can, and roll when you land. The flames are licking the outside of the first floor and your shirt might catch fire."

Eshe nodded and started to climb onto the windowsill, but she'd barely gotten one leg over it when he caught her arm, saying, "Maybe Anders, Bricker, or I should go first."

Recalling that he'd wanted the blood in case the culprit was out there, she knew exactly why he suddenly wanted one of them to go first. Clucking with exasperation, Eshe reminded him, "I'm an enforcer. I'll be fine."

She then tugged her arm free, lifted her second leg over the windowsill, and pushed out with her hands, shoving herself away from the house as much as she could. She landed with a grunt, but without twisting or breaking an ankle, and then dropped and rolled just to be sure she hadn't caught fire. She heard a thud to her right on her third roll and knew it was one of the men following her. Stopping her roll, she got quickly to her feet and then jumped back out of the way as Bricker rolled toward her. Eshe then glanced up to the window in time to see Anders pushing himself out of the window.

Her gaze slid to Armand, a frown claiming her lips when she saw him framed in the window, the blood bags all now gathered to his chest.

"Bricker, keep an eye out for our firebug," she ordered, then stepped closer to the house and held out her hands. "Throw them to me and get out of there."

Armand tossed the first bag at once, the others

quickly followed, and Eshe ended up letting some drop to the ground after catching them so that she could catch the next. She was relieved when he finished tossing the last one, until he suddenly disappeared from the window altogether.

"Armand?" she yelled uncertainly.

"Where the hell did he go?" Anders said, moving to her side. "The fire was licking through the floor when I jumped. He needs to get out of there."

Eshe just shook her head and watched helplessly. She had no idea where the big idiot had gone, but if he didn't return and climb out within the next moment, she was going in after him, she thought grimly, and then sighed with relief when he appeared again and finally climbed onto the windowsill and pushed himself off.

"There's no sign of our firebug," Bricker said quietly, moving to collect the bags she'd let drop.

Eshe merely nodded. She hadn't expected the coward to stick around. For all they knew, he'd taken control of someone and had them start the fire while he watched from a safe distance, she thought with disgust as she moved to help Armand to his feet and check to be sure he was okay.

He stood up easily, uninjured by the jump, and smiled at her crookedly before turning to look at his house.

Eshe sighed and turned to peer at it too, knowing it must be hard for him to watch all his personal possession going up in flames. She was already missing the few she had here; her pants, for instance. But Armand was losing much more, including those portraits and photo albums in his desk.

"I'm sorry," she said quietly, slipping her hands into his.

"It's just a house. We can build another," he murmured, but he sounded weary.

She squeezed his hand and then said, "We should really get out of the sun. You have your choice of the SUV or the woods."

"The SUV," Armand murmured, and then turned away from the house to walk with her toward the vehicle.

"Problem," Anders announced, following. "It's locked and the keys are—"

"In my hand," Armand said, raising his hand and opening his fingers so that the set of keys dangled between his thumb and forefinger. "I saw them on the dresser and grabbed them before I climbed out."

That explained his brief disappearance, Eshe realized, and while it had given her a scary moment, she was glad he'd thought of snatching up those keys. She suspected it wouldn't have been comfortable sitting in the woods without pants on.

Armand handed Anders the keys and he immediately hit the unlock button. They piled into the SUV, Eshe and Armand in the back, Anders and Bricker in the front.

"It's a good thing you woke up, Bricker," Eshe murmured as they watched the fire devour the house.

"I didn't," he admitted grimly, and when she glanced at him with surprise, he explained. "I was up calling hotels until about an hour ago. By the way, they're at the Sofitel," he said, and then continued, "It was of course the last hotel I called. I went to bed after I found that out, but couldn't sleep. I was just dosing off when I smelled smoke."

Eshe smiled wryly and then glanced at Armand and murmured, "See what I mean about the fishbowl?" When he peered back blankly, she pointed out, "I was upset that he forgot to get the name of the hotel when I found out, but in the end it saved our lives."

Armand nodded slowly, his gaze sliding back to the fire.

"What do we do now?" Bricker asked.

Armand opened his mouth to answer and then paused and glanced out the window as the sound of a fire engine suddenly whooped in the distance. They couldn't see it through the trees, but he sighed and turned back. "I guess I should wait here for them," he said reluctantly. "But you three can—"

"I'm not leaving you alone here," Eshe interrupted firmly. "The firebug could still be around."

"We'll all stay," Anders decided.

Satisfied with that, Eshe sat back to wait for the firemen to arrive.

Seventeen

Eshe raised an eyebrow in question when Armand left the firemen gathered in front of his still-smoldering house and headed over to rejoin them by the SUV. It was after four. They'd been sitting in the SUV for most of the afternoon, unable to leave with the fire trucks blocking their vehicle.

"They say it was arson," Armand said dryly as he paused at her side.

"Big surprise," Bricker muttered with disgust.

Armand nodded. "There's nothing more we can do around here, though, and they said we could go."

"Go where?" Anders asked wryly. "Not that run-down motel by the diner? None of us has money."

"I have other farms," Armand said, ushering Eshe toward his pickup. "Follow me in the SUV."

"Do you have keys to the pickup?" Eshe asked with concern as he opened the passenger door for her. It wasn't locked, but then she'd noticed Armand didn't seem to bother much about locks out here. She watched as he paused and felt in his back pocket, and smiled wryly when he pulled out his keys.

"I forgot to take them out last night before you yanked my clothes off and had your way with me," he teased lightly.

"Ha ha," Eshe muttered, climbing up into the pickup. She heard Armand chuckle as he pushed the door closed, and then he hurried around to his side. As he got in, she asked, "Where are we going?"

Armand hesitated. "I considered seeing if we could stay with Agnes and John, their place is bigger, but they'll be sleeping and wouldn't hear the doorbell, so we'll go stay with Cedrick until I figure something else out. I don't like pulling him into it, but it's better than involving one of my mortal managers."

Eshe nodded. She'd liked Cedrick, and he looked like a guy who could handle himself. Besides, at least they'd know he couldn't be controlled and made to attack one of them.

They were silent on the drive over, both of them tired and no doubt fretting over this latest attack. At least Eshe was. It seemed to her that the culprit was getting desperate and desperate meant more dangerous, but it hadn't gotten them any closer to figuring out who he was.

Once they got to the farm Cedrick was managing, Armand made her and the boys wait in the vehicles to avoid standing out in the sun while he went and rousted Cedrick from his bed. The door must have been unlocked, because while he knocked, he also then simply opened the door and entered. He was gone a good ten minutes or more, and Eshe supposed he was explaining everything to Cedrick, which only seemed fair. She wouldn't have had him dragged into the situation blind. It was a hot day, though, and stifling in the pickup. Eshe was relieved when Armand appeared at the front door and waved at them to come in.

"This place reminds me of Armand's," Bricker commented as they met at the front of the vehicles to start toward the house.

"It *is* Armand's," Anders pointed out. "Cedrick just runs it for him."

"You know what I mean," Bricker said with irritation. "It's an old Victorian like his and got the trees around it and everything. It's got heart."

Eshe knew what he meant. John and Agnes had a lovely home, but she preferred the trees and gabled houses. Armand obviously did too.

Armand was waiting to greet them in the entry with a concerned-looking Cedrick at his side. Everyone murmured greetings, and then Cedrick led them upstairs to the bedrooms. This house was laid out much the same as Armand's, but as he'd said, smaller. There were only three bedrooms; Cedrick's room and two guest rooms, which meant Eshe and Armand would share one, and the boys had to bunk together in the other. After showing them the guest bedrooms, Cedrick turned to them and grimaced apologetically as he took in what clothes they'd managed to escape in and the soot covering their faces as well as whatever skin was on display.

"You men can borrow joggers or something from

me," he announced, and then glanced to Eshe and said, "My housekeeper is live-in. She has an apartment over the garage. She probably has something you can wear, Eshe. It'll do until you can buy something else. But we only have the one bathroom here in the house itself and you'll have to take turns." He paused and glanced around the group again and then announced, "Ladies first, of course. You boys can fight over who goes next. Follow me, Eshe, and I'll show you where things are."

When Bricker and Anders groaned at being left sooty for a while longer, Eshe found her first smile since waking up to a house on fire and flashed it at the two of them as she followed Cedrick past them. Sometimes it paid to be the only girl.

"The towels and washcloths are in the cupboard under the sink," Cedrick said pausing to the side of the door to the bathroom so that she could slip past him. "There's soap and shampoo on the tub, you're welcome to it."

"Thank you," she murmured, entering the room decorated in pale blue.

"I'll go see if my housekeeper has anything she can let you wear. I'll set it on the floor outside the door here for you to find," he finished, and then pulled the door closed before she could thank him again.

Sighing, Eshe turned to peer at the room, pausing when she caught sight of herself in the mirror. Her hair was standing on end as if she'd been electrified; there were dark streaks on her face, throat, and legs from the fire; and the white shirt she wore was done up crookedly, one button off, making it look not only ridiculous but even more risqué than it would have been if done up properly. Basically, she was a mess.

Chuckling softly, she turned from the mirror and moved to the tub to open the shower curtain and reach the taps. Within seconds she had a nice steady stream of water coming from the showerhead. Eshe was just undoing Armand's shirt when someone knocked at the door.

Eyebrows rising, she moved to open it and found Armand on the other side, a bundle of clothes in hand with a pair of sandals on top.

"I brought these up for you," he explained, holding them out. "The housekeeper's about your size, believe it or not, so they should fit."

Eshe smiled wryly at his words as she took the bundle of clothes. She was tall for a woman, and lean. It was rare to find someone her size.

"Thank you," she murmured, turning to cross to the counter and set them down. She heard the door close as she did, and assumed Armand had left, so took a moment to examine the booty he'd brought her. A pair of ratty old jeans, faded and with holes in them, and a T-shirt with the dubious logo "Save a tractor, ride a farmer" on it.

"Cute," she said dryly.

"What's that?" Armand said, and Eshe nearly jumped out of her skin with surprise. Whirling, she found he'd entered before closing the door and was now stripped down to just his soot stains.

She let her gaze slide lazily over all that revealed skin and then arched an eyebrow and asked, "Trying to jump the line?"

"It would conserve water if we showered together," he pointed out with a grin, and when she merely stared at him, added, "I could scrub your back for you."

Eshe set down the T-shirt, whipped off his borrowed shirt, and stepped over the lip of the tub and under the spray. When he immediately followed, she warned, "You're only touching my back. I am so not waking up tangled with you in the bottom of this tub with Bricker and Anders pounding at the door."

"Party pooper," he teased, picking up the soap.

Armand behaved himself and was done and out before her. Eshe took a little more time, washing and rinsing her hair before following to find him already dried and dressed. He kissed her as she stepped out of the shower, and then moved to the door, saying, "I'll go see if there's any coffee on."

Eshe nodded and quickly dried and dressed herself, surprised to find that the clothes fit all right. The jeans were a little tight, but a pretty good fit considering they were borrowed. She'd expected Anders and Bricker to be waiting impatiently, but there was no one waiting in the hall when she opened the bathroom door.

Shrugging, she headed downstairs and found Anders and Bricker there. "Where are Armand and Cedrick?" she asked as she moved to the coffeepot to pour herself a cup.

"Cedrick left right after getting some clothes for all of us. He had to go check on one of the other farms or something," Anders said with a shrug.

Bricker then added, "And Armand went over to John's. He called just as Armand came downstairs and asked if he'd come help him with a new cow that seems to be ailing."

"And he went?" she asked with a frown.

Bricker shrugged. "John and Agnes were in Europe when Althea died. It should be safe enough. I offered to go with him, but he said he wanted to talk to John about his drinking and it would be better if he was alone."

"Right," Eshe muttered, thinking that was probably true. Noting the way Bricker was suddenly digging in his pocket, she watched curiously as he pulled out a set of keys and set them on the counter beside Anders.

"The keys to the SUV," he explained, and then moving toward the door, he said, "I'm going for my shower."

"You won the coin toss for who gets to shower first, huh?" Eshe asked lightly, bringing him to a halt.

"Nah. Cedrick's housekeeper is taking me into town to do some shopping after, so Anders said I could go first. I'm picking up clothes and whatever personal stuff everyone wants. You can come too, or just write your clothing size and what you want on that sheet of paper on the table and we'll pick up what we can."

Eshe glanced toward the sheet of paper as he continued out of the room, noting the items already listed beside Anders's and Armand's names. It was written in the same hand; Bricker's, she'd guess. She sat down with her coffee, picked up the pen, and scrawled her clothing sizes and a couple of items, and then glanced around wondering if there was anything to eat.

"The housekeeper, Jean is her name by the way, said there were some scones under that plate cover thing there," Anders told her as she stood up. "She said there was butter on the table, I'm guessing in that glass cow."

Eshe glanced back to the table, smiling faintly when she saw the cow butter dish.

"So what's our next move going to be?" Anders asked as she found a plate in the cupboard and lifted the cover off the plate on the counter to retrieve a scone.

"I'm going to call Mary Harcourt in Montreal," Eshe said quietly, and turned from the counter in time to see him nod. She was glad he didn't protest, but hadn't expected him to. Anders wasn't all that sentimental, and things had gone far enough that the possibility of upsetting Mary on her anniversary didn't seem that important. Besides, she'd approach the subject as carefully as she could. Eshe wouldn't intentionally upset the woman.

Anders settled at the table across from her and kept her company while he waited for the shower to be free. Eshe had finished, gotten herself a second coffee, and dialed the hotel where the Harcourts were staying in Montreal when Bricker came bounding down the stairs to announce the shower was free and grab the paper off the table. He gave her a nod and wave when he noted her on the phone, then turned and hurried back out of the room.

Anders followed, no doubt headed for the shower, and Eshe turned and glanced out the window as she heard Bricker talking to someone. She spotted the tall redhead walking with him toward a van and smiled faintly to herself, suspecting by the way the young woman was laughing that she was soon to be one of his conquests, but her smile faded as the phone was picked up on the other end of the line.

Getting her mind back on business, Eshe asked for the Harcourts' room and then waited, half expecting she wouldn't get any answer or that she'd be put through to a voice mail system. It was after five, but still early for their kind, and they were likely to be sleeping, which meant they'd probably have asked for their calls to be redirected. It was something of a surprise when the phone was picked up on the second ring by a female.

"Mary Harcourt?" she asked uncertainly.

"Yes. Who's this?" the woman said cheerfully.

"This is Eshe d'Aureus. I'm . . ."

"You're Armand's life mate." The woman laughed when she hesitated about how to introduce herself. "I passed you on the way out the night you came and talked to William. He told me all about it. Did that fellow Justin tell you I've invited you all to Sunday dinner?"

"Yes, thank you," Eshe murmured, beginning to feel bad about having to make this call. But knowing it was necessary, she opened her mouth to ask the first question and then changed it to "Is William there?"

"Yes, but I'm afraid he's in the shower. We have an early reservation for a dinner. We're going to a play afterward. Is it important?"

"Actually, no, that's all right. Don't disturb him," she said quickly. She'd only asked that to be sure the woman was alone and would speak freely to her. "Mary, I really wanted to ask you a couple things."

"I see." Some of the good cheer left her voice, replaced with uncertainty.

Eshe hesitated, debating what to ask first, but finally decided to try to stay away from asking her about the night Althea died if she could. Hoping that talking about Annie would be less upsetting, she asked, "Did you ever meet Annie?"

"Nicholas's Annie?" Mary asked, sounding uncertain.

"Yes. We understand she was asking questions about Armand's wives before she died, and wondered if she'd approached you?" There was a long pause, long enough that Eshe was sure the answer was yes and the woman was debating telling the truth, so she murmured, "It's important."

A long sigh slid along the phone line. "Yes, I did meet her. It was accidental really. I was taking something over to Armand for my William and she was there knocking on the door. She introduced herself when I walked up to the porch and explained she was looking to meet her new father-in-law, and I told her he was probably back at the barn or out in the field."

Eshe frowned at this news. Armand had said he'd never met her. "Did she go looking for him?"

"No," Mary murmured, and then hesitated before admitting, "We got talking and then she suddenly rushed to her car, got in, and roared off."

Eshe stiffened, the hairs on the back of her neck prickling. She just knew this was the puzzle piece that would make everything else make sense. "What did you say just before she rushed off, Mary?"

"I . . . I don't recall," she mumbled.

"It's important, Mary," she said firmly. When a stubborn silence reigned from the other end of the line, Eshe tsked with irritation and pulled out the big guns. "I'm a Council enforcer, Mary. I'm here on Council business, and whatever you told Annie pertains to that."

"I don't see how," Mary said, sounding more annoyed than impressed, but then a long sigh sounded down the phone and she said, "Annie was asking a lot of questions about Althea and Armand's other wives. But at the end, the conversation circled back to Althea and how she really disliked Agnes and John. Althea thought they were a pair of leeches taking advantage of Armand's good nature when their sister died. She thought they should have moved out centuries earlier, and her first order of business after they married was to convince Agnes and John to move out. She succeeded and they went to Europe, but she was always afraid they'd come back and pop up like a pair of bad pennies. Althea was becoming obsessed with the idea, to the point that the night we rode into Toronto, she actually thought she saw Agnes and was positive they'd returned and were going to spoil everything she'd managed to achieve."

"Althea saw Agnes?" Eshe asked sharply.

"No, of course she didn't," Mary said firmly. "Agnes and John were in Europe. Everyone knew that. I'm sure she just imagined it or saw someone who looked like her, but it managed to upset Althea enough that she said she couldn't sleep and was going to go for a walk before bed."

"Why didn't William tell me about this?" Eshe asked with a frown.

"Oh, William doesn't know. Althea didn't say anything until I went to collect Thomas from her room. Thomas preferred her to give him his bath, so after we checked in, she took him to her room to bathe him while William and I settled in our rooms, and then I went to collect him. When I arrived, Thomas was sitting in a tub of cold water while Althea paced the room like a caged tiger and kept glancing out the window raving about having seen Agnes as we rode in. I tried to tell her she was mistaken and reminded her that Agnes and John were in Europe, but she wouldn't listen. She never did once she got something in her head," Mary added with exasperation, and it made Eshe think of Althea's being positive that Armand was her life mate because she couldn't read him, and not believing anyone when they tried to tell her she couldn't read him because he was older than she was. It seemed obvious her mother had thought this was another similar case of Althea believing what she wanted to.

"Althea was a bit high-strung," Mary admitted reluctantly, and then rushed on, "It was always best to humor her when she got like that, so I let her have a good rant about it all, and then agreed with some relief that she should go for a walk before bed. Then I took Thomas to our room . . . Of course I've regretted that ever since. William didn't know this, but I know Althea sometimes bit drunken mortals. She said it was only when she was having trouble sleeping, but . . ." There was another unhappy sigh. "Ever since the fire, I've suspected she did so that night too and then went back to her room, and knocked over the lantern as she passed out on her bed."

"Thank you, Mary," Eshe said gently when she fell silent. "You've helped a great deal."

"How?" Mary asked almost plaintively. "Why was Annie so excited about this? And what are you investigating?"

Eshe hesitated, but then shook her head and said, "How about I tell you that at Sunday dinner? I might have more news for you then."

"All right," Mary agreed reluctantly.

"Have a lovely anniversary," Eshe said sincerely, and hung up to immediately begin pacing Cedrick's small kitchen.

While Mary was sure Althea had imagined seeing Agnes, Eshe didn't immediately take the same view. If she *had* seen Agnes, then it meant Agnes and John had returned from Europe earlier than everyone believed, or they'd never left . . . which eliminated their alibi and meant they'd been around for every death. They'd been at the castle when Susanna died, as well as in Toronto the night Althea died, and there had never been any question that they lived in the area when Rosamund and Annie died. And they were certainly here now, able to have caused the fire at the shed, and then the house burning. It was that being-in-Europe business that had taken them off the suspect list, but if Althea really had seen them, then it put them right back on it. Actually, it made them the only suspects, she acknowledged, and then stopped pacing as she realized that Armand was presently out there at John and Agnes's alone.

Eshe turned slowly and peered out the window, staring at the lowering sun. It wasn't nightfall yet. From what she knew about the pair they were never up and about this early and should have been tucked up in their soundproofed basement. She'd assumed John had a day manager as Armand did, and yet he was up today and Armand was out there helping with a sick cow. She hadn't seen any cows at the Maunsell farm.

Cursing, Eshe snatched up the SUV keys Bricker had set on the counter and hurried out of the house.

"I'm surprised you're starting into livestock," Armand commented as he got out of the pickup and walked to meet John in front of his van. His gaze slid over the farm John had led him to. It was quite a distance from the farm where John and Agnes presently lived, and it would have been less of a drive for Armand had John just told Armand to meet him there and given Armand the address. Instead, John had waited for Armand at the main farm and then led him there in his van.

Armand pursed his lips as he peered over the building, another modern ranch house with outbuildings. There were several barns, and he wondered which one held the ailing cow.

"I thought it was time to diversify," John muttered, heading for the house rather than the barns. "I just want to check on something before we go see the cow. Come take a look around."

Armand nodded and followed him to the house, waiting as John unlocked the door and then preceding him inside when John gestured him to.

"I need to check the size and kind of the breakers here. Some of the lights don't work. I think the breakers are burned out and need to know what kind I need to buy," John murmured, following him up the hall as Armand walked along peering into empty rooms. "The basement door is your next on the right."

Armand opened the door and flipped the switch, relieved when a light turned on. He didn't fancy trying to navigate an unknown set of stairs and a basement in pitch dark. Immortals had excellent night vision, but they needed at least a little light to work with and the basement had looked like a great black hole when he'd opened the door.

"Are you going to get any other animals?" Armand asked as he started down the stairs.

"No, just the cow for now," John answered. "I'm working into it gradually."

Armand nodded, and then sighed and brought up the subject he felt he should most approach while here. As he stepped off the last step, he said, "John, Agnes showed Eshe your blood collection when we were over the other night. I think we should talk about it."

There was a heavy sigh from behind him and Armand started to turn to face him, and then grunted with surprise as something slammed into his head. He felt himself falling and reached out instinctively to break his fall, coming to a halt on his hands and knees, but then gave a little moan and collapsed into the waiting darkness as he was hit again.

Eighteen

It was full dark by the time Eshe reached the Maunsell house. As usual the lights were all off, and Eshe's heart sank at the sight. Not sure what else to do, she pulled into the driveway anyway, glad she had when she spotted Agnes just opening the driver's side door of the little yellow car parked by the house. The woman paused and glanced toward the SUV with curiosity, unable to see who was driving through the tinted windows.

Eshe parked and slid out to move around the SUV toward Agnes, managing a weak smile in response to the broad one that graced Agnes's face when she recognized her.

"Eshe," Agnes greeted happily, getting out to meet and hug her. "What a lovely surprise. How are you?"

"Fine," she murmured, automatically hugging the smaller woman back as she glanced around. There was no sign of the van or Armand's pickup and all the barn doors were closed. Forcing a smile, as Agnes stepped back she asked, "Where are John and Armand?"

Agnes's eyebrows rose in surprise. "I imagine John's visiting one of the other farms but I have no idea where Armand is. Was he coming here?"

"Yes, John called and asked him to come take a look at a new dairy cow he's just got. He thought she was ailing."

Agnes frowned. "We don't have any cows. Johnny says they're stupid and useless. We only do agriculture."

"He said he just got it. Perhaps it's at one of the other farms," Eshe suggested, but her heart was sinking again as Agnes shook her head.

"Armand must have misunderstood. The farms are all jointly owned. We both have to sign the checks for purchases and we definitely haven't purchased a cow."

Eshe closed her eyes, just knowing she'd been right . . . which meant Armand was in trouble. Forcing herself to breathe slowly, she tried to calm down and think. After a moment, she said, "Agnes, I need to know if Johnny has someplace he goes alone at times. Somewhere no one else would know to find him."

Agnes tilted her head and asked quietly, "What's happening, Eshe?"

She met her gaze and then asked abruptly, "Were you in Europe when Althea died or here in Canada?"

"We went to Europe after Althea and Armand married," Agnes said evasively. "I told you that."

"Yes, but were you still there at the time of the fire in the hotel?" Eshe asked insistently.

Agnes frowned. "Why are you asking me this?"

"You were here, weren't you?" Eshe said, sure it was true, and then cursed and paced away a few steps before whirling back. "John called and told Armand he had a sick cow he needed help with. If there's no cow, then he's lured him out for another reason, and I think that reason is so he can kill him."

Agnes appeared taken aback by the words and began to shake her head at once. "John wouldn't hurt Armand. He gave us a home for centuries even though Susanna was dead. He treated us like family. He *is* family." She shook her head firmly. "He'd never hurt Armand."

"Well, someone has tried to kill us three times. They locked both Armand and me in the shed and set it on fire and then controlled the housekeeper and had her attack me, and then last night the house was set on fire while we slept. Someone is trying to kill us and I think it's John."

"Why would Johnny—"

"Because we were looking into all the accidents and deaths that have happened around Armand, starting with Susanna's death," she interrupted, knowing it was urgent they get moving quickly.

"Oh dear," Agnes breathed, and then asked almost plaintively, "Why would you do that?"

"To save Nicholas," she answered at once.

"Nicholas?" Agnes blanched. "What's happened to Nicholas?"

Eshe shifted impatiently; they really didn't have time for this. "I need to find Armand, Agnes. Please, think, is there anywhere—"

"Tell me what's happened to Nicholas first," she snapped, showing an unexpected temper.

Eshe paused, but then said, "Annie was murdered fifty years ago and Nicholas was framed for the murder of a mortal. He's been on the run ever since. That's why they haven't been back to visit you."

"Annie murdered?" she whispered with dismay. "But why?"

"Because she was looking into the deaths of Armand's wives."

"Why would she do that?" Agnes cried unhappily.

Eshe shrugged. "I guess she was hoping to find out what had happened in the hopes of getting Armand back in the family for Nicholas's sake. She loved him."

"Of course she did . . . Poor Nicholas, he loved little Annie dearly," she said on a sigh and then asked, "And you say Nicholas was framed for murder?"

Eshe nodded. "We think it was to prevent his looking into what Annie was investigating. He would have been executed if he'd been caught," she pointed out. "Instead, he ran and has been rogue for fifty years. That's why he never visited again and you couldn't reach him." She allowed her a minute to take that in, and then added, "I was sent to see if I could find out what had happened . . . If I can't, they'll execute Nicholas," she added grimly even though she didn't think that was true anymore. After everything they'd learned and all that had gone on here, she didn't really think Lucian would execute Nicholas for a murder they were almost positive he hadn't committed, but she wanted to motivate Agnes.

"The poor boy," Agnes moaned, and then whispered, "Oh, Johnny, what have you done?"

"He's murdered four immortal women, one mortal woman, framed the nephew who is like a son to you, and tried to kill Armand and me repeatedly," Eshe snapped impatiently. "Now he has Armand somewhere, and if we don't find him, he might very well kill him too. So where could he take him, Agnes? Please, think."

Agnes looked torn for a moment, and then sighed and turned to move back to her car.

"Get in," she ordered as she slid behind the wheel.

Eshe didn't hesitate but hurried around the car to the passenger's side and slid in. Judging by the surprise on Agnes's face, the woman hadn't really expected her to obey her order, but Eshe would have walked into hell to drag Armand out. She loved the man, he was her life mate, and she would go wherever the woman said if it would take her to him.

"You have an idea where they might be?" she asked.

"Yes," Agnes said quietly as she started the car and sent it shooting up the driveway. "We haven't purchased a cow, but did buy a new farm a couple months ago. We only got possession last week. Johnny has been interviewing managers for it, but hasn't hired anyone yet. It's the perfect place. No one would be there."

Eshe nodded. That sounded like a likely place to kill someone.

"Why did Armand never tell me about Nicholas and Annie?" Agnes asked, anger in her voice.

"He thought you knew," Eshe told her. "John said

not to bring up the subject around you because it upset you. Armand only found out you didn't know when I told him after our visit the other night." She paused and then admitted, "I wanted to tell you then, but I thought I should talk to Armand first. I didn't know if there was a good reason you hadn't been told."

"Oh, there was a good reason," Agnes said grimly. "Johnny knew I'd never forgive him if I'd found out about Annie and Nicholas." Her mouth tight, she added, "Rosamund was one thing. She was nosy and wasn't a life mate to Armand anyway, but Annie was Nicholas's life mate. She was family and such a sweet girl. And Nicholas . . ." She shook her head grimly. "He never should have hurt Nicholas."

"You knew he killed Rosamund?" Eshe asked carefully.

"Yes. He told me, of course. It gave him something to hold over my head. 'I killed Rosamund for you, blah blah blah,'" she said with disgust, and then cast a dry glance at Eshe. "You don't know how many times he's hammered me over the head with that. He uses it every time we have an argument. I ask him to do something for me he doesn't want to do, and it's 'Haven't I done enough already? I killed Rosamund for you.' I try to get him to stop drinking, and he blames it on me and trying to forget killing Rosamund for me."

"Why would his killing Rosamund be for you?" Eshe asked slowly, afraid she already knew the answer.

Agnes shook her head and heaved out a long sigh, then glanced to her with regret. "Please don't think less of me for this, but John killed Rosamund because she was apparently snooping around about Susanna and Althea's deaths and he was afraid she'd figure out that I killed them."

Armand opened his eyes slowly, at first only aware of the agony in his head and the cramping in his body. He'd sustained a bad head injury and his nanos had used up a lot of blood repairing what damage they could, but he obviously needed more blood for them to finish the job properly or his head wouldn't hurt. The cramping was an indication that he needed that blood for more than just repairing his head.

He came to that conclusion and then became aware of other things. That he was in a brightly lit room with a cement floor. That he was seated on some sort of crate, and that his hands were tied behind his back, which wouldn't be a problem were he at normal strength. Armand could have snapped the ropes with just a quick jerking apart of his wrists then, but he definitely wasn't at normal strength.

He lifted his head to peer around at exactly where he was and paused as he spotted the man lounging on his own crate across the narrow room from him.

"Johnny." The name was a disappointed sigh on his lips.

"I've been waiting here for quite a while for you to wake up," John said quietly.

Armand eyed him silently. John sat with his legs stretched and crossed at the ankles, his upper body leaning back against the wall with arms folded over his chest. His pose suggested he had indeed been waiting a while, but he unfolded his arms and reached down to pick up a bottle of water, and then stood and unscrewed the cap as he brought it to him.

Armand drank when he pressed the bottle to his lips. It was warm, but it was wet and eased the dryness in his mouth. What Armand really needed was blood, but he was pretty sure at that point that Johnny wouldn't bring that to him.

"Why wait?" he asked when Johnny took the bottle away. "Why didn't you just kill me right away?"

Shrugging, John set the bottle down beside him and walked back to his crate. "I wanted to apologize and explain before I kill you. So you'd understand."

"Nice," Armand said bitterly, and then arched an eyebrow. "So, I'm guessing you killed Susanna, Althea, Rosamund, and Annie, as well as framed Nicholas for that mortal's murder?"

"No."

Armand blinked in surprise. "No?"

"I only killed Rosamund and Annie, and framed Nicholas," he explained.

Armand considered that and then asked, "Why?"

Johnny sighed and grimaced. "To protect Agnes."

"From wh—" Eyes widened with realization. "*She* killed Susanna and Althea?"

He nodded solemnly.

Armand stared at him blankly for a minute, finding that hard to believe, and then said, "I know she didn't like Althea, but why would she have killed Susanna? Susanna was her sire."

"Basically, that's why," Johnny said wryly and then

rubbed the back of his neck and said, "Really it was all my fault."

Armand sank back in his seat as Johnny told him what had happened all those years ago.

"Susanna was your sire, Agnes. She was your sister, she loved you. Why would you have killed her?"

Agnes heaved out a deep breath and shook her head before admitting, "I was pretty screwed up back then."

Eshe sank back in her seat with disbelief. "That's your answer? You were pretty screwed up?"

"Well, it's the truth," she said helplessly, and then shook her head and said, "You have to understand, I was a nun, Eshe. A bride of God. I was very religious."

Eshe recalled Cedrick saying that Johnny's betrothed had been very religious and it had made her unable to accept what Johnny had become. She'd thought him demon spawn and would have run off to tell her father and have him appear with an army of soldiers bearing stakes and torches. She supposed being a nun, Agnes would have been even more religious than Johnny's betrothed, and that might have made it hard to accept what she'd become. But then why had she allowed Susanna to turn her?

"I didn't allow it," Agnes said grimly, obviously reading her thoughts. "I was happy at the convent, I was born to it. No one cared there that my face was pockmarked from a childhood illness, no one cared that I was a little clumsy. They accepted me as I was. I blossomed as a nun."

"And then you got sick," Eshe said quietly.

Agnes nodded, and admitted wryly, "I felt horrible every day, worse and worse. But that was okay too. I was going to be with my God. And the sisters all wept for me and prayed by my bed for me to get better, and everyone fussed and tried to cheer me, and they gave me the choicest bits of meat to try to build my strength." She let her breath out on a little sigh. "But then Susanna arrived, beautiful Susanna with her big smiles and easy charm and her fairy-tale romance with Armand. Everyone fussed over her then. They all whispered to her in the corner, telling her how ill I was. And then she sent them all away and came to me and started to tell me the most fantastical tale. Armand was an immortal. He had made her one and she could make me one too and save me."

Agnes's mouth twisted bitterly. "I didn't believe her at first, but then she showed me her fangs and I was terrified. I told her no, to let me be, I was going to be with my God, but Susanna always did what she wanted and just went ahead and did it anyway," she said with irritation. "She ripped open her own arm with her fangs and pressed it to my mouth, and when I refused to swallow, she pinched my nose closed so that I had no choice."

"I'm sorry, Agnes," Eshe said quietly, and meant it. "Susanna shouldn't have done that. We are never supposed to turn one who does not wish it."

Agnes didn't acknowledge hearing her by word or deed, but simply continued. "And then the pain started. It was like I was being burned up and eaten alive at the same time. And the nightmares . . ." She shuddered even now at the memories. "I thought I'd died and gone to hell."

Eshe peered away out the window and silently cursed Susanna. There had been no drugs back then to ease the turn, and to inflict it on someone who did not wish it was just cruel.

"And then I woke up to find my teeth sunk into the abbess's neck," Agnes continued quietly. "And Susanna was there cooing soothing words and running her fingers through my hair as I drained the poor woman's life away."

"She let you feed on the abbess unto death?" Eshe asked with horror. It had always been frowned on to feed on any sort of religious figure, but feeding on any mortal until he died just wasn't allowed anywhere anytime.

"No," Agnes said on a sigh. "But I didn't know it at the time. When the abbess began to sag, I released her and Susanna brought another nun for me to feed on and then another. I didn't want to bite them, but I was in so much pain, I couldn't resist . . . I thought I killed all of them until we left and Susanna assured me I hadn't." She ground her teeth together and added, "I will never forgive her for making me feed on them. They were nuns, my sisters, blessed virgin brides of God."

Eshe sighed. From what she could tell, while Susanna's heart had been in the right place and she'd only wanted to save her sister, she'd done absolutely everything the wrong way.

"When I next opened my eyes it was like waking

from a nightmare into a perfect dream," Agnes said quietly, much of the anger gone from her voice.

"How so?" Eshe asked curiously.

"I felt wonderful," she said simply, and then added, "I felt strong and healthy again, and my skin was perfect. The pocks that had always marked me were gone. My hair shone in the hand mirror Susanna held before me," She smiled slightly at the memory and admitted, "I didn't even mind when Susanna said I'd have to leave the convent. She gave me one of her dresses to wear. It was a little large, but the most beautiful thing I'd ever worn and I felt pretty in it. We rode out the moment the sun had set."

"The next month was wonderful. Armand welcomed me and assured me I would always be welcome in his home, and Susanna threw balls and invited anyone close enough to come. She taught me to hunt and to feed and . . ." Agnes gave a little sigh. "I did miss the sunlight some, but the night was ours, and I was no longer ever afraid to go anywhere without a man to protect me. I felt free."

"What changed that?" Eshe asked quietly.

"Johnny came," she said, her smile fading. "The family had heard that I'd left the convent and Father sent Johnny to find out why. Armand handled him mostly. I realize now he controlled his mind and calmed him, and it was a nice visit until the night he fell off his horse."

"Cedrick said you turned Johnny to save him."

"Yes," Agnes admitted. "I wasn't sure I should. He was unconscious and I couldn't ask him if he wished it, but Susanna kept badgering me to do it, to save him as she'd saved me. And Johnny had always been my favorite. In the end, I did it . . . and everything changed," she added bitterly.

"Oh, it was all right at first. He was pleased to be alive and well when he woke, and the three of us ran the night and laughed so much while he was there. But then he went to see his Elizabeth. He had to have his Elizabeth."

"His betrothed?" Eshe asked. Cedrick had never mentioned the woman's name. When Agnes nodded, she murmured, "Cedrick said she didn't take it well."

"No, she didn't," Agnes agreed. "She spurned him and said some awful things. Johnny was devastated. He was miserable and surly with everyone, but mostly with me. And he kept going down to the village and drinking gallons of ale trying to drink himself to oblivion. Armand had told him it wouldn't work anymore, but he tried . . . and tried . . . and tried," she added wryly and shook her head. "I knew he blamed me for turning him but he never said as much and I tried to be patient and simply wait, hoping it would pass. But months went by and he got no better. I felt like I was forever walking on eggshells waiting for his next outburst of temper. Armand tried to cheer him, but nothing worked. I started regretting turning him, and wishing I'd just let him die. And then I started wishing Susanna had let me die. Then he would never have come, never have broken his neck . . . I'd have been with God, and he with his Elizabeth."

Eshe could hear the despair and depression in her

voice and knew it must have been a hundred times worse at the time.

"And then Susanna had little Nicholas," Agnes said, cheering a little. "Everyone was happy. Johnny even stopped going down to the village to drink, and smiled once or twice. Nicholas was such a beautiful baby. Armand rode off to court and the three of us fussed over the baby. It was almost like it had been right after Johnny was turned . . . and then Marguerite and Jean Claude arrived."

When she paused briefly, Eshe glanced at her curiously, wondering why that visit would have put an end to what had sounded like healing to her.

"It was one little comment," she explained quietly. "A compliment, in fact. As she was saying her good-byes, Marguerite beamed at both Johnny and me, took one of our hands in each of hers, and said, 'You are both wonderful with Nicholas. Susanna is lucky to have you. You'll both make wonderful parents when you have children of your own.' "

Agnes pressed her lips together, her eyes on the road ahead. "I just laughed and said thank you. I didn't realize what effect it had had on Johnny until they were gone and Susanna had gone back inside with Nicholas. I turned to comment to Johnny on how nice the visit had been, and he snarled that he was heading to the village. I had kept my peace on that subject for months, but it had been such a lovely week since Nicholas was born, I just couldn't do it that time. I followed him to the stables, begging him not to go to the village, to come help with Nicholas, it would make him feel better."

"Why, he snapped. So he could see what he would never have? And then he just exploded on me. He had lost his love. He would never have the children they were meant to have. There would never be a life mate for him. We were all soulless devils. I'd fed on nuns, for God's sake. I was the devil's minion and had made him one too. He hated me for it and would never forgive me. Just seeing me made him sick." She paused and turned to arch an eyebrow at Eshe. "You get the idea."

"Yes, I do," Eshe said quietly. Johnny had vomited all his disappointment and frustration on Agnes and no doubt made her feel awful in turn. Eshe seriously disliked people who did that. It was her experience that there were different kinds of people in the world; those who got kicked by life and kicked back, those who were kicked and turned to kick someone else, and those who were kicked and kicked themselves for it. She admired those who kicked back, and could live with those who kicked themselves, but Eshe had no time for those who were kicked and turned around and kicked someone else. It was abuse, and they were abusers, and Johnny had abused Agnes that day in the stables. Unfortunately, already knowing the story, she knew that Agnes had then turned and taken Johnny's abuse of her out on Susanna, and in a much more deadly fashion.

"Yes, I did," she admitted with regret, reading her thoughts again. "When Johnny stormed out I just collapsed in a corner of the stables and wept. I was convinced I was a monster. That I'd ruined his life, and my own was ruined too. We had knives then that served as both weapons and eating utensils that we wore in a scabbard from our belt."

"I remember," Eshe murmured.

"Yes, I suppose you do," Agnes said. "Anyway, I had taken mine out and slit my wrists, but much to my consternation the wounds simply began to close up. It seemed I couldn't even kill myself . . . which infuriated me. Unfortunately, that's when Susanna found me in the stables. She came rushing to kneel beside me, asking what was wrong, and . . . I just exploded. I slashed out at her with the knife and struck her across the throat. She didn't even grab for the wound, she just stared at me, stricken, her blood gushing everywhere, and then I was suddenly on her, stabbing over and over until it stopped hurting."

Eshe assumed Agnes meant until she herself stopped hurting emotionally and not until Susanna stopped hurting. She doubted stabbing someone over and over made their pain stop. Well, when they died it would, she supposed.

"And then I just sat there beside her for a minute, horrified by what I'd done," Agnes continued, not bothering to comment on her thoughts this time. "And then of course I panicked as I realized that Armand would hate me, I'd probably be burned alive for my sins . . . and that's when I thought of fire. It's cleansing. It would hide my sins."

"And you set the stables on fire," she said quietly.

Agnes nodded.

They were both silent for a minute, and then Eshe asked, "And Althea?"

"Oh, Althea." Saying the very name made her mouth twist with disgust. "I don't feel the least bad about killing her. She really was a horrid woman. A spoiled rotten little brat with no thought for anyone but herself and what she wanted."

"Did you ever go to Europe?" Eshe asked.

"Oh yes. We went through France, and Germany and Spain and then finally to England. I thought we could handle it, but that brought back a lot of bad memories. The convent was nothing but a pile of rock when we went there, and Johnny wept for days after visiting Elizabeth's old home and seeing her tomb."

"Why on earth would you go to either place?" Eshe asked with dismay. "You must both be masochists."

"I wondered that myself afterward, but it seemed like a good idea at the time. It just depressed us, though, and made us both long to be back in Canada. So we took a boat back and arrived in Toronto and tried to decide what to do. Should we buy a farm near Armand, or farther away to avoid Althea? That was the big question. We'd been in Toronto about a week when a carriage went riding past us and I glanced up and found myself staring at Althea. She'd seen me too, of course, and I turned to find Johnny but he had stepped into a bar." Her mouth tightened. "He'd learned by then that while drinking the alcohol yourself does not work for us, biting a mortal who had would, and he had begun buying mortals drinks, purely with the intention of then drinking from them.

"I left him to it and followed the carriage to the hotel they booked into, and then waited around out front for Althea to slip away." She glanced to Eshe and said dryly, "I knew she wouldn't be able to resist slipping away to find some man to screw or bite. It was the big city and she was a hedonist."

Agnes turned her gaze back to the road. "I didn't have long to wait. I had positioned myself at the front corner of the hotel so I could watch the front, but also see the alley behind the hotel should she slip out that way, and she did. I followed her, watched her stop to chat up one man, lead him to an alley, and bite him as he screwed her up against the wall. I thought she'd head back then, but she was apparently still hungry. She did the same with three more men before returning to the hotel." Agnes paused and frowned. "Now that I think about it, I think she definitely had a problem. What do they call it? Nymphomania?"

"I believe so," Eshe murmured, thinking Agnes might be right. Biting four men in a night wasn't surprising, but having sex with each one was a bit much.

"Anyway, I followed her back to the hotel when she finally returned there and then trailed her inside and up to her room. I really simply wanted to try to make peace with her. Johnny and I both missed Armand. He was the only family we had, and we wanted to remain family with him. And we wanted it to be easier for Nicholas to visit as well, which was always uncomfortable around Althea. I thought if I explained that to her, perhaps we could come to some sort of agreement where we were at least civil with each other."

"She wasn't amenable?" Eshe suggested dryly. Althea wasn't sounding like someone who cared about other peoples' needs much.

Agnes snorted. "The moment she opened the door, she started spewing the most vile things at me. We were leeches. Armand wasn't our family, he was hers. We should crawl back under the rock we'd come from, or better yet, crawl into Susanna's grave with her. Yada yada yada." She scowled out the windshield and added, "Basically she pissed me off royally."

"It always surprises me when you use such modern terms," Eshe said with wry amusement.

Agnes shrugged. "I watch television."

For some reason that made Eshe laugh, which brought a smile to Agnes's face, and then the other woman glanced to her with an expression that was almost sad and said, "I really do like you Eshe. It's a shame our friendship will be so short."

That gave Eshe pause, but then Agnes continued with her tale. "As I say, she pissed me off and I do have something of a temper when pushed too far. I didn't really think, I just whipped out my knife and had at her."

"You were still carrying a knife with you?" Eshe asked with surprise.

"I always have a knife with me," Agnes assured her. "You never know when it will come in handy."

"Right," Eshe murmured, thinking that might be Agnes's whole problem. A temper was one thing, but if she hadn't had a knife both times she'd lost hers, her life might have gone very differently. So might Armand's, she thought, and asked, "This time you actually removed Althea's head?"

"It offended me," Agnes said with a sniff.

For some reason that brought a startled laugh from Eshe. Her eyes widened in horror at the sound and she quickly covered her mouth in shock at her own response to what was really a horrific event, but Agnes began to chuckle.

"You see? We get on famously," Agnes said with a smile. "I do wish Armand had met you rather than Althea all those centuries ago. We could have been grand friends."

"Except for the part about me being an enforcer and you being a murderer, which makes you one of the rogues I would hunt," Eshe said quietly.

"Yes. Well, no friendship is perfect," Agnes said with a shrug.

Eshe snorted at that with amusement and then said, "So you hacked off Althea's head and started her room on fire."

"And then I went back to the rooms we'd let. Unfortunately, Johnny had returned by then, and while intoxicated when I first entered, seemed to sober up quite quickly when he saw my bloody state." She grimaced with disgust at the memory. "I confessed all, of course; to killing Susanna as well as Althea."

"He didn't know about Susanna by then?" Eshe asked with surprise.

"Did you think I'd tell him?" she asked with surprise of her own. "Good Lord, no. I thought he'd hate me."

"And did he? When you told him after killing Althea?"

Agnes considered that and then shook her head. "No. He mostly felt guilty, I think. My attack on Susanna had been a direct result of his attack on me. Not that he wasn't angry. I mean, he did stomp around shouting a bit, but then he just went out and found another drunk to bite and we never spoke of it again . . . until he killed Rosamund. And then it was all 'It's all your fault I had to do it. If you hadn't killed Susanna and Althea . . .' "

"Yada yada yada?" Eshe suggested when Agnes's voice trailed off.

Agnes gave a dry laugh. "Yes. Basically . . . We're here now," she added, turning into the driveway of a modern ranch farmhouse not dissimilar to the one they lived in.

Much to Eshe's relief, she spotted John's black van and Armand's pickup at once. They were at the right place.

"Stay behind me when we go in," Agnes instructed, shutting off the engine and reaching into the backseat for something. "I don't want you to get hurt. Enough people have been hurt by Johnny and me."

Eshe didn't remind her she was an enforcer and trained for battle, she simply eyed the huge purse Agnes pulled from the backseat, and then quickly scrambled out of the car when Agnes did.

"All right, so Agnes killed Susanna and Althea," Armand said slowly, "But why did you kill Rosamund? She welcomed you as family. She used to have the two of you over for dinner all the time. She was never mean to either of you."

"But she started asking questions about Susanna and Althea's deaths," Johnny said impatiently. "It only made me a little nervous at first. I felt sure there was nothing for her to discover, but then Rosamund came to the house one night asking when exactly we'd returned from Europe. Had it been before Althea's death?"

"Why would she ask that?" Armand asked with surprise. "Everyone thought you'd been in Europe until well after Althea's death."

"Yes, well, it seems Althea's mother told her that Althea thought she'd seen Agnes as they rode into Toronto that night, and it sent Rosamund's little mind churning." He scowled and said, "I had to kill her then. She was getting too close. I killed her on the spot, then loaded her in the wagon and drove to a point about halfway between your farm and town and tried to make it look an accident. Then I tried to set the wagon on fire, but it was pouring rain and wouldn't catch properly, so I had to leave it and hope that everyone would believe the metal slat had decapitated her . . . Fortunately, they did."

"Yes," Armand murmured, thinking of poor, sweet Rosamund. She had been inquisitive, and that had gotten her killed.

"And then almost fifty years later Nicholas's Annie came snooping around with the same damned questions. I hoped that killing her would put an end to it at last, but I stuck around to watch Nicholas for a while, and when I realized his grief was passing enough that he was starting to wonder what Annie had wanted to tell him . . . Well . . ." He shrugged. "I had to act. He was an enforcer. He would have hunted down every lead, every hint and clue, and Agnes and I both would have been staked and baked."

"How did you get Nicholas from the hospital parking lot to his house?" Armand asked grimly.

"Heavy-duty animal tranquilizers," Johnny answered. "I shot him in the neck from my truck. There was a mortal woman passing him at the time and she stopped to see if he was all right when he collapsed. I walked over to them, hefted him over my shoulder, took control of her, and took them both to his place to set it up so it looked like he'd killed her." His lips twisted unhappily, and he explained, "I didn't think another accident so soon would be believed. I thought it would be better if he was found guilty of murder and executed. I was trying to figure out how to get someone over there to discover Nicholas with the dead woman when Decker started pounding at the door. That was pure good luck for me," he added with a faint smile.

Armand stared at him with disbelief. "Nicholas is your nephew. He's Susanna's son. How could you so cold-bloodedly arrange for him to be thought a murderer and executed?"

"I felt bad about it," Johnny assured him solemnly. "But it was better him than me."

"And better me than you too? Right. And who else?" he asked bitterly. "How many more will you murder?"

"Mary Harcourt," Johnny answered at once, and then assured him, "She should be the last. If I'd killed her after Rosamund, Annie wouldn't have had to die. I just never thought that anyone else would come snooping, so I hadn't bothered."

"And why didn't you kill her after Annie?" Armand asked quietly, too weary and in too much pain to be angry anymore.

Johnny shrugged. "Annie's talking to her was purely accidental. It's not like she sought her out to question her. They met by accident on your doorstep. It seemed a fluke. Besides, I do dislike killing. It's unpleasant work with little reward."

"Except for saving your neck," Armand said dryly.

"There is that," Johnny agreed.

Armand scowled at him. "And the shed fire, Mrs. Ramsey attacking Eshe, and my house going up in flames today? You, I presume?"

Johnny nodded. "I was up the first time Bricker and Eshe came to the door. I didn't know who they were and was a bit taken aback when I looked out to see two people all in black with helmets on. I read them, or at least Eshe. As a new life mate she was the easier to read. Once I knew they were there to investigate the deaths I decided I definitely wasn't answering the door. And then I set about trying to get rid of her." He hesitated and then added apologetically, "I am sorry about including you in the two fires, but you two were always together when I came around, and then today when I set the fire I thought it couldn't hurt to get rid of the four of you together. Then there'd be no one to investigate."

"Of course there would," Armand said with disgust.

"A whole ton of people know something is going on now and won't rest until they figure it out. Lucian certainly wouldn't, and he has an army of enforcers to sic on you," he pointed out, thinking Johnny was an idiot and that Agnes had definitely wasted a turn on him.

Thinking of Agnes reminded him of the fact that Johnny hadn't told Agnes about Annie and Nicholas and he asked, "If you told Agnes about Rosamund, why did you never tell her about killing Annie and framing Nicholas?"

Johnny looked at him with disbelief. "Are you kidding? I know she seems sweet and cuddly, but Agnes has one hell of a temper." He shook his head. "She loves Nicholas to death, and she took to Annie right away. She'd kill me if she ever found out what I did to them."

"You're damned right I would."

Armand looked toward the door at that grim comment, and then glanced to John, noting his surprise and horror when Agnes walked in. It about matched his own when Armand glanced back to the door and saw Eshe enter right behind her. His one hope as he'd listened to Johnny had been that at least Eshe was safely away at Cedrick's, but she was here, and now they were both going to die.

Eshe peered over Agnes's shoulder as she followed her into the back room of the basement, the one the voices had been coming from. Much to her relief she spotted Armand at once. He was still alive . . . not looking so hot, maybe, she acknowledged, taking in the dent in his head and the blood covering his face and upper chest. But he was upright, and his eyes were open.

Her eyes slid to John then, noting the antique sword leaning against the wall and the can of gasoline at his side. The plans he'd had for Armand seemed pretty obvious, but he was now staring at Agnes, his mouth working and nothing coming out.

Agnes wasn't having the same problem. Clutching her purse, she crossed the room to stand in front of him and glared straight up his nose as she barked, "How could you? I mean, seriously, John, killing Rosamund was one thing, but little Annie? And to frame Nicholas, your own nephew! What were you thinking? And I suppose you planned to kill Armand too, after all he's done for us!"

"I—You—It's all your fault!" Johnny snapped finally. "If you hadn't killed Susanna and Althea none of this would be necessary! You're the one to blame for this! You're the one who will bear this on your soul. Not me. I've only been trying to protect you. But you . . ."

Eshe's gaze shifted to Agnes as Johnny continued to rant. The other woman turned, a see-what-I-mean? expression on her face, and then turned back, and let her purse drop to reveal a very large and wicked-looking knife that she abruptly plunged into Johnny's chest. It brought an immediate end to his rant.

Eshe watched him peer in horror from the knife in his chest to his sister, shock and wonder on his face, and began to sidle toward Armand.

"It's time to take a little responsibility, John," Agnes

said almost gently. "I made my choices and you made yours, but we can't keep hurting people this way."

Agnes withdrew the knife and Johnny sank to his knees, still looking rather stunned. Leaving him there, she moved to pick up the gas can. As she undid the lid, she said calmly, "You'd better get Armand out of here now, Eshe. I wouldn't want either of you to get hurt."

Eshe hesitated, but when Armand started to stand and then swayed weakly, she hurried to his side, snapped the rope binding his hands, and drew his arm over her shoulder for support. But then she paused to look at Agnes as she began to splash the gasoline around the room and over herself and Johnny.

"Agnes," she began, uncertain what she was going to say. But the other woman looked up and smiled.

"It's okay. Go on. Go tell them everything and get Nicholas his life back. Maybe he'll find another life mate someday and find it in his heart to forgive us."

"He already has found another life mate," Eshe told her.

That made Agnes pause. "Really?"

"Her name's Josephine Willan. She goes by Jo." She hesitated and then added, "She seems nice."

"Oh, I wish I could have met her." Agnes sagged briefly at the thought that she wouldn't, and then glanced to Johnny when he groaned and tried to get up. Sighing, she dropped the can, letting what was left of the liquid run out where it would and pulled out a Zippo lighter. Holding it in one hand, she then took up Johnny's sword before glancing to them again. "Get going now. And give Nicholas my love."

Eshe debated setting Armand down, knocking out Agnes and John, and taking them both in, but it seemed a ridiculous idea. While she found she actually liked Agnes, it didn't change the fact that she was a murderer, and the Council would simply order their execution anyway. Letting out a sad sigh, she turned Armand toward the door and half walked and half dragged him to it.

They'd barely slid through the door when a "whoosh" sounded behind them and heat radiated at their back. Eshe glanced back to see the brother and sister surrounded by a circle of flame that was running toward them, and then hurried Armand along a little faster.

They'd reached the stairs when Johnny began to scream. By the time they got to the top, he'd stopped, and Eshe recalled Agnes picking up the sword and suspected she'd beheaded him rather than make him suffer being burned alive. She couldn't behead herself, however, and yet there was not a sound from Agnes. Eshe couldn't help but admire her for that as she and Armand staggered from the house.

By the time Eshe and Armand stumbled over to lean against the pickup, flames were beginning to lick out of the first floor windows of the house. Eshe glanced back at it, but then leaned into the back of the pickup and opened the cooler there, relieved to find several bags inside. She grabbed all of them and gave them to Armand one at a time as they watched the house burn.

"Better?" she asked as he finished the last one.

"Sort of," he ground out, and she knew that while he would no longer be cramping from lack of blood, the healing would be taking place and he probably had one hell of a headache. She doubted he'd be on his feet long.

"Let's get you back to Cedrick's," she said, helping him to the passenger side of the truck. She got him inside and then moved around to the driver's side to get in, not surprised to see him slumped against the door, unconscious, by the time she slid behind the steering wheel. He'd probably bc in and out of consciousncss for the next twenty-four hours. More out than in, since she planned to keep the man drugged. There was no need for him to suffer the healing.

"I love you, Armand Argeneau," she whispered, and then gave a start when his eyes slid open.

"I love you too, Eshe," he growled and then his eyes closed again and he slid off the seat to rest crumpled in the small space between the seat and the dashboard.

Eshe started to move to lift him back up into the seat, but when she touched him, he moaned, and she decided to just leave him where he was and get him to Cedrick's.

Sighing, Eshe turned and glanced at the steering column, relieved to see his keys dangling there. She gave them a twist and started the engine, and then began to back away from the now fully aflame house.

Epilogue

"Isn't that mutt finished yet?" Lucian asked with disgust. "Everyone is waiting."

"He isn't a mutt," Armand said firmly, peering down at the pale puppy at his feet, a gift from Eshe. "He's a golden retriever and his name is Lucky."

"We named him after you, Lucian," Eshe said with a goading grin. "But we're calling him Lucky for short."

Lucian's response was a grunt of disgust as he whirled back into the house and slammed the door behind him.

"You are an evil woman, Eshe." Armand chuckled, winding the hand holding hers behind her back to draw her nearer. "I like it."

"Good, because you're stuck with me," she said softly, leaning against his chest and toying with the buttons there with her free hand as she glanced down at the puppy.

"Eshe?" he said quietly.

"Hmm?" She raised her gaze to his in query.

"Your name means life."

She smiled crookedly. "I know."

"I'm sure you did," he said easily. "But I didn't until I looked it up on the Internet last night. Eshe means life and d'Aureus means gold. It's fitting. You're my golden girl who saved my son's life and gave me back my life as well. I'm very very grateful," he assured her.

Eshe's eyes sparkled, a wicked smile curving her lips as she said, "Good. You can show me just how grateful when we get back to the hotel." When Armand chuckled at the suggestion, and urged her closer to press against him, she added, "And then I'll show you how grateful I am that you brought joy and color back into my life."

"I love you," Armand said, smiling.

"And I love you," she assured him.

They kissed again, this time the kiss deepening until they heard the door open again and Lucian bellowed, "Goddammit, isn't that dog done yet? The natives are getting restless in here."

Armand pulled back with a sigh, and turned a scowl on his brother. "We're coming. He's nearly done."

Muttering under his breath, Lucian stomped back inside and slammed the door with some vigor.

"Maybe we should go in now," Eshe said wryly, her gaze dropping to Lucky, who had come over and plopped to sit on their feet where there shoes were toe to toe. "I think he's done now."

"Hmm." Armand looked down at the puppy as she eased away from him, but didn't immediately make a move to go inside. Instead, he glanced toward the door and swallowed the sudden ball of dread in his throat.

"You're nervous," Eshe said with surprise, taking in his expression.

"What if she hates me?" Armand asked with a grimace. "I'm a stranger to her, and as far as she knows, I just dumped her on her aunt like unwanted garbage. And then there's Nicholas. He might blame me for—"

"Your daughter isn't going to hate you," Eshe interrupted quietly. "They were already speculating that you'd sent her away to keep her safe before I was sent to you. She knows. And Nicholas will not blame you for anything. None of it was your fault."

Armand sucked in a breath and nodded, then allowed her to lead him to the door, the puppy following happily on his lead. Once there, Armand stepped forward to open the door for her, pausing when it swung open to reveal Lucian on the other side.

"Finally," his brother muttered with disgust. "Come on."

Armand shook his head and ushered Eshe and Lucky in, but when he urged her to follow Lucian, she shook her head and gestured for him to go first. Straightening his shoulders, he moved after Lucian, pausing when the other man stopped in a doorway, blocking his entrance.

"Well?" someone asked from inside. "How did you find out Nicholas was innocent? Who killed Annie and the mortal? Are you going to tell us now or what?"

Armand smiled faintly as he recognized Thomas's

voice, but his smile disappeared abruptly when Lucian answered, "No. I'm going to let your father do that."

And then Lucian was stepping aside, leaving him the focus of several pairs of curious eyes. Armand slid his gaze around the room, recognizing his sister-in-law Marguerite and guessing the dark-haired man at her side was her life mate, Julius. He'd heard the tale of the man who had replaced Lucian's twin but not yet met the man. He spotted Bricker and Anders by Leigh as Lucian moved to stand behind her chair and offered all three a faint smile, and then his gaze swung to Nicholas in another chair at the opposite end of the room. There was a German shepherd curled up at his feet, and a cute brunette on his lap, his Jo. They exchanged smiles, and then Armand recognized Mortimer standing behind their seat with another brunette, this one similar in looks to the girl on Nicholas's lap. She would be Jo's sister and Mortimer's life mate, Sam, he guessed, noting that she was unhealthily skinny. But he knew she'd put off the turn for a bit and suspected the nanos would take care of that when she was finally ready.

Finally his gaze slid to the people on the couch in the middle. Thomas and his mate, Inez; she was more attractive in person than in the pictures, he noted, smiling at them, and then finally he turned his gaze to the dark-haired woman at the other end of the couch. She looked just like her mother, Rosamund, and he sighed her name, "Jeanie."

"My name's Jeanne Louise, sir," she said a bit stiffly, as if suspecting he didn't know it.

Armand hesitated, but then Eshe gave him a little

nudge and he caught her hand and moved across the room to stand in front of this daughter he hadn't seen in a century. Peering down at her, he cleared a suddenly tight throat and said, "We named you Jeanne Louise, but your mother and I called you Jeanie while we had you when you were a baby, and I've thought of you as Jeanie ever since."

"Oh," she murmured uncertainly, looking as if she didn't know what to do or say.

Armand could sympathize, he was unsure himself, but Eshe squeezed his hand reassuringly and he cleared his throat again and said, "I'm very glad to finally be able to meet you, Jeanie. The pictures Nicholas and then Thomas sent me when I asked for them over the years just weren't the same as being in your life. I'm sorry I missed seeing you walk for the first time, and talk for the first time, and I would have really liked to be at your graduation. You looked beautiful in your blue dress. I wish I'd been there to tell you how proud I was and that your mother would have been too. I—"

Armand stopped on a grunt as Jeanne Louise suddenly catapulted upward off the couch, throwing herself at him. He released Eshe to catch his daughter to his chest, felt her body quake with silent sobs, and closed his eyes as he held his daughter for the first time since she was just months old.

"You'll be there for other important occasions," she said in a voice muffled by his chest. "You can walk me down the aisle when I meet my life mate, and you can pick him up when he faints at the birth of our first child, and . . . and just all that stuff," she assured him, patting his shoulder as if he were the one needing the comforting.

"You're upsetting my Leigh, Armand," Lucian said suddenly, sounding put out. "Sit down and put Nicholas out of his misery."

"He isn't upsetting me, darling," Leigh said in a watery voice. "I'm just crying because I'm happy for Jeanne Louise."

"So am I." Marguerite sighed.

"And me," Inez added, and Armand glanced around to see that all the women were wiping away tears. Even Eshe had glassy eyes.

"He's right though," Jeanne Louise murmured, pulling away to wipe her face. "We should let you tell us who framed Nicholas."

Catching his hand, she sat down, tugging at him to sit beside her. Armand caught Eshe's hand again as he dropped onto the couch beside his daughter, pulling her off balance and down with him. Thomas started to laugh and shifted Inez onto his lap to make room for them all to crowd together, and then Armand simply sat there for a moment, his gaze sliding from Jeanne Louise to Eshe as he squeezed each hand he held. He then glanced at the rest of the people in the room and for a moment was overwhelmed. It had been a long time since he'd been surrounded by family.

Movement on the ground drew his attention then, distracting him briefly as he saw that Lucky was nosing at the German shepherd. When the bigger dog merely looked at him with disinterest and then laid his head back on his paws, Lucky apparently took that as an invitation and curled up next to him.

Smiling, Armand finally glanced to Nicholas and Jo, who smiled back, their expressions expectant.

Armand hesitated, and then cleared his throat and started with "Your aunt Agnes sends her love."

Turn the page for a sneak peek of

LYNSAY SANDS'S

HUNGRY FOR YOU

Available December 2010
From

Avon Books

"You have to be kidding me." Alex Willan stared at the man standing on the other side of her desk. Peter Cunningham, or Pierre as he preferred to be called, was her head cook. He was also short, bearded, and had beady little eyes. She'd always thought he resembled a weasel, but never so much as she did at that moment. "You can't quit just like that. The new restaurant opens in two weeks."

"Yes I know." He gave her a sad little moue. "But really, Alexandra, he is offering a king's ransom for me to— "

"Of course he is. He's trying to ruin me," she snapped.

Peter shrugged. "Well, if you were to beat their offer . . ."

Alex's eyes narrowed. She couldn't help noticing that he'd said beat rather than match or even come close. The little creep really was a weasel with no loyalty at all . . . but she needed him.

"How much?" she asked sharply, barely managing to keep from hyperventilating at the amount he murmured. Dear God, that was three times what she was paying him and twice what she could afford . . . which he knew, of course. It was a ridiculous sum. No chef earned that, and he wasn't worth it. Peter was good, but not that good. It didn't make any sense that Jacques Tournier, the owner of Chez Joie, would offer him that much. But then Alex could suddenly see what the plan was. Jacques was luring the man away in a deliberate attempt to leave her high and dry. He'd keep him on for two or three weeks, just long enough to cause scads of trouble for her, then he'd fire him under some pretext or other.

Alex opened her mouth, prepared to warn Pierre, but the smug expression on his face stopped her. Peter had always been an egotistical bastard. It was bad enough when he was only the sous chef, but in the short time since she'd promoted him to head chef, his ego had grown to ten times its previously bloated state. No, she thought with a sigh, he wouldn't believe her. He'd think it just sour grapes.

"I know you can't afford it," Peter said pityingly. Then with something less than sympathy he added, "Just admit it so I can stop wasting my time and get out of here."

Alex's mouth tightened. "Well, if you knew, why even bother suggesting it?"

"I didn't want you to think I was totally without loyalty," he admitted with a shrug. "Were you to beat their offer, I would have stayed."

"Thanks," she said dryly.

"*De rien*," he said, and turned toward the door.

Alex almost let him walk out, but her conscience got the better of her. Whether he'd believe her or not, she had to at least try to warn him that he was setting himself up for a fall. Once Jacques fired him—and she didn't doubt for a minute he would—Peter would be marked. The entire industry would know that he'd left her for them, then lost that job. Even if people didn't suspect the truth of what happened and labeled him a putrid little weasel, they would think he'd been fired for *something.*

Alex had barely begun to speak her thoughts, however, before Peter was shaking his head. Still, she rushed on with it, warning him as her conscience dictated. The moment she fell silent, he sneered at her derisively.

"I knew you would be upset, Alexandra, but making up such a ridiculous story to get me to stay is just sad. The truth is, I have been selling myself cheap for some time now. I've built up a reputation as an amazing chef these last several weeks while cooking in your stead—"

"Two weeks," Alex corrected impatiently. "It's only been two weeks since I promoted you to head chef. And you're cooking *my* recipes, not coming up with brilliant ones of your own. Surely you can see how ridiculous it is that someone would pay you that kind of money for—"

"No, I do not see it as ridiculous. I am brilliant. Jacques sees my potential and that I deserve to be paid my value. But you obviously don't. You have been trying to keep me under. Now I will get paid what I deserve and enjoy some of the profits produced by my skills." Mouth tightening, he added, "And you're not going to trick me into staying here with such stupid stories."

With a little sniff of disgust, Peter turned on his heel and sailed out of her office with his nose up and a self-righteous air that made her want to gag.

Alex closed her eyes. At the moment, she wanted nothing more than to yell a string of obscenities after the man. She would definitely enjoy his fall when it came. Unfortunately, her own fall would come first.

Cursing, she pulled her Rolodex toward her and began to rifle through the numbers. Perhaps one of her old friends from culinary school could help for a night or two. Christ, she was ruined if she didn't find someone quickly.

An hour later, Alex reached the Ws in her Rolodex with no prospects when the phone rang. Irritated with the interruption when she was having a crisis, Alex snapped it up. She barked "hello," the fingers of her free hand still flipping through the Rolodex cards one after the other in quick succession.

"I have someone I want you to meet."

Alex frowned at the strange greeting, slow to recognize her sister's voice. Once she did, a deep sigh slid from her lips and she shook her head wearily. She really didn't need this right now. She was heartily sick of the parade of men Sam had been presenting her with over the last eight months. It had been bad enough when she and their younger sister, Jo, had both been single and available, but now that Jo had Nicholas, Sam was focusing all of her attention on finding Alex a man. She supposed it wouldn't be so bad if even one of the men Sam had insisted on introducing her to had shown some mild interest in her, but after barely more than a moment, and sometimes as little as a few seconds, every single one had simply ignored her, or in some cases, even walked away. It was giving her a complex. She'd even started dieting, something she'd sworn she'd never do, and exercising, a pastime she detested, as well as trying different makeup and fashion choices in an effort to boost her now flagging ego.

This really was the last thing she needed, but knowing Sam's heart was in the right place, Alex forced herself to hang on to her patience, even managing to keep her tone to only mildly exasperated. "Sam, honey, my head chef just quit and I have one hour to replace him before the dinner set start to arrive. I don't have time for your matchmaking right now."

"Oh, but, Alex, I'm pretty sure this is the one," she protested.

"Right. Well, maybe he is, but if he isn't a world class chef, I'm not interested," Alex said grimly. "I'm hanging up now."

"He is!"

Alex paused with the phone halfway back to its cradle and pulled it back to her ear. "What? He is what?"

"A chef?" Sam said, but it sounded like a question rather than an announcement. It was enough to make Alex narrow her eyes.

"For real?" she asked suspiciously.

"Yes." Sam sounded more certain this time.

"Where did he last work?" she asked cautiously.

"I—I'm not sure," Sam hedged. "He's from Europe."

"Europe?" Alex asked, her interest growing. They had some fine culinary schools in Europe. She'd attended one of them.

"Yes," Sam assured her. "Actually, that's why I was sure he would be the one. He's into cooking and fine cuisine like you."

Alex drummed her fingers thoughtfully on the desk. It seemed like just too much good fortune that her sister wanted to introduce her to a chef the very day she was in desperate need of one. On the other hand, she'd suffered enough bad luck the last few months that a bit of good luck was surely in order. Finally, she asked, "What's his name?"

"Cale."

"I've never heard of him." Alex murmured, then realized how stupid it was to say that. She didn't know every single chef in France. In fact, she only knew a few from her days in culinary school . . . and the names of the famous ones, of course.

"Look, he's a chef and you need one. What can it hurt to meet him?" Sam asked. "I swear you won't be sorry. I really think this will work out. Marguerite is never wrong. You have to meet him."

"Marguerite?" Alex asked with confusion, recognizing the name. She was the aunt of one of Mortimer's bandmates, Decker Argeneau. Alex had never met her, but Sam mentioned her a lot. However, she had no idea what the woman had to do with any of this.

"Just meet him," Sam pleaded.

Alex sighed, her fingers tapping a rapid tattoo. She could sense that Sam was lying about something in her determination to get her to meet the man, and really, she didn't have time to waste at the moment. On the other hand, Sam hadn't hesitated to say he could cook and had even said it was why she'd thought they might hit it off, so Alex suspected that part of it was at least true. At least she hoped it was. The fact was, she was desperate. And frankly, beggars couldn't be choosers. If the man could cook even half decently she was definitely interested in him, though not the way Sam was obviously hoping she would be.

"Send him over," she barked, then slammed the phone back on its cradle before she could change her mind.

"I can't believe Sam told her sister I am a chef," Cale muttered for probably the sixth time since finding himself bundled into the passenger seat of his rental car and riding away from the enforcer house with Justin Bricker at the wheel.

"Believe it," Bricker said dryly. "Sam is desperate to see her sister settled with an immortal. She and her sisters are as thick as thieves. She'll do everything and anything she can to ensure Alex doesn't have to be left behind at some point in the future."

"Hmm." Cale supposed he could understand that. He had often thought it must be hard for mortals to give up their family and friends to claim the immortals they loved. They gained a lot in return, of course: eternal youth and a love and passion most mortals could only dream of. Still, family was important to his clan, and to his mind it spoke well of Sam and her sisters that they also deemed family important.

"Still . . . a chef? Just the sight of food makes my stomach turn, and the smell . . ." He grimaced and shuddered, growing nauseated at just the thought of it. His reaction to food was one of the reasons Cale didn't much bother with mortals anymore. Their very lives seemed to revolve around food or beverages. They did business over coffee or drinks and held feasts to celebrate every event. It was for that reason Cale had funneled most of his business interests into areas where he need only deal with immortals. Of course, some of them ate, too—those who were still young or were mated, but he ran into it much less dealing with immortals.

"This is the first time I've heard of an immortal with that kind of reaction to food," Bricker commented, then cast him a curious glance and asked, "Just how old are you?"

Cale scowled. The older he got, the more he detested answering that question, and supposed he was starting to feel his age. Not physically, of course, but mentally. The truth was, lately Cale was bored to tears. It was why he'd agreed to a long visit in Canada. He hadn't had any real change in his life for a very long time. Running companies that catered to immortals' needs and that had mostly immortal employees meant he hadn't had to change his name or job for some time. He also lived on a country estate just outside Paris where there were no neighbors to notice his lack of aging. It had allowed him to avoid moving as well.

Cale knew that while doing so had been convenient, it had also allowed him to stagnate. Lately, he'd been thinking that a major rearranging of his life was in order. He'd been contemplating leaving his company in the hands of one of his capable senior employees and taking up a different line of work but simply hadn't decided on what he wanted to do. He'd considered several things, but most of them necessitated attending college to gain the necessary skills, which meant being around mortals and their ever-present love of food.

Another option he'd considered was hiring himself out as a mercenary. Cale had enjoyed battle in his youth, and while he couldn't become a proper soldier because he couldn't risk daylight, he understood they still hired mercenaries to fight in Third World countries. He supposed it spoke of how low his mood had sunk that the idea of a bloody battlefield appealed to him.

"If you're Martine and Darius's son, you have to have been born before Christ," Bricker said thoughtfully. "Your father died in 300 B.C. or something, didn't he?"

"230 B.C.," Cale said tightly. It was not a day he liked to recall. He had lost not only his father, but several brothers that year, all in the same battle. Actually, slaughter was the better word, since they'd been lured into a trap by an immortal who vied for the same mercenary contracts they did and had decided to eliminate the competition. Cale's father, Darius, had been a great warrior and raised his sons with the same skills, then made a living by hiring himself and his sons out for battle.

Including Cale, his mother had borne eleven children with his father, all sons. The pair had met and become life mates in 1180 B.C., when his father was two hundred years old and his mother three hundred. While they'd adhered to the rule of one child every century, they'd also had two sets of twins, and—so far—the council didn't punish parents for having twins by making them wait an extra century to have another child. Of those eleven sons only three still survived. The rest had died alongside their father on a bloody battlefield in 230 B.C. Cale still ached at the memory of the mammoth loss.

"Well, then, maybe your reaction to food is because you're so old," Bricker murmured with concern. Apparently, the idea of having such an extreme distaste for food was bothersome to the younger immortal. Shrugging, he said more cheerfully, "But if Marguerite's right about this—and she always is—once you meet Alex, you're going to find yourself craving food."

When Cale merely peered at him dubiously, Bricker chuckled and added, "Trust me. By tonight you're going to be stuffing your face like a mortal after a week-long fast."

Cale scowled, not pleased at the suggestion. Really, he wasn't any more delighted to find himself trapped in a vehicle with the younger immortal. Food eaters always had a similar stench. Normally that smell didn't bother him so much, but then he wasn't usually trapped in an airless car with one. Wrinkling his nose, he sighed and asked, "Why are you driving me there again?"

"Because you don't know your way around Toronto and Sam didn't want to take the chance of your getting lost," Bricker reminded him with amusement. "She also worried you might crack up your car on the icy roads and didn't want to risk that either. And Mortimer wanted to discuss her turning and wouldn't let her drive you herself, so she reluctantly decided I should deliver you to Alex. I'm to report back to her on every word that passes between you," he announced with amusement.

"Right," Cale muttered, beginning to wonder what he'd got himself into. Perhaps it really wasn't worth it to humor Marguerite after all. Not if it meant going to a restaurant where he would be surrounded by the stench of mortal food . . . and this Alex woman thought he was a chef for God's sake! What on earth had possessed Sam to claim he could cook? He didn't know the first damned thing about cooking and didn't want to. On the other hand, if it turned out Marguerite was right and this woman was his life mate . . . Well, he supposed that might make it worth it . . . and he really might start to like food again.

"Here." Bricker reached blindly into the back seat to retrieve a book. He offered the large volume to Cale, saying, "Sam thought it might help if you gave this a quick once-over on the way."

"*Cooking for Dummies*?" Cale read with something akin to horror as his gaze moved with distaste over the picture of the dead, headless, featherless, and trussed-up roasted chicken on the plate next to a bunch of equally roasted vegetables.

"Well, it can't hurt," Bricker said with amusement. "Alex is expecting a world-class chef."

Cale tossed the book back on the seat behind him with disgust. "I have no intention of cooking. I'll just go there, meet the woman, see if I can read her, and leave when I can't."

"Or," Bricker drawled, "you're going to go there, discover Marguerite was on the mark *again*, that you can't read Alex, and will be desperate for an excuse to stay close to her as you try to lay claim to her as a life mate."

Cale snorted. "If I can't read her and she is my life mate, I won't need an excuse to stay close to her. She'll want me there."

"Oh, man do you have a lot to learn about mortal women," Bricker said dryly.

Cale glanced at him sharply. "Surely if she is my life mate, she will—"

"What? Drop into your palm like a plum ripe for the picking?" Bricker tore his gaze from the road to glance at Cale with obvious amusement. When Cale merely scowled, he shook his head and turned his attention back to the road. "You weren't paying attention back there at the house, were you? Didn't you catch the fact that Mortimer and Sam are life mates, have been together for eight months, and yet she's only now agreeing to the turn? Mortal women do have free will you know."

Cale's eyes widened as he realized that was true.

"And contrary to what the movie claims, Earth girls *aren't* easy."

"What?" Cale asked, completely bewildered by the reference.

"Never mind," Bricker muttered with disgust. "The point is, while *we* grow up with the knowledge that some day we will meet that special someone who can't read us and whom we can't read and so will therefore be our perfect life mate, mortal women *don't*. They grow up being taught that men are cheating, lying bastards and being told that they will have to kiss a lot of toads before they find the one that will be their prince. And *then* they're taught to be cautious because some princes are actually wolves in princely clothing."

Cale peered at the younger immortal with dismay. "Are you serious?"

"You don't watch much TV, do you?" Bricker asked dryly, then suggested, "Get a clue, watch a movie or two tonight. It will bring you up-to-date on the state of the war of the sexes."

"War?"

"Yes, war," Bricker said solemnly. "Women aren't the sweet, little biddable gals pleased just to have a bit of attention anymore. If they have a man in their lives it's because they want him there, not because they need him to take care of them. Today's women can take care of themselves. At least a lot of them can. And as a successful businesswoman, Alex is one of the ones who can. In fact, dragging her attention away from her business is most likely going to be more of a struggle than anything. Especially right now," he added grimly.

"Why especially right now?" Cale asked.

"She's in the midst of opening a second restaurant," Bricker informed him. "She started with this little hole in the wall. It was fancy," he added in case Cale got the wrong impression. "But small. Only she's one hell of a cook and it was a raging success. You had to book months ahead to get a table. So she decided she needed a larger venue, only from what Sam said that's been one problem after another and Alex has been running in circles trying to get it together in time for opening night."

"When is that?" Cale asked.

"In two weeks," Bricker said dryly. "Trust me, she'll be running around like a chicken with her head cut off, and life mate or no life mate, you'll be lucky if she gives you the time of day if she finds out you're *not* a chef."

Cale was silent for a moment, then undid his seatbelt and shifted around to reach in the back for the cookbook. It seemed to him it was better to be safe than sorry.